ROBERT E. HOWARD

Introduction by Michael A. Stackpole
Edited by Rob Roehm and Paul Herman

THE
Robert E. Howard
FOUNDATION PRESS

For Glenn Lord (1931-2011), preserver of Howard's typescripts and manuscripts, godfather of Howard studies, and the greatest fan that ever lived.

ISBN: 978-1-955446-15-0 (Paperback)
ISBN: 978-1-955446-14-3 (Hardcover)
ISBN: 978-1-955446-30-3 (eBook)

Published by the REH Foundation Press, LLC by arrangement with Robert E. Howard Properties Inc.

https://rehfoundation.org
https://rehfpress.com

https://markwheatleygallery.com

Book prepared for publication by Ståle Gismervik, Savage Studios.

Version 2.2 - Ultimate Edition.

Acknowledgments

All of the Howard stories, poems, letters and portions thereof contained in *Adventures in Science Fiction* come from Howard's original typescripts, manuscripts, and carbons. Virtually all of them were scanned from the Glenn Lord collection, now at the University of Texas, Austin; the Robert E. Howard collection at Texas A&M University; or the typescript collection at Cross Plains Library.

The exeption is Almuric which was serialized in *Weird Tales* (Popular Publications) from May to August 1939.

CHANGES FROM THE 1ST EDITION: King of the Forgotten People, synopsis and an early draft, are new to this edition.

Contents

The Science Fiction of Robert E. Howard

introduction by Michael A. Stackpole

I was first introduced to the work of Robert E. Howard when I was thirteen, through the Lancer reprints of the Conan stories. I took to them immediately. I'd already burned through every Edgar Rice Burroughs book I could find, and devoured Doc Savage and Shadow novels as they were reprinted. I was firmly locked into pulp-era fiction. Howard provided wonderful adventure stories which carried with them more raw passion than the other writers I was enjoying.

I was hooked.

In reading over the stories in the present collection, I had two reactions. The first was to be transported back to the age of thirteen, getting to thrill again at wonderful adventure tales. The second, to which I want to devote the bulk of this essay, involves my being able to look at Howard's work through the eyes of a writer. I was first published in 1978 and down through the years I've had well over four million words published. In 2011, I had the honor of writing *Conan the Barbarian*, the novelization of the movie by the same name. This means my career has lasted longer than Howard's life, though my output has only just overtaken his. In reading these tales as a writer, I got to see new and fascinating aspects of how he worked, which made me enjoy them even more.

A truth has to be acknowledged: science fiction ages very quickly. That's not really true of the science in these stories, however, because Howard was writing at the infancy of science's development. Science at that time was more the triumph of engineering than it was the technological sorcery we live with every day. Howard's stories do not adhere to one definition of science fiction, which holds that science must be part of the solution of any problem. In fact, in most of these stories, the application of science is the genesis of the problem, and man's heroic spirit is the solution.

Because science fiction ages so quickly, it provides ample targets for guardians of literature who want to dismiss it. With the arrogance of hindsight, they can laugh at the flawed futures others have imagined. Opposing these meanspirited folk are apologists who will bend over backward to point out the slimmest glimmer of reality and thereby sanctify the whole of a story as prophecy. Both camps, to my mind, do the author a disservice because they root their judgment of his success or failure in their hopes and fears. It really isn't about them.

Two stories in this volume, *The Last White Man* and *The Last Man*, are clearly set in the same world, just at different points in time. In this world Howard presupposes the ascent of black men and their conquest over all the other races, especially including the degenerate white race. It would be easy to look at this world and suggest that Howard was, as the term was then, a racialist; but this would be to judge him by our standards and not look at the work for what it is.

First, in his time, the science of eugenics had a great many adherents. While World War II and Nazi atrocities makes it abhorrent now, then it was as brilliant and as full of promise as gene therapy is today—it would make supermen of us all. Howard could look at it and look at the grand sweep of history. He used it to overlay on western civilization the same destruction faced by the Roman and Byzantine empires, or on China under the assault of the Mongols, and chose Africa as the likely point from which a new ascendant people would rise. In *The Last Man* he even points to radical Islam as the driving force behind this revolution.

As writers do today, he trusted that what he was told were *facts*. For him, the idea that there were human races, of differing abilities, was a simple fact. No science existed to dissuade him of that notion. In the same way, until twenty years ago, mental disorders were thought to be a defect of the psyche, not genetic disorders or neurobiological imbalances which drugs could cure. An author's job, and one Howard does well, is to look at the existing facts and extrapolate from them. That our vision is later undercut by reality is really no more remarkable than a baseball player being fooled by a curve ball when he's looking for a fast ball. Unfortunately, for writers, our errors are frozen in print, while baseball players move on to the next pitch, next inning and next game.

Within Howard's work is the recurring theme that civilization is a thin veneer over our more base natures. Howard believes in the heart of iron, whereas others believe in a heart of gold, or the noble savage. For Howard, there is no inherent nobility in being a savage, there's just honesty. He also holds as true the idea that any society which has risen to great heights will likely tumble from them. Yet, for him, the struggle is not to regain civilization, but to be true to one's nature and fight against the one true enemy: Death.

There are critics that would see Howard's emphasis on these two points in story after story as psychotic obsession, or a lack of sufficient wit to move past them. Anyone who does that is self-deluding. The stories *The Supreme Moment* and *The Gondarian Man* touch on these points, but in entirely different and even uncharacteristic ways for Howard. He's able to reveal these truths in a manner that emphasizes them without resorting to rip-roaring combat and savagery as we might otherwise expect. I suspect, when editors looked at these two tales, their initial reaction was, "But these are not Robert E. Howard stories."

Yet they came from his pen.

Those who would denigrate Howard for revisiting these themes are those who dare not look at how little we've progressed from our animal beginnings. As Howard came of age, stories of Hun atrocities in Belgium and France shocked and angered the world. Most people today think of World War One as the war where a dog flying a doghouse shot down the Red Baron, or the war in which someone should have killed Hitler early on. For Howard, as depicted in countless books from that era, the war was a savage time when men wallowed in muddy trenches with dead bodies bobbing up, climbing into No Man's Land to be blasted to pieces by shells or raked by unrelenting machine-gun fire. Shell shock reduced men to quivering animals, and no civility existed when men met across bayonets.

Modern critics would like to suggest we've gotten better, but that's not true. Ethnic cleansing still occurs, and is accomplished with a mechanical efficiency that Hitler and Stalin would have envied. In war men revert to their most base nature, desecrating dead enemies, humiliating captured enemies, pillaging, plundering, raping and slaughtering. Domestic violence is no less savage. While these acts are declared evil, and their perpetrators are often declared insane, I find the Howardian notion that they've simply shrugged off the bonds of our consensual civilized reality much easier to accept.

In looking at these tales I see plenty of signs of Howard as a working writer, drawing from other authors, and producing work targeted toward specific audiences. One aspect of the pulp era that I have long envied is the legion of markets. All of the pulp writers I've had the privilege to know down through the years described having stacks of stories that they would keep in circulation. They'd turn out new stories, and send the rejected ones right back out. Howard's letters point out his search for new markets, and frustration at not being able to crack others.

In this regard, *Almuric* is a wonderful example. One cannot help but be struck by the parallels to Edgar Rice Burroughs' *A Princess of Mars*, at least at the opening. I have no doubt that Howard wanted to appeal to Burroughs' audience in the same way that so many writers today are trying to cash in on *Twilight* and the whole paranormal romance field. In fact, were Howard writing today, I am certain he'd take his stab at it, but in his own way. He'd have his hero living in that grey area between the unawares civilization and the savagery of the supernatural world.

Truth be told, Solomon Kane actually occupied that niche. Bring him forward in time to the early 21st century, outfit him in a leather trenchcoat, give him a katana and a .45 with silver bullets, and both Team Edward and Team Jacob would be heading for the hills. I'd pay money to read those stories and, I'm sure, that's exactly what Howard would hope I'd say.

While, on the surface, *Almuric*'s opening maps really well over *A Princess of Mars*' opening, the stories diverge quickly and significantly. Burroughs always believed in the noble savage; he believed that civilization would win out and tame men. John Carter is a southern gentleman and a master of the sword, who finds himself imbued with superhuman abilities by virtue of Mars' reduced gravity. By contrast, Esau Cairn's arrival on Almuric thrusts him immediately into a savage battle with a man who is bigger and stronger than he—something he's never faced during his life on Earth. From there Cairn descends into savagery and ascends again into the society of men.

It's this difference between the stories which earns my admiration for what Howard did. There are countless writers—then and now—who would have simply looked at the earlier work, changed some names, numbers of arms, colors and creatures, then proclaimed it a new work. As I tell writing students, turning out 90% of someone else's story is not turning out a new story. All you do is prove yourself a thief and an inept one at that. Those writers do nothing to make the story their own.

Howard, on the other hand, saw a market for a story with an earth man set on a distant shore. In that way *Almuric* owes as much to *Robinson Crusoe* or *Gulliver's Travels* as it does *A Princess of Mars*. The convention of such a story back then was the somewhat miraculous translation of the man from our world to the other. John Carter takes a nap, Cairn is transported through a technological device. Howard starts there so readers of these kinds of stories will feel comfortable at the beginning, and then he whisks them off on an adventure that would have left John Carter broken and weeping.

And imagine what would have happened to Barsoom if Esau Cairn ended up there!

There is no question that Howard knew of Burroughs and his work. In *The Last Man*, Burroughs is mentioned by name. It's not really a surprise since Howard's work reveals both a knowledge of his contemporaries and a love for what they do. His voluminous correspondence, along with evidence like *The Challenge from Beyond*, makes apparent his awareness and willingness to work with others.

You don't collaborate with other writers closely or even at a remove if you do not respect their work. And you certainly don't take steps to push your work beyond the foundations they laid down if you don't know what others have done. *Almuric* could not have sailed past *A Princess of Mars* without knowledge and understanding of the earlier book.

One secret about writing is this: writers learn how to write from reading other writers. Burroughs, for example, clearly learned from Edwin L. Arnold's *Gullivar of Mars* (1905) or books like George Griffiths' *The Outlaws of the Air* (1895). Howard clearly learned from Burroughs and Harold Lamb. It's easy for me to point to Howard, Burroughs, Lamb and many others as authors through whose work I learned to tell stories.

What pleases me a great deal about Howard is that it's evident that he did not settle for being *as good as* these authors. He didn't just want to present 90% of their stories. He knew two things: what his audience liked, and what *he* liked, and that latter point is more important than the former. An author who only knows what his audience likes will continue to grind out that same sort of story with nothing new tossed in. A writer who knows what *he* likes, and who allows his taste to change, who challenges himself to get better and do more, *will* get better. Howard clearly does, and this forces him to do more than what other authors do. He can take their kinds of stories and tell them in his unique voice.

Best of all in this collection are the characters. The vast majority of heroes are cast from a similar mold. These are not gentlemen who would prefer death before dishonor. That's not to suggest they are dishonorable. Quite the opposite. They are men possessed of great honor, but their preference is to kill the other guy before dishonor, and that differentiates them from many another hero.

We get the most of Esau Cairn in this volume. I marvel at the contrast between a man who describes himself as a savage and barbarian, yet who shows such erudition in chronicling his exploits. It's a great contrast which shows a complexity of character and brutal honesty within the character. Those who view what he does and the savage efficiency with which he does it, and ignore the language he uses to describe it all are missing the essence of the character. In this way Cairn and all the other characters are unique, even if they are all of a recognizable brotherhood.

Were I asked to choose favorites from among these tales, I would point to *The Gondarian Man* and *The King of the Forgotten People*. I like *The Gondarian Man* because of the subtle way in which Howard uses contrast to describe the race of humans inhabiting our Earth (presumably) in the future. He tells us just enough to get across the idea that by progressing mentally we sacrifice physicality, yet the vision of that future is not dystopian or of a world in decline. Surely a decline happened—at least two—but things appear to be on the upswing again.

The King of the Forgotten People I love because I enjoy—and lament the loss of—hidden world stories. With 24 hour news channels and cameras everywhere, it's hard to believe there could be an uncharted island or hidden mountain valley where a human population could have existed undiscovered for centuries. This story also offers a strong "what-if" element concerning the ability to read vibrations and access the impressions left by long-dead people. It doesn't matter that modern science has cast cold water on such an idea, the romance of it still excites.

Robert E. Howard is justifiably best known for his fantasy fiction. Some would certainly class the present works as science fantasy more than science fiction, but that distinction is really immaterial. Once you look past the labels, what you have is pure Howard: iron-hearted, steel-thewed heroes who defy the entropy that threatens to destroy them, and laugh at those who think themselves so elevated by civilization that they will never fall. This is Howard plying his trade in arenas for which he is not known, and doing it well.

As only Robert E. Howard could.

Adventures in Science Fantasy

The Last Laugh

The rising sun was behind the wild figure. He threw back his black mane and laughed, the wild, ribald laughter of humanity that has mocked the gods for a million years. All life and wine and madness roared in that mirth. All the passion and lust and ribald rebellious mirth that has trod the long road up from the jungle. Feet widebraced, he heaved up the great sword and yelled down at the surging mass of upturned faces; he spat down at them and his wild laughter thundered out across the throng again, all the ribaldry and the obscenity and the wit and the mirth and the courage and the glory that is humanity.

"Dogs!" he yelled, and his voice carried like the roll of drums, like the blare of a clarion, like the roar of a trumpet. "Look at me! I am Man! My great-grandfather was a savage and his great-grandfather was an ape! We came up from the slime and the mud and the blind black squalid chaos of the jungle, and we brought its reek with us all the way! We knew bloodlust and fear and bellyhunger! We knew laughter and tears and the feel of the dirt under our feet and the feel of the rain on our hands!

"We laughed and we lusted, we hated and we loved, we lived like dogs and died like flies. We broke the heads of the wolves and the jackals, and we ripped the bellies of the lions and elephants. We glutted our hunger on beasts that thought to master us. We leveled the forests, and we dammed the rivers, we strangled the volcanoes, we broke down the mountains, we ripped the guts out of the earth, and we pulled up the bottoms of the seas!

"We were the Conquerors! We trampled life redhanded and heavy-footed. We destroyed all before us, and we destroyed one another. You dogs! I'm the last man on earth, but I am a conqueror yet! Did you think to conquer us, you bloodless, gutless, brainless mechanisms? You never suffered and you never joyed. You never felt the bite of lust or grief or hate, nor the madness of love or power or exultation. Aye, we were faulty; we were mad as all things that spring from the earth. Our brains were imperfect, our bodies were imperfect. We were fools and clowns and madmen—and we were the Conquerors of the world! Hah! hah! hah!" Again his wild laugh shouted out over the throng. Below him shapes were climbing swiftly toward him. He spat down at them and laughed. His eyes blazed; he shook back his mane and his lips curled with boisterous mockery. He was the very epitome of mankind, a grotesque, leaping, posturing, ape-like ribald gesticulating and crowing defiance into the teeth of the wondering cosmos.

"Man!" he yelled, brandishing his sword. "A million generations lived and died. We destroyed all before us. Destruction is on you all! Fools! The last atom of life to glow on this planet shall be a man!" And with a wild yell he swung the great sword in a flaming arc and crashed down on the metal hood. Metal gave way with a splintering crash, and there was an explosion, a burst of flame. One great groan sighed up from below where grey shapes were falling like sheaves of wheat under the reaper. The sun went out in a glare of lurid flame that turned the sky copper.

The destroyer reeled back, staggering on the great hood. The sword in his hands was a twisted shard of blackened metal, hanging in charred fingers. From his belt up, the cloth of his garment had vanished and his broad breast showed, burned black. His glazing eyes swept the scene; blackened lips parted and over the world for the last time, the last sound of the life that was extinct, thundered the senseless, defiant, joyful laughter of a man.

The Gondarian Man

(originally untitled)

As we worked, we were impressed with the evident age of the thing. Some of the men, expert metal workers, vowed that this material was not of the earth, and hazarded a guess that it dropped from some other planet.

At last it was open, and a terrible sight met our eyes. A monster lay in the case. As you have seen it, it is needless to describe the thing, but I only wish to say that I disagree with the scientists who claim it to be some form of a human.

We stood spellbound, and then as I hope for a future Life, I saw a flicker of the Thing's eyelids! It was as if the air, rushing into its nostrils, had revived it from its long sleep!

Of course, now, every child is familiar with the process by which our scientists produce a death-like sleep which may last for years or for a few seconds only, but this hideous being, dead for the gods only know how many thousands of years, was coming to life before our eyes!

The eyes opened and stared up at me, freezing the very blood in my veins! The long terrible fingers or talons opened and closed, and the frightful thing rose sluggishly and emerged from its case, like a dragon coming from its shell. A kind of cloth on it, crumbled as the air struck it.

We stood silent, motionless, our flesh crawling with a fear too intense to put into words. The thing stood on its hind legs, like a human being, glaring at us with those fearful eyes; then, terrible and unthinkable as it seems, I swear I saw a flash of fear in those eyes! They flared wide with an intolerable expression of horror, and then the thing went into ferocious action.

With one sweeping blow of its taloned hand it killed one of the metal workers, and, dodging a blow aimed at it by another, seized and crushed him. All was confusion amounting to insanity, men screaming and running, and striking wildly and blindly. And in the midst of them, that fiend raging silently and dealing out death with lashing arms. At last I managed to bring my ray projector to bear upon it, and with one inhuman screech, it fell and died.

Four of the workers lay dead, broken and mangled in a hideous manner, and others had suffered broken bones and torn flesh. The case and the corpse of the monster, we sent to the Lord of Science Society at Gledhah.

Amser Ram
At Burt, chief city of Gondar.

The Report of the Lord of Science
Concerning the Recent Discovery

As to the exact origin of the specimen which the Society has named the Gondarian Man, the authorities differ, but that it is some form of human or prehuman life is evident, and agreed upon by all. The formation of the spinal bones alone show this.

The Society agrees that this prehistoric man was a member of some race which developed highly enough to understand the secret of preserving life for many ages, in which respect they were further advanced than the men of today.

This being the case, a stupendous thought comes to life: *that there were civilizations on earth before our race developed from the Monad.*

This cannot be denied, because this man is indisputably of a type which existed before the coming of men as we know them, since not even in the wild legends of the ancients have we any description of giant or demon which approaches this reality. Nor have there been any bones found by which to reconstruct such a frame.

This means that his tribe perished so long ago that the brain reels when seeking to contemplate that lapse of time. And for some reason, men of his race sealed him into a metal case, the construction of which we know nothing about, then sealed him into a rock cave and left him for Eternity. What was their purpose? Was it a punishment? Was it some strange religious rite? Or was this man some priest or hero who was to come again in time of need?

We do not know. We cannot know. But we know this much: that millions on countless millions of years must have passed before the workers of Gurt burst his metal shell and let him into the light, for the moments that were his before he was again plunged into darkness—the real dark, this time.

Between the time of his sealing up and the time of his release and death, the earth must have passed through many changes. What a grand and terrible panorama for his eyes, could they have but seen through the stone and metal walls of his prison!

Oceans rose and continents heaved up out of the deeps. Whole races died—his presence proves that—mighty civilizations were lost, and vanished without leaving a trace. Time erased all marks. Men again came up the long slow climb from the primal slime of the seas. And all the while this one, this last survivor of the elder world, lay in his strange case and slept away the ages as if they were seconds.

What magnificent vistas this finding opens to the eye of science! How colossal a thought! To this time we had supposed ourselves to be the first men to inhabit the world! Now we see that men have come before us, just as they shall come after us, when we have vanished without a trace!

Returning to the Gondarian Man, one cannot look at him and wonder that the workers were overcome with horror. This creature is of strange and uncanny appearance. Standing upright, he would measure something over six feet in height—a remarkable contrast to the true human of today, who has never stood over five feet in height. The limbs are long and muscular, the skin very rough as compared to human skin, and sparsely covered with hair, such as is sometimes found growing on the eyebrows of some of the more primitive races.

His skull, instead of being bare like ours, is topped with a heavy shock of this hair, being of a strange golden hue. Moreover, there is a profuse growth of hair on his chin and along his jawbones. His eyes are of a strange indefinable color, grey, but not as we are used to the color. His nose is far more pronounced than the man's of today, and the skin of his face is filled out and padded by the flesh beneath, instead of being drawn tightly against the skull so as to outline the bony structure, as ours is.

His forehead is low and broad, nearly twice as broad as modern man's, but less than half as high. His skull is rounded rather than conical, his lips thick compared to ours, and altogether, his features present a monstrous aspect.

His shoulders are wide and square instead of narrow and rounded, and his neck is short and thick, rather than long and slender as is the present-day man's. His arms are long and curiously jointed in the middle, with a sort of hinge affair, as are his legs. His limbs can be bent backward, but not forward.

Instead of seven fingers with four joints each, he has only five on each hand, four of which have three joints, counting the joint which fastens the finger to the hand; the fifth is set opposite to the rest in a curious manner and has but two joints. On each finger are talons of a curious nature, thin and flat, with rounded points.

The feet are much like the hand in bony structure, except the toes are shorter and the fifth toe is set side by side with the others, instead of opposite them.

There are no horns on his skull, not the slightest trace of even the most rudimentary ones.

As for his enormous strength, the fact that he slaughtered the workmen is proof enough. His vitals seem to differ greatly from the true human, and we expect to have other sensational communications to offer upon dissecting the body.

After all, it is to be pitied that he was killed. Amser Ram speaks of the fear in his eyes; and indeed, who can deny that we would probably appear as horrible in appearance to him, as he to us? No one can deny this.

The Supreme Moment

"The future of the race depends upon it."

The speaker was a man whose every appearance spoke of power. He fairly radiated authority.

In fact, there was but one man in the strangely furnished room who did not somehow give the impression of wealth and power. There were six of them, and five sat facing the sixth.

He was the most insignificant in appearance of them all. Small and deformed he was, his legs twisted, his shoulders humped. Small weak eyes peered from beneath a great bulging dome of a forehead.

"But why do you come to me?" a thin, high-pitched voice, strangely mingled with abasement and defiance.

The others looked at him contemptuously, almost loathingly.

"You know," said the first speaker, rising and striding up and down the room, "that you are the only man on earth who has what we want. What we must have. As you know, a strange new form of fungi has sprung up near the equator. Nothing seems to check its growth. It spreads over fields, farms, buildings. What it touches, it destroys. Before it fertile lands spread, covered with rich vegetation; behind it lies a barren wilderness. It grows and spreads with astonishing rapidity, covering miles in a day. Nothing can stop it. It feeds on flesh as upon vegetation. Forests and cities alike melt before its approach. Oceans cannot stay it, for it spreads over their surfaces like a vast, unthinkable Sargasso, clogging the seas, destroying the fish and entangling and devouring all shipping. Like a monstrous octopus, it is sending its tentacles out to clutch the world. All this you know, doubtless."

"Some hint of it has drifted into my secluded laboratories from the outside world."

"Very good. Now, you are the acknowledged authority on all parasitic plants. You have spent a lifetime in the study of fungi. Years ago it was announced to the world that you had stumbled upon a plant formula which would check the growth of, and destroy, any fungus, no matter of what nature. Though skeptical, certain capitalists offered you a great sum for the formula, which you refused. Now, in the interest of ourselves, of yourself, of the whole world, we come to you to purchase at any price, or in any manner, the formula which will save the world from becoming an uninhabited wilderness."

The aged scientist rose and walked to a window, gazed out for a moment.

Then, turning, "Why should I give up my priceless formula?"

"Because the lives of all the world depend upon it, including your own."

"I am old."

"You owe it to the world, which gave you birth."

"Ha!" A strange light sprang up in the strange old man's eyes. "I owe to the world—Listen, and I will tell you something of the life of Zan Uller, the crazed scientist.

"I was born in a wretched tenement in London. My mother, deserted when I was but a few months old, was thrown into prison for attempting to steal milk for her starving children. She never came out. After a wretched babyhood in an alms house, I was kicked forth into the world at the age of ten to earn my living as best I could. Working at the looms in the factories ruined my health, what little I had, and a brutal employer's kicks and beatings made me a twisted cripple. I managed to keep body and soul together by begging and stealing and eventually became a newsboy, selling papers and earning a few cents a day. Even then the flame of science burned brightly within my starved soul and when the other newsboys beat me and drove me away, I went to a great university and begged and obtained leave to work there, sweeping, cleaning, doing all sorts of vile work. I got only scant meals and a hovel in which to sleep, but there I had the chance to read and to study. Daily I toiled and slaved, and nightly I worshipped at the altar of science, reading the books I had stolen and borrowed, by the light of candle stubs salvaged from sweeping the floors. It is not my intention to relate to you of the long, hard upward climb. Every obstacle, every hindrance was set in my path by greed, by prejudice, and by stupidity and jealousy. But I overcame them all, battling my way up by pure strength and resolution of spirit alone. From one position and another I was ousted, only to gain better ones. The spite of a rival caused an explosion in a laboratory which permanently impaired my eyesight.

"My book, *Evolution of Animal Life from Plant Life*, became a center of persecution and I, as its author, was subjected to the vilest kind of treatment. Driven from my house in London by a fanatical mob, I sought seclusion in the country. But even there, a reporter scenting a story, sought me out, and a clergyman—" here his voice shook with passion and an almost fanatical gleam lighted his weak eyes—"a clergyman incited a mob to attack me. I barely escaped with my life.

"Eventually, after many long hard struggles, I rose to a place of eminence, and no longer had to endure the abuses and insults of the world. The world to which you say I owe so much." A cynical, mocking note, almost savage in its irony, crept into his tone.

"I could then devote all my time to my study. As you say, I studied plants, and especially the fungi. I saw what you fools did not: that the fungi is a living, devouring organism, a menace to the race of man.

"Years ago, in a book which you never saw, which has gone out of print, I warned the race. They laughed at me! I was branded as a fool, caricatured and scoffed at.

"So I ceased to seek to serve the race which had ostracized me, but I did not cease to carry on my studies.

"You say I 'stumbled' upon a fungi destroyer. *Stumbled!* It was the product of years of labor, of days of toil and nights of study. My whole soul went into the work. I made it, perfected it.

"And years ago, I saw in one of my exploration tours in search of new plants, the beginnings of the growth that is now overrunning the world. I saw its possibilities. I could have checked it. I chose not to. Why should I? Who am I to seek to turn aside the path of Nature's destiny?

"Even now I could destroy it. If I chose."

"You admit then, that you have such a formula as of which we speak?"

"Certainly."

"What is your price, if you must demand a price for what most men would gladly give?"

"I have no price."

"You will not part with it?"

"Of that, I am the judge."

"We are authorized to search you, to search your laboratories if necessary, and take the formula by force."

"It will avail you little. The substance and the formula I long ago destroyed. I carefully memorized the formula, however, and can put it into effect at any time I choose."

The leader of the party arose.

"Old man," he said sternly, "it will little avail you to thwart us. We come from a world on the edge of destruction. We are prepared to secure what we ask, by fair means or foul. No matter what we do, we will have the sanction of the whole race."

The aged scientist shrugged his shoulders.

"If necessary, fire and torture shall make you divulge your secret."

The others added passionate assent, crowding forward. The whole scene was grotesquely similar to a wolf pack surging in upon a crippled caribou. The faces of the men, high bred and intellectual, were now twisted and vicious. For they were shaking with the fury of Fear. Fear that is the greatest tyrant of them all.

The old scientist raised a hand. Somehow, twisted and deformed as he was, he seemed to dominate the group.

"This is the moment for which I have lived," he said, and his voice was thrilled with suppressed exultation.

"The world which hurled me forth, which maimed, crippled, abused me, the world, I say, is at my feet. Yet it is not the height.

"I am the only man on earth who can rescue the world. Is it not true? Now, look you, I, whom the world has ever kicked and trampled, I who owe nothing to the world, I, to be its savior!

"If I should refuse to give you the formula, you will torture me?"

Five voices answered assent.

"But what if I do not refuse? Is it not godlike to forgive? Who am I to leave the world to destruction?

"Gentlemen, this is my vengeance, this, *the supreme moment!*"

His twisted hand jerked from behind him, twitching to his hairless head.

The five men staggered back with hoarse shrieks as the shot crashed.

The echoes rebounded through the room like mocking, devilish laughter.

The People of the Black Coast

This comes of idle pleasure seeking and—now what prompted that thought? Some Puritanical atavism lurking in my crumbling brain, I suppose. Certainly, in my past life I never gave much heed to such teachings. At any rate, let me scribble down here my short and hideous history, before the red hour breaks and Death shouts across the beaches.

There were two of us, at the start. Myself, of course, and Gloria, who was to have been my bride. Gloria had an airplane, and she loved to fly the thing—that was the beginning of the whole horror. I tried to dissuade her that day—I swear I did!—but she insisted, and we took off from Manila with Guam as our destination. Why? The whim of a reckless girl who feared nothing and always burned with the zest for some new adventure—some untried sport.

Of our coming to the Black Coast there is little to tell. One of those rare fogs rose—we soared above it and lost our way among thick billowing clouds. We struggled along, how far out of our course God alone knows, and finally fell into the sea just as we sighted land through the lifting fog.

We swam ashore from the sinking craft, unhurt, and found ourselves in a strange and forbidding land. Broad beaches sloped up from the lazy waves to end at the foot of vast cliffs. These cliffs seemed to be of solid rock and were—are—hundreds of feet high. The material was basalt or something similar. As we descended in the falling aircraft, I had had time for a quick glance shoreward, and it had seemed to me that beyond these cliffs, rose other, higher cliffs, as if in tiers, rampart above rampart. But of course, standing directly beneath the first tier, we could not tell. As far as we looked in either direction, we could see the narrow strip of beach running along at the foot of the black cliffs, in silent monotony.

"Now that we're here," said Gloria, somewhat shaken by our recent experience, "what are we to do? Where are we?"

"There isn't any telling," I answered. "The Pacific is full of unexplored islands. We're on one. I only hope that we haven't a gang of cannibals for neighbors."

I wished then that I had not mentioned cannibals, but Gloria did not seem frightened—at that.

"I'm not afraid of natives," she said uneasily. "I don't think there are any here."

I smiled to myself, reflecting how women's opinions merely reflected their wishes. But there was something deeper, as I learned in a hideous manner soon, and I believe now in feminine intuition. Their brain fibers are more delicate than ours—more readily disturbed and reached by psychic influences. But I had no time to theorize.

"Let's stroll along the beach and see if we can find some way of getting up these cliffs and back on the island."

"But the island is all cliffs, isn't it?" she asked.

Somehow I was startled. "Why do you say that?"

"I don't know," she answered rather confusedly. "That was the impression I had, that this island is just a series of high cliffs, like stairs, one on top of the other, all bare black rock."

"If that's the case," said I, "we're out of luck, for we can't live on seaweed and crabs—"

"Oh!" Her exclamation was sharp and sudden.

I caught her in my arms, rather roughly in my alarm, I fear.

"Gloria! What is it?"

"I don't know." Her eyes stared at me rather bewilderedly, as if she were emerging from some sort of nightmare.

"Did you see or hear anything?"

"No." She seemed to be averse to leaving my sheltering arms. "It was something you said—no, that wasn't it. I don't know. People have daydreams. This must have been a nightmare."

God help me, I laughed in my masculine complacency and said:

"You girls are a queer lot in some ways. Let's go up the beach a way—"

"No!" she exclaimed emphatically.

"Then let's go down the beach—"

"No, no!"

I lost patience.

"Gloria, what's come over you? We can't stay here all day. We've got to find a way to go up those cliffs and find what's on the other side. Don't be so foolish; it isn't like you."

"Don't scold me," she returned with a meekness strange to her. "Something seems to keep clawing at the outer edge of my mind, something that I can't translate—do you believe in transmission of thought waves?"

I stared at her. I'd never heard her talk in this manner before.

"Do you think somebody's trying to signal you by sending thought waves?"

"No, they're not thoughts," she murmured absently, "not as I know thoughts, at least."

Then, like a person suddenly coming out of a trance, she said:

"You go on and look for a place to go up the cliffs, while I wait here."

"Gloria, I don't like the idea. You come along—or else I'll wait until you feel like going."

"I don't think I'll ever feel that way," she answered forlornly. "You don't need to go out of sight—one can see a long way here. Did you ever see such black cliffs—this is a black coast, sure enough. Did you ever read Tevis Clyde Smith's poem—'The long black coasts of death—' something? I can't remember exactly."

I felt a vague uneasiness to hear her talk in this manner but sought to dismiss the feeling with a shrug of my shoulders.

"I'll find a trail up," I said, "and maybe get something for our meal—clams or a crab—"

She shuddered violently.

"Don't mention crabs," said she. "I've hated them all my life, but I didn't realize it until you spoke. They eat dead things, don't they? I know the Devil looks just exactly like a monstrous crab."

"All right," said I, to humor her. "Stay right here; I won't be gone long."

"Kiss me before you go," she said with a wistfulness that caught at my heart, I knew not why. I drew her tenderly into my arms, joying in the feel of her slim young body so vibrant with life and loveliness. She closed her eyes as I kissed her, and I noted how strangely white she seemed.

"Don't go out of sight," she said as I released her. A number of rough boulders dotted the beach, fallen, no doubt, from the overhanging cliff face, and on one of these she sat down.

With some misgivings, I turned to go. I went along the beach close to the great black wall which rose into the blue like a monster against the sky, and at last came to a number of unusually large boulders. Before going among these I glanced back and saw the girl sitting where I had left her. I know my eyes softened as I looked on that slim, brave little figure—for the last time.

I wandered in among the boulders and lost sight of the beach behind me. I often wonder just why I so thoughtlessly ignored her last plea. A man's brain fabric is coarser than a woman's, not so susceptible to outer influence. Yet I wonder if even then, pressure was being brought to bear upon me—

At any rate, I wandered along, gazing up at the towering black mass until it seemed to have a sort of mesmeric effect upon me. One who has never seen these cliffs cannot possibly form any true conception of them, nor can I breathe into my description the invisible aura of malignity which seemed to emanate from them. I say, they rose so high above me that their edges seemed to cut through the sky—that I felt like an ant crawling beneath a Babylonian wall—that their monstrous serrated faces seemed like the breasts of dusky gods of unthinkable age—this I can say, this much I can impart to you. But if any man ever reads this, let him not think that I have given here a true portrait of the Black Coast. For the reality of the thing lay, not in sight and sense nor even in the thoughts which they induced—but in the things you know without thinking—the feelings and the stirrings of consciousness—the faint clawings at the outer edge of the mind which were not thoughts at all—

But these things I discovered later. At the moment, I walked along like a man in a daze, almost mesmerized by the stark monotony of the black ramparts above me. At times I shook myself, blinked and looked out to sea to get rid of this mazy feeling, but even the sea seemed shadowed by the great walls. The further I went, the more threatening they seemed. My reason told me that they could not fall, but the instinct at the back of my brain whispered that they would suddenly hurtle down and crush me.

Then suddenly I found some fragments of driftwood which had washed ashore. I could have shouted for elation. The mere sight of them proved that man at least *existed* and that there was a world far removed from these dark and sullen cliffs, which seemed to fill the whole universe. I found a long fragment of iron attached to a piece of the wood and tore it off; if the necessity arose, it would make a very serviceable iron bludgeon. Rather heavy for the ordinary man, it is true, but in size and strength, I am no ordinary man.

At this moment, too, I decided I had gone far enough. Gloria was long out of sight and I retraced my steps hurriedly. As I went I noted a few tracks in the sand and reflected with amusement that if a spider crab, something larger than a horse, had crossed the beach here, it would make just such a track. Then I came in sight of the place where I had left the girl and gazed along a bare and silent beach.

I had heard no scream, no cry. Utter silence had reigned as it reigned now, when I stood beside the boulder where she had sat and looked in the sand of the beach. Something small and slim and white lay there, and I dropped to my knees beside it. It was a woman's hand, severed at the wrist, and as I saw upon the second finger the engagement ring I had placed there myself, my heart withered in my breast and the sky became a black ocean which drowned the sun.

How long I crouched over that pitiful fragment like a wounded beast, I do not know. Time ceased to be for me, and from its dying minutes was born Eternity. What are days, hours, years, to a shattered heart, to whose empty hurt each instant is an Everlasting Forever? But when I rose and reeled down to the sea edge, holding that little hand close to my hollow bosom, the sun had set and the moon had set and the hard white stars looked scornfully at me across the immensity of space.

There I pressed my lips again and again to that pitiful cold flesh and laid the slim little hand on the flowing tide which carried it out to the clean, deep sea, as I trust, merciful God, the white flame of her soul found rest in the Everlasting Sea. And the sad and ancient waves that know all the sorrows of men seemed to weep for me, for I could not weep. But since, many have shed tears, oh God, and the tears were of blood!

I staggered along the mocking whiteness of the beach like a drunken man or a lunatic. And from the time that I rose from the sighing tide to the time that I dropped exhausted and became unconscious seems centuries on countless centuries, during which I raved and screamed and staggered along huge black ramparts which frowned down on me in cold inhuman disdain—which brooded above the squeaking ant at their feet.

The sun was up when I awoke, and I found I was not alone. I sat up. On every hand I was ringed in by a strange and horrible throng. If you can imagine spider crabs larger than a horse—yet they were not true spider crabs, outside the difference in the size. Leaving that difference out, I should say that there was as much difference in these monsters and the true spider crab as there is between a highly developed European and an African bushman. These were more highly developed, if you understand me.

They sat and looked at me. I remained motionless, uncertain just what to expect—and a cold fear began to steal over me. This was not caused by any especial fear of the brutes killing me, for I felt somehow that they would do that, and did not shrink from the thought. But their eyes bore in on me and turned my blood to ice. For in them I recognized an intelligence infinitely higher than mine, yet terribly different. This is hard to conceive, harder to explain. But as I looked into those frightful eyes, I knew that keen, powerful brains lurked behind them, brains which worked in a higher sphere, a different dimension than mine.

There was neither friendliness nor favor in those eyes, no sympathy or understanding—not even fear or hate. It is a terrible thing for a human being to be looked at in that manner. Even the eyes of a human enemy who is going to kill us have understanding in them, and a certain acceptance of kindred. But these fiends gazed upon me in something of the manner in which cold-hearted scientists might look at a worm about to be stuck on a specimen board. They did not—they could not—understand me. My thoughts, sorrows, joys, ambitions, they never could fathom, any more than I could fathom theirs. We were of different species! And no wars of humankind can ever equal in cruelty the constant warfare that is waged between living things of diverging order. Is it possible that all life came from one stem? I cannot now believe it.

There was intelligence and power in the cold eyes which were fixed on me, but not intelligence as I knew it. They had progressed much further than mankind in their ways, but they progressed along different lines. Further than this, I cannot say. Their minds and reasoning faculties are closed doors to me and most of their actions seem absolutely meaningless; yet I know that these actions are guided by definite, though inhuman, thoughts, which in turn are the results of a higher stage of development than the human race may ever reach in *their way*.

But as I sat there and these thoughts were borne in on me—as I felt the terrific force of their inhuman intellects crashing against my brain and willpower, I leaped up, cold with fear; a wild unreasoning fear which wild beasts must feel when first confronted by men. I knew that these things were of a higher order than myself, and I feared to even threaten them, yet with all my soul I hated them.

The average man feels no compunction in his dealings with the insects underfoot. He does not feel, as he does in his dealings with his brother man, that the Higher Powers will call upon him for an accounting—of the worms on which he treads, nor the fowls he eats. Nor does a lion devour a lion, yet feasts nobly on buffalo or man. I tell you, Nature is most cruel when she sets the species against each other.

These thinking-crabs, then, looking upon me as God only knows what sort of prey or specimen, were intending me God only knows what sort of evil, when I broke the chain of terror which held me. The largest one, whom I faced, was now eyeing me with a sort of grim disapproval, a sort of anger, as if he haughtily resented my threatening actions—as a scientist might resent the writhing of a worm beneath the dissecting knife. At that, fury blazed in me and the flames were fanned by my fear. With one leap I reached the largest crab and with one desperate smash I crushed and killed him. Then bounding over his writhing form, I fled.

But I did not flee far. The thought came to me as I ran that these were they whom I sought for vengeance. Gloria—no wonder she started when I spoke the accursed name of "crab" and conceived the Devil to be in the form of a crab, when even then those fiends must have been stealing about us, tingling her sensitive thoughts with the psychic waves which always flowed from their horrid brains. I turned then and came back a few steps, my bludgeon raised. But the throng had bunched together, as cattle do upon the approach of a lion. Their claws were raised menacingly, and their cruel thought emanations struck me so like a power of physical force that I staggered backward and was unable to proceed against it. I knew then that in their way they feared me, for they backed slowly away, toward the cliffs, ever fronting me.

My history is long, but I must draw it to a close shortly. Since that hour I have waged a fierce and merciless warfare against a race I knew to be higher in culture and intellect than I. Scientists, they are, and in some horrid experiment of theirs, Gloria must have perished; I cannot say.

This I have learned. Their city is high up among those lofty tiers of cliffs which I cannot see because of the overhanging crags of the first tier. I suppose the whole island is like that, a mere base of basaltic rock, rising to a high flung pinnacle, no doubt, this pinnacle being the last tier of innumerable tiers of rocky walls. The monsters descend by a secret way which I have only just discovered. They have hunted me, and I have hunted them.

I have found this, also: the one point in common between these beasts and the human is that the higher the race develops mentally, the less acute become the physical faculties. I, who am as much lower than they mentally as a gorilla is lower than a human professor, am as deadly in single combat with them as a gorilla would be with an unarmed professor. I am quicker, stronger, of keener senses. I possess coordinations which they do not. In a word, there is a strange reversion here—I am the wild beast and they are the civilized and developed beings. I ask no mercy and I give none. What are my wishes and desires to them? I would never have molested them, any more than an eagle molests men, had they not taken my mate. But to satisfy some selfish hunger or to evolve some useless scientific theory, they took her life and ruined mine.

And now I have been, and shall be, the wild beast with a vengeance. A wolf may wipe out a herd, a man-eating lion has destroyed a whole village of men, and I am a wolf, a lion, to the people of the Black Coast. I have lived on such clams as I have found, for I have never been able to bring myself to eat of crab flesh. And I have hunted my foes, along the beaches, by sunlight and by starlight, among the boulders, and high up in the cliffs as far as I could climb. It has not been easy, and I must shortly admit defeat. They have fought me with psychic weapons against which I have no defense, and the constant crashing of their wills against mine has weakened me terribly, mentally and physically. I have lain in wait for single enemies and have even attacked and destroyed several, but the strain has been terrific.

Their power is mainly mental, and far, far exceeds human mesmerism. At first it was easy to plunge through the enveloping thought waves of one crab-man and kill him, but they have found weak places in my brain.

This I do not understand, but I know that of late I have gone through Hell with each battle. Their thought-tides have seemed to flow into my skull in waves of molten metal, freezing, burning, withering my brain and my soul. I lie hidden and when one crab-man approaches, I leap and I must kill quickly, as a lion must kill a man with a rifle before the victim can aim and fire.

Nor have I always escaped physically unscathed, for only yesterday the desperate stroke of a dying crab-man's claws tore off my left arm at the elbow. This would have killed me at one time, but now I shall live long enough to consummate my vengeance. Up there, in the higher tiers, up among the clouds where the crab city of horror broods, I must carry doom. I am a dying man—the wounds of my enemies' strange weapons have shown me my Fate, but my left arm is bound so that I shall not bleed to death, my crumbling brain will hold together long enough, and I still have my right hand and my iron bludgeon. I have noted that at dawn the crab-people keep closer to their high cliffs, and such as I have found at that time are very easy to kill. Why, I do not know, but my lower reason tells me that these Masters are at a low ebb of vitality at dawn, for some reason.

I am writing this by the light of a low-hanging moon. Soon dawn will come, and in the darkness before dawn, I shall go up the secret trail I have found which leads to the clouds—and above. I shall find the demon city and as the east begins to redden, I shall begin the slaughter. Oh, it will be a great battle! I will crush and crash and kill, and my foes will lie in great shattered heaps, and at last I too shall die. Good enough. I shall be content. I have scattered death like a lion. I have littered the beaches with their corpses. Before I die, I shall slay many more.

Gloria, the moon swings low. Dawn will be here soon. I do not know if you look in approval, from shadowland, on my red work of vengeance, but it has to some extent brought ease to my frozen soul. After all, these creatures and I are of different species, and it is Nature's cruel custom that the diverging orders may never live in peace with each other. They took my mate; I take their lives.

King of the Forgotten People

Jim Brill licked his parched lips, staring about him with bloodshot eyes. Behind him lay the sand, blown in curving ridges and long riffles; before him rose the stark outlines of the nameless mountains which were his goal. The sun hung above the western horizon, dull gold in the veil of dust which turned the sky a sickly yellow and lent its taste to the very air he breathed.

Yet he was thankful for it. But for the sandstorm he would have shared the fate which had overtaken his guides and servants.

The attack had come at dawn. From behind a bare ridge which had concealed their approach, a swarm of squat riders on shaggy horses had rushed the camp, howling like devils, shooting and slashing. In the midst of the fight the storm had brought blinding clouds of dust rolling over the desert, and through it Jim Brill had fled, knowing that he alone remained alive of the expedition which had toiled so far on its strange quest.

Now, after a grind that had taxed to the uttermost the powers of himself and his steed, he saw nothing of his pursuers, though the dust which still hung over the desert limited the range of his vision considerably.

He had been the only white man in the expedition. His previous experiences with Mongol bandits told him that they would not let him escape if they could help it.

Brill's equipment consisted of the .45 at his hip, a canteen with a few drops of water remaining in it, and the weary horse which drooped under his weight after the long flight.

Mindful of this, the man swung down from the saddle and plodded on, leading the animal. He scanned the rugged slopes ahead of him without hope. Sure death awaited him in the desert; what the mountains held, he could not know. No man knew what lay in this unexplored region. If any white man had ever entered it, he had never come out alive to tell what he had found.

The horse snorted suddenly and threw up its head, pulling back on the rein. Brill swore wearily and tried to quiet it. Its eyes rolled and its haunches quivered. Uneasily he looked about him. They were entering the narrow mouth of a canyon, the rocky floor of which sloped upward. The sides were steep, broken by jutting ledges. On one of these ledges, that overhung the canyon mouth, *something* moved, scuttled behind a boulder. Brill had a vague impression of something bulky and hairy that moved in a manner which suggested neither man nor beast.

He swung wide of that ledge, hugging the opposite wall. When they were even with it, the horse shied and snorted, but quieted after they had passed on. Whatever the animal feared was crouching up there among the boulders.

Brill was meditating on that matter as he went on up the canyon, when it was swept out of his mind by a sound that galvanized him—the drum of hoofs! He wheeled, the fear of a trapped wolf clutching him. Over the sands, heading for the canyon mouth, raced a cluster of riders—ten squat figures in wolf skins, flogging their horses and brandishing their sabers in exultation. The storm had not thrown them off his track. Now they had seen him, and they gave tongue stridently.

Brill let go the reins and dropped behind a rock, drawing his .45. They did not pull their rifles from the boots beneath their knees. They knew their prey was trapped, and their lust for slaughter with cold steel overcame their caution.

Brill sighted across the crest of the boulder at the foremost horseman. He mechanically judged the distance, intending to shoot just as the man came even with the overhanging ledge, under which his course was taking him. But that shot was never fired.

Just as the Mongol swept under the ledge, some sound or instinct caused him to look upward. As he did so, his yellow face went ashy; with a scream he threw up his arms. And simultaneously something black and hairy shot from the ledge and struck full on his breast, knocking him from his horse.

The men behind yelled in dismay and jerked their mounts back on their haunches. Above their clamor rose a scream of mortal agony. The horses wheeled and bolted, neighing shrilly.

The fallen Mongol writhed on the canyon floor, pinned beneath a shape that was like the figment of a nightmare. Brill glared at it, frozen with amazement. It was a spider, beyond the maddest dreams of spiders.

It was like a tarantula, with a gross body bristling with stiff hairs, and crouching black legs. But it was fully as big as a hog. Beneath it the shrieks of the Mongol ceased in a bubbling gurgle and his straining limbs went limp.

The other desert men had halted outside the canyon mouth, and one lifted a rifle and fired at the thing, but obviously his nerves were badly shaken. The bullet splatted harmlessly on a rock. As if disturbed by the sound, the monster turned in their direction, and with wild yells, the Mongols wheeled away and raced off across the sands in ignominious flight.

Brill watched them dwindle to black dots in the dust, then he rose gingerly from behind his rock. His horse had bolted away up the canyon. Twilight was approaching, and he was alone in the gorge with that hairy monstrosity which crouched like a black ogre over the man it had killed.

He hoped to steal away up the canyon without molestation. But the moment he rose into full view, the monster abandoned its prey and scuttled toward him at appalling speed.

Sweating with candid fright, Brill sighted at the oncoming black bulk and pulled the trigger. The impact of the big bullet knocked the thing sidewise, but it righted itself and came on, its eyes gleaming redly among its black bristles. Again and again the gun cracked, waking the echoes among the cliffs, before the monster tumbled over, working its hairy legs vainly. Then from all sides sounded a sinister rustling, and Brill shivered as he saw a grisly horde swarm down into the canyon. They seemed to emerge from every cranny, all converging on the stricken bulk quivering on the gorge floor. None were so large as it, but all were big enough and horrible enough to make a man doubt his sanity.

They ignored Brill, and fell on their mangled king as wolves fall on the wounded pack-leader. The giant was hidden in a writhing, working mass of black and grey-banded bodies, and Brill hurried up the canyon before they could finish their grisly repast and turn their attention to him.

He went up into the mountains because he dared not go down the gorge past that working hill of death; because only death by thirst lay in the desert beyond the canyon; and because it was to find these hills that he had plunged into the Gobi in the first place. Jim Brill was looking for a man; a man whom he hated more than anyone else on earth, yet for whom he was ready to risk his life.

It was certainly not love for Richard Barlow, eminent scientist and explorer, which had sent Brill on his quest; he had his own reasons and they were sufficient. Following dim clues and cryptic hints dropped by natives, he had concluded that the man he sought, if he still lived, was to be found in the mysterious hills which stood in an unmapped region of the Gobi. And he believed that these were the hills for which he had sought.

He emerged from the canyon into a wild tangle of cliffs and ravines. There was no vegetation, no water. The ridges rose grim and stark and black in the dusk about him. He thought of the great spiders, and strained his ears for the stealthy rustle of hairy legs. But the land lay desolate as the earth before man's creation, and the rising moon carved out black shadows of turreted cliffs, and showed him a dim path winding dizzily upward. A manmade trail that betokened human habitation somewhere.

He followed it; it wound up between sheer cliffs to a notch that showed a square of star-flecked sky. When he reached this he halted, panting from his exertions, and grunted with surprize. A heavy chain was stretched across the notch. With his hands resting on it, he gazed through the pass. It was narrow, and beyond it a long slope fell away into a valley where water gleamed in the moonlight among dense groves of trees. And something else gleamed among the trees—towers and walls, apparently of white marble.

Then the native tales were true, and there was a city among these hills. But what manner of men dwelt there? Even as the thought crossed his mind, something moved in the shadow of the cliffs. He caught a glimpse of a tall black figure with a curiously misshapen head, from which blazed eyes like balls of balefire. A choking cry escaped his lips. No human ever had eyes like that.

Gripping the chain to steady himself, he snatched at his revolver. And in that instant the universe burst around him, showering the sky with red sparks which were instantly quenched in the blackness of utter oblivion.

When Jim Brill regained his senses, his first impression was that he was lying on something soft and yielding to his rugged frame. There floated before him the soft pale oval of a face with dark, oblique eyes. A voice spoke somewhere, a familiar voice, but framed in an unfamiliar accent, and the face vanished. And then Jim Brill was fully conscious, and staring about him.

He lay on a satin divan in a chamber whose ceiling was a fretted dome. Satin hangings, worked with gilt dragons, adorned the walls, and thick carpets littered the floor.

This he saw in a sweeping glance, before his whole attention was riveted on the figure which sat before him. This was a heavily built man, whose incongruous robe of watered silk did not conceal the muscularity of his frame. A velvet cap was on his head, and from under this gleamed cold grey eyes, matching the rugged hardness of his features. It was the aggressive jut of the jaw that woke recognition in Brill.

"Barlow!"

He sat up, gripping the edge of the divan, glaring at the other as at one risen from the dead.

"Yes, it's me." The man's voice was sardonic. "Fancy *you* dropping in on me like this."

"I was hunting you, blast you!" bristled Brill; yes, this was Barlow, all right, with his gift of putting Brill's teeth on edge.

"Hunting me?" The surprize in Barlow's tone was genuine.

"Oh, it wasn't through any love of you," growled Brill. "I wasn't losing any sleep over you."

"Why, then?"

"Great Judas, man, can't you guess?" exclaimed Brill irritably. "Gloria—"

"Oh!" Barlow's expression was strange, as if he had just had recalled to his mind something he had forgotten. "So my wife sent you?"

"Naturally. She waited four years. Nobody knew whether you were alive or dead. You'd simply vanished into inner Mongolia. No word ever came back. Gloria came to me, because she knew no one else to come to. She financed the expedition, and here I am."

"And disgusted to find me alive," bantered Barlow. Brill merely grunted; he was too straightforward for hypocrisy.

"What happened to me?" he demanded. "What was that devil-thing I glimpsed just before I went out?"

"Just one of my servants in a robe and hood, with phosphorescent eyes painted on it. A little trick to discourage our superstitious neighbors, the Mongols. This faithful servant knocked you out by merely doing as I have taught him to do. He's one of the guards of the pass. He pushed a little handle and sent some electricity shooting along the chain you were leaning against. If he hadn't seen you were white, you'd be dead now."

Brill glanced at his hand. He knew nothing about electricity, but he had a vague idea that a shock hard enough to knock him senseless would be enough to burn his hand off.

"No burns on you," Barlow assured him. "You've seen men knocked cold by lightning without being burnt, haven't you? Same principle. I can control electricity as easily as I write my name. I know more about it than any other man in the world."

"Modest as usual," grunted Brill.

Barlow smiled with contemptuous tolerance. He had changed subtly in four years. There was more poise about him, a greater air of superiority. And there was a dim difference in his face: in his complexion, or the shape of his eyes—Brill could not place it, but it was there, somewhere. And his voice sounded almost unfamiliar at times.

"What is this dump, anyway?" Brill offered a strong contrast, in his dust-stained shirt, breeches and boots, to the exotic chamber and the figure in the embroidered silk. Brill was as tall and heavy as Barlow, a broad-shouldered, thick-chested man, with muscular arms and a nervous energy that could fire him to the quickness of a big cat.

"This is the city of Khor," said Barlow, as if that explained everything.

"Khor's a myth," grunted Brill. "I've heard the Mongols spinning their lies about it—"

Barlow smiled coldly. "You are in the position of the man who looked at a camel and refused to admit its existence. Khor exists and you are at this instant lying in its royal palace."

"Then where's the king?" demanded Brill sarcastically.

Barlow bowed with mock modesty, then folded his hands in his lap and looked at Brill with eyes that glinted between slitted lids. Brill was aware of a vague uneasiness. There was something wrong with his appearance.

"You mean you're the boss of this city?" he asked incredulously.

"And of this valley. Oh, it was not difficult. The people are grossly superstitious. I brought a whole laboratory on camels. My electrical devices alone convinced them that I was a mighty magician. I was the power behind the throne of their king, old Khitai Khan, until he was killed in a Mongol raid. Then I stepped into his shoes without any trouble; he had no heirs. I'm not only the big sorcerer of Khor, I'm Ak Khan, the White King."

"Who are these people?"

"A mixed race, Mongolian and Turkish, originally, with a strain of Chinese. Did you ever hear of Genghis Khan?"

"Who hasn't?" snapped Brill impatiently.

"Well, as you know, he conquered most of Asia in the early thirteenth century. He destroyed many cities, but he also built a few. This was his pleasure city, and was erected by skilled Persian architects. He filled it with slaves, both men and women. When he died, the world forgot about Khor, far up in these isolated mountains. The descendants of those slaves have lived on here ever since, under their own *khans*, raising their food in the valley, getting other things they wanted from the few Mongol traders who visited the hills."

He clapped his hands. "I was forgetting. You'll be hungry."

Brill's eyes widened as a slender silk-clad figure glided lithely into the chamber. "Then she wasn't a dream," he muttered.

"Scarcely!" Barlow laughed. "The Mongols stole her from a Chinese caravan, and sold her to me. Her name is Lala Tzu."

Chinese women held no attraction for Brill, but this girl was undeniably beautiful. Her oblique eyes glowed with a soft fire, her features were delicately molded, and her slender body was a marvel of suppleness.

"Dancing girl," decided Brill, as he set to work ravenously on the food and wine she set before him. From the corner of his eye, he saw her pass a slender arm about Barlow's shoulder and whisper some soft endearment into his ear. The man shrugged away from her with a show of impatience, and motioned her out of the room. Her slender shoulders drooped as if from a rebuke as she obeyed.

"Feel like seeing the city?" Barlow asked abruptly. Brill rose with a snort of disgust that such a question should be deemed necessary.

But as they left the chamber he realized that he had lain senseless for hours. Outside it was full daylight. Barlow led him through a series of hallways and out into a small open court, surrounded on three sides by galleries letting on to the palace, and on the fourth by a low wall. Over this wall Brill looked down into the city, in the midst of which the palace stood on a low hill. It was much like other Oriental towns, with market squares, open stalls with goods displayed, and flat-topped houses. The main differences were in the unusual cleanliness and the richness of the buildings. The houses were of marble instead of mud, and the streets were paved with the same material.

"Quarries of marble in these hills," grunted Barlow, as if reading Brill's thoughts. "Made them clean things up after I got to be *khan*. Didn't want plagues breeding in filth."

Brill had a good view of the valley, which was walled in by sheer cliffs. Besides the pass through which he had been brought, and up to which a sort of natural ramp led, there was no break in the massive palisades. A stream flowed through the valley, and the vegetation which crowded its banks was relieving after the barren monotony of the outer desert. Gardens, with small huts, checkered the valley floor, and sheep and cattle grazed up to the very wall of the city, which was of no great extent, though rather densely populated.

The inhabitants moved indolently through the streets in their silk garments. Their skins were yellowish, their faces round and flat, their slanted eyes dreamy. They seemed to Brill the remnants of a race which had fulfilled their destiny and now waited drowsily for death.

Barlow's servants were of a different breed, lean, dark-skinned men from Tonkin, who seldom spoke but looked quick and dangerous as cats. Barlow said he had brought them with him to Khor.

"I suppose you're wondering why I came here in the first place," the scientist remarked. "Well, I was always cramped in America. Fools with their stupid laws were always interfering. I heard of this place and it sounded ideal for my purposes. It is. I've gone beyond the wildest dreams of western scientists. Nobody interferes with me. Here human life means nothing; the will of the ruler everything."

Brill scowled at the implication.

"You mean you experiment with human subjects?"

"Why not? These servants of mine live only to do my bidding, and the Khoranese consider me a priest of Erlik, the god they have worshipped since time immemorial. The subjects I demand of them are no more than offerings to the god, according to their way of thinking. I only sacrifice them to the cause of science."

"To the cause of the devil!" growled Brill, revolted. "Don't pull that stuff with me. You care nothing about the progress of humanity. All you've ever considered has been your own ambitions."

Barlow laughed without resentment.

"At any rate, my will is the only law there is in Khor—a fact you'll do well to remember. If I occasionally use one of these fat fools in an experiment from which he fails to recover, I also protect them. They used to suffer from the raids of the Mongols before I came. The only way into the valley is through that pass, but even so, the raiders often cut their way through and devastated everything outside the city walls. Sooner or later they'd have destroyed the city itself.

"I barred the pass with that electric chain, and have done other things that scared the Mongols so badly they seldom venture into the hills. I have a machine in a dome of this palace, for instance, that any world power would pay a fortune for if they knew of it."

"Those big spiders—" began Brill.

"More of my work. They were originally tiny creatures which inhabited caves in the hills. I used my science to make carnivorous monsters out of them. Good watch dogs. The Mongols fear them out of all proportion to their actual ability to do harm. Developing them was a triumph, but I've gone far beyond that now. I am now exploring the profoundest of all mysteries."

"What's that?"

"The human mind; the ego, spirit, soul. Call it what you will. It remains the primary essence of life. Too long men have dabbled in what they called the occult, after the fashion of witch doctors. It's time the mystery was approached in a scientific manner. I have so approached it."

"Well, listen," said Brill abruptly. "I came a long way to find you, thinking you were a prisoner of a hill tribe. Now I find you master of the tribe, and here of your own free will. You might at least have sent word to Gloria."

"How?" demanded Barlow. "None of my servants could have got through alive, and I couldn't trust a Mongol trader to get a letter outside. Anyway, when a man is absorbed in his life's work, he can't worry himself about a woman."

"Not even his wife, eh?" sneered Brill, his resentment growing every minute. "Well, now I've found you, I want to know, are you coming back to America with me?"

"Certainly not."

"What shall I tell Gloria?"

"Tell her whatever you choose; you will anyway."

Brill's big fists clenched. The man's attitude was intolerable. But before he could make the savage reply which framed itself on his lips, Barlow said: "I'll show you my latest triumph. You won't understand it, and maybe you won't believe it. But it's too big for me to keep still about. I've got to show it to some white man, even you."

As Barlow led the way back through the corridors, Brill saw a slim hand draw aside a hanging, and the face of Lala Tzu was framed in the dark velvet. Her eyes rested meltingly on Barlow, then grew hard and bright with anger as they turned toward Brill. Evidently the girl resented his presence. Doubtless she understood English and had overheard enough of their conversation to fear that Brill was going to take her master back to America with him.

Barlow halted before an arched door of lacquered teak on which writhed a golden dragon. An antique lock was manipulated by an equally antique key, and Barlow led Brill into the chamber.

Above it rose a dome inlaid with gold and ivory. The walls, of a strange, softly glistening green stone, were not tapestried. The floor was of the same material. There were no windows, the dome being craftily pierced so as to let in enough light dimly to illuminate the interior. The only furniture was a satin divan.

"This is the meditation chamber of the great khan, Genghis," said Barlow. "He alone entered it during his lifetime, and after his death none crossed the threshold until I came. Here he sat and dreamed the dreams induced by wine, opium and *bhang*. Here I first conceived my great discovery.

"Everything leaves its impression on its surroundings, sights, sounds, even thought, for thought is a tangible force, invisible only because on a different plane than visible substance. When a man occupies a room, he leaves the imprints of his personality on that room as surely as his fleshly feet leave their imprints in mud or sand. Wood, steel, stone, all are, in effect, potential camera films and phonograph whereon are imperishably recorded all sounds and scenes that have been in their vicinity. But, in the case of the man in the room, other people come and go, leaving their impressions too, and all these different impressions overlie each other and become hopelessly mixed and muddled.

"Naturally, some substances retain impressions longer and more clearly than others, just as mud retains a footprint more clearly than stone. These walls possess that quality to a phenomenal extent. There is no stone like this natural to the earth. I think it came from a meteorite which fell in this valley long ago, and which was sawed up and used for this purpose by the builders of Khor.

"These walls hold the thought-impressions of Genghis Khan, overlaid by no others, except mine, which are so few they scarcely count. They contain, indelibly imprinted, all the thoughts and dreams and ideas that made up the personality of the great conqueror. Imagine these walls as a camera film. On them I shall develop the pictures invisibly recorded by them!"

Brill grunted scornfully.

"How? By waving a magic wand?"

"By processes I can no more make you understand than I could make a Congo savage understand television," answered Barlow imperturbably. "I'll tell you this much, that even you may be able to understand: only a novice needs mechanical contrivances to aid him in psychic experiments. A master dispenses with artificial aids. He no more needs them than an athlete needs crutches, to use an example concrete enough for your low-grade mind to grasp.

"I have developed my psychic energy—I use the term for lack of a more explicit one. That energy is the real power of life; the brain itself is but one of its emanations, a machine through which it works. It needs no mechanical devices. Mechanics are but channels for its release. I have discovered how to release its terrific energy naturally.

"I will admit that the experiment I am now about to perform is made possible only by a strange series of circumstances, depending, ultimately, upon the marvelous quality of these walls. On this planet some people are psychic; here is an inanimate substance which is definitely psychic."

"But an abstract thought—"

"What is any personality but a material appearance embodying myriad abstractions? The universe is a giant chain, with each link inseparably interlocked with every other link. Some of these links we are cognizant of by our external senses, others only through our psychic powers, and then only when these are specially developed. I merely frame an unseen link into a form recognizable by our external faculties.

"It is merely a matter of transmutation, of reduction to basic principles. Thoughts deal, ultimately, with material things. Emanations of the mentality which leave their impressions on material things, are transmutable into forms recognizable by the external senses. Watch!"

Barlow sank upon the divan and resting his elbows on his knees, dropped his chin in his hands and stared hypnotically at the opposite wall. A peculiar change passed over the atmosphere of the room; the light faded to a twilight grey. The even hue of the green walls altered with interchanging shades, like clouds passing over a dusky sky. Brill stared about uneasily. He saw only the bare, changing walls, the dim grey dome above them, and that cryptic figure sitting statue-like on the divan.

He looked again at the walls. Shadows flowed across them in endless procession; shapeless, nebulous, swiftly they passed. Sometimes a distortion of the dim light lent them the appearance of misshapen human figures. All converged upon the spot on which Barlow's mesmeric gaze was riveted. And at that point the green substance began to glow, to deepen, to take on the appearance of translucency. In its depths there was movement and unrest, a merging of dim anthropomorphic shapes. As the shadows flowed into it, this amalgamation took on more distinct outlines. Brill smothered a cry. It was as if he looked into a deep green lake, and in its depths, mistily, he saw a human figure, a squat giant in silk robes. The outlines of the garments and body were vague and unstable, but the face stood out more distinctly beneath the velvet skullcap.

It was a broad, immobile face, with slanted grey eyes, and a wisp of a moustache drooping over wide thin lips. *It was—*

The cry escaped Brill in spite of himself. He was on his feet, shaking like a leaf. Abruptly the image vanished. The shadows faded, leaving the smooth green surface of the walls unclouded. Barlow was watching him cynically.

"Well?" inquired the scientist.

"It's a trick," snapped Brill. "You've got a picture projector hidden somewhere. I've seen Genghis Khan's face on old Chinese coins, and so have you. It wouldn't be hard for you to fake up something." But as he spoke he was uncomfortably aware of the cold sweat pouring off his skin.

"I didn't expect you to believe it," retorted Barlow, sitting like a silk-clad Buddha. In the dim light the unpleasant change in his countenance was more noticeable. It almost amounted to a deformity, and still Brill could not place it.

"What you believe matters little," said Barlow placidly. "I *know* the figure was Genghis Khan. No, not his ghost; not a phantom resurrected from the dead. But the combined total of his thoughts, dreams and memories, which together make up a sum as real and vital as the man himself. It *is* the man; for what is a man besides the total of his feelings, emotions, sensations and thoughts? Genghis Khan's body has been dust for centuries; but the immortal parts of him slumber in these walls. When they are materialized upon a visible plane, naturally they take on the aspect of the physical man from which they emanated.

"I have sat here for hours and watched the great khan grow more and more distinct until walls and chamber and time seemed to fade, until only he and my own mind seemed the only realities in the universe—until he seemed to flow into and merge with my own ego! I understand his dreams, conceptions, the secret of his power.

"To all great conquerors, to Caesar, Alexander, Napoleon, Genghis Khan, nature gave powers not possessed by other men. And I am acquiring the uncanny genius by which Genghis Khan, who was born in a nomad's horsehide tent, overthrew armies, kings, cities, empires!"

He had risen to his feet in his excitement, and now strode out into a curtained corridor, closing the lacquered door behind him.

"And what of it?" demanded Brill, who had naturally followed him.

"I too will become a conqueror! My ego absorbs all the impressions left by his. I shall be emperor of Asia!"

"Bunkum!" snorted Brill. "I'm sick of listening to your pipe dreams. What I want to know is, are you ever coming back to America, and Gloria?"

"No; you are going to bring Gloria to me."

"What!" exclaimed Brill.

"Yes, I've decided. She'll fit very nicely into my schemes. She'll come if I send her a message, for she is a dutiful wife."

"Entirely too much so," snarled Brill. "Otherwise she'd have gotten a divorce long ago. Yes, she'd come. Not because she loves you. Her parents forced her into marrying you when she was only a child, and you've treated her like a dog; but she has an overdeveloped sense of duty. That's why she sent me looking for you. She and I have always loved one another. I hoped I'd find you dead. I'm sorry you're alive. But I'm not going to bring Gloria into this God-forsaken valley. What about that Chinese girl, Lala Tzu? You have the nerve to—"

"Silence!" roared Barlow imperiously. "You shall bring my wife to me!"

"Why, you—!" Brill was on his feet, his big fists clenched. But before either could move, a slim figure darted into the scene from behind a hanging. It was Lala Tzu, her beautiful features contorted with fury.

"I heard!" she shrilled at Barlow. "You shall not bring another woman here! You shall not put me aside for a white woman! I will kill—"

With his face convulsed with passion, Barlow struck her savagely in the face with his open hand, ripping out a volley of staccato gutturals Brill did not understand. Three lean silent Tonkinese glided into the hallway, laid hands on Lala Tzu and dragged her, kicking and screaming, through a curtained archway. There was the sound of a blow, a shriek of pain, then her passionate sobs dwindled as she was carried away.

Barlow stood posed like an image of imperial Oriental wrath, and Brill glared at him, his hair bristling with incredulous horror.

"I know now!" the explorer roared. "I've sensed a change in you, from the beginning! Your accent—it's Mongol! Your eyes have begun to slant; there's a copperish cast to your skin. Those impressions you've raved about—you've absorbed them until they're changing you! *Changing you!* You damned devil—*you're changing into a Mongol!*"

A wild flood of devilish exultation lit Barlow's countenance.

"Yes!" he bellowed. "I said I was absorbing the mental emanations of Genghis Khan. *I will be Genghis Khan!* His personality will replace mine, because his is the stronger. Like him I will conquer the world. I will fight the Mongols no longer, because I am becoming one of them. They will be my people; all Asians will be my people! I will make a gift to the chief of the Mongols and win his friendship. You shall return to America and bring me the little fool I married in a moment of weakness; she is beautiful; she shall be my gift to Togrukh Khan, the Mongol chief—"

With a maddened roar Brill drove at him, every nerve of his big muscular body straining with a primitive passion to smash and break and rip. With a guttural snarl the powerful scientist met him breast to breast.

Brill scarcely felt the blows that rained on his face and body. In a red mist of berserk fury he drove Barlow backward, smashing his iron fists again and again into the hated features of his enemy, until the scientist crashed over backwards among the ruins of a table, and Brill fell on him and sank his fingers into Barlow's bull throat. A worrying, wordless mouthing snarled from Brill's lips as he drove all the power of heavy shoulders and corded arms into his strangling hands. Blood from Barlow's torn throat trickled over Brill's fingers; the scientist's tongue protruded between blue lips; his eyes were glazing.

Men were swarming into the corridor, but Brill, in the fog of his wrath, was scarcely aware of their shouts, or of the hands which tore vainly at his corded forearms. Then a gun butt, swung with desperate force, crashed on his head and the lights went out.

Brill came to himself with a clear understanding of all that had occurred, and a fervent desire to renew the combat. But he was bound into a chair, hand and foot. Blood trickled into his eyes from a wound in his scalp. He shook his head to clear his vision, and saw Barlow facing him. Brill grinned wolfishly when he saw the damage he had done to the scientist's features. He knew that Barlow's nose was broken, and at least one of his ribs cracked. His face looked like a mask of raw beef, and his one good eye blazed fiendishly.

"Get out!" he croaked, choking with passion, and the impassive Tonkinese glided from the chamber. Twisting his head to stare about, Brill decided that he had been brought to Barlow's laboratory. Scientific appliances of all kinds littered the large room, and huge glass jars contained grisly relics at which Brill did not care to look twice. He glanced back at Barlow, from whom all sanity seemed to have departed.

"You hoped to find me dead," the man was raving, "so you could go back and marry my wife! Well, I'm going to send you back to her. Do you see that thing there? That stuffed ape? Well, that's what you're going to look like within the hour. Laugh, you ignorant fool! Less than a month ago that ape was a man, as intelligent and well developed as you are. I have discovered a process of degeneration that retrogrades the human into the beast which was his progenitor. I could go still further, and revert him to the protozoa which fathered us all.

"But I will leave you an ape. That specimen died, but you shall live—to prance and gibber in some zoo or circus!" His voice rose to a scream. "You fool, do you realize what I'm saying? You'll be a beast! A filthy, hairy, verminous anthropoid! I'll send you back to my loving wife with my compliments—*aaah!*"

It happened so quickly it blurred Brill's sight. From a curtained arch a lithe, tigerish figure had sprung, wielding a gleaming shard of steel. He heard the impact of the blow, the scientist's grunt of agony. Then Barlow, his face a death-mask, took one reeling step and crumpled. His hands, emerging from the wide silk sleeves, worked spasmodically and were still. And Brill shuddered, for those hands were yellow-tinted and the nails were not those of a white man. Barlow's dead features were scarcely recognizable; their aspect was alien and unnatural.

Lala Tzu stood over the man she had killed, grasping her dagger, and staring with a fixed, wide-eyed stare at Brill. He gave back her stare in fascinated dread; this lovely, soulless young animal was just as likely to kill him as she had killed the man she once had loved. Creatures of whims, these dancing girls, beautiful, vagrant, cruel and passionate. Then he cried out an instinctive warning. Over her shoulder a yellow face peered through parted hangings. One of the Tonkinese servants glared at the body of his master. Lala Tzu cried out shrilly and sprang at him, lifting her dagger, but the face vanished, and in the corridor outside sounded a strident screaming. Lala Tzu stood uncertainly.

"Cut me loose, girl!" Brill roared, tearing at his bonds. "I'll help you!"

In an instant she had reached him and slashed his cords. Casting about for a weapon, he saw a great Mongol scimitar hanging on the wall. He tore it free just as the Tonkinese rushed in, daggers in their hands. Gripping the ponderous weapon with both hands, he heaved it above his head and flailed right and left. The razor edge sheared through flesh and bone, severing a yellow man's head and shoulder from his body. Another screamed as his arm jumped from his shoulder on a spurting fountain of blood. The others gave back, appalled, then ran shrieking from the chamber. Brill glared after them, sickened at the havoc he had wrought, but fighting mad. Lala Tzu tugged at his arm.

"They have gone for guns!" she cried shrilly. "They will shoot us down like dogs! We can not escape from the palace, but there is a place where we can take refuge!"

He followed her out of the chamber and along a corridor. Behind them the palace was in an uproar, and somewhere sounded a popping like that of many firecrackers. It seemed to come from outside the palace, but the din within was so furious Brill could not be certain. The girl's little feet pattered swiftly along the marble tiles ahead of him, until she came to a winding stair. Up this she went without hesitation. It wound up and up into a lofty dome. Brill's breath came in gasps before he reached the top. Their pursuers were closer on their heels than he realized. Just as he reached the head of the stair and turned, a howling Tonkinese charged up and around the last turn with such headlong recklessness that he was thrusting a pistol into Brill's face before the American could move. The scimitar fell as the gun cracked; powder burnt Brill's face, and the Oriental's head caved in like an eggshell beneath the shearing blade. The impact of the stroke knocked the body backward down the stair where it demoralized the men storming up it.

Guns spat and bullets spattered against the wall, but Brill and the girl were out of sight around the last bend of the stair, and the natives dared not charge up around it in the teeth of those terrible sword-strokes. As he waited, sweat dripping from his face and both hands gripping the long hilt, Brill heard a sudden uproar beyond the palace walls. Those below heard it, and a sudden silence fell upon the stair. In the hush Brill heard a rising clamor of yells, and the cracking of many rifles. Lala Tzu cried out to him, and he risked his life by whirling and looking where she pointed.

They were under the arch of a lofty dome which was the pinnacle of the palace. On a platform was set what seemed to be a huge telescope, its muzzle protruding through a kind of loophole. Looking through a small window beside it, Brill could see the city streets below him, and the walls and the valley beyond. And he saw that doom had fallen on Khor.

Down the ramp that led from the pass swarmed chanting riders, and others raced around the valley, firing huts and shooting cattle in pure wantonness. Several hundred more were thronged outside the great gate. Swinging a huge log between their horses like a battering ram, some were assailing the portal, while others kept up a withering fire at the defenders on the walls who strove to return their volleys. The Mongols were in the valley at last, despite all Barlow's barriers!

In the palace below the clamor burst out afresh, and Brill wheeled toward the stair, sword lifted. But the attack did not come. A strident voice screamed in desperate urgency, and Lala Tzu, listening, turned to Brill.

"They say the Mongols will break down the gate and cut all their throats," she said. "They beg you to save them. You, too, are a white magician, they think. They say a Mongol climbed the cliffs and shot the watcher at the pass before he could push the handle and make the chain impassable. They came in such numbers they did not fear the spiders. They are led by Togrukh Khan, who does not fear the white man's magic. They swear they will obey you if you save them from the Mongols."

"How can I?" he asked helplessly.

"I will show you!" She caught his hand and drew him toward the great machine on the platform. "*He* always said he would use this if the Mongols reached the wall. See, it is aimed like a gun at the gate. He showed me—hold it so and pull this trigger!"

"Make them swear first they won't harm us," said Brill, and she called to the terrified Khoranese below. There was an answering babble, wild shouts, the sudden sound of heavy blows, then one voice shouting triumphantly.

"What was that?" he demanded nervously.

"The Tonkinese wished to kill us," she answered. "The men of Khor have slain them, and swear to obey you. Fear not. They will keep their word. Haste, the gate begins to buckle!"

It was true. The wretched Khoranese who had been trying to hold the portal scattered screaming. The gate crashed inward and the riders began swarming through, howling like wolves as they saw their helpless prey before them. Brill sighted along the great barrel and pulled the trigger. He expected some kind of a report, an explosion accompanied by a recoil. There was nothing of the sort. But from the flaring muzzle a long beam of blue light shot to the gate and the horde which thronged it. The result was hideous.

For an instant there was a blurring in which nothing was distinct. Then an awful cry arose. The gate was choked with a blackened mass of disintegrated flesh and blackened bone that had been a hundred men and horses. That ray had neither burned nor shattered, by some awful force it had blasted into Eternity all that were crowded in the gate, and had cut a wide swatch through the hordes massed outside. An instant the survivors sat stunned, then with mad screams they wheeled and flogged their steeds toward the hills, fighting like madmen to gain the pass. Brill watched, his soul revolted, until Lala Tzu touched his arm. On the stair below rose a paean of exultation.

"The people of Khor give thanks for their deliverance," said Lala Tzu, "and beg you mount the throne of Khitai Khan, which was the throne of Ak Khan, whom you have slain."

"Whom *I* have slain?" grunted Brill. "That's a good one! Well, you tell the people of Khor that I thank them kindly, but all I want is horses and food and canteens of water. I want to get out of this country while the Mongols are still running in another direction, and I want to get back to America as quick as I can. Somebody's waiting for me there."

Almuric

Foreword

It was not my original intention ever to divulge the whereabouts of Esau Cairn, or the mystery surrounding him. My change of mind was brought about by Cairn himself, who retained a perhaps natural and human desire to give his strange story to the world which had disowned him and whose members can now never reach him. What he wishes to tell is his affair. One phase of my part of the transaction I refuse to divulge; I will not make public the means by which I transported Esau Cairn from his native Earth to a planet in a solar system undreamed of by even the wildest astronomical theorists. Nor will I divulge by what means I later achieved communication with him, and heard his story from his own lips, whispering ghostily across the cosmos.

Let me say that it was not premeditated. I stumbled upon the Great Secret quite by accident in the midst of a scientific experiment, and never thought of putting it to any practical use, until that night when Esau Cairn groped his way into my darkened observatory, a hunted man, with the blood of a human being on his hands. It was chance led him there, the blind instinct of the hunted thing to find a den wherein to turn at bay.

Let me state definitely and flatly, that, whatever the appearances against him, Esau Cairn is not, and was never, a criminal. In that specific case he was merely the pawn of a corrupt political machine which turned on him when he realized his position and refused to comply further with its demands. In general, the acts of his life which might suggest a violent and unruly nature simply sprang from his peculiar mental make-up.

Science is at last beginning to perceive that there is sound truth in the popular phrase, "born out of his time." Certain natures are attuned to certain phases or epochs of history, and these natures, when cast by chance into an age alien to their reactions and emotions, find difficulty in adapting themselves to their surroundings. It is but another example of nature's inscrutable laws, which sometimes are thrown out of stride by some cosmic friction or rift, and result in havoc to the individual and the mass.

Many men are born outside their century; Esau Cairn was born outside his epoch. Neither a moron nor a lowclass primitive, possessing a mind well above the average, he was, nevertheless, distinctly out of place in the modern age. I never knew a man of intelligence so little fitted for adjustment in a machine-made civilization. (Let it be noted that I speak of him in the past tense; Esau Cairn lives, as far as the cosmos is concerned; as far as the earth is concerned, he is dead, for he will never again set foot upon it.)

He was of a restless mold, impatient of restraint and resentful of authority. Not by any means a bully, he at the same time refused to countenance what he considered to be the slightest infringement on his rights. He was primitive in his passions, with a gusty temper and a courage inferior to none on this planet. His life was a series of repressions. Even in athletic contests he was forced to hold himself in, lest he injure his opponents. Esau Cairn was, in short, a freak—a man whose physical body and mental bent leaned back to the primordial.

Born in the Southwest, of old frontier stock, he came of a race whose characteristics were inclined toward violence, and whose traditions were of war and feud and battle against man and nature. The mountain country in which he spent his boyhood carried out the tradition. Contest—physical contest—was the breath of life to him. Without it he was unstable and uncertain. Because of his peculiar physical make-up, full enjoyment in a legitimate way, in the ring or on the football field was denied him. His career as a football player was marked by crippling injuries received by men playing against him, and he was branded as an unnecessarily brutal man, who fought to maim his opponents rather than win games. This was unfair. The injuries were simply resultant from the use of his great strength, always so far superior to that of the men opposed to him. Cairn was not a great sluggish lethargic giant as so many powerful men are; he was vibrant with fierce life, ablaze with dynamic energy. Carried away by the lust of combat, he forgot to control his powers, and the result was broken limbs or fractured skulls for his opponents.

It was for this reason that he withdrew from college life, unsatisfied and embittered, and entered the professional ring. Again his fate dogged him. In his training-quarters, before he had had a single match, he almost fatally injured a sparring partner. Instantly the papers pounced upon the incident, and played it up beyond its natural proportions. As a result Cairn's license was revoked.

Bewildered, unsatisfied, he wandered over the world, a restless Hercules, seeking outlet for the immense vitality that surged tumultuously within him, searching vainly for some form of life wild and strenuous enough to satisfy his cravings, born in the dim red days of the world's youth.

Of the final burst of blind passion that banished him forever from the life wherein he roamed, a stranger, I need say little. It was a nine-days' wonder, and the papers exploited it with screaming headlines. It was an old story— a rotten city government, a crooked political boss, a man chosen, unwittingly on his part, to be used as a tool and serve as a puppet.

Cairn, restless, weary of the monotony of a life for which he was unsuited, was an ideal tool—for a while. But Cairn was neither a criminal nor a fool. He understood their game quicker than they expected, and took a stand surprisingly firm to them, who did not know the real man.

Yet, even so, the result would not have been so violent if the man who had used and ruined Cairn had any real intelligence. Used to grinding men under his feet and seeing them cringe and beg for mercy, Boss Blaine could not understand that he was dealing with a man to whom his power and wealth meant nothing.

Yet so schooled was Cairn to iron self-control that it required first a gross insult, then an actual blow on the part of Blaine, to rouse him. Then for the first time in his life, his wild nature blazed into full being. All his thwarted and repressed life surged up behind the clenched fist that broke Blaine's skull like an eggshell and stretched him lifeless on the floor, behind the desk from which he had for years ruled a whole district.

Cairn was no fool. With the red haze of fury fading from his glare, he realized that he could not hope to escape the vengeance of the machine that controlled the city. It was not because of fear that he fled Blaine's house. It was simply because of his primitive instinct to find a more convenient place to turn at bay and fight out his death fight.

So it was that chance led him to my observatory.

He would have left, instantly, not wishing to embroil me in his trouble, but I persuaded him to remain and tell me his story. I had long expected some catastrophe of the sort. That he had repressed himself as long as he did, shows something of his iron character. His nature was as wild and untamed as that of a maned lion.

He had no plan—he simply intended to fortify himself somewhere and fight it out with the police until he was riddled with lead.

I at first agreed with him, seeing no better alternative. I was not so naïve as to believe he had any chance in the courts, with the evidence that would be presented against him. Then a sudden thought occurred to me, so fantastic and alien, and yet so logical, that I instantly propounded it to my companion. I told him of the Great Secret, and gave him proof of its possibilities.

In short, I urged him to take the chance of a flight through space, rather than meet the certain death that awaited him.

And he agreed. There was no place in the universe which would support human life. But I had looked beyond the knowledge of men, in universes beyond universes. And I chose the only planet I knew on which a human being could exist—the wild, primitive, and strange planet I named Almuric.

Cairn understood the risks and uncertainties as well as I. But he was utterly fearless—and the thing was done. Esau Cairn left the planet of his birth, for a world swimming afar in space, alien, aloof, strange.

Esau Cairn's Narrative

The transition was so swift and brief, that it seemed less than a tick of time lay between the moment I placed myself in Professor Hildebrand's strange machine, and the instant when I found myself standing upright in the clear sunlight that flooded a broad plain. I could not doubt that I had indeed been transported to another world. The landscape was not so grotesque and fantastic as I might have supposed, but it was indisputably alien to anything existing on the Earth.

But before I gave much heed to my surroundings, I examined my own person to learn if I had survived that awful flight without injury. Apparently I had. My various parts functioned with their accustomed vigor. But I was naked. Hildebrand had told me that inorganic substance could not survive the transmutation. Only vibrant, living matter could pass unchanged through the unthinkable gulfs which lie between the planets. I was grateful that I had not fallen into a land of ice and snow. The plain seemed filled with a lazy summer-like heat. The warmth of the sun was pleasant on my bare limbs.

On every side stretched away a vast level plain, thickly grown with short green grass. In the distance this grass attained a greater height, and through it I caught the glint of water. Here and there throughout the plain this phenomenon was repeated, and I traced the meandering course of several rivers, apparently of no great width. Black dots moved through the grass near the rivers, but their nature I could not determine. However, it was quite evident that my lot had not been cast on an uninhabited planet, though I could not guess the nature of the inhabitants. My imagination peopled the distances with nightmare shapes.

It is an awesome sensation to be suddenly hurled from one's native world into a new strange alien sphere. To say that I was not appalled at the prospect, that I did not shrink and shudder in spite of the peaceful quiet of my environs, would be hypocrisy. I, who had never known fear, was transformed into a mass of quivering, cowering nerves, starting at my own shadow. It was that man's utter helplessness was borne in upon me, and my mighty frame and massive thews seemed frail and brittle as the body of a child. How could I pit them against an unknown world? In that instant I would gladly have returned to Earth and the gallows that awaited me, rather than face the nameless terrors with which imagination peopled my newfound world. But I was soon to learn that those thews I now despised were capable of carrying me through greater perils than I dreamed.

A slight sound behind me brought me around to stare amazedly at the first inhabitant of Almuric I was to encounter. And the sight, awesome and menacing as it was, yet drove the ice from my veins and brought back some of my dwindling courage. The tangible and material can never be as grisly as the unknown, however perilous.

At my first startled glance I thought it was a gorilla which stood before me. Even with the thought I realized that it was a man, but such a man as neither I nor any other Earthman had ever looked upon.

He was not much taller than I, but broader and heavier, with a great spread of shoulders, and thick limbs knotted with muscles. He wore a loin-cloth of some silklike material, girdled with a broad belt which supported a long knife in a leather sheath. High-strapped sandals were on his feet. These details I took in at a glance, my attention being instantly fixed in fascination on his face.

Such a countenance it is difficult to imagine or describe. The head was set squarely between the massive shoulders, the neck so squat as to be scarcely apparent. The jaw was square and powerful, and as the wide thin lips lifted in a snarl, I glimpsed brutal tusklike teeth. A short bristly beard masked the jaw, set off by fierce, up-curving mustaches. The nose was almost rudimentary, with wide flaring nostrils. The eyes were small, bloodshot, and an icy gray in color. From the thick black brows the forehead, low and receding, sloped back into a tangle of coarse, bushy hair. The ears were small and very close-set.

The mane and beard were very blue-black, and the creature's limbs and body were almost covered with hair of the same hue. He was not, indeed, as hairy as an ape, but he was hairier than any human being I had ever seen.

I instantly realized that the being, hostile or not, was a formidable figure. He fairly emanated strength—hard, raw, brutal power. There was not an ounce of surplus flesh on him. His frame was massive, with heavy bones. His hairy skin rippled with muscles that looked iron-hard. Yet it was not altogether his body that spoke of dangerous power. His look, his carriage, his whole manner reflected a terrible physical might backed by a cruel and implacable mind. As I met the blaze of his bloodshot eyes, I felt a wave of corresponding anger. The stranger's attitude was arrogant and provocative beyond description. I felt my muscles tense and harden instinctively.

But for an instant my resentment was submerged by the amazement with which I heard him speak in perfect English!

"Thak! What manner of man are you?"

His voice was harsh, grating and insulting. There was nothing subdued or restrained about him. Here were the naked primitive instincts and manners, unmodified. Again I felt the old red fury rising in me, but I fought it down.

"I am Esau Cairn," I answered shortly, and halted, at a loss how to explain my presence on his planet.

His arrogant eyes roved contemptuously over my hairless limbs and smooth face, and when he spoke, it was with unbearable scorn.

"By Thak, are you a man or a woman?"

My answer was a smash of my clenched fist that sent him rolling on the sward.

The act was instinctive. Again my primitive wrath had betrayed me. But I had no time for self-reproach. With a scream of bestial rage my enemy sprang up and rushed at me, roaring and frothing. I met him breast to breast, as reckless in my wrath as he, and in an instant was fighting for my life.

I, who had always had to restrain and hold down my strength lest I injure my fellow men, for the first time in my life found myself in the clutches of a man stronger than myself. This I realized in the first instant of impact, and it was only by the most desperate efforts that I fought clear of his crushing embrace.

The fight was short and deadly. The only thing that saved me was the fact that my antagonist knew nothing of boxing. He could—and did—strike powerful blows with his clenched fists, but they were clumsy, ill-timed and erratic. Thrice I mauled my way out of grapples that would have ended with the snapping of my spine. He had no knack of avoiding blows; no man on Earth could have survived the terrible battering I gave him. Yet he incessantly surged in on me, his mighty hands spread to drag me down. His nails were almost like talons, and I was quickly bleeding from a score of places where they had torn the skin.

Why he did not draw his dagger I could not understand, unless it was because he considered himself capable of crushing me with his bare hands—which proved to be the case. At last, half blinded by my smashes, blood gushing from his split ears and splintered teeth, he did reach for his weapon, and the move won the fight for me.

Breaking out of a half-clinch, he straightened out of his defensive crouch and drew his dagger. And as he did so, I hooked my left into his belly with all the might of my heavy shoulders and powerfully driving legs behind it. The breath went out of him in an explosive gasp, and my fist sank to the wrist in his belly. He swayed, his mouth flying open, and I smashed my right to his sagging jaw. The punch started at my hip, and carried every ounce of my weight and strength. He went down like a slaughtered ox and lay without twitching, blood spreading out over his beard. That last smash had torn his lip open from the corner of his mouth to the rim of his chin, and must surely have fractured his jawbone as well.

Panting from the fury of the bout, my muscles aching from his crushing grasp, I worked my raw, skinned knuckles, and stared down at my victim, wondering if 1 had sealed my doom. Surely, I could expect nothing now but hostility from the people of Almuric. Well, I thought, as well be hanged for a sheep as a goat. Stooping, I despoiled my adversary of his single garment, belt and weapon, and transferred them to my own frame. This done, I felt some slight renewal of confidence. At least I was partly clothed and armed.

I examined the dagger with much interest. A more murderous weapon I have never seen. The blade was perhaps nineteen inches in length, double-edged, and sharp as a razor. It was broad at the haft, tapering to a diamond point. The guard and pommel were of silver, the hilt covered with a substance somewhat like shagreen. The blade was indisputably steel, but of a quality I had never before encountered. The whole was a triumph of the weapon-maker's art, and seemed to indicate a high order of culture.

From my admiration of my newly-acquired weapon, I turned again to my victim, who was beginning to show signs of returning consciousness. Instinct caused me to sweep the grasslands, and in the distance, to the south, I saw a group of figures moving toward me. They were surely men, and armed men. I caught the flash of the sunlight on steel. Perhaps they were of the tribe of my adversary. If they found me standing over their senseless comrade, wearing the spoils of conquest, their attitude toward me was not hard to visualize.

I cast my eyes about for some avenue of escape or refuge, and saw that the plain, some distance away, ran up into low green-clad foothills. Beyond these in turn, I saw larger hills, marching up and up in serried ranges. Another glance showed the distant figures to have vanished among the tall grass along one of the river courses, which they must cross before they reached the spot where I stood.

Waiting for no more, I turned and ran swiftly toward the hills. I did not lessen my pace until I reached the foot of the first foothills, where I ventured to look back, my breath coming in gasps, and my heart pounding suffocatingly from my exertions. I could see my antagonist, a small shape in the vastness of the plain. Further on, the group I was seeking to avoid had come into the open and were hastening toward him.

I hurried up the low slope, drenched with sweat and trembling with fatigue. At the crest I looked back once more, to see the figures clustered about my vanquished opponent. Then I went down the opposite slope quickly, and saw them no more.

An hour's journeying brought me into as rugged a country as I have ever seen. On all sides rose steep slopes, littered with loose boulders which threatened to roll down upon the wayfarer. Bare stone cliffs, reddish in color, were much in evidence. There was little vegetation, except for low stunted trees, of which the spread of their branches was equal to the height of the trunk, and several varieties of thorny bushes, upon some of which grew nuts of peculiar shape and color. I broke open several of these, finding the kernel to be rich and meaty in appearance, but I dared not eat it, although I was feeling the bite of hunger.

My thirst bothered me more than my hunger, and this at least I was able to satisfy, although the satisfying nearly cost me my life. I clambered down a precipitous steep and entered a narrow valley, enclosed by lofty cliffs, at the foot of which the nut-bearing bushes grew in great abundance. In the middle of the valley lay a broad pool, apparently fed by a spring. In the center of the pool the water bubbled continuously, and a small stream led off down the valley.

I approached the pool eagerly, and lying on my belly at its lush-grown marge, plunged my muzzle into the crystalclear water. It, too, might be lethal for an Earthman, for all I knew, but I was so maddened with thirst that I risked it. It had an unusual tang, a quality I have always found present in Almuric water, but it was deliciously cold and satisfying. So pleasant it was to my parched lips that after I had satisfied my thirst, I lay there enjoying the sensation of tranquility. That was a mistake. Eat quickly, drink quickly, sleep lightly, and linger not over anything—those are the first rules of the wild, and his life is not long who fails to observe them.

The warmth of the sun, the bubbling of the water, the sensuous feeling of relaxation and satiation after fatigue and thirst—these wrought on me like an opiate to lull me into semi-slumber. It must have been some subconscious instinct that warned me, when a faint swishing reached my ears that was not part of the rippling of the spring. Even before my mind translated the sound as the passing of a heavy body through the tall grass, I whirled on my side, snatching at my poniard.

Simultaneously my ears were stunned with a deafening roar, there was a rushing through the air, and a giant form crashed down where I had lain an instant before, so close to me that its outspread talons raked my thigh. I had no time to tell the nature of my attacker—I had only a dazed impression that it was huge, supple, and cat-like. I rolled frantically aside as it spat and struck at me sidewise; then it was on me, and even as I felt its claws tear agonizingly into my flesh, the icecold water engulfed us both. A cat-like yowl rose half strangled, as if the yowler had swallowed a large amount of water; there was a great splashing and thrashing about me; then as I rose to the surface, I saw a long, bedraggled shape disappearing around the bushes near the cliffs. What it was I could not say, but it looked more like a leopard than anything else, though it was bigger than any leopard I had ever seen.

Scanning the shore carefully, I saw no other enemy, and crawled out of the pool, shivering from my icy plunge. My poniard was still in its scabbard. I had had no time to draw it, which was just as well. If I had not rolled into the pool, just when I did, dragging my attacker with me, it would have been my finish. Evidently the beast had a true cat-like distaste for water.

I found that I had a deep gash in my thigh and four lesser abrasions on my shoulder, where a great talon-armed paw had closed. The gash in my leg was pouring blood, and I thrust the limb deep into the icy pool, swearing at the excruciating sting of the cold water on the raw flesh. My leg was nearly numb when the bleeding ceased.

I now found myself in a quandary. I was hungry, night was coming on, there was no telling when the leopard-beast might return, or another predatory animal attack me; more than that, I was wounded. Civilized man is soft and easily disabled. I had a wound such as would be considered, among civilized people, ample reason for weeks of an invalid's existence. Strong and rugged as I was, according to Earth standards, I despaired when I surveyed the wound, and wondered how I was to treat it. The matter was quickly taken out of my hands.

I had started across the valley toward the cliffs, hoping I might find a cave there, for the nip of the air warned me that the night would not be as warm as the day, when a hellish clamor up near the mouth of the valley caused me to wheel and glare in that direction. Over the ridge came what I thought to be a pack of hyenas, except for their noise, which was more infernal than an earthly hyena, even, could produce. I had no illusions as to their purpose. It was I they were after.

Necessity recognizes few limitations. An instant before I had been limping painfully and slowly. Now I set out on a mad race for the cliff as if I were fresh and unwounded. With every step a spasm of agony shot along my thigh, and the wound, bleeding afresh, spurted red, but I gritted my teeth and increased my efforts.

My pursuers gave tongue and raced after me with such appalling speed that I had almost given up hope of reaching the trees beneath the cliffs before they pulled me down. They were snapping at my heels when I lurched into the low stunted growths, and swarmed up the spreading branches with a gasp of relief. But to my horror the hyenas climbed after me! A desperate downward glance showed me that they were not true hyenas; they differed from the breed I had known just as everything on Almuric differed subtly from its nearest counterpart on Earth. These beasts had curving cat-like claws, and their bodily structure was cat-like enough to allow them to climb as well as a lynx.

Despairingly, I was about to turn at bay, when I saw a ledge on the cliff above my head. There the cliff was deeply weathered, and the branches pressed against it. A desperate scramble up the perilous slant, and I had dragged my scratched and bruised body up on the ledge and lay glaring down at my pursuers, who loaded the topmost branches and howled up at me like lost souls. Evidently their climbing ability did not include cliffs, because after one attempt, in which one sprang up toward the ledge, clawed frantically for an instant on the sloping stone wall, and then fell off with an awful shriek, they made no effort to reach me.

Neither did they abandon their post. Stars came out, strange unfamiliar constellations, that blazed whitely in the dark velvet skies, and a broad golden moon rose above the cliffs and flooded the hills with weird light; but still my sentinels sat on the branches below me and howled up at me their hatred and belly-hunger.

The air was icy, and frost formed on the bare stone where I lay. My limbs became stiff and numb. I had knotted my girdle about my leg for a tourniquet; the run had apparently ruptured some small veins laid bare by the wound, because the blood flowed from it in an alarming manner.

I never spent a more miserable night. I lay on the frosty stone ledge, shaking with cold. Below me the eyes of my hunters burned up at me. Throughout the shadowy hills sounded the roaring and bellowing of unknown monsters. Howls, screams and yapping cut the night. And there I lay, naked, wounded, freezing, hungry, terrified, just as one of my remote ancestors might have lain in the Paleolithic Age of my own planet.

I can understand why our heathen ancestors worshipped the sun. When at last the cold moon sank and the sun of Almuric pushed its golden rim above the distant cliffs, I could have wept for sheer joy. Below me the hyenas snarled and stretched themselves, bayed up at me briefly, and loped away in search of easier prey. Slowly the warmth of the sun stole through my cramped, numbed limbs, and I rose stiffly up to greet the day, just as that forgotten forbear of mine might have stood up in the youth-dawn of the Earth.

After a while I descended, and fell upon the nuts clustered in the bushes near by. I was faint from hunger, and decided that I had as soon die from poisoning as from starvation. I broke open the thick shells and munched the meaty kernels eagerly, and I cannot recall any Earthly meal, howsoever elaborate, that tasted half as good. No ill effects followed; the nuts were good and nutritious. I was beginning to overcome my surroundings, at least so far as food was concerned. I had surmounted one obstacle of life on Almuric.

It is needless for me to narrate the details of the following months. I dwelt among the hills in such suffering and peril as no man on Earth has experienced for thousands of years. I make bold to say that only a man of extraordinary strength and ruggedness could have survived as I did. I did more than survive. I came at last to thrive on the existence.

At first I dared not leave the valley, where I was sure of water and food. I built a sort of nest of branches and leaves on the ledge, and slept there at night. Slept? The word is misleading. I crouched there, trying to keep from freezing, grimly lasting out the night. In the daytime I snatched naps, learning to sleep anywhere, or at any time, and so lightly that the slightest unusual noise would awaken me. The rest of the time I explored my valley and the hills about, and picked and ate nuts. Nor were my humble explorations uneventful. Time and again I raced for the cliffs or the trees, winning sometimes by shuddery hair-breadths. The hills swarmed with beasts, and all seemed predatory.

It was that fact which held me to my valley, where I at least had a bit of safety. What drove me forth at last was the same reason that has always driven forth the human race, from the first ape-man down to the last European colonist—the search for food. My supply of nuts became exhausted. The trees were stripped. This was not altogether on my account, although I developed a most ravenous hunger, what of my constant exertions; but others came to eat the nuts—huge, shaggy bear-like creatures, and things that looked like fur-clad baboons. These animals ate nuts, but they were omnivorous, to judge by the attention they accorded me. The bears were comparatively easy to avoid; they were mountains of flesh and muscle, but they could not climb, and their eyes were none too good. It was the baboons I learned to fear and hate. They pursued me on sight, they could both run and climb, and they were not balked by the cliff.

One pursued me to my eyrie, and swarmed up onto the ledge with me. At least such was his intention, but man is always most dangerous when cornered. I was weary of being hunted. As the frothing apish monstrosity hauled himself up over my ledge, man-like, I drove my poniard down between his shoulders with such fury that I literally pinned him to the ledge; the keen point sinking a full inch into the solid stone beneath him.

The incident showed me both the temper of my steel, and the growing quality of my own muscles. I who had been among the strongest on my own planet, found myself a weakling on primordial Almuric. Yet the potentiality of mastery was in my brain and my thews, and I was beginning to find myself.

Since survival was dependent on toughening, I toughened. My skin, burnt brown by the sun and hardened by the elements, became more impervious to both heat and cold than I had deemed possible. Muscles I had not known I possessed became evident. Such strength and suppleness became mine as Earthmen have not known for ages.

A short time before I had been transported from my native planet, a noted physical culture expert had pronounced me the most perfectly developed man on Earth. As I hardened with my fierce life on Almuric, I realized that the expert honestly had not known what physical development was. Nor had I. Had it been possible to divide my being and set opposite each other the man that expert praised, and the man I had become, the former would have seemed ridiculously soft, sluggish and clumsy in comparison to the brown, sinewy giant opposed to him.

I no longer turned blue with the cold at night, nor did the rockiest way bruise my naked feet. I could swarm up an almost sheer cliff with the ease of a monkey. I could run for hours without exhaustion; in short dashes it would have taken a racehorse to out-foot me. My wounds, untended except for washing in cold water, healed of themselves, as Nature is prone to heal the hurts of such as live close to her.

All this I narrate in order that it may be seen what sort of a man was formed in the savage mold. Had it not been for the fierce forging that made me steel and rawhide, I could not have survived the grim and bloody episodes through which I was to pass on that wild planet.

With new realization of power came confidence. I stood on my feet and stared at my bestial neighbors with defiance. I no longer fled from a frothing, champing baboon. With them, at least, I declared feud, growing to hate the abominable beasts as I might have hated human enemies. Besides, they ate the nuts I wished for myself.

They soon learned not to follow me to my eyrie, and the day came when I dared to meet one on even terms. I will never forget the sight of him frothing and roaring as he charged out of a clump of bushes, and the awful glare in his man-like eyes. My resolution wavered, but it was too late to retreat, and I met him squarely, skewering him through the heart as he closed in with his long clutching arms.

But there were other beasts which frequented the valley, and which I did not attempt to meet on any terms: the hyenas; the saber-tooth leopards, longer and heavier than an Earthly tiger and more ferocious; giant mooselike creatures, carnivorous, with alligator-like tusks; the monstrous bears; gigantic boars, with bristly hair which looked impervious to a sword-cut. There were other monsters, which appeared only at night, and the details of which I was not able to make out. These mysterious beasts moved mostly in silence, though some emitted high-pitched weird wails, or low earth-shaking rumbles. As the unknown is most menacing, I had a feeling that these nighted monsters were even more terrible than the familiar horrors which harried my day-life.

I remember one occasion on which I awoke suddenly and found myself lying tensely on my ledge, my ears strained to a night suddenly and breathlessly silent. The moon had set and the valley was veiled in darkness. Not a chattering baboon, not a yelping hyena disturbed the sinister stillness. *Something* was moving through the valley; I heard the faint rhythmic swishing of the grass that marked the passing of some huge body, but in the darkness I made out only a dim gigantic shape, which somehow seemed infinitely longer than it was broad—out of natural proportion, somehow. It passed away up the valley, and with its going, it was as if the night audibly expelled a gusty sigh of relief. The nocturnal noises started up again, and I lay back to sleep once more with a vague feeling that some grisly horror had passed me in the night.

I have said that I strove with the baboons over the possession of the life-giving nuts. What of my own appetite and those of the beasts, there came a time when I was forced to leave my valley and seek far afield in search of nutriment. My explorations had become broader and broader, until I had exhausted the resources of the country close about. So I set forth at random through the hills in a southerly and easterly direction. Of my wanderings I will deal briefly. For many weeks I roamed through the hills, starving, feasting, threatened by savage beasts, sleeping in trees or perilously on tall rocks when night fell. I fled, I fought, I slew, I suffered wounds. Oh, I can tell you my life was neither dull nor uneventful.

I was living the life of the most primitive savage; I had neither companionship, books, clothing, nor any of the things which go to make up civilization. According to the cultured viewpoint, I should have been most miserable. I was not. I reveled in my existence. My being grew and expanded. I tell you, the natural life of mankind is a grim battle for existence against the forces of nature, and any other form of life is artificial and without realistic meaning.

My life was not empty; it was crowded with adventures calling on every ounce of intelligence and physical power. When I swung down from my chosen eyrie at dawn, I knew that I would see the sun set only through my personal craft and strength and speed. I came to read the meaning of every waving grass tuft, each masking bush, each towering boulder. On every hand lurked Death in a thousand forms. My vigilance could not be relaxed, even in sleep. When I closed my eyes at night it was with no assurance that I would open them at dawn. I was fully alive. That phrase has more meaning than appears on the surface. The average civilized man is never fully alive; he is burdened with masses of atrophied tissue and useless matter. Life flickers feebly in him; his senses are dull and torpid. In developing his intellect he has sacrificed far more than he realizes.

I realized that I, too, had been partly dead on my native planet. But now I was alive in every sense of the word; I tingled and burned and stung with life to the finger tips and the ends of my toes. Every sinew, vein, and springy bone was vibrant with the dynamic flood of singing, pulsing, humming life. My time was too much occupied with foodgetting and preserving my skin to allow the developing of the morbid and intricate complexes and inhibitions which torment the civilized individual. To those highly complex persons who would complain that the psychology of such a life is over-simple, I can but reply that in my life at that time, violence and continual action and the necessity of action crowded out most of the gropings and soul-searchings common to those whose safety and daily meals are assured them by the toil of others. My life *was* primitively simple; I dwelt altogether in the present. My life on Earth already seemed like a dream, dim and far away.

All my life I had held down my instincts, had chained and enthralled my over-abundant vitalities. Now I was free to hurl all my mental and physical powers into the untamed struggle for existence, and I knew such zest and freedom as I had never dreamed of.

In all my wanderings—and since leaving the valley I had covered an enormous distance—I had seen no sign of humanity, or anything remotely resembling humanity.

It was the day I glimpsed a vista of rolling grassland beyond the peaks, that I suddenly encountered a human being. The meeting was unexpected. As I strode along an upland plateau, thickly grown with bushes and littered with boulders, I came abruptly on a scene striking in its primordial significance.

Ahead of me the earth sloped down to form a shallow bowl, the floor of which was thickly grown with tall grass, indicating the presence of a spring. In the midst of this bowl a figure similar to the one I had encountered on my arrival on Almuric was waging an unequal battle with a saber-tooth leopard. I stared in amazement, for I had not supposed that any human could stand before the great cat and live.

Always the glittering wheel of a sword shimmered between the monster and its prey, and blood on the spotted hide showed that the blade had been fleshed more than once. But it could not last; at any instant I expected to see the swordsman go down beneath the giant body.

Even with the thought, I was running fleetly down the shallow slope. I owed nothing to the unknown man, but his valiant battle stirred newly plumbed depths in my soul. I did not shout but rushed in silently and murderously, my poniard gleaming in my hand. Even as I reached them, the great cat sprang, the sword went spinning from the wielder's hand, and he went down beneath the hurtling bulk. And almost simultaneously I disemboweled the saber-tooth with one tremendous ripping stroke.

With a scream it lurched off its victim, slashing murderously as I leaped back, and then it began rolling and tumbling over the grass, roaring hideously and ripping up the earth with its frantic talons, in a ghastly welter of blood and streaming entrails.

It was a sight to sicken the hardiest, and I was glad when the mangled beast stiffened convulsively and lay still.

I turned to the man, but with little hope of finding life in him. I had seen the terrible saber-like fangs of the giant carnivore tear into his throat as he went down.

He was lying in a wide pool of blood, his throat horribly mangled. I could see the pulsing of the great jugular vein which had been laid bare, though not severed. One of the huge taloned paws had raked down his side from arm-pit to hip, and his thigh had been laid open in a frightful manner; I could see the naked bone, and from the ruptured veins blood was gushing. Yet to my amazement the man was not only living, but conscious. Yet even as I looked, his eyes glazed and the light faded in them.

I tore a strip from his loin-cloth and made a tourniquet about his thigh which somewhat slackened the flow of blood; then I looked down at him helplessly. He was apparently dying, though I knew something of the stamina and vitality of the wild and its people. And such evidently this man was; he was as savage and hairy in appearance, though not quite so bulky, as the man I had fought during my first day on Almuric.

As I stood there helplessly, something whistled venomously past my ear and thudded into the slope behind me. I saw a long arrow quivering there, and a fierce shout reached my ears. Glaring about, I saw half a dozen hairy men running fleetly toward me, fitting shafts to their bows as they came.

With an instinctive snarl I bounded up the short slope, the whistle of the missiles about my head lending wings to my heels. I did not stop, once I had gained the cover of the bushes surrounding the bowl, but went straight on, wrathful and disgusted. Evidently men as well as beasts were hostile on Almuric, and I would do well to avoid them in the future.

Then I found my anger submerged in a fantastic problem. I had understood some of the shouts of the men as they rushed toward me. The words had been in English, just as the antagonist of my first encounter had spoken and understood that language. In vain I cudgeled my mind for a solution. I had found that while animate and inanimate objects on Almuric often closely copied things on Earth, yet there was almost a striking difference somewhere, in substance, quality, shape or mode of action. It was preposterous that certain conditions on the separate planets could run such a perfect parallel as to produce an identical language. Yet I could not doubt the evidence of my ears. With a curse I abandoned the problem as too fantastic to waste time on.

Perhaps it was this incident, perhaps the glimpse of the distant savannas, which filled me with a restlessness and distaste for the barren hill country where I had fared so hardily. The sight of men, strange and alien as they were, stirred in my breast a desire for human companionship, and this frustrated longing became in turn a sudden feeling of repulsion for my surroundings. I did not hope to meet friendly humans on the plains; but I determined to try my chances upon them, nevertheless, though what perils I might meet there I could not know. Before I left the hills some whim caused me to scrape from my face my heavy growth and trim my shaggy hair with my poniard, which had lost none of its razor edge. Why I did this I cannot say, unless it was the natural instinct of a man setting forth into new country to look his "best."

The next morning I descended into the grassy plains, which swept eastward and southward as far as sight could reach. I continued eastward and covered many miles that day, without any unusual incident. I encountered several small winding rivers, along whose marges the grass stood taller than my head. Among this grass I heard the snorting and thrashing of heavy animals of some sort, and gave them a wide berth—for which caution I was later thankful.

The rivers were thronged in many cases with gailycolored birds of many shapes and hues, some silent, others continually giving forth strident cries as they wheeled above the waters or dipped down to snatch their prey from its depths.

Further out on the plain I came upon herds of grazing animals—small deer-like creatures, and a curious animal that looked like a pot-bellied pig with abnormally long hind legs, and that progressed in enormous bounds, after the fashion of a kangaroo. It was a most ludicrous sight, and I laughed until my belly ached. Later I reflected that it was the first time I had laughed—outside of a few short barks of savage satisfaction at the discomfiture of an enemy—since I had set foot on Almuric.

That night I slept in the tall grass not far from a water course, and might have been made the prey of any wandering meat-eater. But fortune was with me that night. All across the plains sounded the thunderous roaring of stalking monsters, but none came near my frail retreat. The night was warm and pleasant, strikingly in contrast with the nights in the chill grim hills.

The next day a momentous thing occurred. I had had no meat on Almuric, except when ravenous hunger had driven me to eat raw flesh. I had searched in vain for some stone that would strike a spark. The rocks were of a peculiar nature, unknown to Earth. But that morning on the plains, I found a bit of greenish-looking stone lying in the grass, and experiments showed that it had some of the qualities of flint. Patient effort, in which I clinked my poniard against the stone, rewarded me with a spark of fire in the dry grass, which I soon fanned to a blaze—and had some difficulty in extinguishing.

That night I surrounded myself with a ring of fire which I fed with dry grass and stalked plants which burned slowly, and I felt comparatively safe, though huge forms moved about me in the darkness, and I caught the stealthy pad of great paws, and the glimmer of wicked eyes.

On my journey across the plains I subsisted on fruit I found growing on green stalks, which I saw the birds eating. It was pleasant to the taste, though lacking in the nutritive qualities of the nuts in the hills. I looked longingly at the scampering deer-like animals, now that I had the means of cooking their flesh, but saw no way of securing them.

And so for days I wandered aimlessly across those vast plains, until I came in sight of a massive walled city.

I sighted it just at nightfall, and eager though I was to investigate it further, I made my camp and waited for morning. I wondered if my fire would be seen by the inhabitants, and if they would send out a party to discover my nature and purpose.

With the fall of night I could no longer make it out, but the last waning light had shown it plainly, rising stark and somber against the eastern sky. At that distance no evidence of life was visible, but I had a dim impression of huge walls and massive towers, all of a greenish tint.

I lay within the circle of my fire, while great sinuous bodies rustled through the grass and fierce eyes glared at me, and my imagination was at work as I strove to visualize the possible inhabitants of that mysterious city. Would they be of the same race as the hairy ferocious troglodytes I had encountered? I doubted it, for it hardly seemed possible that these primitive creatures would be capable of rearing such a structure. Perhaps there I would find a highly developed type of cultured man. Perhaps—here imaginings too dark and shadowy for description whispered at the back of my consciousness.

Then the moon rose behind the city, etching its massive outlines in the weird golden glow. It looked black and somber in the moonlight; there was something distinctly brutish and forbidding about its contours. As I sank into slumber I reflected that if ape-men could build a city, it would surely resemble that colossus in the moon.

2

Dawn found me on my way across the plain. It may seem like the height of folly to have gone striding openly toward the city, which might be full of hostile beings, but I had learned to take desperate chances, and I was consumed with curiosity; weary at last of my lonely life.

The nearer I approached, the more rugged the details stood out. There was more of the fortress than the city about the walls, which, with the towers that loomed behind and above them, seemed to have been built of huge blocks of greenish stone, very roughly cut. There was no apparent attempt at smoothing, polishing, or otherwise adorning this stone. The whole appearance was rude and savage, suggesting a wild fierce people heaping up rocks as a defense against enemies.

As yet I had seen nothing of the inhabitants. The city might have been empty of human life. But a broad road leading to the massive gate was beaten bare of grass, as if by the constant impact of many feet. There were no fields or gardens about the city; the grass waved to the foot of the walls. All during that long march across the plain to the gates, I saw nothing resembling a human being. But as I came under the shadow of the great gate, which was flanked on either hand by a massive tower, I caught a glimpse of tousled black heads moving along the squat battlements. I halted and threw back my head to hail them. The sun had just topped the towers and its glare was full in my eyes. Even as I opened my lips, there was a cracking report like a rifle shot, a jet of white smoke spurted from a tower, and a terrific impact against my head dashed me into unconsciousness.

When I came to my senses it was not slowly, but quickly and clear-headedly, what of my immense recuperative powers. I was lying on a bare stone floor in a large chamber, the walls, ceiling and floor of which were composed of huge blocks of green stone. From a barred window high up in one wall sunlight poured to illumine the room, which was without furnishing, except for a bench, crudely and massively built.

A heavy chain was looped about my waist and made fast with a strange, heavy lock. The other end of the chain was fastened to a thick ring set in the wall. Everything about that fantastic city seemed massive.

Lifting a hand to my head, I found it was bandaged with something that felt like silk. My head throbbed. Evidently whatever missile it was that had been fired at me from the wall had only grazed my head, inflicting a scalp wound and knocking me senseless. I felt for my poniard, but naturally it was gone.

I cursed heartily. When I had found myself on Almuric I had been appalled by my prospects; but then at least I had been free. Now I was in the hands of God only knew what manner of beings. All I knew was that they were hostile. But my inordinate self-confidence would not go down, and I felt no great fear. I did feel a rush of panic, common to all wild things, at being confined and shackled, but I fought down this feeling, and it was succeeded by one of red unreasoning rage. Springing to my feet, which movement the chain was long enough to allow, I began jerking and tearing at my shackle.

It was while engaged in this fruitless exhibition of primitive resentment that a slight noise caused me to wheel, snarling, my muscles tensed for attack or defense. What I saw froze me in my tracks.

Just within the doorway stood a girl. Except in her garments she differed little from the type of girls I had known on Earth, except that her slim figure exhibited a suppleness superior to theirs. Her hair was intensely black, her skin white as alabaster. Her lissome limbs were barely concealed by a light, tunic-like garment, sleeveless, lownecked, revealing the greater part of her ivory breasts. This garment was girdled at her lithe waist, and came to within a few inches above her knees. Soft sandals encased her slender feet. She was standing in an attitude of awed fascination, her dark eyes wide, her crimson lips parted. As I wheeled and glared at her she gave back with a quick gasp of surprise or fear, and fled lightly from the chamber.

I stared after her. If she were typical of the people of the city, then surely the effect produced by the brutish masonry was an illusion, for she seemed the product of some gentle and refined civilization, allowing for a certain barbaric suggestion about her costume.

While so musing, I heard the tramp of feet, harsh voices were lifted in argument, and the next instant a group of men strode into the chamber, halting as they saw me conscious and on my feet. Still thinking of the girl, I glared at them in surprise. They were of the same type as the others I had seen, huge, hairy, ferocious, with the same ape-like forward-thrust heads and formidable faces. Some, I noticed, were darker than others, but all were dark and fierce, and the whole effect was one of somber and ferocious savagery. They were instinct with ferocity; it blazed in their icy-gray eyes, reflected in the snarling lift of their bristling lips, rumbled in their rough voices.

All were armed, and their hands seemed instinctively to seek their hilts as they stood glaring at me, their shaggy heads thrust forward in their ape-like manner.

"Thak!" one exclaimed, or rather roared—all their voices were as gusty as a sea wind—"he's conscious!"

"Do you suppose he can speak or understand human language?" rumbled another.

All this while I had stood glaring back at them, wondering anew at their speech. Now I realized that they were not speaking English.

The thing was so unnatural that it gave me a shock. They were not speaking any Earthly language, and I realized it; yet I understood them, except for various words which apparently had no counterpart on Earth. I made no attempt to understand this seemingly impossible phenomenon, but answered the last speaker.

"I can speak and understand," I grunted. "Who are you? What city is this? Why did you attack me? Why am I in chains?"

They rumbled in amazement, with much tugging of mustaches, shaking of heads, and uncouth profanity.

"He talks, by Thak!" said one. "I tell you, he is from beyond the Girdle!"

"From beyond my hip!" broke in another rudely. "He is a freak, a damned, smooth-skinned degenerate misfit which should not have been born, or allowed to exist."

"Ask him how he came by the Bonecrusher's poniard," requested yet another.

At that one of them advanced, and, fixing me with a stern and accusing eye, held out a sheathed weapon which I recognized as my poniard.

"Did you steal this from Logar?" he demanded.

"I stole nothing!" I snapped, feeling like a wild beast being prodded through the bars of a cage by unfeeling and critical spectators. My rages, like all the emotions on that wild planet, were without restraint.

"I took that poniard from the man who carried it, and I took it in a fair fight," I added.

"Did you slay him?" they demanded unbelievingly.

"No," I growled. "We fought with our bare hands, until he tried to knife me. Then I knocked him senseless."

A roar greeted my words. I thought at first they were clamoring with rage; then I made out that they were arguing among themselves.

"I tell you, he lies!" one bull's bellow rose above the tumult. "We all know that Logar the Bonecrusher is not the man to be thrashed and stripped by a smooth-skinned hairless brown man like this. Ghor the Bear might be a match for Logar. No one else."

"Well, there's the poniard," someone pointed out.

The clamor rose again, and in an instant the disputants were yelling and cursing, and brandishing their hairy fists in one another's faces, hands fumbled at sword-hilts, and challenges and defiances were exchanged freely.

I looked to see a general throat-cutting, but presently one who seemed in some authority drew his sword and began banging the hilt on the rude bench, at the same time drowning out the voices of the others with his bull-like bellowing.

"Shut up! Shut up! Let another man open his mouth and I'll split his head!" As the clamor subsided and the disputants glared venomously at him, he continued in a voice as calm as if nothing had occurred. "It's neither here nor there about the poniard. He might have caught Logar sleeping and brained him, or he might have stolen it, or found it. Are we Logar's brothers, that we should seek after his welfare?"

A general snarl answered this. Evidently the man called Logar was not popular among them.

"The question is, what shall we do with this creature? We've got to hold a council and decide. He's evidently uneatable." He grinned as he said this, which was apparently meant as a bit of grim humor.

"His hide would make good leather," suggested another in a tone that did not sound as though he was joking.

"Too soft," protested another.

"He didn't feel soft while we were carrying him in," returned the first speaker. "He was hard as steel springs."

"Tush," deprecated the other. "I'll show you how tender his flesh is. Watch me slice off a few strips." He drew his dagger and approached me while the others watched with interest.

All this time my rage had been growing, until the chamber seemed to swim in a red mist. Now, as I realized that the fellow really intended trying the edge of his steel on my skin I went berserk. Wheeling, I gripped the chain with both hands, wrapping it around my wrists for more leverage. Then, bracing my feet against the floor and walls I began to strain with all my strength. All over my body the great muscles coiled and knotted; sweat broke out on my skin, and then with a shattering crash the stone gave way, the iron ring was torn out bodily, and I was catapulted on my back onto the floor, at the feet of my captors who roared with amazement and fell on me *en masse*.

I answered their bellows with one strident yell of bloodthirsty gratification, and heaving up through the mêlée, began swinging my heavy fists like caulking mallets. Oh, that was a rough-house while it lasted! They made no attempt to knife me, striving to swamp me with numbers. We rolled from one side of the chamber to the other, a gasping, thrashing, cursing, hammering mass, while with the yells, howls, earnest profanity, and impact of heavy bodies, it was a perfect bedlam. Once I seemed to catch a fleeting glimpse of the door thronged with the heads of women similar to the one I had seen, but I could not be sure; my teeth were set in a hairy ear, my eyes were full of sweat and stars from a vicious punch on the nose, and what with a gang of heavy forms romping all over me my sight was none too good.

Yet I gave a good account of myself. Ears split, noses crumpled and teeth splintered under the crushing impact of my iron-hard fists, and the yells of the wounded were music to my battered ears. But that damnable chain about my waist kept tripping me and coiling about my legs, and pretty soon the bandage was ripped from my head, my scalp wound opened anew and deluged me with blood. Blinded by this I floundered and stumbled, and gasping and panting they bore me down and bound my arms and legs.

The survivors then fell away from me and lay or sat in positions of pain and exhaustion while I, finding my voice, cursed them luridly. I derived ferocious satisfaction at the sight of all the bloody noses, black eyes, torn ears and smashed teeth which were in evidence, and barked in vicious laughter when one announced with many curses that his arm was broken. One of them was out cold, and had to be revived, which they did by dumping over him a vessel of cold water that was fetched by someone I could not see from where I lay. I had an idea that it was a woman who came in answer to a harsh roar of command.

"His wound is open again," said one, pointing at me. "He'll bleed to death."

"I hope he does," snarled another, lying doubled up on the floor. "He's burst my belly. I'm dying. Get me some wine."

"If you're dying you don't need wine," brutally answered the one who seemed a chief, as he spat out bits of splintered teeth. "Tie up his wound, Akra."

Akra limped over to me with no great enthusiasm and bent down.

"Hold your damnable head still," he growled.

"Keep off!" I snarled. "I'll have nothing from you. Touch me at your peril."

He exasperatedly grabbed my face in his broad hand and shoved me violently down. That was a mistake. My jaws locked on his thumb, evoking an ear-splitting howl, and it was only with the aid of his comrades that he extricated the mangled member. Maddened by the pain, he howled wordlessly, then suddenly gave me a terrific kick in the temple, driving my wounded head with great violence back against the massive bench leg. Once again I lost consciousness.

When I came to myself again I was once more bandaged, shackled by the wrists and ankles, and made fast to a fresh ring, newly set in the stone, and apparently more firmly fixed than the other had been. It was night. Through the window I glimpsed the star-dotted sky. A torch which burned with a peculiar white flame was thrust into a niche in the wall, and a man sat on the bench, elbows on knees and chin on fists, regarding me intently. On the bench near him stood a huge gold vessel.

"I doubted if you'd come to after that last crack," he said at last.

"It would take more than that to finish me," I snarled. "You are a pack of cursed weaklings. But for my wound and that infernal chain, I'd have bested the whole mob of you."

My insults seemed to interest rather than anger him. He absently fingered a large bump on his head on which blood was thickly clotted, and asked: "Who are you? Whence do you come?"

"None of your business," I snapped.

He shrugged his shoulders, and lifting the vessel in one hand drew his dagger with the other.

"In Koth none goes hungry," he said. "I'm going to place this food near your hand and you can eat. But I warn you, if you try to strike or bite me, I'll stab you."

I merely snarled truculently, and he bent and set down the bowl, hastily withdrawing. I found the food to be a kind of stew, satisfying both thirst and hunger. Having eaten I felt in somewhat better mood, and upon my guard renewing his questions, I answered: "My name is Esau Cairn. I am an American, from the planet Earth."

He mulled over my statements for a space, then asked: "Are these places beyond the Girdle?"

"I don't understand you," I answered.

He shook his head. "Nor I you. But if you do not know of the Girdle, you cannot be from beyond it. Doubtless it is all fable, anyway. But whence did you come when we saw you approaching across the plain? Was that your fire we glimpsed from the towers last night?"

"I suppose so," I replied. "For many months I have lived in the hills to the west. It was only a few weeks ago that I descended into the plains."

He started and stared at me.

"In the hills? Alone, and with only a poniard?"

"Well, what about it?" I demanded.

He shook his head as if in doubt or wonder. "A few hours ago I would have called you a liar. Now I am not sure."

"What is the name of this city?" I asked.

"Koth, of the Kothan tribe. Our chief is Khossuth Skullsplitter. I am Thab the Swift. I am detailed to guard you while the warriors hold council."

"What's the nature of their council?" I inquired.

"They discuss what shall be done with you; and they have been arguing since sunset, and are no nearer a solution than before."

"What is their disagreement?"

"Well," he answered. "Some want to hang you, and some want to shoot you."

“I don’t suppose it’s occurred to them that they might let me go,” I suggested with some bitterness.

He gave me a cold look. “Don’t be a fool,” he said reprovingly.

At that moment a light step sounded outside, and the girl I had seen before tiptoed into the chamber. Thab eyed her disapprovingly.

“What are you doing here, Altha?” he demanded.

“I came to look again at the stranger,” she answered in a soft musical voice. “I never saw a man like him. His skin is nearly as smooth as mine, and he has no hair on his countenance. How strange are his eyes! Whence does he come?”

“From the Hills, he says,” grunted Thab.

Her eyes widened. “Why, none dwells in the Hills, except wild beasts! Can it be that he is some sort of animal? They say he speaks and understands speech.”

“So he does,” growled Thab, fingering his bruises. “He also knocks out men’s brains with his naked fists, which are harder and heavier than maces. Get away from there.

“He’s a rampaging devil. If he gets his hands on you he won’t leave enough of you for the vultures to pick.”

“I won’t get near him,” she assured him. “But, Thab, he does not look so terrible. See, there is no anger in the gaze he fixes on me. What will be done with him?”

“The tribe will decide,” he answered. “Probably let him fight a sabertooth leopard bare-handed.”

She clasped her own hands with more human feeling than I had yet seen shown on Almuric.

“Oh, Thab, why? He has done no harm; he came alone and with empty hands. The warriors shot him down without warning—and now—”

He glanced at her in irritation. “If I told your father you were pleading for a captive—”

Evidently the threat carried weight. She visibly wilted.

“Don’t tell him,” she pleaded. Then she flared up again. “Whatever you say, it’s beastly! If my father whips me until the blood runs over my heels, I’ll still say so!”

And so saying, she ran quickly out of the chamber.

"Who is that girl?" I asked.

"Altha, the daughter of Zal the Thrower."

"Who is he?"

"One of those you battled so viciously a short time ago."

"You mean to tell me a girl like that is the daughter of a man like—" Words failed me.

"What's wrong with her?" he demanded. "She differs none from the rest of our women."

"You mean all the women look like her, and all the men look like you?"

"Certainly—allowing for their individual characteristics. Is it otherwise among your people? That is, if you are not a solitary freak."

"Well, I'll be—" I began in bewilderment, when another warrior appeared at the door, saying, "I'm to relieve you, Thab. The warriors have decided to leave the matter to Khossuth when he returns on the morrow."

Thab departed and the other seated himself on the bench. I made no attempt to talk to him. My head was swimming with the contradictory phenomena I had heard and observed, and I felt the need of sleep. I soon sank into dreamless slumber.

Doubtless my wits were still addled from the battering I had received. Otherwise I would have snapped awake when I felt something touch my hair. As it was, I woke only partly. From under drooping lids I glimpsed, as in a dream, a girlish face bent close to mine, dark eyes wide with frightened fascination, red lips parted. The fragrance of her foamy black hair was in my nostrils. She timidly touched my face, then drew back with a quick soft intake of breath, as if frightened by her action. The guard snored on the bench. The torch had burned to a stub that cast a weird dull glow over the chamber. Outside, the moon had set. This much I vaguely realized before I sank back into slumber again, to be haunted by a dim beautiful face that shimmered through my dreams.

3

I awoke again in the cold gray light of dawn, at a time when the condemned meet their executioners. A group of men stood over me, and one I knew was Khossuth the Skullsplitter.

He was taller than most, and leaner—almost gaunt in comparison to the others. This circumstance made his broad shoulders seem abnormally huge. His face and body were seamed with old scars. He was very dark, and apparently old; an impressive and terrible image of somber savagery.

He stood looking down at me, fingering the hilt of his great sword. His gaze was gloomy and detached.

"They say you claim to have beaten Logar of Thugra in open fight," he said at last, and his voice was cavernous and ghostly in a manner I cannot describe.

I did not reply, but lay staring up at him, partly in fascination at his strange and menacing appearance, partly in the anger that seemed generally to be with me during those times.

"Why do you not answer?" he rumbled.

"Because I'm weary of being called a liar," I snarled.

"Why did you come to Koth?"

"Because I was tired of living alone among wild beasts. I was a fool. I thought I would find human beings whose company was preferable to the leopards and baboons. I find I was wrong."

He tugged his bristling mustaches.

"Men say you fight like a mad leopard. Thab says that you did not come to the gates as an enemy comes. I love brave men. But what can we do? If we free you, you will hate us because of what has passed, and your hate is not lightly to be loosed."

"Why not take me into the tribe?" I remarked, at random.

He shook his head. "We are not Yagas, to keep slaves."

"Nor am I a slave," I grunted. "Let me live among you as an equal. I will hunt and fight with you. I am as good a man as any of your warriors."

At this another pushed past Khossuth. This fellow was bigger than any I had yet seen in Koth—not taller, but broader, more massive. His hair was thicker on his limbs, and of a peculiar rusty cast instead of black.

"That you must prove!" he roared, with an oath. "Loose him, Khossuth! The warriors have been praising his power until my belly revolts! Loose him and let us have a grapple!"

"The man is wounded, Ghor," answered Khossuth.

"Then let him be cared for until his wound is healed," urged the warrior eagerly, spreading his arms in a curious grappling gesture.

"His fists are like hammers," warned another.

"Thak's devils!" roared Ghor, his eyes glaring, his hairy arms brandished. "Admit him into the tribe, Khossuth! Let him endure the test! If he survives—well, by Thak, he'll be worthy even to be called a man of Koth!"

"I will go and think upon the matter," answered Khossuth after a long deliberation.

That settled the matter for the time being. All trooped out after him. Thab was last, and at the door he turned and made a gesture which I took to be one of encouragement. These strange people seemed not entirely without feelings of pity and friendship.

The day passed uneventfully. Thab did not return. Other warriors brought me food and drink, and I allowed them to bandage my scalp. With more human treatment, the wild beast fury in me had been subordinated to my human reason. But that fury lurked close to the surface of my soul, ready to blaze into ferocious life at the slightest encroachment.

I did not see the girl Altha, though I heard light footsteps outside the chamber several times, whether hers or another's I could not know.

About nightfall a group of warriors came into the room and announced that I was to be taken to the council, where Khossuth would listen to all arguments and decide my fate. I was surprised to learn that arguments would be presented on my behalf. They got my promise not to attack them, and loosed me from the chain that bound me to the wall, but they did not remove the shackles on my wrists and ankles.

I was escorted out of the chamber into a vast hall, lighted by the white fire torches. There were no hangings or furnishings, nor any sort of ornamentation—just an almost oppressive sense of massive architecture.

We traversed several halls, all equally huge and windy, with rugged walls and lofty ceilings, and came at last into a vast circular space, roofed with a dome. Against the back wall a stone throne stood on a block-like dais, and on the throne sat old Khossuth in gloomy majesty, clad in a spotted leopard-skin. Before him in a vast three-quarters circle sat the tribe, the men cross-legged on skins spread on the stone floor, and behind them the women and children seated on fur-covered benches.

It was a strange concourse. The contrast was startling between the hairy males and the slender, white-skinned, dainty women. The men were clad in loin-cloths and highstrapped sandals; some had thrown panther-skins over their massive shoulders. The women were dressed similar to the girl Altha, whom I saw sitting with the others. They wore soft sandals, or none, and scanty tunics girdled about their waists. That was all. The difference of the sexes was carried out down to the smallest babies. The girl children were quiet, dainty and pretty. The young males looked even more like monkeys than did their elders.

I was told to take my seat on a block of stone in front and somewhat to the side of the dais. Sitting among the warriors I saw Ghor, squirming impatiently as he unconsciously flexed his thick biceps.

As soon as I had taken my seat, the proceedings went forward. Khossuth simply announced that he would hear the arguments, and pointed out a man to represent me, at which I was again surprised, but this apparently was a regular custom among these people. The man chosen was the lesser chief who had commanded the warriors I had battled in the cell, and they called him Gutchluk Tigerwrath. He eyed me venomously as he limped forward with no great enthusiasm, bearing the marks of our encounter.

He laid his sword and dagger on the dais, and the foremost warriors did likewise. Then he glared at the rest truculently, and Khossuth called for arguments to show why Esau Cairn—he made a marvelous jumble of the pronunciation—should not be taken into the tribe.

Apparently the reasons were legion. Half a dozen warriors sprang up and began shouting at the top of their voice, while Gutchluk dutifully strove to answer them. I felt already doomed. But the game was not played out, or even well begun. At first Gutchluk went at it only halfheartedly, but opposition heated him to his task. His eyes blazed, his jaw jutted, and he began to roar and bellow with the best of them. From the arguments he presented, or rather thundered, one would have thought he and I were lifelong friends.

No particular person was designated to protest against me. Everybody who wished took a hand. And if Gutchluk won over anyone, that person joined his voice to Gutchluk's. Already there were men on my side. Thab's shout and Ghor's bellow vied with my attorney's roar, and soon others took up my defense.

That debate is impossible for an Earth man to conceive of, without having witnessed it. It was sheer bedlam, with from three voices to five hundred voices clamoring at once. How Khossuth sifted any sense out of it, I cannot even guess. But he brooded somberly above the tumult, like a grim god over the paltry aspirations of mankind.

There was wisdom in the discarding of weapons. Dispute frequently became biting, and criticisms of ancestors and personal habits entered into it. Hands clutched at empty belts and mustaches bristled belligerently. Occasionally Khossuth lifted his weird voice across the clamor and restored a semblance of order.

My attempts to follow the arguments were vain. My opponents went into matters seemingly utterly irrelevant, and were met by rebuttals just as illogical. Authorities of antiquity were dragged out, to be refuted by records equally musty.

To further complicate matters, disputants frequently snared themselves in their own arguments, or forgot which side they were on, and found themselves raging frenziedly on the other. There seemed no end to the debate, and no limit to the endurance of the debaters. At midnight they were still yelling as loudly, and shaking their fists in one another's beards as violently as ever.

The women took no part in the arguments.

They began to glide away about midnight, with the children. Finally only one small figure was left among the benches. It was Altha, who was following—or trying to follow—the proceedings with a surprising interest.

I had long since given up the attempt. Gutchluk was holding the floor valiantly, his veins swelling and his hair and beard bristling with his exertions. Ghor was actually weeping with rage and begging Khossuth to let him break a few necks. Oh, that he had lived to see the men of Koth become adders and snakes, with the hearts of buzzards and the guts of toads! he bawled, brandishing his huge arms to high heaven.

It was all a senseless madhouse to me. Finally, in spite of the clamor, and the fact that my life was being weighed in the balance, I fell asleep on my block and snored peacefully while the men of Koth raged and pounded their hairy breasts and bellowed, and the strange planet of Almuric whirled on its way under the stars that neither knew nor cared for men, Earthly or otherwise.

It was dawn when Thab shook me awake and shouted in my ear: "We have won! You enter the tribe, if you'll wrestle Ghor!"

"I'll break his back!" I grunted, and went back to sleep again.

4

So began my life as a man among men on Almuric. I, who had begun my new life as a naked savage, now took the next step on the ladder of evolution and became a barbarian. For the men of Koth were barbarians, for all their silks and steel and stone towers. Their counterpart is not on Earth today, nor has it ever been. But of that later. Let me tell first of my battle with Ghor the Bear.

My chains were removed and I was taken to a stone tower on the wall, there to dwell until my wounds had healed. I was still a prisoner. Food and drink were brought me regularly by the tribesmen, who also tended carefully to my wounds, which were unimportant, considering the hurts I had had from wild beasts, and had recovered from unaided. But they wished me to be in prime condition for the wrestling, which was to decide whether I should be admitted into the tribe of Koth, or—well, from what they said of Ghor, if I lost there would be no problem as to my disposition. The wolves and vultures would take care of that.

Their manner toward me was noncommittal, with the exception of Thab the Swift, who was frankly cordial to me. I saw neither Khossuth, Ghor, nor Gutchluk during the time I was imprisoned in the tower, nor did I see the girl Altha.

I do not remember a more tedious and wearisome time. I was not nervous because of any fear of Ghor; I frankly doubted my ability to beat him, but I had risked my life so often and against such fearful odds, that personal fear had been stamped out of my soul. But for months I had lived like a mountain panther, and now to be caged up in a stone tower, where my movements were limited, bounded and restricted—it was intolerable, and if I had been forced to put up with it a day longer, I would have lost control of myself, and either fought my way to freedom or perished in the attempt. As it was, all the constrained energy in me was pent up almost to the snapping point, giving me a terrific store of nervous power which stood me in good stead in my battle.

There is no man on Earth equal in sheer strength to any man of Koth. They lived barbaric lives, filled with continuous peril and warfare against foes human and bestial. But after all, they lived the lives of men, and I had been living the life of a wild beast.

As I paced my tower chamber, I thought of a certain great wrestling champion of Europe with whom I had once contested in a friendly private bout, and who pronounced me the strongest man he had ever encountered. Could he have seen me now, in the tower of Koth! I am certain that I could have torn out his biceps like rotten cloth, broken his spine across my knee, or caved in his breast-bone with my clenched fist; and as for speed, the most finely trained Earth athlete would have seemed awkward and sluggish in comparison to the tigerish quickness lurking in my rippling sinews.

Yet for all that, I knew that I would be strained to the uttermost even to hold my own with the giant they called Ghor the Bear. He did, indeed, resemble a shaggy rustyhued cave-bear.

Thab the Swift narrated some of his triumphs to me, and such a record of personal mayhem I never heard; the man's progress through life was marked by broken limbs, backs and necks. No man had yet stood before him in barehanded battle, though some swore Logar the Bonecrusher was his equal.

Logar, I learned, was chief of Thugra, a city hostile to Koth. All cities on Almuric seemed to be hostile to each other, the people of the planet being divided into many small tribes, incessantly at war. The chief of Thugra was called the Bonecrusher because of his terrible strength. The poniard I had taken from him had been his favorite weapon, a famous blade, forged, Thab said, by a supernatural smith. Thab called this being a *gorka*, and I found in tales concerning the creature an analogy to the dwarfish metalworkers of the ancient Germanic myths of my own world.

Thab told me much concerning his people and his planet, but of these things I will deal later. At last Khossuth came, found my wounds completely cured, eyed my bronzed sinews with a shadow of respect in his cold brooding eyes, and pronounced me fit for battle.

Night had fallen when I was led into the streets of Koth. I looked with wonder at the giant walls towering above me, dwarfing their human inhabitants. Everything in Koth was built on a heroic scale. Neither the walls nor the edifices were unusually high, in comparison to their bulk, but they were so massive. My guides led me to a sort of amphitheater near the outer wall. It was an oval space surrounded by huge stone blocks, rising tier upon tier, and forming seats for the spectators. The open space in the center was hard ground, covered with short grass. A sort of bulwark was formed about it out of woven leather thongs, apparently to keep the contestants from dashing their heads against the surrounding stones. Torches lighted the scene.

The spectators were already there, the men occupying the lower blocks, the women and children the upper. My gaze roved over the sea of faces, hairy or smooth, until it rested on one I recognized, and I felt a strange throb of pleasure at the sight of Altha sitting there watching me with her intent dark eyes.

Thab indicated for me to enter the arena, and I did so, thinking of the old-time bare-knuckle bouts of my own planet, which were fought in crude rings pitched, like this, on the naked turf. Thab and the other warriors who had escorted me remained outside. Above us brooded old Khossuth on a carven stone elevated above the first tier, and covered with leopard-skins.

I glanced beyond him to that dusky star-filled sky whose strange beauty never failed to fascinate me, and I laughed at the fantasy of it all—where I, Esau Cairn, was to earn by sweat and blood my right to exist on this alien world, the existence of which was undreamed by the people of my own planet.

I saw a group of warriors approaching from the other side, a giant form looming among them. Ghor the Bear glared at me across the ring, his hairy paws grasping the thongs, then with a roar he vaulted over them and stood before me, an image of truculence incarnate—angry because I had chanced to reach the ring before him.

On his rude throne above us, old Khossuth lifted a spear and cast it earthward. Our eyes followed its flight, and as it sheathed its shining blade in the turf outside the ring, we hurled ourselves at each other, iron masses of bone and thew, vibrant with fierce life and the lust to destroy.

We were each naked except for a sort of leather loinclout, which was more brace than garment. The rules of the match were simple: we were not to strike with our fists or open hands, knees or elbows, kick, bite or gouge. Outside of that, anything went.

At the first impact of his hairy body against mine, I realized that Ghor was stronger than Logar. Without my best natural weapons—my fists—Ghor had the advantage.

He was a hairy mountain of iron muscle, and he moved with the quickness of a huge cat. Accustomed to such fighting, he knew tricks of which I was ignorant. Lastly, his bullet head was set so squarely on his shoulders that it was practically impossible to strangle that thick squat neck of his.

What saved me was the wild life I had lived which had toughened me as no man, living as a man, can be toughened. Mine was the superior quickness, and ultimately, the superior endurance.

There is little to be said of that fight. Time ceased to be composed of intervals of change, and merged into a blind mist of tearing, snarling eternity. There was no sound except our panting gasps, the guttering of the torches in the light wind, and the impact of our feet on the turf, of our hard bodies against each other. We were too evenly matched for either to gain a quick advantage. There was no pinning of shoulders, as in an Earthly wrestling match. The fight would continue until one or both of the contestants were dead or senseless.

When I think of our endurance and stamina, I stand appalled. At midnight we were still rending and tearing at each other. The whole world was swimming red when I broke free out of a murderous grapple. My whole frame was a throb of wrenched, twisted agony. Some of my muscles were numbed and useless. Blood poured from my nose and mouth. I was half blind and dizzy from the impact of my head against the hard earth. My legs trembled and my breath came in great gulps. But I saw that Ghor was in no better case. He too bled at the nose and mouth, and more, blood trickled from his ears. He reeled as he faced me, and his hairy chest heaved spasmodically. He spat out a mouthful of blood, and with a roar that was more a gasp, he hurled himself at me again. And steeling my ebbing strength for one last effort, I caught his outstretched wrist, wheeled, ducking low and bringing his arm over my shoulder, and heaved with all my last ounce of power.

The impetus of his rush helped my throw. He whirled headlong over my back and crashed to the turf on his neck and shoulder, slumped over and lay still. An instant I stood swaying above him, while a sudden deep-throated roar rose from the people of Koth, and then a rush of darkness blotted out the stars and the flickering torches, and I fell senseless across the still body of my antagonist.

Later they told me that they thought both Ghor and I were dead. They worked over us for hours. How our hearts resisted the terrible strain of our exertions is a matter of wonder to me. Men said it was by far the longest fight ever waged in the arena.

Ghor was badly hurt, even for a Kothan. That last fall had broken his shoulder-bone and fractured his skull, to say nothing of the minor injuries he had received before the climax. Three of my ribs were broken, and my joints, limbs and muscles so twisted and wrenched that for days I was unable even to rise from my couch. The men of Koth treated our wounds and bruises with all their skill, which far transcends that of the Earth; but in the main it was our remarkable primitive vitality that put us back on our feet. When a creature of the wild is wounded, he generally either dies quickly or recovers quickly.

I asked Thab if Ghor would hate me for his defeat, and Thab was at a loss; Ghor had never been defeated before.

But my mind was soon put at rest on this score. Seven brawny warriors entered the chamber in which I had been placed, bearing a litter on which lay my late foe, wrapped in so many bandages he was scarcely recognizable. But his bellowing voice was familiar. He had forced his friends to bring him to see me as soon as he was able to stir on his couch. He held no malice. In his great, simple, primitive heart there was only admiration for the man who had given him his first defeat. He recounted our Homeric struggle with a gusto that made the roof reverberate, and roared his impatient eagerness for us to fare forth and do battle together against the foes of Koth.

He was borne back to his own chamber, still bellowing his admiration and gory plans for the future, and I experienced a warm glow in my heart for this great-hearted child of nature, who was far more of a man than many sophisticated scions of civilization that I had met.

And so I, Esau Cairn, took the step from savagery to barbarism. In the vast domed council hall before the assembled tribesmen, as soon as I was able, I stood before the throne of Khossuth Skullsplitter, and he cut the mysterious symbol of Koth above my head with his sword. Then with his own hands he buckled on me the harness of a warrior— the broad leather belt with the iron buckle, supporting my poniard and a long straight sword with a broad silver guard. Then the warriors filed past me, and each chief placed his palm against mine, and spoke his name, and I repeated it, and he repeated the name they had given me: Ironhand. That part was most wearisome, for there were some four thousand warriors, and four hundred of these were chiefs of various rank. But it was part of the ritual of initiation, and when it was over I was as much a Kothan as if I had been born into the tribe.

In the tower chamber, pacing like a caged tiger while Thab talked, and later as a member of the tribe, I learned all that the people of Koth knew of their strange planet.

They and their kind, they said, were the only true humans on Almuric, though there was a mysterious race of beings dwelling far to the south called Yagas. The Kothans called themselves Guras, which applied to all cast in their mold, and meant no more than "man" does on Earth. There were many tribes of Guras, each dwelling in its separate city, each of which was a counterpart of Koth. No tribe numbered more than four or five thousand fighting-men, with the appropriate number of women and children.

No man of Koth had ever circled the globe, but they ranged far in their hunts and raids, and legends had been handed down concerning their world—which, naturally, they called by a name simply corresponding to the word "Earth"; though after a while some of them took up my habit of speaking of the planet as Almuric. Far to the north there was a land of ice and snow, uninhabited by human beings, though men spoke of weird cries shuddering by night from the ice crags, and of shadows falling across the snow. A lesser distance to the south rose a barrier no man had ever passed—a gigantic wall of rock which legend said girdled the planet; it was called, therefore, the Girdle. What lay beyond that Girdle, none knew. Some believed it was the rim of the world, and beyond it lay only empty space. Others maintained that another hemisphere lay beyond it. They believed, as seemed to me most logical, that the Girdle separated the northern and southern halves of the world, and that the southern hemisphere was inhabited by men and animals, though the exponents of this theory could give no proof, and were generally scoffed at as overimaginative romanticists.

At any rate, the cities of the Guras dotted the vast expanse that lay between the Girdle and the land of ice. The northern hemisphere possessed no great body of water. There were rivers, great plains, a few scattered lakes, occasional stretches of dark, thick forests, long ranges of barren hills, and a few mountains. The larger rivers ran southward, to plunge into chasms in the Girdle.

The cities of the Guras were invariably built on the open plains, and always far apart. Their architecture was the result of the peculiar evolution of their builders—they were, basically, fortresses of rocks heaped up for defense. They reflected the nature of their builders, being rude, stalwart, massive, despising gaudy show and ornamentation, and knowing nothing of the arts.

In many ways the Guras are like the men of Earth, in other ways bafflingly different. Some of the lines on which they have evolved are so alien to Earthly evolution that I find it difficult to explain their ways and their development.

Specifically, Koth—and what is said of Koth can be said of every other Gura city—the men of Koth are skilled in war, the hunt, and weapon-making. The latter science is taught each male child, but now seldom used. It is seldom found necessary to manufacture new arms, because of the durability of the material used. Weapons are handed down from generation to generation, or captured from enemies.

Metal is used only for weapons, in building, and for clasps and buckles on garments. No ornaments are worn, either by men or women, and there are no such things as coins. There is no medium of exchange. No trade between cities exists, and such "business" as goes on within the city is a matter of barter. The only cloth worn is a kind of silk, made from the fiber of a curious plant grown within the city walls. Other plants furnish wine, fruit, and seasonings. Fresh meat, the principal food of the Guras, is furnished by hunting, a pastime at once a sport and an occupation.

The folk of Koth, then, are highly skilled in metalworking, in silk-weaving, and in their peculiar form of agriculture. They have a written language, a simple hieroglyphic form, scrawled on leaves like papyrus, with a dagger-like pen dipped in the crimson juice of a curious blossom, but few except the chiefs can read or write. Literature they have none; they know nothing of painting, sculpturing, or the "higher" learning. They have evolved to the point of culture needful for the necessities of life, and they progress no further. Seemingly defying laws we on Earth have come to regard as immutable, they remain stationary, neither advancing nor retrogressing.

Like most barbaric people, they have a form of rude poetry, dealing almost exclusively with battle, mayhem and rapine. They have no bards or minstrels, but every man of the tribe knows the popular ballads of his clan, and after a few jacks of ale is prone to bellow them forth in a voice fit to burst one's eardrums.

These songs are never written down, and there is no written history. As a result, events of antiquity are hazy, and mixed with improbable legends.

No one knows how old is the city of Koth. Its gigantic stones are impervious to the elements, and might have stood there ten years or ten thousand years. I am of the opinion that the city is at least fifteen thousand years old. The Guras are an ancient race, in spite of their exuberant barbarism which gives them the atmosphere of a new young people. Of the evolution of the race from whatever beast was their common ancestor, of their racial splittings-off and tribal drifts, of their development to their present condition, nothing whatever is known. The Guras themselves have no idea of evolution. They suppose that, like eternity, their race is without beginning and without end, that they have always been exactly as they are now. They have no legends to explain their creation.

I have devoted most of my remarks to the men of Koth. The women of Koth are no less worthy of detailed comment. I found the difference in the appearance of the sexes not so inexplicable after all. It is simply the result of natural evolution, and its roots lie in a fierce tenderness on the part of the Gura males for their women. It was to protect their women that they first, I am certain, built those brutish heaps of stone and dwelt among them; for the innate nature of the Gura male is definitely nomadic.

The woman, carefully guarded and shielded both from danger and from the hard work that is the natural portion of the women of Earthly barbarians, evolved by natural process into the type I have described. The men, on the other hand, lead incredibly active and strenuous lives. Their existence has been a savage battle for survival, ever since the first ape stood upright on Almuric. And they have evolved into a special type to fit their needs. Their peculiar appearance is not a result of degeneration or under-development. They are, indeed, a highly specialized type, finely adapted to the wild life they follow.

As the men assume all risks and responsibility, they naturally assume all authority. The Gura woman has no say whatever in the government of the city and tribe, and her mate's authority over her is absolute, with the exception that she has the right to appeal to the council and chief in case of oppression. Her scope is narrow; few women ever set foot outside the city in which they are born, unless they are carried off in a raid.

Yet her lot is not so unhappy as it might seem. I have said that one of the characteristics of the Gura male is a savage tenderness for his women. Mistreatment of a woman is very rare, and not tolerated by the tribe.

Monogamy is the rule. The Guras are not given to hand-kissing and pretty compliments, and the other superficial adjuncts of chivalry, but there is justice and a rough kindness in their dealing with women, somewhat similar to the attitude of the American frontiersman.

The duties of the Gura women are few, concerned mainly with child-bearing and child-rearing. They do no work heavier than the manufacturing of silk from the silk plants. They are musically inclined, and play on a small, stringed affair, resembling a lute, and they sing. They are quicker-witted, and of much more sensitive mind than the men. They are witty, merry, affectionate, playful and docile. They have their own amusements, and time does not seem to drag for them. The average woman could not be persuaded to set foot outside the city walls. They well know the perils that hem the cities in, and they are content in the protection of their ferocious mates and masters.

The men are, as I have said, in many ways like barbaric peoples on Earth. In some respects they resemble, I imagine, the ancient Vikings. They are honest, scorning theft and deceit. They delight in war and the hunt, but are not wantonly cruel, except when maddened by rage or bloodlust. Then they can be screaming fiends. They are blunt in speech, rough in their manners, easily angered, but as easily pacified, except when confronted by an hereditary enemy. They have a definite, though crude, sense of humor, a ferocious love for tribe and city, and a passion for personal freedom.

Their weapons consist of swords, daggers, spears, and a firearm something like a carbine—a single-shot, breechloading weapon of no great range, but deadly and accurate within its range. The combustible material is not powder, as we know it. Its counterpart is not found on Earth. It possesses both percussion and explosive qualities. The bullet is of a substance much like lead. These weapons were used mainly in war with men; for hunting, bows and arrows were most often used.

Hunting parties are always going forth, so that the full force of warriors is seldom in the city at once. Hunters are often gone for weeks or months. But there are always a thousand fighting-men in the city to repel possible attack, though it is not often that the Guras lay siege to a hostile city. Those cities are difficult to storm, and it is impossible to starve out the inhabitants, since they produce so much of their food supply within the walls, and in each city is an unfailing spring of pure water. The hunters frequently sought their prey in the Hills which I had haunted, and which were reputed to contain more and varied forms of ferocious bestial life than any other section of the globe. The boldest hunters went in strong parties to the Hills, and seldom roamed there more than a few days. The fact that I had lived among the Hills alone for months won me even more respect and admiration among those wild fightingmen than had my fight with Ghor.

Oh, I learned much of Almuric. As this is a chronicle and not an essay, I can scarcely skim the surface of customs, ways and traditions. I learned all they could tell me, and I learned much more. The Guras were not first on Almuric, though they considered themselves to be. They told me of ancient ruins, never built by Guras, relics of vanished races, who, they supposed, were contemporary with their distant ancestors, but which, as I came to learn, had risen and vanished awfully before the first Gura began to heap up stones to build his primordial city. And how I learned what no Gura knew, is part of this strange narrative.

But they spoke of strange unhuman beings or survivals. They told me of the Yagas, a terrible race of winged black men, dwelling far to the south, within sight of the Girdle, in the grim city of Yugga, on the rock Yuthla, by the river Yogh, in the land of Yagg, where living man had never set foot. The Yagas, the Guras said, were not true men, but devils in a human form. From Yugga they swooped periodically, bearing the sword of slaughter and the torch of destruction, to carry young Gura girls into a slavery the manner of which none knew, because none had ever escaped from the land of Yagg. Some men thought that they were fed to a monster worshiped by the Yagas as a god, though some swore that the fiends worshiped nothing except themselves. This was known: their ruler was a black queen, named Yasmeena, and for more than a thousand years she had reigned on the grim rock of Yuthla, her shadow falling across the world to make men shudder.

The Guras told me other things, things weird and terrible: of dog-headed monstrosities skulking beneath the ruins of nameless cities; of earth-shaking colossals stalking through the night; of fires flitting like flaming bats through the shadowy skies; of things that haunted midnight forests, crawling, squamous things that were never seen, but which tracked men down in the dank depths. They told me of great bats whose laughter drove men mad, and of gaunt shapes shambling hideously through the dusk of the hills. They told me of such things as do not even haunt the dreams of men on my native planet. For Life has taken strange shapes on Almuric, and natural Life is not the only Life there.

But the nightmares told to me and the nightmares seen by me unfold in their place, and I have already lingered too long in my narrative. Be patient a little, because events move swiftly on Almuric, and my chronicle moves no less swiftly when well under way.

For months I dwelt in Koth, fitting into the life of hunting, feasting, ale-guzzling, and brawling, as if I had been born into it. There life was not restrained and bound down, as it is on Earth. As yet no tribal war had tested my powers, but there was fighting enough in the city with naked hands, in friendly bouts, and drunken brawls, when the fighting-men dashed down their foaming jacks and bellowed their challenges across the ale-stained boards. I reveled in my new existence. Here, as in the Hills, I threw my full powers unleashed into life; and here, unlike as in the Hills, I had human companionship, of a sort that suited my particular make-up. I felt no need of art, literature or intellectuality; I hunted, I gorged, I guzzled, I fought; I spread my massive arms and clutched at life like a glutton. And in my brawling and reveling I all but forgot the slender figure which had sat so patiently in the council chamber beneath the great dome.

5

I had wandered far in my hunting. Alone I had spent several nights on the plains. Now I was returning leisurely, but I was still many miles from Koth, whose massive towers I could not yet glimpse across the waving savannas. I cannot say what my thoughts were as I swung along, my carbine in the crook of my arm, but they were likely concerned with spoors in the water's edge, crushed-down grass marking the passing of some large animal, or the scents born on the light wind.

Whatever my thoughts may have been, they were interrupted suddenly by a shrill cry. Wheeling, I saw a slim white figure racing across the grassy level toward me. Behind her, gaining with every stride, came one of those giant carnivorous birds which are among the most dangerous of all the grisly denizens of the grasslands. They tower ten feet in height and somewhat resemble an ostrich except for the beak, which is a huge curving weapon, three feet in length, pointed and edged like a scimitar. A stroke of that beak can slash a man asunder, and the great taloned feet of the monster can tear a human limb from limb.

This mountain of destruction was hurtling along behind the flying girl at appalling speed, and I knew it would overtake her long before I could hope to reach them. Cursing the necessity for depending on my none too accurate marksmanship, I lifted my carbine and took as steady an aim as possible. The girl was directly in line with the brute, and I could not risk a shot at the huge body, lest I hit her instead. I had to chance a shot at the great head that bobbed bafflingly on the long arching neck.

It was more luck than skill that sent my bullet home. At the crack of the shot the giant head jerked backward as if the monster had run into an unseen wall. The stumpy wings thrashed thunderously, and staggering erratically, the brute pitched to the earth.

The girl fell at the same instant, as if the same bullet had brought them both down. Running forward to bend over her, I was surprised to see Altha, daughter of Zal, looking up at me with her dark enigmatic eyes. Quickly satisfying myself that she was not injured, outside of fright and exhaustion, I turned to the thunder-bird and found it quite dead, its few brains oozing out of a hole in its narrow skull.

Turning back to Altha, I scowled down at her.

"What are you doing outside the city?" I demanded. "Are you quite mad, to venture so far into the wilderness alone?"

She made no reply, but I sensed a hurt in her dark eyes, and I repented the roughness of my speech. I dropped down on one knee beside her.

"You are a strange girl, Altha," I said. "You are not like the other women of Koth. Folk say you are willful and rebellious without reason. I do not understand you. Why should you risk your life like this?"

"What will you do now?" she demanded.

"Why, take you back to the city, of course."

Her eyes smoldered with a curious sullenness.

"You will take me back, and my father will whip me. But I will run away again—and again—and again!"

"But why should you run away?" I asked in bewilderment. "There is nowhere for you to go. Some beast will devour you."

"So!" she answered. "Perhaps it is my wish to be devoured."

"Then why did you run from the thunder-bird?"

"The instinct to live is hard to conquer," she admitted.

"But why should you wish to die?" I expostulated. "The women of Koth are happy, and you have as much as any."

She looked away from me, out across the broad plains.

"To eat, drink and sleep is not all," she answered in a strange voice. "The beasts do that."

I ran my fingers through my thick hair in perplexity. I had heard similar sentiments voiced in many different ways on Earth, but it was the first time I had ever heard them from the lips of an inhabitant on Almuric. Altha continued in a low detached voice, almost as if she were speaking to herself rather than to me:

"Life is too hard for me. I do not fit, somehow, as the others do. I bruise myself on its rough edges. I look for something that is not and never was."

Uneasy at her strange words, I caught her heavy locks in my hand and forced back her head to look into her face. Her enigmatic eyes met mine with a strange glimmer in them such as I had never seen.

"It was hard before you came," she said. "It is harder now."

Startled, I released her, and she turned her head away.

"Why should I make it harder?" I asked bewilderedly.

"What constitutes life?" she countered. "Is the life we live all there is? Is there nothing outside and beyond our material aspirations?"

I scratched my head in added perplexity.

"Why," I said, "on Earth I met many people who were always following some nebulous dream or ideal, but I never observed that they were happy. On my planet there is much grasping and groping for unseen things, but I never knew there was such full content as I have known on Almuric."

"I thought you different," she said, still looking away from me. "When I saw you lying wounded and in chains, with your smooth skin and strange eyes, I thought you were more gentle than other men. But you are as rough and fierce as the rest. You spend your days and nights in slaying beasts, fighting men, and in riotous wassail."

"But they all do," I protested.

She nodded. "And so I do not fit in life, and were better dead."

I felt unreasonably ashamed. It had occurred to me that an Earth woman would find life on Almuric intolerably crude and narrow, but it seemed beyond reason that a native woman would have such feelings. If the other women I had seen desired more superficial gentleness on the part of their men, they had not made it known. They seemed content with shelter and protection, and cheerfully resigned to the rough manners of the males. I sought for words but found none, unskilled as I was in polite discourse. I suddenly felt my roughness, crudity and raw barbarism, and stood abashed.

"I'll take you back to Koth," I said helplessly.

She shrugged her shapely shoulders. "And you can watch my father whip me, if you will."

At that I found my tongue.

"He won't whip you," I retorted angrily. "Let him lay a hand on you, and I'll break his back."

She looked up at me quickly, with eyes widened in sudden interest. My arm had found its way about her slim form, and I was glaring into her eyes, with my face very close to hers. Her lips parted, and had that breathless instant lasted a little longer, I know not what would have happened. But suddenly the color went from her face, and from her parted lips rang a terrible scream. Her gaze was fixed on something beyond and above me, and the thrash of wings suddenly filled the air.

I wheeled on one knee, to see the air above me thronged with dark shapes. The Yagas! The winged men of Almuric! I had half believed them a myth; yet here they were in all their mysterious terror.

I had but a glance as I reared up, clubbing my empty carbine. I saw that they were tall and rangy in build, sinewy and powerful, with ebon skins. They seemed made like ordinary men, except for the great leathery bat-like wings which grew from their shoulders. They were naked except for loin-cloths, and were armed with short curved blades.

I rose on my toes as the first swooped in, scimitar lifted, and met him with a swing of my carbine that broke off the stock and crushed his narrow skull like an eggshell. The next instant they were whirling and thrashing about me, their curved blades licking at me like jets of lightning from all sides, the very number of their broad wings hampering them.

Whirling the carbine barrel in a wheel about me, I broke and beat back the flickering blades, and in a furious exchange of strokes, caught another a glancing blow on the head that stretched him senseless at my feet. Then a wild despairing cry rang out behind me, and abruptly the rush slackened.

The whole pack was in the air, racing southward, and I stood frozen. In the arms of one of them writhed and shrieked a slender white figure, stretching out imploring arms to me. Altha! They had snatched her up from behind my back, and were carrying her away to whatever doom awaited her in that black citadel of mystery far to the south. The terrific velocity with which the Yagas raced through the sky was already taking them out of my sight.

As I stood there baffled, I felt a movement at my feet. Looking down I saw one of my victims sit up and feel his head dazedly. I vengefully lifted my carbine barrel to dash out his brains; then a sudden thought struck me, inspired by the ease with which Altha's captor had carried both his weight and hers in the air.

Drawing my poniard, I dragged my captive to his feet. Standing erect he was taller than I, with shoulders equally broad, though his limbs were lean and wiry rather than massive. His dark eyes, which slanted slightly, regarded me with the unblinking stare of a venomous serpent.

The Guras had told me the Yagas spoke a tongue similar to their own.

"You are going to carry me through the air in pursuit of your companions," I said.

He shrugged his shoulders and spoke in a peculiarly harsh voice.

"I cannot carry your weight."

"Then that's bad for you," I answered grimly, and whirling him about, I leaped upon his back, locking my legs about his waist. My left arm was hooked about his neck; the poniard in my right hand pricked his side. He had kept his feet under the impact of my bulk, spreading his great wings.

"Take the air!" I snarled in his ear, sinking the dagger point into his flesh. "Fly, damn you, or I'll cut your heart out!"

His wings began to thrash the air, and we rose slowly from the earth. It was a most sensational experience, but one to which I gave scant thought at the time, being so engrossed in my fury at the abduction of Altha.

When we had risen to a height of about a thousand feet, I looked for the abductors, and saw them far away, a mere group of black dots in the southern sky. After them I steered my reluctant steed.

In spite of my threats and urging for greater speed the flying dots soon vanished. Still I kept on due southward, feeling that even if I failed to overtake them, I would eventually come to the great dusky rock where legend placed their habitation.

Inspired by my poniard, my bearer made good time, considering the burden he was carrying. For hours we sped over the savannas, and by the middle of the afternoon, the landscape changed. We were flying over a forest, the first I had seen on Almuric. The trees seemed to tower to a vast height.

It was near sundown when I saw the farther limits of the forest, and in the grasslands beyond, the ruins of a city. From among these ruins smoke curled upward, and I asked my steed if his companions were cooking their evening meal there. His only answer was a snarl.

We were flying low over the forest, when a sudden uproar caused me to look down. We were just passing over a narrow glade, and in it a terrific battle was taking place. A pack of hyenas had attacked a giant unicorn-like beast, as big as a bison. Half a dozen mangled, trampled bodies attested the fury of the beast's defense, and even as I peered down, he caught the single survivor on his long sword-like ivory horn, and cast it a score of feet in the air, broken and torn.

In the brief fascination of the sight, I must have involuntarily loosened my grasp on my captive. For at that instant, with a convulsive bucking heave and twist, he wrenched free and hurled me sideways. Caught off guard, I clutched vainly at empty air, and rushing earthward, crashed with a stunning impact on the loamy leaf-carpeted earth, directly in front of the maddened unicorn!

I had a dazed brief glimpse of his mountainous bulk looming over me, as his massive lowered head drove his horn at my breast. Then I lurched up on one knee, simultaneously grasping that ivory sword with my left hand and seeking to deflect it, while my right hand drove my poniard up toward the great jugular. Then there came a terrific impact against my skull, and consciousness was blotted out in darkness.

6

I could have been senseless only a few minutes. When I regained consciousness my first sensation was that of a crushing weight upon my limbs and body. Struggling weakly, I found that I was lying beneath the lifeless body of a unicorn. At the instant my poniard had torn open his great jugular vein, the base of his horn must have struck my head, while the vast body collapsed upon me. Only the soft spongy ground beneath me had saved me from being crushed to a pulp. Working myself out from under that bulk was a Herculean task, but eventually I accomplished it, and stood up, bruised and breathless, with the half-dried blood of the monster clotted in my hair and smearing my limbs. I was a grisly sight to look at, but I wasted no time on my appearance. My erstwhile steed was nowhere in evidence, and the circling trees limited my view of the sky.

Selecting the tallest of these trees, I climbed it as swiftly as possible, and on the topmost branches, looked out over the forest. The sun was setting. I saw that perhaps an hour's swift walk to the south, the forest thinned out and ceased. Smoke still drifted thinly up from the deserted city. And I saw my former captive just dropping down among the ruins. He must have lingered, after he had overthrown me, possibly to see if I showed any signs of life, probably to rest his wings after that long grind.

I cursed; there went my chance of stealing up on them unsuspected. Then I got a surprise. No sooner had the Yaga vanished than he reappeared, shooting up out of the city like a rocket. Without hesitation he raced off southward, speeding through the sky at a rate that left me gaping. What was the reason for his flight? If it had been his companions who were among the ruins, why had he not alighted? Perhaps he had found them gone, and was merely following them. Yet his actions seemed strange, considering the leisurely way he had approached the ruins. His flight had the earmarks of panic.

Shaking my head in puzzlement, I descended the tree and set out for the ruins as swiftly as I could make my way through the dense growth, paying no heed to the rustling in the leaves about me, and the muttering of rousing life, that grew as the shadows deepened.

Night had fallen when I emerged from the forest, but the moon was rising, casting a weird unreal glow over the plains. The ruins glimmered ghostily in the near distance. The walls were not of the rough greenish material used by the Guras. As I approached I saw they were of marble, and that fact caused a vague uneasiness to stir in my mind. I remembered legends told by the Kothans of ruined marble cities haunted by ghoulish beings. Such ruins were found in certain uninhabited places, and none knew their origin.

A brooding silence lay over the broken walls and columns as I entered the ruins. Between the gleaming white tusks and surfaces, deep black shadow floated, almost liquid in its quality. From one dusky pool to the other I glided silently, sword in hand, expecting anything from an ambush by the Yagas to an attack by some lurking beast of prey. Utter silence reigned, as I had never encountered it anywhere on Almuric before. Not a distant lion roared, not a night fowl voiced its weird cry. I might have been the last survivor on a dead world.

In silence I came to a great open space, flanked by a circle of broken pillars, which must have been a plaza. Here I halted, motionless, my skin crawling.

In the midst of the plaza smoldered the dying coals of a fire over which, on spits planted in the earth, were roasting pieces of meat. The Yagas had evidently built that fire and prepared to sup; but they had not eaten of their meal. They lay strewn about the plaza in a way to appall the hardiest.

I had never gazed on such a scene of organic devastation. Hands, feet, grinning heads, bits of flesh, entrails, clots of blood littered the whole plaza. The heads were like balls of blackness, rolled out of the shadows against the snowy marble; their teeth grinned, their eyes glimmered palely in the moonlight. *Something* had come upon the winged men as they sat about their fire and had torn them limb from limb. On the remnants of flesh were the marks of fangs, and some of the bones had been broken, apparently to get the marrow.

A cold ripple went up and down my spine. What animal but man breaks bones in that fashion? But the scattering of the bloody remnants seemed not the work of beasts; it seemed too vindictive, as if it were the work of vengeance, fury or bestial blood-thirstiness.

Where, then, was Altha? Her remains were not among those of her captors. Glancing at the flesh on the spit, the configuration of the pieces set me to shuddering. Shaken with horror, I saw that my dark suspicions were correct. It was parts of a human body the accursed Yagas had been roasting for their meal. Sick with revulsion and dread, I examined the pitiful remnants more closely, and breathed a deep sigh of relief to see the thick muscular limbs of a man, and not the slender parts of a woman. But after that I looked unmoved at the torn bloody bits that had been Yagas.

But where was the girl? Had she escaped the slaughter and hidden herself, or had she been taken by the slayers? Looking about at the towers and fallen blocks and pillars, bathed in the weird moonlight, I was aware of a distinct aura of evil, of lurking menace. I felt the glare of hidden eyes.

But I began casting about the plaza, and came upon a trail of blood drops, lying blackly in the moon, leading through a maze of drunken pillars, and for want of better occupation, I followed it. At least it might lead me to the slayers of the winged men.

I passed under the shadows of leaning pillars which dwarfed my human frame with their brute massiveness, and came into a crumbling edifice, overgrown with lichen. Through the broken roof and the gaping windows the moon poured a fungus-white light that served to make the shadows blacker. But a square of moonlight fell across the entrance of a corridor, and leading into it, I saw the sprinkle of dark clotted drops on the cracked vine-grown marble. Into the corridor I groped, and almost broke my neck on the stairs that lay within. Down them I went, and striking a level, hesitated and was about to retrace my steps when I was electrified by a sound that stopped my heart, and then sent the blood pounding madly through my veins. Through the darkness, faint and far away, sounded the call: *"Esau! Esau Cairn!"*

Altha! Who else could it be? Why should an icy shuddering pass over me, and the short hairs bristle at the back of my neck? I started to answer; then caution clutched my tongue. She could not know I was within hearing, surely. Perhaps she was calling as a frightened child will cry for someone far out of hearing. I went as swiftly down the black tunnel as I dared, in the direction I had heard the cry. And as I went I felt beads of clammy sweat form on my skin, and was gagged by a tendency toward nausea.

My groping hand encountered a doorway and I halted, sensing, as a wild thing does, a living presence of some sort near me. Straining my eyes in the pitch dark, I spoke Altha's name in a low urgent voice. Instantly two lights burned in the darkness, yellowish glows at which I stared for an instant before I realized that they were two eyes. They were broad as my hand, round, and of a scintillance I cannot describe. Behind them I got a vague impression of a huge shapeless bulk. Simultaneously such a wave of instinctive fear swept over me, that I withdrew quickly into the tunnel and hastened along it in the direction I had been going. Back in the cell I heard a faint movement, like the shifting of some great pulpy mass, mingled with a soft rasping sound, as of bristles scraping against stone.

A few score paces more and I halted. The tunnel seemed endless, and besides, judging from the feel, other tunnels branched off from it in the darkness, and I had no way of knowing which was the right one. As I stood there I again heard the call: "Esau! Esau Cairn!"

Steeling myself against something, I knew not what, I set off once more in the direction of the ghostly voice. How far I went I do not know, until I stopped once more baffled. Then from near by the voice rang out again: "Esau! Esau CairNNNN!" It rose to a high-pitched note, trailing off into an awful burst of inhuman laughter that froze the blood in my veins.

That was not Altha's voice. I had known all the time that it was not—that it could not be. Yet the alternative was so inexplicable that I had refused to heed what my intuition affirmed and my reason denied.

Now from every direction, on every hand rose a medley of shrill demoniac voices, all shrieking my name with the mockery of devils. The tunnels that had been so silent now rang and re-echoed with strident clamor. I stood bewildered and terrified, as the damned must stand in the clamorous halls of hell. I passed through the stages of icy terror, bewildered horror, desperation, berserk fury. With a maddened roar I plunged blindly at the sounds that seemed nearest, only to collide with a solid wall, while a thousand inhuman voices rose in hideous mirth. Wheeling like a wounded bull, I charged again, this time into the mouth of another tunnel. Racing down this, mad to come to grips with my tormenters, I burst into a vast shadowy space, into which a beam of moonlight cast a ghostly shaft. And again I heard my name called, but in human tones of fear and anguish:

"Esau! Oh, Esau!"

Even as I answered the piteous cry with a savage bellow, I saw her, Altha, etched in the dim moonlight. She was stretched out on the floor, her hands and feet in the shadow. But I saw that at each outstretched member squatted a dim misshapen figure.

With a blood-thirsty yell I charged, and the darkness sprang into nauseous life, flooding my knees with tangible shapes. Sharp fangs gashed me, apish hands clawed at me. They could not halt me. Swinging my sword in great arcs that cut a path through solid masses of writhing shapes, I forged toward the girl that twisted and screamed on the floor in that square of moonlight.

I waded through a rolling, surging mire of squirming biting things that washed about me waist-high, but they could not drag me down. I reached the moonlit square, and the creatures that held Altha gave back before the whistling menace of my sword edge, and the girl sprang up and clung to me. Even as the shadowy horde rolled in to drag us down I saw a crumbling stair leading up, and I thrust her upon it, wheeling to cover her retreat.

It was dark on the stairs, though they led up into a chamber flooded with light through a broken roof. That battle was fought in utter darkness, with only my senses of feeling and hearing to guide my strokes. And it was fought in silence, too, except for my panting, and the whir and crunch of my blade.

Up that drunken stair I backed, battling every inch of the way, the skin between my shoulders crawling with the expectancy of an attack from the rear. If they had come upon us from above, we had been lost, but evidently all were below me. What manner of creatures I was fighting I did not know, except that they were taloned and fanged. Otherwise, from the feel of them, they were stunted and misshapen, furry and apish.

When I came out into the chamber above the tunnels I could see little more. The moonlight streaming through the broken roof made only a white shaft in the darkness. I could only make out vague forms in the dimness about me—a heaving, writhing and lashing of shadows, that surged up against me, clawing and tearing, and fell back beneath my lashing sword.

Thrusting Altha behind me, I backed across that shadowy chamber toward a wide rift that showed in the crumbling wall, reeling and stumbling in the whirlpool of battle that swirled and eddied about me. As I reached the rift through which Altha had already slipped, there was a concerted rush to drag me down. Panic swept over me at the thought of being pulled down in that shadowy room by that dim horde. A blasting burst of fury, a gasping, straining plunge, and I catapulted through the rift, carrying half a dozen attackers with me.

Reeling up, I shook the clinging horrors from my shoulders as a bear might shake off wolves, and bracing my feet slashed right and left. Now for the first time I saw the nature of my foes.

The bodies were like those of deformed apes, covered with sparse dirty white fur. Their heads were dog-like, with small close-set ears. But their eyes were those of serpents— the same venomous steady lidless stare.

Of all the forms of life I had encountered on that strange planet, none filled me with as much loathing as these dwarfish monstrosities. I backed away from the mangled heap on the earth, as a nauseous flood poured through the rift in the wall.

The effect of those vermin emerging from that broken wall was almost intolerably sickening; the suggestion was that of maggots squirming out of a cracked and bleached skull.

Turning, I caught Altha up in one arm and raced across the open space. They followed fleetly, running now on all fours, and now upright like a man. And suddenly they broke out into their hellish laughter again, and I saw we were trapped. Ahead of me were more emerging from some other subterranean entrance. We were cut off.

A giant pedestal, from which the column had been broken, stood before us. With a bound I reached it, set the girl on the jagged pinnacle, and wheeled on the lower base to take such toll of our pursuers as I might. Blood streaming from a score of gashes trickled down the pedestal on which I stood, and I shook my head violently to rid my eyes of blinding sweat.

They ringed me in a wide semicircle, deliberate now that their prey seemed certain, and I cannot recall a time when I was more revolted by horror and disgust, than when I stood with my back to that marble pillar and faced those verminous monsters of the lower world.

Then my attention was caught by a movement in the shadows under the wall through which we had just come. Something was emerging from the rift—something huge and black and bulky. I caught the glitter of a yellowish spark. Fascinated, I watched, even while the furred devils were closing in. Now the thing had emerged entirely from the rift. I saw it crouching in the shadow of the wall, a squat mass of blackness from which glimmered a pair of yellowish lights. With a start I recognized the eyes I had seen in the subterranean cell.

With a clamor of fiendish yells the furry devils rushed in, and at the same instant the unknown creature ran out into the moonlight with surprising speed and agility. I saw it plainly then—a gigantic spider, bigger than an ox. Moving with the swiftness characteristic of its breed, it was among the dog-heads before the first had felt my lifted sword. An awful scream rose from its first victim, and the rest, turning, broke and fled shrieking in all directions. The monster raged among them with appalling quickness and ferocity. Its huge jaws crunched their skulls, its dripping mandibles skewered them, it crushed their bodies by its sheer weight. In an instant the place was a shambles, inhabited only by the dead and dying. Crouching among its victims, the great black hairy thing fixed its horribly intelligent eyes on me.

I was the one it was trailing. I had awakened it underground, and it had followed the scent of the dried blood on my sandals. It had slaughtered the others simply because they stood in its way.

As it crouched on its eight bent legs, I saw that it differed from Earthly spiders not only in size, but in the number of its eyes and the shape of its jaws. Now Altha screamed as it ran swiftly toward me.

But where the fangs and claws of a thousand beastthings were futile against the venom dripping from those black mandibles, the brain and thews of a single man prevailed. Catching up a heavy block of masonry, I poised it for an instant, and then hurled it straight into the onrushing bulk. Full among those branching hairy legs it crushed, and a jet of nauseous green stuff gushed into the air from the torn torso. The monster, halted in his rush, writhed under the pinning stone, cast it aside and staggered toward me again, dragging broken legs, its eyes glittering hellishly. I tore another missile from the crumbling stone, and another and another, raining huge chunks of marble on the writhing horror until it lay still in a ghastly mess of squirming hairy black legs, entrails and blood.

Then, catching Altha in my arms, I raced away through the shadows of monolith and tower and pillar, nor did I halt until the city of silence and mystery lay behind us, and we saw the moon setting across the broad waving grasslands.

No word had passed between us since I had first come upon the girl in that ghoulish tunnel. Now when I looked down to speak to her I saw her dark head drooping against my arm; her white face was upturned, her eyes shut. A quick throb of fear went through me, but a swift examination showed me that she had merely fainted. That fact showed the horror of what she had been through. The women of Koth do not faint easily.

I laid her at full length on the turf, and gazed at her helplessly, noting, as if for the first time, the white firmness of her slender limbs, the exquisite molding of her supple figure. Her dark hair fell in thick glossy clusters about her alabaster shoulders, a strap of her tunic, slipped down, revealed her firm, pink-tipped young breasts. I was aware of a vague unrest that was almost a pain.

Altha opened her eyes and looked up at me. Then her dark eyes flared with terror, and she cried out and clutched at me frantically. My arms closed about her instinctively, and within their iron-thewed clasp I felt the pulsating of her lithe body, the wild fluttering of her heart.

"Don't be afraid," my voice sounded strange, scarcely articulate. "Nothing is going to harm you."

I could feel her heart resuming its normal beat, so closely she clung to me, before her quick pants of fright ceased. But for a while she lay in my arms, looking up at me without speaking, until, embarrassed, I released her and lifted her to a sitting position on the grass.

"As soon as you feel fit," I said, "we'll put more distance between us and—that." I jerked my head in the direction of the distant ruins.

"You are hurt," she exclaimed suddenly, tears filling her eyes. "You are bleeding! Oh, I am to blame. If I had not run away—" She was weeping now in earnest, like any Earthly girl.

"Don't worry about these scratches," I answered, though privately I was wondering if the fangs of the vermin were venomous. "They are only flesh wounds. Stop crying, will you?"

She obediently stifled her sobs, and naïvely dried her eyes with her skirt. I did not wish to remind her of her horrible experience, but I was curious on one point.

"Why did the Yagas halt at the ruins?" I asked. "Surely they knew of the things that haunt such cities."

"They were hungry," she answered with a shudder. "They had captured a youth—they dismembered him alive, but never a cry for mercy they got, only curses. Then they roasted—" she gagged, smitten with nausea.

"So the Yagas are cannibals," I muttered.

"No. They are devils. While they sat about the fire the Dogheads fell upon them. I did not see them until they were on us. They swarmed over the Yagas like jackals over deer. Then they dragged me into the darkness. What they meant to do, Thak only knows. I have heard—but it is too obscene to repeat."

"But why did they shriek my name?" I marveled.

"I cried it aloud in my terror," she answered. "They heard and mimicked me. When you came, they knew you. Do not ask me how. They too are devils."

"This planet is infested with devils," I muttered. "But why did you call on me, in your fright, instead of your father?"

She colored slightly, and instead of answering, began pulling her tunic straps in place.

Seeing that one of her sandals had slipped off, I replaced it on her small foot, and while I was so occupied she asked unexpectedly: "Why do they call you Ironhand? Your fingers are hard, but their touch is as gentle as a woman's. I never had men's fingers touch me so lightly before. More often they have hurt me."

I clenched my fist and regarded it moodily—a knotted iron mallet of a fist. She touched it timidly.

"It's the feeling behind the hand," I answered. "No man I ever fought complained that my fists were gentle. But it is my enemies I wish to hurt, not you."

Her eyes lighted. "You would not hurt me? Why?"

The absurdity of the question left me speechless.

7

It was past sunrise when we started back on the long trek toward Koth, swinging far to the west to avoid the devil city from which we had escaped. The sun came up unusually hot. The air was breathless, the light morning wind blew fitfully, and then died down entirely. The always cloudless sky had a faint copperish tint. Altha eyed that sky apprehensively, and in answer to my question said she feared a storm. I had supposed the weather to be always clear and calm and hot on the plains, clear and windy and cold in the hills. Storms had not entered into my calculations.

The beasts we saw shared her uneasiness. We skirted the edge of the forest, for Altha refused to traverse it until the storm had passed. Like most plains-dwellers, she had an instinctive distrust of thick woods. As we strode over the grassy undulations, we saw the herds of grazers milling confusedly. A drove of jumping pigs passed us, covering the ground with gargantuan bounds of thirty and forty feet. A lion started up in front of us with a roar, but dropped his massive head and slunk hurriedly away through the tall grass.

I kept looking for clouds, but saw none. Only the copperish tint about the horizons grew, discoloring the whole sky. It turned from light color to dull bronze, and from bronze to black. The sun smoldered for a little like a veiled torch, veining the dusky dome with fire; then it was blotted out. A tangible darkness seemed to hover an instant in the sky, then rush down, cloaking the world in utter blackness, through which shone neither sun, moon, nor star. I had never guessed how impenetrable darkness could be. I might have been a blind, disembodied spirit wandering through unlighted space, but for the swish of the grasses under my feet, and the soft warm contact of Altha's body against mine. I began to fear we might fall into a river, or blunder against some equally blind beast of prey.

I had been making for a mass of broken boulders, such a formation as occasionally occurs on the plains. Darkness fell before we reached them, but groping on, I stumbled upon a sizable rock, and placing my back to it, drew Altha against it and stood sheltering her with my body as well as I could. Out on the dark plains breathless silence alternated with the sounds of varied and widespread movement— rustling of grass, shuffle of padded hoofs, weird lowing and low-pitched roaring. Once a vast herd of some sort swept by us, and I was thankful for the protection of the boulders that kept us from being trampled. Again all sounds ceased and the silence was as complete as the darkness. Then from somewhere came a weird howling.

"What's that?" I asked uneasily, unable to classify it.

"The wind!" she shivered, snuggling closer to me.

It did not blow with a steady blast; here and there it swept in mad fitful gusts. Like lost souls it wailed and moaned. It ripped the grasses near us, and finally a puff of it struck us squarely, knocking us off our feet and bruising us against the boulder behind us. Just that one abrupt blast, like a buffet from an unseen giant's fist.

As we regained our feet I froze. Something was passing near our refuge—something mountain-huge, beneath whose tread the earth trembled. Altha caught me in a desperate clutch, and I felt the pounding of her heart. My hair prickled with nameless fear. The *thing* was even with us. It halted, as if sensing our presence. There was a curious leathery sound, as of the movement of great limbs. Something waved in the air above us; then I felt a touch on my elbow. The same object touched Altha's bare arm, and she screamed, her taut nerves snapping.

Instantly our ears were deafened by an awful bellow above us, and something swept down through the darkness with a clashing of gigantic teeth. Blindly I lashed out and upward, feeling my sword-edge meet tangible substance. A warm liquid spurted along my arm, and with another terrible roar, this time more of pain than rage, the invisible monster shambled away, shaking the earth with its tread, dimming the shrieking wind with its bellowing.

"What was it, in God's name?" I panted.

"It was one of the Blind Ones," she whispered. "No man has ever seen them; they dwell in the darkness of the storm. Whence they come, whither they go, none knows. But look, the darkness melts."

"Melts" was the right word. It seemed to shred out, to tear in long streamers. The sun came out, the sky showed blue from horizon to horizon. But the earth was barred fantastically with long strips of darkness, tangible shadows floating on the plain, with broad spaces of sunlight between. The scene might have been a dream landscape of an opium-eater. A hurrying deer flitted across a sunlight band and vanished abruptly in a broad streamer of black; as suddenly it flashed into light and sight again. There was no gradual shading into darkness; the borders of the torn strips of blackness were as clear-cut and definite as ribbons of ebony on a background of gold and emerald. As far as I could see, the world was stripped and barred with those black ribbons. Sight could not pierce them, but they were thinning, dividing, vanishing.

Directly before me one of the streamers of darkness ripped apart and disappeared, revealing the figure of a man—a hairy giant, who stood glaring at me, sword in hand, as surprised as I. Then several things happened all at once. Altha screamed: "A Thugran!"; the stranger leaped and slashed, and his sword clanged on my lifted blade.

I have only a brief chaotic memory of the next few seconds. There was a whirl of strokes and parries, a brief clanging of steel; then my sword-point sank under his heart and stood out behind his back. I wrenched the blade free as he sank down, and stood glaring down at him bewilderedly. I had secretly wondered what the outcome would be when I was called upon to face a seasoned warrior with naked steel. Now it had occurred and was over with, and I was absolutely unable to remember how I had won. It had been too fast and furious for conscious thought; my fighting instinct had acted for me.

A clamor of angry cries burst on me, and wheeling I saw a score of hairy warriors swarming out from among the rocks. It was too late to flee. In an instant they were on me, and I was the center of a whirling, flashing maelstrom of swords. How I parried them even for a few seconds I cannot say. But I did, and even had the satisfaction of feeling my blade grate around another, and sever the wielder's shoulderbone. A moment later one stooped beneath my thrust and drove the spear through the calf of my leg. Maddened by the pain, I dealt him a stroke that split his skull to the chin, and then a carbine stock descended on my head. I partially parried the blow, else it had smashed my skull. But even so, it beat down on my crown with murderous impact, and the lights went out.

I came to with the impression that I was lying in a small boat which was rocking and tossing in a storm. Then I discovered that I was bound hand and foot, and being borne on a litter made of spear-shafts. Two huge warriors were bearing me between them, and they made no effort to make the traveling any easier for me. I could see only the sky, the hairy back of the warrior in front of me, and by drawing back my head the bearded face of the warrior behind. This person, seeing my eyes open, growled a word to his mate, and they promptly dropped the litter. The jolt set my damaged head to throbbing, and the wound in my leg to hurting abominably.

"Logar!" bawled one of them. "The dog is conscious. Make him walk, if you must bring him to Thugra. I've carried him as far as I'm going to."

I heard footsteps, and then above me towered a giant form and a face that seemed familiar. It was a fierce, brutal face, and from the corner of the snarling mouth to the rim of the square jaw, ran a livid scar.

"Well, Esau Cairn," said this individual, "we meet again."

I made no reply to this obvious comment.

"What?" he sneered, "do you not remember Logar the Bone-crusher, you hairless dog?"

He punctuated his remarks by a savage kick in my ribs. Somewhere there rang out a feminine shriek of protest, the sound of a scuffle, and Altha broke through the ring of warriors and fell to her knees beside me.

"Beast!" she cried, her beautiful eyes blazing. "You kick him when he is helpless, when you would not dare face him in fair battle."

"Who let this Kothan cat loose?" roared Logar. "Thal, I told you to keep her away from this dog."

"She bit my hand," snarled the big warrior, striding forward and shaking a drop of blood from his hairy paw. "I'd as soon try to hold a spitting wildcat."

"Well, haul him to his feet," directed Logar. "He walks the rest of the way."

"But he is wounded in the leg!" wailed Altha. "He cannot walk."

"Why don't you finish him here?" demanded one of the warriors.

"Because that would be too easy!" roared Logar, red lights flickering in his blood-shot eyes. "The thief struck me foully with a stone, from behind, and stole my poniard"— here I saw that he was wearing it once more at his girdle. "He shall go to Thugra, and there I'll take my time about killing him. Drag him up!"

They loosened my legs, none too gently, but the wounded one was so stiff I could hardly stand, much less walk. They encouraged me with blows, kicks, and prods from spears and swords, while Altha wept in helpless fury, and at last turned on Logar.

"You are both a liar and a coward!" she screamed. "He did not strike you with a stone—he beat you down with his naked fists, as all men know, though your slaves dare not acknowledge it—"

Logar's knotty fist crashed against her jaw, knocking her off her feet, to fall in a crumpled heap a dozen feet away. She lay without moving, blood trickling from her lips. Logar grunted in savage satisfaction, but his warriors were silent. Moderate corporal correction for women was not unknown among the Guras, but such excessive and wanton brutality was repugnant to any warrior of average decency. So Logar's braves looked glum, though they made no verbal protest.

As for me, I went momentarily blind with the red madness of fury that swept over me. With a blood-thirsty snarl I jerked convulsively, upsetting the two men who held me; so we all went down in a heap. The other Thugrans came and boosted us up, glad to vent their outraged feelings on my carcass, which they did lustily, with sandal heels and sword-hilts. But I did not feel the blows that rained upon me. The whole world was swimming red to my sight, and speech had utterly failed me. I could only snarl bestially as I tore in vain at the thongs which bound me. When I lay exhausted, my captors hauled me up and began beating me to make me walk.

"You can beat me to death," I snarled, finding my voice at last, "but I won't move until some of you see to the girl."

"The slut's dead," growled Logar.

"You lie, you dog!" I spat. "You miserable weakling, you couldn't hit hard enough to kill a new-born babe!"

Logar bellowed in wordless fury, but one of the others, panting from his exertions of hammering me, stepped over to Altha, who was showing signs of life.

"Let her lie!" roared Logar.

"Go to the devil!" snarled his warrior. "I love her no more than you do, but if bringing her along will make that smooth-skinned devil walk of his own accord, I'll bring her, if I have to carry her all the way. He's not human; I've pummeled him till I'm ready to drop dead, and he's in better shape than I."

So Altha, wobbly on her legs and very groggy, accompanied us as we marched to Thugra.

We were on the road several days, during which time walking was agony to my wounded leg. Altha persuaded the warriors to let her bandage my wounds, and but for that I very probably should have died. I was marked in many places by the gashes received in the haunted ruins, battered and bruised from head to foot by the beating the Thugrans gave me. Just enough food and water was given me to keep me alive. And so, dazed, weary, harassed by thirst and hunger, crippled, stumbling along over those endless rolling plains, I was even glad at last to see the walls of Thugra looming in the distance, even though I knew they spelled my doom. Altha had not been badly treated on the march, but she had been prevented from giving me aid and comfort, beyond bandaging my wounds, and all through the nights, waking from the beast-like sleep of utter exhaustion, I heard her sobbing. Among the hazy, tortured impressions of that dreary trek, that stands out most clearly—Altha sobbing in the night, terrible with loneliness and despair in the immensity of shadowed world and moaning darkness.

And so we came to Thugra. The city was almost exactly like Koth—the same huge tower-flanked gates, massive walls built of rugged green stone, and all. The people, too, differed none in the main essentials from the Kothans. But I found that their government was more like an absolute monarchy than was Koth's. Logar was a primitive despot, and his will was the last power. He was cruel, merciless, lustful and arrogant. I will say this for him: he upheld his rule by personal strength and courage. Thrice during my captivity in Thugra I saw him kill a rebellious warrior in hand-to-hand combat—once with his naked hands against the other's sword. Despite his faults, there was force in the man, a gusty, driving, dynamic power that beat down opposition with sheer brutality. He was like a roaring wind, bending or breaking all that stood before him.

Possessed of incredible vitality, he was intensely vain of his physical prowess—in which, I believe, his superiority of personality was rooted. That was why he hated me so terribly. That was why he lied to his people and told them that I struck him with a stone. That was why, too, he refused to put the matter to test. In his heart lurked fear—not of any bodily harm I might do him, but fear lest

I overcome him again, and discredit him in the eyes of his subjects. It was his vanity that made a beast of Logar.

I was confined in a cell, chained to the wall. Logar came every day to curse and taunt me. It was evident that he wished to exhaust all mental forms of torment before he proceeded to physical torture. I did not know what had become of Altha. I had not seen her since first we entered the city. He swore that he had taken her to his palace, and described to me with great detail the salacious indignities to which he swore he subjected her. I did not believe him, for I felt he would be more likely to bring her to my cell and torture her before me. But the fury into which his obscene narrations threw me could not have been much more violent if the scenes he described had been enacted before me.

It was easy to see that the Thugrans did not relish Logar's humor, for they were no worse than other Guras, and all Guras possess, as a race, an innate decency in regard to women. But Logar's power was too complete for any to venture a protest. At last, however, the warrior who brought me food told me that Altha had disappeared immediately after we reached the city, and that Logar was searching for her, but unable to find her. Apparently she had either escaped from Thugra, or was hiding somewhere in the city.

And so the slow days crawled by.

8

It was midnight when I awoke suddenly. The torch in my cell was flickering and guttering. The guard was gone from my door. Outside, the night was full of noise. Curses, yells and shots mingled with the clash of steel, and over all rose the screaming of women. This was accompanied by a curious thrashing sound in the air above. I tore at my bonds, mad to know what was happening. There was fighting in the city, beyond the shadow of a doubt, but whether civil war or alien invasion, I could not know.

Then quick light steps sounded outside, and Altha ran swiftly into my cell. Her hair was in wild disorder, her scanty garment torn, her eyes ablaze with terror.

"Esau!" she cried. "Doom from the sky has fallen on Thugra! The Yagas have descended on the city by the thousands! There is fighting in the streets and on the house tops—the gutters are running red, and the streets are strewn with corpses! Look! The city is burning!"

Through the high-set barred windows I saw a smoldering glow. Somewhere sounded the dry crackling of flames. Altha was sobbing as she fumbled vainly at my bonds. That day Logar had begun the physical torture, and had had me hauled upright and suspended from the roof by a rawhide thong bound about my wrists, my toes just touching a huge block of granite. But Logar had not been so wise. They had used a new thong of hide, and it had stretched, allowing my feet to rest on the block, in which position I had suffered no unbearable anguish, and had even fallen asleep, though naturally the attitude was not conducive to great comfort.

As Altha worked futilely to free me, I asked her where she had been, and she answered that she had slipped away from Logar when we had reached the city, and that kind women, pitying her, had hidden and fed her. She had been waiting for an opportunity to aid me in escaping. "And now," she wailed, wringing her hands, "I can do nothing! I cannot untie this wretched noose!"

"Go find a knife!" I directed. "Quick!"

Even as she turned, she cried out and shrank back, trembling, as a terrible figure lurched through the door.

It was Logar, his mane and beard matted and singed, the hair on his great breast crisped and blackened, blood streaming from his limbs. His bloodshot eyes glared madness as he reeled toward me, lifting the poniard I had taken from him so long before.

"Dog!" he croaked. "Thugra is doomed! The winged devils drop from the skies like vultures on a dead ox! I have slain until I die of weariness, yet still they come. But I remembered you. I could not rest easy in Hell, knowing you still lived. Before I go forth again to die, I'll send you before me!"

Altha shrieked and ran to shield me, but he was before her. Rising on his toes he caught at my girdle, lifting the poniard on high. And as he did so, I drove my knee with terrific force up against his jaw. The impact must have broken his bull-neck like a twig. His shaggy head shot back between his shoulders, his bearded chin pointing straight up. He went down like a slaughtered ox, his head crashing hard on the stone floor.

A low laugh sounded from the doorway. Etched in the opening stood a tall ebony shape, wings half lifted, a dripping scimitar in a crimsoned hand. Limned in the murky red glare behind him, the effect was that of a blackwinged demon standing in the flame-lit door of Hell. The passionless eyes regarded me enigmatically, flitted across the crumpled form on the floor, then rested on Altha, cowering at my feet.

Calling something over his shoulder, the Yaga advanced into the room, followed by a score of his kind. Many of them bore wounds, and their swords were notched and dripping.

"Take them," the first comer indicated Altha and myself.

"Why the man?" demurred one.

"Who ever saw a white man with blue eyes before? He will interest Yasmeena. But be careful. He has the thews of a lion."

One of them grasped Altha's arm and dragged her away, struggling vainly and twisting her head to stare back at me with terrified eyes, and the others from a safe distance cast a silken net about my feet. While my limbs were so enmeshed, they seized me, bound me with silken cords that a lion could not have broken, and cut the thong by which I was suspended. Then two of them lifted me and bore me out of the cell. We emerged into a scene of frenzy in the streets.

The stone walls were of course immune to flame, but the woodwork of the buildings was ablaze. Smoke rolled up in great billowing clouds, shot and veined by tongues of flame, and against this murky background black shapes twisted and contorted like figments of nightmare. Through the black clouds shot what appeared to be blazing meteors, until I saw they were winged men bearing torches.

In the streets, among falling sparks and crashing walls, in the burning buildings, on the roofs, desperate scenes were being hideously enacted. The men of Thugra were fighting with the fury of dying panthers. Any one of them was more than a match for a single Yaga, but the winged devils far outnumbered them, and their fiendish agility in the air balanced the superior strength and courage of the apemen. Swooping down through the air, they slashed with their curved swords, soaring out of reach again before the victim could return the stroke. When three or four devils were striking thus at a single enemy, the butchery was certain and swift. The smoke did not seem to bother them as it did their human adversaries. Some, perched on points of vantage, bent bows and sent arrows singing down into the struggling masses in the streets.

The killing was not all on one side. Winged bodies as well as hairy shapes lay strewn in the blood-splashed streets. Carbines cracked and more than a few flying fiends crashed earthward in a frantic thrashing of wings. Madly lashing swords found their target, and when the desperate hands of a Gura closed on a Yaga, that Yaga died horribly.

But by far the greater slaughter was among the Thugrans. Blinded and half strangled, most of their bullets and arrows went wild. Outnumbered and bewildered by the hawk-like tactics of their merciless foes, they fought vainly, were cut down or feathered with arrows.

The main object of the Yagas seemed to be women captives. Again and again I saw a winged man soar up through the whirling smoke, gripping a shrieking girl in his arms.

Oh, it was a sickening sight! I do not believe that the utter barbarism and demoniac cruelty of the scene could be duplicated on Earth, vicious as its inhabitants can be at times. It was not like humans fighting humans, but like members of two different forms of life at war, utterly without sympathy or any common plane of understanding.

But the massacre was not complete. The Yagas were quitting the city they had ruined, sweeping up into the skies laden with naked writhing captives. The survivors still held the streets, and fired blindly at the departing victors, evidently preferring to risk killing their captives rather than to let them be carried to the fate that awaited them.

I saw a knot of perhaps a hundred struggling fighters slashing and gasping on the highest roof in the city, the Yagas to tear away and escape, the Guras to drag them down. Smoke billowed about them, flames caught at their hair; then with a thunderous roar the roof fell in, bearing victors and vanquished alike to a fiery death. The deafening thunder of the devouring flames was in my ears as my captors whirled me through the air away from the reeking city of Thugra.

When my dazed faculties adjusted themselves sufficiently for me to take note of my surroundings, I found myself sailing through the sky at terrific speed, while below, above and about me sounded the steady beat of mighty wings. Two Yagas were bearing me with perfect ease, and I was in the midst of the band, which was flying southward in a wedge-shaped formation, like that of wild geese. There were fully ten thousand of them. They darkened the morning sky, and their gigantic shadow swept over the plain beneath them as the sun rose.

We were flying at an altitude of about a thousand feet. Many of the winged men bore girls and young women, and carried them with an ease that spoke of incredible wingpower. No match in sheer muscularity for the Guras, yet those winged devils have unbelievable powers of endurance in the air. They can fly for hours at top speed, and in the wedge formation, with unburdened leaders cleaving the air ahead of them, can carry weights almost equal their own at almost the same velocity.

We did not pause to rest or eat until nightfall, when our captors descended to the plain, where they built fires and spent the night. That night lives in my memory as one of the greatest horrors I have ever endured. We captives were given no food, but the Yagas ate.

And their food was their miserable captives. Lying helpless, I shut my eyes to that butchery, wished that I were deaf that I might not hear the heart-rending cries. The butchery of men I can endure, in battle, even in red massacre. The wanton slaughter of helpless women who can only shriek for mercy until the knife silences their wails, that is more than I can stand. Nor did I know but that Altha was among those chosen for the grisly feast. With each hiss and crunch of the beheading blade I winced, seeing in fancy her lovely dark head roll on the blood-soaked ground. For what was going on at the other fires I could not know.

After it was over and the gorged demons lay about the fires in slumber, I lay sick at heart, listening to the roaring of the prowling lions, and reflecting how kinder and more gentle is any beast, than any thing molded in the form of man. And out of my sick horror grew a hate that steeled me for whatever might come, in the grim determination to ultimately repay these winged monsters for all the suffering they had inflicted.

Dawn was only a hint in the sky when we took the air again. There was no morning meal. I was to learn that the Yagas ate only at intervals, gorging themselves to capacity every few days. After several hours hurtling over the usual grasslands, we came suddenly in sight of a broad river spanning the savannas from horizon to horizon, fringed on the northern bank by a narrow belt of forest. The waters were of a curious purple, glimmering like watered silk. On the farther bank appeared a tall thin tower of a black shiny material that glittered like polished steel.

As we whirled over the river I saw that it was rushing with terrific velocity. Its roar came up to us, and I saw the seething of eddying whirlpools in its racing current. Crossing the stream at the point where the tower stood, reared numbers of huge stones, among which the waters foamed and thundered. Looking down at the tower, I saw half a dozen winged men on the battlemented roof, who tossed up their arms as if hailing our captors. From the river southward stretched desert—bare, dusty, grayish, strewn occasionally with bleached bones here and there. Far away on the horizon I saw a giant black bulk growing in the sky.

It stood out boldly as we raced toward it. In a few hours we had reached it, and I was able to make out all its details. It was a gigantic block of black basalt-like rock rising sheer out of the desert, a broad river flowing about its feet, its summit crowned with black towers, minarets and castles. It was no myth, then, but a fantastic reality—Yugga, the Black City, the stronghold of the winged people.

The river, cutting through the naked desert, split on that great rock and passed about it on either side, forming a natural moat. On every side but one the waters lapped the sheer walls of the cliffs. But on one side a broad beach had been formed, and there stood another town. Its style of architecture was very different from that of the edifices on the rock. The houses were mere stone huts, squat, flat-roofed, and one-storied. Only one building had any pretensions—a black temple-like edifice built against the cliff wall. This lower town was protected by a strong stone wall built about it at the water's edge, and connecting at each end with the cliff behind the town.

I saw the inhabitants, and saw that they were neither Yagas nor Guras. They were short and squat of build, and of a peculiar blue color. Their faces, while more like those of Earthly humans than were those of the Gura males, lacked the intelligence of the latter. The countenances were dull, stupid and vicious, the women being little more prepossessing than the men. I saw these curious people, not only in their town at the foot of the cliff, but at work in fields along the river.

I had little opportunity for observing them, however, since the Yagas swept straight up to the citadel, which towered five hundred feet above the river. I was bewildered by the array of battlements, pinnacles, minarets and roof gardens that met my gaze, but got the impression that the city on the rock was built like one huge palace, each part connected with the rest. Figures lounging on couches on the flat roofs lifted themselves on elbow, and from scores of casements the faces of women looked at us as we sank down on a broad flat roof that was something like a landingfield. There many of the winged men dispersed, leaving the captives guarded by three or four hundred warriors, who herded them through a gigantic door. There were about five hundred of these wretched girls, Altha among them. I was carried, still bound, along with them. By this time my whole body was numb from having circulation cut off so long, but my mind was intensely active.

We traversed a stairway down which half a dozen elephants could have stalked abreast, and came into a corridor of corresponding vastness. Walls, stair, ceiling and floor were all of the gleaming black stone, which I decided had been cut out of the rock on which Yugga was built, and highly polished. So far I had seen no carvings, tapestries, or any attempt at ornamentation; yet it could not be denied that the effect of those lofty walls and vaulted ceilings of polished ebony was distinctly one of splendor. There was an awe-inspiring majesty about the architecture which seemed incongruous, considering the beastliness of the builders. Yet the tall black figures did not seem out of place, moving somberly through those great ebony halls. The Black City—not alone because its walls were dusky hued did humans give it that sinister name.

As we passed through those lofty halls I saw many of the inhabitants of Yugga. Besides the winged men, I saw, for the first time, the women of the Yagas. Theirs was the same lithe build, the same glossy black skin, the same faintly hawk-like cast of countenance. But the women were not winged. They were clad in short silken skirts held up with jewel-crusted girdles, and in filmy sashes bound about their breasts. But for the almost intangible cruelty of their faces, they were beautiful. Their dusky features were straight and clear-cut, their hair was not kinky.

I saw other women, hundreds of the black-haired, white-skinned daughters of the Guras. But there were others: small, dainty, yellow-skinned girls, and coppercolored women—all, apparently, slaves to the black people. These women were something new and unexpected. All the fantastic forms of life I had encountered so far had been mentioned in tales or legends of the Kothans. The Dogheads, the giant spider, the winged people with their black citadel and their blue-skinned slaves—all these had been named in legendry, at least. But no man or woman of Koth had ever spoken of women with yellow or copper skins. Were these exotic prisoners from another planet, just as I was from an alien world?

While meditating the matter I was carried through a great bronze portal at which stood a score of winged warriors on guard, and found myself with the captive girls in a vast chamber, octagonal in shape, the walls hung with dusky tapestries. It was carpeted with some sort of rich fur-like stuff, and the air was heavy with perfumes and incense.

Toward the back of the chamber, broad steps of beaten gold led up to a fur-covered dais, on which lounged a young black woman. She alone, of all the Yaga women, was winged. She was dressed like the rest, wearing no ornaments except her gem-crusted girdle, from which jutted a jeweled dagger-hilt. Her beauty was marvelous and disquieting, like the beauty of a soulless statue. I sensed that of all the inhuman denizens of Yugga, she was least human. Her brooding eyes spoke of dreams beyond the boundaries of human consciousness. Her face was the face of a goddess, knowing neither fear nor mercy.

Ranged about her couch in attitudes of humility and servitude were twenty naked girls, white, yellow and copper-skinned.

The leader of our captors advanced toward the royal dais, and bowing low, at the same time extending his hands, palms down and fingers spread wide, he said: "Oh, Yasmeena, Queen of the Night, we bring you the fruits of conquest."

She raised herself on her elbow, and as her terribly impersonal gaze passed over her cringing captives, a shudder swept across their ranks as a wind passes over rows of wheat. From earliest childhood Gura girls were taught, by tales and tradition, that the worst fate that could befall them was to be captured by the people of the Black City. Yugga was a misty land of horror, ruled by the arch-fiend Yasmeena. Now those trembling girls were face to face with the vampire herself. What wonder that many of them fainted outright?

But her eyes passed over them and rested on me, where I stood propped up between a couple of warriors. I saw interest grow in those dark luminous eyes, and she spoke to the chief:

"Who is that barbarian, whose skin is white, yet almost as hairless as ours, who is clad like a Gura, and yet unlike them?"

"We found him a captive among the Thugrans, oh mistress of Night," he answered. "Your majesty shall herself question him. And now, oh dark beauty, be pleased to designate the miserable wenches who shall serve your loveliness, that the rest may be apportioned among the warriors who made the raid."

Yasmeena nodded, her eyes still on me, and with a few waves of her hand she indicated a dozen or so of the handsomest girls, among these being Altha. They were drawn aside, and the rest were herded out.

Yasmeena eyed me a space without speaking, and then said to him who appeared to be her major-domo: "Gotrah, this man is weary and stained with travel and captivity, and there is an unhealed wound in his leg. The sight of him, as he now is, offends me. Take him away, let him bathe and eat and drink, and let his leg be bandaged. Then bring him to me again."

So my captors, with a weary sigh, heaved me up again, and carried me from the royal chamber, down a winding corridor, along a flight of stairs, and halted finally in a chamber where a fountain bubbled in the floor. There they fastened gold chains to my wrists and ankles, and then cut the cords that bound me. In the excruciating pain of the returning circulation, I scarcely noticed when they splashed me in the fountain, bathing the sweat, dirt and dried blood from my limbs and body, and clad me in a new loin-cloth of scarlet silk. They likewise dressed the wound in my calf, and then a copper-skinned slave-girl entered with gold vessels of food. I would not touch the meat, what with my grisly suspicions, but I ate ravenously of the fruit and nuts, and drank deeply of a green wine which I found most delicious and refreshing.

After that I felt so drowsy that I sank down on a velvet couch and passed instantly into deep slumber, from which I was roused by someone shaking me. It was Gotrah bending over me with a short knife in his hand; and, all my wild instincts aroused, I did my best to brain him with my clenched fist, and failed only because of the chain on my wrist. He recoiled, cursing.

"I have not come to cut your throat, barbarian," he snapped, "though nothing would please me better. The Kothan girl has told Yasmeena that it is your habit to scrape the hair from your face, and it is the Queen's desire to see you thus. Here, take this knife and scrape yourself. It has no point, and I will be careful to stay out of your reach. Here is a mirror."

Still half asleep—by which I believe the green wine was drugged, though for what reason I cannot say—I propped the silver mirror up against the wall, and went to work on my beard, which had reached no mean proportions during my captivities. It was a dry shave, but my skin is as durable as tanned leather, and the knife had an edge keener than I ever found on an Earthly razor. When I had finished, Gotrah grunted at my changed appearance and demanded the knife again. As there was no point in retaining it, it being useless as a weapon, I threw it at him, and immediately fell asleep again.

The next time I awoke naturally, and rising, took in my surroundings more minutely. The chamber was unadorned, furnished only with the couch, a small ebony table, and a fur-covered bench. There was a single door, which was closed and doubtless bolted on the outside, and one window. My chains were fastened to a gold ring in the wall behind the couch, but the strand that linked me to it was long enough to allow me to take a few steps, to the fountain, and to the window. This window was barred with gold, and I looked out over flat roofs, at towers and minarets which limited my view.

So far the Yagas had treated me well enough; I wondered how Altha was faring, and if the position of member of the Queen's retinue carried any special privileges or safety.

Then Gotrah entered again, with half a dozen warriors, and they unlocked my chain from the wall and escorted me down the corridor, up the winding stair. I was not taken back to the great throne chamber, but to a smaller room high up in a tower. This room was so littered with furs and cushions that it was almost stuffed. I was reminded of the soft, padded nest of a spider, and the black spider was there—lounging on a velvet couch and staring at me with avid curiosity. This time she was not attended by slaves. The warriors chained me to the wall—every wall in that accursed palace seemed to have rings for captives—and left us alone.

I leaned back among the furs and pillows, finding their downy contact irksome to my iron-hard frame, unaccustomed to soft living of any kind, and for a wearisome time the Queen of Yugga surveyed me without speaking. Her eyes had a hypnotic quality; I distinctly felt their impact. But I felt too much like a chained beast on exhibition to be aware of any feeling but one of rising resentment. I fought it down. A burst of berserk fury might break the slender chains that held me, and rid the world of Yasmeena, but Altha and I would still be prisoners on that accursed rock from which legend said there was no escape save through the air.

"Who are you?" Yasmeena demanded abruptly. "I have seen men with skins smoother even than yours, but never a hairless white man before."

Before I could ask her where she had seen hairless men, if not among her own people, she continued: "Nor have I seen eyes like yours. They are like a deep cold lake, yet they blaze and smolder like the cold blue flame that dances forever above Xathar. What is your name? Whence come you? The girl Altha said you came out of the wilderness and dwelt in her city, defeating its mighty men in single combat. But she does not know from what land you came, she says. Speak, and do not lie."

"I'll speak but you'll think I lie," I grunted. "I am Esau Cairn, whom the men of Koth call Ironhand. I come from another world in another solar system. Chance, or the whim of a scientist whom you would call a magician, cast me on this planet. Chance again threw me among the Kothans. Chance carried me to Yugga. Now I have spoken. Believe me or not, as you will."

"I believe you," she answered. "Of old, men passed from star to star. There are beings now which traverse the cosmos. I would study you. You shall live—for a while, at least. But you must wear those chains, for I read the fury of the beast in your eyes, and know you would rend me if you could."

"What of Altha?" I asked.

"Well, what of her?" She seemed surprised at the question.

"What have you done with her?" I demanded.

"She will serve me with the rest, until she displeases me. Why do you speak of another woman, when you are talking to me? I am not pleased."

Her eyes began to glitter. I never saw eyes like Yasmeena's. They changed with every shift of mood and whim, and they mirrored passions and angers and desires beyond the maddest dreams of humanity.

"You do not blench," she said softly. "Man, do you know what it is for Yasmeena to be displeased? Then blood flows like water, Yugga rings with screams of agony, and the very gods hide their heads in horror."

The way she said it turned my blood cold, but the red anger of the primitive would not down. The feel of my strength came upon me, and I knew that I could tear that golden ring from the stone and rip out her life before she could leap from her couch, if it came to that. So I laughed, and my laughter thrummed with blood-lust. She started up and eyed me closely.

"Are you mad, to laugh?" she asked. "No, that was not mirth—it was the growl of a hunting leopard. It is in your mind to leap and kill me, but if you do, the girl Altha will suffer for your crime. Yet you interest me. No man has ever laughed at me before. You shall live—for a while." She clapped her hands and the warriors entered. "Take him back to his chamber," she directed. "Keep him chained there until I send for him again."

And so began my third captivity on Almuric, in the black citadel of Yugga, on the rock Yuthla, by the river of Yogh, in the land of Yagg.

9

Much I learned of the ways of that terrible people, who have reigned over Almuric since ages beyond the memory of man. They might have been human once, long ago, but I doubt it. I believe they represented a separate branch on the tree of evolution, and that it is only an incredible freak of coincidence which cast them in a mold so similar to man, instead of the shapes of the abysmal, howling, blasphemous dwellers of Outer Darkness.

In many ways they seemed, superficially, human enough, but if one followed their lines of consciousness far enough, he would come upon phases inexplicable and alien to humanity. As far as pure intellect went, they were superior to the hairy Guras. But they lacked altogether the decency, honesty, courage, and general manliness of the apemen. The Guras were quick to wrath, savage and brutal in their anger; but there was a studied cruelty about the Yagas which made the others seem like mere rough children. The Yagas were merciless in their calmest moments; roused to anger, their excesses were horrible to behold.

They were a numerous horde, the warriors alone numbering some twenty thousand. There were more women than men, and with their slaves, of which each male and female Yaga possessed a goodly number, the city of Yugga was fully occupied. Indeed, I was surprised to learn of the multitudes of people who dwelt there, considering the comparative smallness of the rock Yuthla on which the city was built. But its space was greater vertically than horizontally. The castles and towers soared high into the air, and several tiers of chambers and corridors were sunk into the rock itself. When the Yagas felt themselves crowded for space, they simply butchered their slaves. I saw no children; losses in war were comparatively slight, and plagues and diseases unknown. Children were produced only at regular intervals, some three centuries apart. The last flock had come of age; the next brood was somewhere in the dim distance of the future.

The lords of Yugga did no sort of work, but passed their lives in sensual pleasures. Their knowledge and adeptness at debauchery would have shamed the most voluptuous libertine in later Rome. Their debauches were interrupted only by raids on the outer world in order to procure women slaves.

The town at the foot of the cliff was called Akka, the blue people Akki, or Akkas. They had been subject to the Yagas as far back as tradition extended. They were merely stupid work-animals, laboring in the irrigated fields of fruits and edible plants, and otherwise doing the will of their masters, whom they considered superior beings, if not veritable gods. They worshipped Yasmeena as a deity. Outside of continual toil, they were not mistreated. Their women were ugly and beast-like. The winged people had a keen aesthetic sense, though their interest in the beauty of the lower orders was sadistic and altogether beastly. The Akkas never came into the upper city, except when there was work to be done there, too heavy for the women slaves. Then they ascended and descended by means of great silken ladders let down from the rock. There was no road leading up from below, since the Yagas needed none. The cliffs could not be scaled; so the winged people had no fear of an Akka uprising.

The Yaga women were likewise prisoners on the rock Yuthla. Their wings were carefully removed at birth. Only the infants destined to become queens of Yugga were spared. This was done in order to keep the male sex in supremacy, and indeed, I was never able to learn how, and at what distant date, the men of Yugga gained supremacy over their women; for, judging from Yasmeena, the winged women were superior to their mates in agility, endurance, courage and even in strength. Clipping their wings kept them from developing their full superiority.

Yasmeena was an example of what a winged woman could be. She was taller than the other Yaga females, who in turn were taller than the Gura women, and though voluptuously shaped, the steel thews of a wildcat lurked in her slender rounded limbs. She was young—all the women of Yugga looked young. The average life-span of the Yaga was nine hundred years. Yasmeena had reigned over Yugga for four hundred years. Three winged princesses of royal blood had contested with her for the right to rule, and she had slain each of them, fighting with naked hands in the regal octagonal chamber. As long as she could defend her crown against younger claimants, she would rule.

The lot of the slaves in Yugga was hideous. None ever knew when she would be dismembered for the cookingpot, and the lives of all were tormented by the cruel whims of their masters and mistresses. Yugga was as like Hell as any place could be. I do not know what went on in the palaces of the nobles and warriors, but I do know what took place daily in the palace of the Queen. There was never a day or night that those dusky walls did not re-echo screams of agony and piteous wails for mercy, mingled with vindictive maledictions, or lascivious laughter.

I never became accustomed to it, hard as I was physically and mentally. I think the only thing that kept me from going mad was the feeling that I must keep my sanity in order to protect Altha if I could. That was precious little; I was chained in my chamber; where the Kothan girl was, I had not the slightest idea, except that she was somewhere in the palace of Yasmeena, where she was protected from the lust of the winged men, but not from the cruelty of her mistress.

In Yugga I heard sounds and saw sights not to be repeated—not even to be remembered in dreams. Men and women, the Yagas were open and candid in their evil. Their utter cynicism banished ordinary scruples of modesty and common decency. Their bestialities were naked, unhidden and shameless. They followed their desires with one another, and practiced their tortures on their wretched slaves with no attempt at concealment. Deeming themselves gods, they considered themselves above the considerations that guide ordinary humans. The women were more vicious than the men, if such a thing were possible. The refinements of their cruelties toward their trembling slaves cannot be even hinted at. They were versed in every art of torture, both mental and physical. But enough. I can but hint at what is unrepeatable.

Those days of captivity seem like a dim nightmare. I was not badly treated, personally. Each day I was escorted on a sort of promenade about the palace—something on the order of giving a confined animal exercise. I was always accompanied by seven or eight warriors armed to the teeth, and always wore my chains. Several times on these promenades I saw Altha, going about her duties, but she always averted her gaze and hurried by. I understood, and made no attempt to speak to her. I had placed her in jeopardy already by speaking of her to Yasmeena. Better let the Queen forget about her, if possible. Slaves were safest when the Queen of Yagg remembered them least.

Somewhere, somehow, I found in me power to throttle my red rage and blind fury. When my very brain reeled with the lust to break my chains and explode into a holocaust of slaughter, I held myself with iron grasp. And the fury ate inward into my soul, crystallizing my hate. So the days passed, until the night that Yasmeena again sent for me.

10

Yasmeena cupped her chin in her slim hands and fixed her great dark eyes on me. We were alone in a chamber I had never entered before. It was night. I sat on a divan opposite her, my limbs unshackled. She had offered me temporary freedom if I would promise not to harm her, and to go back into shackles when she bade me. I had promised. I was never a clever man, but my hate had sharpened my wits. I was playing a game of my own.

"What are you thinking of, Esau Ironhand?" she asked.

"I'm thirsty," I answered.

She indicated a crystal vessel near at hand. "Drink a little of the golden wine—not much, or it will make you drunk. It is the most powerful drink in the world. Not even I can quaff that vessel without lying senseless for hours. And you are unaccustomed to it."

I sipped a little of it. It was indeed heady liquor.

Yasmeena stretched her limbs out on her couch, and asked: "Why do you hate me? Have I not treated you well?"

"I have not said that I hated you," I countered. "You are very beautiful. But you are cruel."

She shrugged her winged shoulders. "Cruel? I am a goddess. What have I to do with either cruelty or mercy? Those qualities are for men. Humanity exists for my pleasure. Does not all life emanate from me?"

"Your stupid Akkis may believe that," I replied, "but I know otherwise, and so do you."

She laughed, not offended. "Well, I may not be able to create life, but I can destroy life at will. I may not be a goddess, but you would find it difficult to convince these foolish wenches who serve me that I am not all-powerful. No, Ironhand; the gods are only another name for *Power*. I am Power on this planet; so I am a goddess. What do your hairy friends, the Guras, worship?"

"They worship Thak; at least they acknowledge Thak as the creator and preserver. They have no regular ritual of worship, no temples, altars or priests. Thak is the Hairy One, the god in the form of man. He bellows in the tempest, and thunders in the hills with the voice of the lion. He loves brave men, and hates weaklings, but he neither harms nor aids. When a male child is born, he blows into it courage and strength; when a warrior dies, he ascends to Thak's abode, which is a land of celestial plains, river and mountains, swarming with game, and inhabited by the spirits of departed warriors, who hunt, fight and revel forever as they did in life."

She laughed. "Stupid pigs. Death is oblivion. We Yagas worship only our own bodies. And to our bodies we make rich sacrifices with the bodies of the foolish little people."

"Your rule cannot last forever," I was moved to remark.

"It *has* lasted since beyond the gray dawn of Time's beginning. On the dark rock Yuthla my people have brooded through ages uncountable. Before the cities of the Guras dotted the plains, we dwelt in the land of Yagg. We were always masters. As we rule the Guras, so we ruled the mysterious race which possessed the land before the Guras evolved from the ape: the race which reared their cities of marble whose ruins now affright the moon, and which perished in the night.

"Tales! I could tell you tales to blast your reason! I could tell you of races which appeared from the mist of mystery, moved across the world in restless waves, and vanished in the midst of oblivion. We of Yugga have watched them come and go, each in turn bending beneath the yoke of our godship. We have endured, not centuries or millenniums, but cycles.

"Why should not our rule endure forever? How shall these Gura-fools overcome us? You have seen how it is when my hawks swoop from the air in the night on the cities of the apemen. How then shall they attack us in our eyrie? To reach the land of Yagg they must cross the Purple River, whose waters race too swiftly to be swum. Only at the Bridge of Rocks can it be crossed, and there keen-eyed guards watch night and day. The watchers brought word of their coming once, and the men of Yagg were prepared. In the midst of the desert they fell on the invaders and destroyed them by thirst and madness and arrows showering upon them from the skies.

"Suppose a horde should fight its way through the desert and reach the rock Yuthla? They have the river Yogh to cross, and when they have crossed it, in the teeth of the Akki spears, what then? They could not scale the cliffs. No; no foreign foe will ever set foot in Yugga. If, by the wildest whim of the gods, such a thing *should* come to pass"—her beautiful features became even more cruel and sinister— "rather than submit to conquest I would loose the *Ultimate Horror*, and perish in the ruins of my city," she whispered, more to herself than to me.

"What do you say?" I asked, not understanding.

She lifted her head and fixed me with an enigmatic stare.

"There are secrets beneath the velvet coverings of the darkest secrets," she said. "Tread not where the very gods tremble. I said nothing—you heard nothing. Remember that!"

There was silence for a space, and then I asked a question I had long mulled over: "Whence come these red girls and yellow girls among your slaves?"

"You have looked southward from the highest towers on clear days, and seen a faint blue line rimming the sky far away? That is the Girdle that bands the world. Beyond that Girdle dwell the races from which come those alien slaves. We raid across the Girdle just as we raid the Guras, though less frequently."

I was about to ask more concerning these unknown races, when a timid tap came on the outer door. Yasmeena, frowning at the interruption, called a sharp question, and a frightened feminine voice informed her that the lord Gotrah desired audience. Yasmeena spat an oath at her, and bade her tell the lord Gotrah to go to the devil.

"No, I must see the fellow," she said, rising. "Theta! Oh, Theta! Where has the little minx gone? I must do my own biddings, must I? Her buttocks shall smart for her insolence. Wait here, Ironhand. I'll see to Gotrah."

She crossed the cushion-strewn chamber with her lithe long stride, and passed through the door. As it closed behind her, I was struck by what was nothing less than an inspiration. No especial reason occurred to me to urge me to feign drunkenness. It was intuition or blind chance that prompted me. Snatching up the crystal jug which contained the golden wine, I emptied it into a great golden vessel which stood half hidden beneath the fringe of a tapestry. I had drunk enough for the scent to be on my breath.

Then, as I heard footsteps and voices without, I extended myself quickly on a divan, the jug lying on its side near my outstretched hand. I heard the door open, and there was an instant's silence so intense as to be almost tangible. Then Yasmeena spat like an angry cat. "By the gods, he's emptied the jug! See how he lies in brutish slumber! Faugh! The noblest figure is abominable when besotted. Well, let us to our task. We need not fear to be overheard by him."

"Had I not better summon the guard and have him dragged to his cell?" came Gotrah's voice. "We cannot afford to take chances with this secret, which none has ever known except the Queen of Yugga and her major-domo."

I sensed that they came and stood over me, looking down. I moved vaguely and mumbled thickly, as if in drunken dreams.

Yasmeena laughed.

"No fear. He will know nothing before dawn. Yuthla could split and fall into Yogh without breaking his sottish dreams. The fool! This night he would have been lord of the world, for I would have made him lord of the Queen of the world—for one night. But the lion changes not his mane, nor the barbarian his brutishness."

"Why not put him to the torture?" grunted Gotrah.

"Because I want a man, not a broken travesty. Besides, his is a spirit not to be conquered by fire or steel. No. I am Yasmeena and I will make him love me before I feed him to the vultures. Have you placed the Kothan Altha among the Virgins of the Moon?"

"Aye, Queen of the dusky stars. A month and a half from this night she dances the dance of the Moon with the other wenches."

"Good. Keep them guarded day and night. If this tiger learns of our plans for his sweetheart, chains and bolts will not hold him."

"A hundred and fifty men guard the virgins," answered Gotrah. "Not even the Ironhand could prevail against them."

"It is well. Now to this other matter. Have you the parchment?"

"Aye."

"Then I will sign it. Give me the stylus."

I heard the crackle of papyrus and the scratch of a keen point, and then the Queen said:

"Take it now, and lay it on the altar in the usual place. As I promise in the writing, I will appear in the flesh tomorrow night to my faithful subjects and worshippers, the blue pigs of Akka. Ha! ha! ha! I never fail to be amused at the animal-like awe on their stupid countenances when I emerge from the shadows of the golden screen, and spread my arms above them in blessing. What fools they are, not in all these ages, to have discovered the secret door and the shaft that leads from their temple to this chamber."

"Not so strange," grunted Gotrah. "None but the priest ever comes into the temple except by special summons, and he is far too superstitious to go meddling behind the screen. Anyway, there is no sign to mark the secret door from without."

"Very well," answered Yasmeena. "Go."

I heard Gotrah fumbling at something, then a slight grating sound. Consumed by curiosity, I dared open one eye a slit, in time to glimpse Gotrah disappearing through a black opening that gaped in the middle of the stone floor, and which closed after him. I quickly shut my eye again and lay still, listening to Yasmeena's quick pantherish tread back and forth across the floor.

Once she came and stood over me. I felt her burning gaze and heard her curse beneath her breath. Then she struck me viciously across the face with some kind of jeweled ornament that tore my skin and started a trickle of blood. But I lay without twitching a muscle, and presently she turned and left the chamber, muttering.

As the door closed behind her I rose quickly, scanning the floor for some sign of the opening through which Gotrah had gone. A furry rug had been drawn aside from the center of the floor, but in the polished black stone I searched in vain for a crevice to denote the hidden trap. I momentarily expected the return of Yasmeena, and my heart pounded within me. Suddenly, under my very hand, a section of the floor detached itself and began to move upward. A pantherish bound carried me behind a tapestried couch, where I crouched, watching the trap rise upward. The narrow head of Gotrah appeared, then his winged shoulders and body.

He climbed up into the chamber, and as he turned to lower the lifted trap, I left the floor with a cat-like leap that carried me over the couch and full on his shoulders.

He went down under my weight, and my gripping fingers crushed the yell in his throat. With a convulsive heave he twisted under me, and stark horror flooded his face as he glared up at me. He was down on the cushioned stone, pinned under my iron bulk. He clawed for the dagger at his girdle, but my knee pinned it down. And crouching on him, I gutted my mad hate for his cursed race. I strangled him slowly, gloatingly, avidly watching his features contort and his eyes glaze. He must have been dead for some minutes before I loosed my hold.

Rising, I gazed through the open trap. The light from the torches of the chamber shone down a narrow shaft, into which was cut a series of narrow steps, that evidently led down into the bowels of the rock Yuthla. From the conversation I had heard, it must lead to the temple of the Akkis, in the town below. Surely I would find Akka no harder to escape from than Yugga. Yet I hesitated, my heart torn at the thought of leaving Altha alone in Yugga. But there was no other way. I did not know in what part of that devil-city she was imprisoned, and I remembered what Gotrah had said of the great band of warriors guarding her and the other virgins.

Virgins of the Moon! Cold sweat broke out on me as the full significance of the phrase became apparent. Just what the festival of the Moon was I did not fully know, but I had heard hints and scattered comments among the Yaga women, and I knew it was a beastly saturnalia, in which the full frenzy of erotic ecstasy was reached in the dying gasps of the wretches sacrificed to the only god the winged people recognized—their own inhuman lust.

The thought of Altha being subjected to such a fate drove me into a berserk frenzy, and steeled my resolution. There was but one chance—to escape myself, and try to reach Koth and bring back enough men to attempt a rescue. My heart sank as I contemplated the difficulties in the way, but there was nothing else to be done.

Lifting Gotrah's limp body I dragged it out of the chamber through a door different from that through which Yasmeena had gone; and traversing a corridor without meeting anyone, I concealed the corpse behind some tapestries. I was certain that it would be found, but perhaps not until I had a good start. Perhaps its presence in another room than the chamber of the trap might divert suspicion from my actual means of escape, and lead Yasmeena to think that I was merely hiding somewhere in Yugga.

But I was crowding my luck. I could not long hope to avoid detection if I lingered. Returning to the chamber, I entered the shaft, lowering the trap above me. It was pitchdark, then, but my groping fingers found the catch that worked the trap, and I felt that I could return if I found my way blocked below. Down those inky stairs I groped, with an uneasy feeling that I might fall into some pit or meet with some grisly denizen of the underworld. But nothing occurred, and at last the steps ceased and I groped my way along a short corridor that ended at a blank wall. My fingers encountered a metal catch, and I shot the bolt, feeling a section of the wall revolving under my hands. I was dazzled by a dim yet lurid light, and blinking, gazed out with some trepidation.

I was looking into a lofty chamber that was undoubtedly a shrine. My view was limited by a large screen of carved gold directly in front of me, the edges of which flamed dully in the weird light.

Gliding from the secret door, I peered around the screen. I saw a broad room, made with the same stern simplicity and awesome massiveness that characterized Almuric architecture. It was a temple, the first I had encountered on Almuric. The ceiling was lost in the brooding shadows; the walls were black, dully gleaming, and unadorned. The shrine was empty except for a block of ebon stone, evidently an altar, on which blazed the lurid flame I had noted, and which seemed to emanate from a great somber jewel set upon the altar. I noticed darkly stained channels on the sides of that altar, and on the dusky stone lay a roll of white parchment—Yasmeena's word to her worshippers. I had stumbled into the Akka holy of holies—uncovered the very root and base on which the whole structure of Akka theology was based: the supernatural appearances of revelations from the goddess, and the appearance of the goddess herself in the temple. Strange that a whole religion should be based on the ignorance of the devotees concerning a subterranean stair! Stranger still, to an Earthly mind, that only the lowest form of humanity on Almuric should possess a systematic and ritualistic religion, which Earth people regard as sure token of the highest races!

But the cult of the Akkas was dark and weird. The whole atmosphere of the shrine was one of mystery and brooding horror. I could imagine the awe of the blue worshippers to see the winged goddess emerging from behind the golden screen, like a deity incarnated from cosmic emptiness.

Closing the door behind me, I glided stealthily across the temple. Just within the door a stocky blue man in a fantastic robe lay snoring lustily on the naked stone. Presumably he had slept tranquilly through Gotrah's ghostly visit. I stepped over him as gingerly as a cat treading wet earth, Gotrah's dagger in my hand, but he did not awaken. An instant later I stood outside, breathing deep of the riverladen night air.

The temple lay in the shadow of the great cliffs. There was no moon, only the myriad millions of stars that glimmer in the skies of Almuric. I saw no lights anywhere in the village, no movement. The sluggish Akkis slept soundly.

Stealthily as a phantom I stole through the narrow streets, hugging close to the sides of the squat stone huts. I saw no human until I reached the wall. The drawbridge that spanned the river was drawn up, and just within the gate sat a blue man, nodding over his spear. The senses of the Akkis were dull as those of any beasts of burden. I could have knifed the drowsy watchman where he sat, but I saw no need of useless murder. He did not hear me, though I passed within forty feet of him. Silently I glided over the wall, and silently I slipped into the water.

Striking out strongly, I forged across the easy current, and reached the farther bank. There I paused only long enough to drink deep of the cold river water; then I struck out across the shadowed desert at a swinging trot that eats up miles—the gait with which the Apaches of my native Southwest can wear out a horse.

In the darkness before dawn I came to the banks of the Purple River, skirting wide to avoid the watch-tower which jutted dimly against the star-flecked sky. As I crouched on the steep bank and gazed down into the rushing swirling current, my heart sank. I knew that, in my fatigued condition, it was madness to plunge into that maelstrom. The strongest swimmer that either Earth or Almuric ever bred had been helpless among those eddies and whirlpools. There was but one thing to be done—try to reach the Bridge of Rocks before dawn broke, and take the desperate chance of slipping across under the eyes of the watchers. That, too, was madness, but I had no choice.

But dawn began to whiten the desert before I was within a thousand yards of the Bridge. And looking at the tower, which seemed to swim slowly into clearer outline, etched against the dim sky, I saw a shape soar up from the turrets and wing its way toward me. I had been discovered. Instantly a desperate plan occurred to me. I began to stagger erratically, ran a few paces, and sank down in the sand near the river bank. I heard the beat of wings above me as the suspicious harpy circled; then I knew he was dropping earthward. He must have been on solitary sentry duty, and had come to investigate the matter of a lone wanderer, without waking his mates.

Watching through slitted lids, I saw him strike the earth near by, and walk about me suspiciously, scimitar in hand. At last he pushed me with his foot, as if to find if I lived. Instantly my arm hooked about his legs, bringing him down on top of me. A single cry burst from his lips, half stifled as my fingers found his throat; then in a great heaving and fluttering of wings and lashing of limbs, I heaved him over and under me. His scimitar was useless at such close quarters. I twisted his arm until his numbed fingers slipped from the hilt; then I choked him into submission. Before he regained his full faculties, I bound his wrists in front of him with his girdle, dragged him to his feet, and perched myself astride his back, my legs locked about his torso. My left arm was hooked about his neck, my right hand pricked his hide with Gotrah's dagger.

In a few low words I told him what he must do, if he wished to live. It was not the nature of a Yaga to sacrifice himself, even for the welfare of his race. Through the rosepink glow of dawn we soared into the sky, swept over the rushing Purple River, and vanished from the sight of the land of Yagg, into the blue mazes of the northwest.

11

I drove that winged devil unmercifully. Not until sunset did I allow him to drop earthward. Then I bound his feet and wings so he could not escape, and gathered fruit and nuts for our meal. I fed him as well as I fed myself. He needed strength for the flight. That night the beasts of prey roared perilously close to us, and my captive turned ashy with fright, for we had no way of making a protecting fire, but none attacked us. We had left the forest of the Purple River far, far behind, and were among the grasslands. I was taking the most direct route to Koth, led by the unerring instinct of the wild. I continually scanned the skies behind me for some sign of pursuit, but no winged shapes darkened the southern horizon.

It was on the fourth day that I spied a dark moving mass in the plains below, which I believed was an army of men marching. I ordered the Yaga to fly over them. I knew that I had reached the vicinity of the wide territory dominated by the city of Koth, and there was a chance that these might be men of Koth. If so, they were in force, for as we approached I saw there were several thousand men, marching in some order.

So intense was my interest that it almost proved my undoing. During the day I left the Yaga's legs unbound, as he swore that he could not fly otherwise, but I kept his wrists bound. In my engrossment I did not notice him furtively gnawing at the thong. My dagger was in its sheath, since he had shown no recent sign of rebellion. My first intimation of revolt was when he wheeled suddenly sidewise, so that I lurched and almost lost my grip on him. His long arm curled about my torso and tore at my girdle, and the next instant my own dagger gleamed in his hand.

There ensued one of the most desperate struggles in which I have ever participated. My near fall had swung me around, so that instead of being on his back, I was in front of him, maintaining my position only by one hand clutching his hair, and one knee crooked about his leg. My other hand was locked on his dagger wrist, and there we tore and twisted, a thousand feet in the air, he to break away and let me fall to my death, or to drive home the dagger in my breast, I to maintain my grip and fend off the gleaming blade.

On the ground my superior weight and strength would quickly have settled the issue, but in the air he had the advantage. His free hand beat and tore at my face, while his unimprisoned knee drove viciously again and again for my groin. I hung grimly on, taking the punishment without flinching, seeing that our struggles were dragging us lower and lower toward the earth.

Realizing this, he made a final desperate effort. Shifting the dagger to his free hand, he stabbed furiously at my throat. At the same instant I gave his head a terrific downward wrench. The impetus of both our exertions whirled us down and over, and his stroke, thrown out of line by our erratic convulsion, missed its mark and sheathed the dagger in his own thigh. A terrible cry burst from his lips, his grasp went limp as he half fainted from the pain and shock, and we rushed plummet-like earthward. I strove to turn him beneath me, and even as I did, we struck the earth with a terrific concussion.

From that impact I reeled up dizzily. The Yaga did not move; his body had cushioned mine, and half the bones in his frame must have been splintered.

A clamor of voices rang on my ears, and turning, I saw a horde of hairy figures rushing toward me. I heard my own name bellowed by a thousand tongues. I had found the men of Koth.

A hairy giant was alternately pumping my hand and beating me on the back with blows that would have staggered a horse, while bellowing: "Ironhand! By Thak's jawbones, *Ironhand!* Grip my hand, old war-dog! Hell's thunders, I've known no such joyful hour since the day I broke old Khush of Tanga's back!"

There was old Khossuth Skullsplitter, somber as ever, Thab the Swift, Gutchluk Tigerwrath—nearly all the mighty men of Koth. And the way they smote my back and roared their welcome warmed my heart as it was never warmed on Earth, for I knew there was no room for insincerity in their great simple hearts.

"Where have you been, Ironhand?" exclaimed Thab the Swift. "We found your broken carbine out on the plains, and a Yaga lying near it with his skull smashed; so we concluded that you had been done away with by those winged devils. But we never found your body—and now you come tumbling through the skies locked in combat with another flying fiend! Say, have you been to Yugga?" He laughed as a man laughs when he speaks a jest.

"Aye, to Yugga, on the rock Yuthla, by the river Yogh, in the land of Yagg," I answered. "Where is Zal the Thrower?"

"He guards the city with the thousand we left behind," answered Khossuth.

"His daughter languishes in the Black City," I said. "On the night of the full moon, Altha, Zal's daughter, dies with five hundred other girls of the Guras—unless we prevent it."

A murmur of wrath and horror swept along the ranks. I glanced over the savage array. There were a good four thousand of them; no bows were in evidence, but each man bore his carbine. That meant war, and their numbers proved it was no minor raid.

"Where are you going?" I asked.

"The men of Khor move against us, five thousand strong," answered Khossuth. "It is the death grapple of the tribes. We march to meet them afar off from our walls, and spare our women the horrors of the war."

"Forget the men of Khor!" I cried passionately. "You would spare the feelings of your women—yet thousands of your women suffer the tortures of the damned on the ebon rock of Yuthla! Follow me! I will lead you to the stronghold of the devils who have harried Almuric for a thousand ages!"

"How many warriors?" asked Khossuth uncertainly.

"Twenty thousand."

A groan rose from the listeners.

"What could our handful do against that horde?"

"I'll show you!" I exclaimed. "I'll lead you into the heart of their citadel!"

"Hai!" roared Ghor the Bear, brandishing his broadsword, always quick to take fire from my suggestions. "That's the word! Come on, sir brothers! Follow Ironhand! He'll show us the way!"

"But what of the men of Khor?" expostulated Khossuth. "They are marching to attack us. We must meet them."

Ghor grunted explosively as the truth of this assertion came home to him, and all eyes turned toward me.

"Leave them to me," I proposed desperately. "Let me talk with them—"

"They'll hack off your head before you can open your mouth," grunted Khossuth.

"That's right," admitted Ghor. "We've been fighting the men of Khor for fifty thousand years. Don't trust them, comrade."

"I'll take the chance," I answered.

"The chance you shall have, then," said Gutchluk grimly. "For there they come!" In the distance we saw a dark moving mass.

"Carbines ready!" barked old Khossuth, his cold eyes gleaming. "Loosen your blades, and follow me." "Will you join battle tonight?" I asked.

He glanced at the sun. "No. We'll march to meet them, and pitch camp just out of gunshot. Then with dawn we'll rush them and cut their throats."

"They'll have the same idea," explained Thab. "Oh, it will be great fun!"

"And while you revel in senseless bloodshed," I answered bitterly, "your daughters and theirs will be screaming vainly under the tortures of the winged people over the river Yogh. Fools! Oh, you fools!"

"But what can we do?" expostulated Gutchluk.

"Follow me!" I yelled passionately. "We'll march to meet them, and I'll go on to them alone."

I wheeled and strode across the plain, and the hairy men of Koth fell in behind me, with many head-shakes and mutterings. I saw the oncoming mass, first as a mingled blur; then the details stood out—hairy bodies, fierce faces, gleaming weapons—but I swung on heedlessly. I knew neither fear nor caution; my whole being seemed on fire with the urgency of my need and desire.

Several hundred yards separated the two hosts when I dashed down my single weapon—the Yaga dagger—and shaking off Ghor's protesting hands, advanced alone and unarmed, my hands in the air, palms toward the enemy.

These had halted, drawn up ready for action. The unusualness of my actions and appearance puzzled them. I momentarily expected the crack of a carbine, but nothing happened until I was within a few yards of the foremost group, the mightiest men clustered about a tall figure that was their chief—old Bragi, Khossuth had told me. I had heard of him, a hard, cruel man, moody and fanatical in his hatreds.

"Stand!" he shouted, lifting his sword. "What trick is this? Who are you who comes with empty hands in the teeth of war?"

"I am Esau Ironhand, of the tribe of Koth," I answered. "I would parley with you."

"What madman is this?" growled Bragi. "Than—a bullet through his head."

But the man called Than, who had been staring eagerly at me, gave a shout instead and threw down his carbine.

"Not if I live!" he exclaimed, advancing toward me his arms outstretched. "By Thak, it is he! Do you not remember me, Than Swordswinger, whose life you saved in the Hills?"

He lifted his chin to display a great scar on his corded neck.

"You are he who fought the sabertooth! I had not dreamed you survived those awful wounds."

"We men of Khor are hard to kill!" he laughed joyously, throwing his arms about me in a bear-like embrace. "What are you doing among the dogs of Koth? You should be fighting with us!"

"If I have my way there will be no fighting," I answered. "I wish only to talk with your chiefs and warriors. There is nothing out of the way about that."

"True!" agreed Than Swordswinger. "Bragi, you will not refuse him this?"

Bragi growled in his beard, glaring at me.

"Let your warriors advance to that spot." I indicated the place I meant. "Khossuth's men will come up on the other side. There both hordes will listen to what I have to say. Then, if no agreement can be reached, each side shall withdraw five hundred yards and after that follow its own initiative."

"You are mad!" Old Bragi jerked his beard with a shaking hand of rage. "It is treachery. Back to your kennel, dog!"

"I am your hostage," I answered. "I am unarmed. I will not move out of your sword reach. If there is treachery, strike me down on the spot."

"But why?"

"I have been captive among the Yagas!" I exclaimed. "I have come to tell the Guras what things occur in the land of Yagg!"

"The Yagas took my daughter!" exclaimed a warrior, pushing through the ranks. "Did you see her in Yagg?"

"They took my sister"—"And my young bride"— "And my niece!" shouts rose in chorus, as men swarmed about me, forgetful of their enemies, shaking me in the intensity of their feeling.

"Back, you fools!" roared Bragi, smiting with the flat of his sword. "Will you break your ranks and let the Kothans cut you down? Do you not see it is a trick?"

"It is no trick!" I cried. "Only listen to me, in God's name!"

They swept away Bragi's protests. There was a milling and stamping, during which only a kindly Providence kept the nerve-taut Kothans from pouring a volley into the surging mass of their enemies, and presently a sort of order was evolved. A shouted conference finally resulted in approximately the position I had asked for—a semicircle of Khorans over against a similar formation composed of Kothans. The close proximity almost caused the tribal wrath to boil over. Jaws jutted, eyes blazed, hairy hands clutched convulsively at carbine stocks. Like wild dogs those wild men glared at each other, and I hastened to begin my say.

I was never much of a talker, and as I strode between those hostile hordes I felt my fire die out in cold ague of helplessness. A million ages of traditional war and feud rose up to confound me. One man against the accumulated ideas, inhibitions, and customs of a whole world, built up through countless millenniums—the thought crushed and paralyzed me. Then blind rage swept me at the memory of the horrors of Yugga, and the fire blazed up again and enveloped the world and made it small, and on the wings of that conflagration I was borne to heights of which I had never dreamed.

No need for fiery oratory to tell the tale I had to tell. I told it in the plainest, bluntest language possible, and the knowledge and feeling that lay behind the telling made those naked words pulse, and burn like acid.

I told of the hell that was Yugga. I told of young girls dying beneath the excesses of black demons—of women lashed to gory ribbons, mangled on the wheel, sundered on the rack, flayed alive, dismembered alive—of the torments that left the body unharmed, but sucked the mind empty of reason and left the victim a blind, mowing imbecile. I told them—oh God, I cannot repeat all I told them, at the memory of which I am even now sickened almost unto death.

Before I had finished, men were bellowing and beating their breasts with their clenched fists, and weeping in agony of grief and fury.

I lashed them with a last whip of scorpions. "These are your women, your own flesh and blood, who scream on the racks of Yugga! You call yourselves men—you strut and boast and swagger, while these winged devils mock you. Men! Ha!" I laughed as a wolf barks, from the depths of my bitter rage and agony. "Men! Go home and don the skirts of women!"

A terrible yell arose. Clenched fists were brandished, bloodshot eyes flamed at me, hairy throats bayed their anguished fury. "You lie, you dog! Damn you, you lie! We *are* men! Lead us against these devils or we will rend you!"

"If you follow me," I yelled, "few of you will return. You will suffer and you will die in hordes. But if you had seen what I have seen, you would not wish to live. Soon approaches the time when the Yagas will clean their house. They are weary of their slaves. They will destroy those they have, and fare forth into the world for more. I have told you of the destruction of Thugra. So it will be with Khor; so it will be with Koth—when winged devils swoop out of the night. Follow me to Yugga—I will show you the way. If you are men, follow me!"

Blood burst from my lips in the intensity of my appeal, and as I reeled back, in a state of complete collapse from overwrought nerves and strain, Ghor caught me in his mighty arms.

Khossuth rose like a gaunt ghost. His ghostly voice soared out across the tumult.

"I will follow Esau Ironhand to Yugga, if the men of Khor will agree to a truce until our return. What is your answer, Bragi?"

"No!" roared Bragi. "There can be no peace between Khor and Koth. The women in Yugga are lost. Who can war against demons? Up, men, back to your place! No man can twist me with mad words to forget old hates."

He lifted his sword, and Than Swordswinger, tears of grief and fury running down his face, jerked out his poniard and drove it to the hilt in the heart of his king. Wheeling to the bewildered horde, brandishing the bloody dagger, his body shaken with sobs of frenzy, he yelled:

"So die all who would make us traitors to our own women! Draw your swords, all men of Khor who will follow me to Yugga!"

Five thousand swords flamed in the sun, and a deepthroated thunderous roar shook the very sky. Then wheeling to me, his eyes coals of madness:

"Lead us to Yugga, Esau Ironhand!" cried Than Swordswinger. "Lead us to Yagg, or lead us to Hell! We will stain the waters of Yogh with blood, and the Yagas will speak of us with shudders for ten thousand times a thousand years!"

Again the clangor of swords and the roar of frenzied men maddened the sky.

12

Runners were sent to the cities, to give word of what went forward. Southward we marched, four thousand men of Koth, five thousand of Khor. We moved in separate columns, for I deemed it wise to keep the tribes apart until the sight of their oppressors should again drown tribal feelings.

Our pace was much swifter than that of an equal body of Earth soldiers. We had no supply trains. We lived off the land through which we passed. Each man bore his own armament—carbine, sword, dagger, canteen, and ammunition pouch. But I chafed at every mile. Sailing through the air on the back of a captive Yaga had spoiled me for marching. It took us days to cover ground the flying men had passed over in hours. Yet we progressed, and some three weeks from the time we began the march, we entered the forest beyond which lay the Purple River and the desert that borders the land of Yagg.

We had seen no Yagas, but we went cautiously now. Leaving the bulk of our force encamped deep in the forest, I went forward with thirty men, timing our march so that we reached the bank of the Purple River a short time after midnight, just before the setting of the moon. My purpose was to find a way to prevent the tower guard from carrying the news of our coming to Yugga, so that we might cross the desert without being attacked in the open, where the numbers and tactics of the Yagas would weigh most heavily against us.

Khossuth suggested that we lie in wait among the trees along the bank, and pick the watchers off at long range at dawn, but this I knew to be impossible. There was no cover along the water's edge, and the river lay between. The men in the tower were out of our range. We might creep near enough to pick off one or two, but it was imperative that all should perish, since the escape of one would be enough to ruin our plans.

So we stole through the woods until we reached a point a mile upstream, opposite a jutting tongue of rock, toward which, I believed, a current set in from the center of the stream. There we placed in the water a heavy, strong catamaran we had constructed, with a long powerful rope. I got upon the craft with four of the best marksmen of the combined horde—Thab the Swift, Skel the Hawk, and two warriors of Khor. Each of us bore two carbines, strapped to our backs.

We bent to work with crude oars, though our efforts seemed ludicrously futile in the teeth of that flood. But the raft was long enough and heavy enough not to be spun by every whirlpool we crossed, and by dint of Herculean effort we worked out toward the middle of the stream. The men on shore paid out the rope, and it acted as a sort of brace, swinging us around in a wide arc that would have eventually brought us back to the bank we had left, had not the current we hoped for suddenly caught us and hurled us at dizzy speed toward the projecting tongue of rock. The raft reeled and pitched, driving its nose under repeatedly, until sometimes we were fully submerged. But our ammunition was waterproof, and we had lashed ourselves to the logs; so we hung on like drowned rats, until our craft was dashed against the rocky point.

It hung there for a breathless instant, in which time it was touch and go. We slashed ourselves loose, jumped into the water which swirled arm-pit deep about us, and fought our way along the point, clinging tooth and nail to every niche or projection, while the foaming current threatened momentarily to tear us away and send us after our raft which had slid off the ledge and was dancing away down the river.

We did make it, though, and hauled ourselves on the shore at last, half dead from buffeting and exhaustion. But we could not stop to rest, for the most delicate part of our scheme was before us. It was necessary that we should not be discovered before dawn gave us light enough to see the sights of our carbines, for the best marksman in the world is erratic by starlight. But I trusted to the chance that the Yagas would be watching the river, and paying scant heed to the desert behind them.

So in the darkness that precedes dawn, we stole around in a wide half-circle, and the first hint of light found us lying in a depression we had scraped in the sand not over four hundred yards to the south of the tower.

It was tense waiting, while the dawn lifted slowly over the land, and objects became more and more distinct. The roar of the water over the Bridge of Rocks reached us plainly, and at last we were aware of another sound. The clash of steel reached us faintly through the water tumult. Ghor and others were advancing to the river bank, according to my instructions. We could not see any Yagas on the tower; only hints of movement along the turrets. But suddenly one whirled up into the morning sky and started south at headlong speed. Skel's carbine cracked and the winged man, with a loud cry, pitched sideways and tumbled to earth.

There followed an instant of silence; then five winged shapes darted into the air, soaring high. The Yagas sensed what was occurring, and were chancing all on a desperate rush, hoping that at least one might get through. We all fired, but I scored a complete miss, and Thab only slightly wounded his man. But the others brought down the man I had missed, while Thab's second shot dropped the wounded Yaga. We reloaded hastily, but no more came from the tower. Six men watched there, Yasmeena had said. She had spoken the truth.

We cast the bodies into the river. I crossed the Bridge of Rocks, leaping from boulder to boulder, and told Ghor to take his men back into the forest, and to bring up the host. They were to camp just within the fringe of woods, out of sight from the sky. I did not intend to start across the desert until nightfall.

Then I returned to the tower and attempted to gain entrance, but found no doors, only a few small barred windows. The Yagas had entered it from the top. It was too tall and smooth to be climbed, so we did the only thing left to do. We dug pits in the sand and covered them with branches, over which we scattered dust. In these pits we concealed our best marksmen, who lay all day, patiently scanning the sky. Only one Yaga came winging across the desert. No human was in sight, and he was not suspicious until he poised directly over the tower. Then, when he saw no watchmen, he became alarmed, but before he could race away, the reports of half a dozen carbines brought him tumbling to the earth in a whirl of limbs and wings.

As the sun sank, we brought the warriors across the Bridge of Rocks, an accomplishment which required some time. But at last they all stood on the Yaga side of the river, and with our canteens well filled, we started at quick pace across the narrow desert. Before dawn we were within striking distance of the river.

Having crossed the desert under cover of darkness, I was not surprised that we were able to approach the river without being discovered. If any had been watching from the citadel, alert for anything suspicious, they would have discerned our dark mass moving across the sands under the dim starlight. But I knew that in Yugga no such watch was ever kept, secure as the winged people felt in the protection of the Purple River, of the watchmen in the tower, and of the fact that for centuries no Gura raid had dared the bloody doom of former invaders. Nights were spent in frenzied debauchery, followed by sodden sleep. As for the men of Akka, these slow-witted drudges were too habitually drowsy to constitute much menace against our approach, though I knew that once roused they would fight like animals.

So three hundred yards from the river we halted, and eight thousand men under Khossuth took cover in the irrigation ditches that traversed the fields of fruit. The waving fronds of the squat trees likewise aided in their concealment. This was done in almost complete silence. Far above us towered the somber rock Yuthla. A faint breeze sprang up, forerunner of dawn. I led the remaining thousand warriors toward the river bank. Halting them a short distance from it, I wriggled forward on my belly until my hands were at the water's edge. I thanked the Fates that had given me such men to lead. Where civilized men would have floundered and blundered, the Guras moved as easily and noiselessly as stalking panthers.

Across from me rose the wall, sheer from the steep bank, that guarded Akka. It would be hard to climb in the teeth of spears. At the first crack of dawn, the bridge, which towered gauntly against the stars, would be lowered so that Akkis might go into the fields to work. But before then the rising light would betray our forces.

With a word to Ghor, who lay at my side, I slid into the water and struck out for the farther shore, he following. Reaching a point directly below the bridge, we hung in the water, clutching the slippery wall, and looked about for some way of climbing it. There the water, near the bank, was almost as deep as in midstream. At last Ghor found a crevice in the masonry, wide enough to give him a grip for his hands. Then bracing himself, he held fast while I clambered on his shoulders. Standing thus I managed to reach the lower part of the lifted bridge, and an instant later I drew myself up. The erected bridge closed the gap in the wall. I had to clamber over the barrier. One leg was across, when a figure sprang out of the shadows, yelling a warning. The watchman had not been as drowsy as I had expected.

He leaped at me, the starlight glinting on his spear. With a desperate twist of my body I avoided the whistling blade, though the effort almost toppled me from the wall. My outthrown hand gripped his lank hair as he fell against the coping with the fury of his wasted thrust, and jerking myself back into balance, I dealt him a crushing buffet on the ear with my clenched fist. He crumpled, and the next instant I was over the wall.

Ghor was bellowing like a bull in the river, mad to know what was taking place above him, and in the dim light the Akkis were swarming like bees out of their stony hives. Leaning over the barrier I stretched Ghor the shaft of the watchman's spear, and he came heaving and scrambling up beside me. The Akkis had stared stupidly for an instant; then realizing they were being invaded, they rushed, howling madly.

As Ghor sprang to meet them, I leaped to the great windlass that controlled the bridge. I heard the Bear's thunderous war-cry boom above the squalling of the Akkis, the strident clash of steel and the crunch of splintered bone. But I had no time to look; it was taking all my strength to work the windlass. I had seen five Akkis toiling together at it; yet in the stress of the moment I accomplished its lowering single-handed, though sweat burst out on my forehead and my muscles trembled with the effort. But down it came, and the farther end touched the other bank in time to accommodate the feet of the warriors who sprang up and rushed for it.

I wheeled to aid Ghor, whose panting gasps I still heard amidst the clamor of the mêlée. I knew the din in the lower town would soon rouse the Yagas and it was imperative that we gain a foothold in Akka before the shafts of the winged men began to rain among us.

Ghor was hard pressed when I turned from the bridgehead. Half a dozen corpses lay under his feet, and he wielded his great sword with a berserk lustiness that sheared through flesh and bone like butter, but he was streaming blood, and the Akkis were closing in on him.

I had no weapon but Gotrah's dagger, but I sprang into the fray and ripped a sword from the sinking hand of one whose heart my slim blade found. It was a crude weapon, such as the Akkis forge, but it had edge and weight, and swinging it like a club, I wrought havoc among the swarming blue men. Ghor greeted my arrival with a gasping roar of pleasure, and redoubled the fury of his tremendous strokes, so that the dazed Akkis momentarily gave back.

And in that fleeting interval, the first of the Guras swarmed across the bridge. In an instant fifty men had joined us. But there the matter was deadlocked. Swarm after swarm of blue men rushed from their huts to fall on us with reckless fury. One Gura was a match for three or four Akkis, but they swamped us by numbers. They crushed us back into the bridge mouth, and strive as we could, we could not advance enough to clear the way for the hundreds of warriors behind us who yelled and struggled to come to sword-strokes with the enemy. The Akkis pressed in on us in a great crescent, almost crushing us against the men behind us. They lined the walls, yelling and screaming and brandishing their weapons. There were no bows or missiles among them; their winged masters were careful to keep such things out of their hands.

In the midst of the carnage dawn broke, and the struggling hordes saw their enemies. Above us, I knew, the Yagas would be stirring. Indeed I thought I could already hear the thrash of wings above the roar of battle, but I could not look up. Breast to breast we were locked with the heaving, grunting hordes, so closely there was no room for sword-strokes. Their teeth and filthy nails tore at us beastlike; their repulsive body odor was in our nostrils. In the crush we writhed and cursed, each man striving to free a hand to strike.

My flesh crawled in dread of the arrows I knew must soon be raining from above, and even with the thought the first volley came like a whistling sheet of sleet. At my side and behind me men cried out, clutching at the feathered ends protruding from their bodies. But then the men on the bridge and on the farther bank, who had held their fire for fear of hitting their comrades in the uncertain light, began loosing their carbines at the Akkis. At that range their fire was devastating. The first volley cleared the wall, and climbing on the bridge rails the carbineers poured a withering fusillade over our heads into the close-massed horde that barred our way. The result was appalling. Great gaps were torn in the struggling mob, and the whole horde staggered and tore apart. Unsupported by the mass behind, the front ranks caved in, and over their mangled bodies we rushed into the narrow streets of Akka.

Opposition was not at an end. The stocky blue men still fought back. Up and down the streets sounded the clash of steel, crack of shots, and yells of pain and fury. But our greatest peril was from above.

The winged men were swarming out of their citadel like hornets out of a nest. Several hundred of them dropped swiftly down into Akka, swords in their hands, while others lined the rim of the cliff and poured down showers of arrows. Now the warriors hidden in the shrub-masked ditches opened fire, and as that volley thundered, a rain of mangled forms fell on the flat roofs of Akka. The survivors wheeled and raced back to cover as swiftly as their wings could carry them.

But they were more deadly in defense than in attack. From every casement, tower and battlement above they rained their arrows; a hail of death showered Akka, striking down foe and serf alike. Guras and Akkis took refuge in the stone-roofed huts, where the battling continued in the lowceilinged chambers until the gutters of Akka ran red. Four thousand Guras battled four times their number of Akkis, but the size, ferocity and superior weapons of the apemen balanced the advantage of numbers.

Across the river Khossuth's carbineers kept up an incessant fire at the towers of Yugga, but with scant avail. The Yagas kept well covered, and their arrows, arching down from the sky, had a greater range and accuracy than the carbines of the Guras. But for their position among the ditches, Khossuth's men would have been wiped out in short order, and as it was, they suffered terribly. They could not join us in Akka; it would have been madness to try to cross the bridge in the teeth of that fire.

Meanwhile, I ran straight for the temple of Yasmeena, cutting down those who stood in my way. I had discarded the clumsy Akka sword for a fine blade dropped by a slain Gura, and with this in my hand I cut my way through a swarm of blue spearmen who made a determined stand before the temple. With me were Ghor, Thab the Swift, Than Swordswinger and a hundred other picked warriors.

As the last of our foes were trampled under foot, I sprang up the black stone steps to the massive door, where the bizarre figure of the Akka priest barred my way with shield and spear. I parried his spear and feinted a thrust at his thigh. He lowered the great gold-scrolled shield, and before he could lift it again I slashed off his head, which rolled grinning down the steps. I caught up the shield as I rushed into the temple.

I rushed across the temple and tore aside the golden screen. My men crowded in behind me, panting, bloodstained, their fierce faces lighted by the weird flame from the altar jewel. Fumbling in my haste, I found and worked the secret catch. The door began to give, reluctantly. It was this reluctance which fired my brain with sudden suspicion, as I remembered how easily it had opened before. Even with the thought I yelled, "Back!" and hurled myself backward as the door gaped suddenly.

Instantly my ears were deafened by an awful roar, my eyes blinded by a terrible flash. Something like a spurt of hell's fire passed so close by me it seared my hair in passing. Only my recoil, which carried me behind the opening door, saved me from the torrent of liquid fire which flooded the temple from the secret shaft.

There was a blind chaotic instant of frenzy, shot through with awful screams. Then through the din I heard Ghor bellowing my name, and saw him stumbling blindly through the whirling smoke, his beard and bristling hair burned crisp. As the lurid murk cleared somewhat, I saw the remnants of my band—Ghor, Thab and a few others who by quickness or luck had escaped. Than Swordswinger had been directly behind me, and was knocked out of harm's way when I leaped back. But on the blackened floor of the temple lay three-score shriveled forms, burned and charred out of all human recognition. They had been directly in the path of that devouring sheet of flame as it rushed to dissipate itself in the outer air.

The shaft seemed empty now. Fool to think that Yasmeena would leave it unguarded, when she must have suspected that I escaped by that route. On the edges of the door and the jamb I found bits of stuff like wax. Some mysterious element had been sealed into the shaft which the opening of the door ignited, sending it toward the outer air in a rush of flame.

I knew the upper trap would be made fast. I shouted for Thab to find and light a torch, and for Ghor to procure a heavy beam for a ram. Then, telling Than to gather all the men he could find in the streets and follow, I raced up the stair in the blackness. As I thought, I found the upper trap fastened—bolted above, I suspected; and listening closely, I caught a confused mumbling above my head, and knew the chamber must be filled with Yagas.

An erratic flame bobbing below me drew my attention, and quickly Thab reached my side with a torch. He was followed by Ghor and a score of others, grunting under the weight of a heavy log-like beam, torn from some Akka hut. He reported that fighting was still going on in the streets and buildings, but that most of the Akka males had been put to the sword, and others, with their women and children, had leaped into the river and swum for the south shore. He said some five hundred swordsmen were thronging the temple.

"Then burst this trap above our heads," I exclaimed, "and follow me through. We must win our way into the heart of the hold, before the arrows of the Yagas on the towers overwhelm Khossuth."

It was difficult in that narrow shaft, where only one man could stand on each step, but gripping the heavy beam like a ram, we swung it and dashed it against the trap. The thunder of the blows filled the shaft deafeningly, the jarring impact stung our hands and quivered the wood, but the trap held. Again—and again—panting, grunting, thews cracking, we swung the beam—and with a final terrific drive of hard-braced knotty legs and iron shoulders, the trap gave with a splintering crash, and light flooded the shaft from above.

With a wordless yell I heaved up through the splinters of the trap, the gold shield held above my head. A score of swords descended on it, staggering me; but desperately keeping my feet, I heaved up through a veritable rain of shattering blades, and burst into the chamber of Yasmeena. With a yell the Yagas swarmed on me, and I cast the bent and shattered shield in their faces, and swung my sword in the wheel that flashed through breasts and throats like a mowing blade through corn. I should have died there, but from the opening behind me crashed a dozen carbines, and the winged men went down in heaps.

Then up into the chamber came Ghor the Bear, bellowing and terrible, and after him the killers of Khor and of Koth, thirsting for blood.

That chamber was full of Yagas, and so were the adjoining rooms and corridors. But in a compact circle, back to back, we held the shaft entrance, while scores of warriors swarmed up the stair to join us, widening and pushing out the rim of the circle. In that comparatively small chamber the din was deafening and terrifying—the clang of swords, the yelling, the butcher's sound of flesh and bones parting beneath the chopping edge.

We quickly cleared the chamber, and held the doors against attack. As more and more men came up from below, we advanced into the adjoining rooms, and after perhaps a half-hour of desperate fighting, we held a circle of chambers and corridors, like a wheel of which the chamber of the shaft was the axle, and more and more Yagas were leaving the turrets to take part in the hand-to-hand fighting. There were some three thousand of us in the upper chambers now, and no more came up the shaft. I sent Thab to tell Khossuth to bring his men across the river.

I believed that most of the Yagas had left the turrets. They were massed thick in the chambers and corridors ahead of us, and were fighting like demons. I have mentioned that their courage was not of the type of the Guras', but any race will fight when a foe has invaded its last stronghold, and these winged devils were no weaklings.

For a time the battle was at a gasping deadlock. We could advance no farther in any direction, nor could they thrust us back. The doorways through which we slashed and thrust were heaped high with bodies, both hairy and black. Our ammunition was exhausted, and the Yagas could use their bows to no advantage. It was hand to hand and sword to sword, men stumbling among the dead to come to hand grips.

Then, just when it seemed that flesh and blood could stand no more, a thunderous roar rose to the vaulted ceilings, and up through the shaft and out through the chambers poured streams of fresh, eager warriors to take our places. Old Khossuth and his men, maddened to frenzy by the arrows that had been showering upon them as they lay partly hidden in the ditches, foamed like rabid dogs to come to hand-grips and glut their fury. Thab was not with them, and Khossuth said he had been struck down by an arrow in his leg, as he was following his king across the bridge in that dash from the ditches to the temple. There had been few losses in that reckless rush, however; as I had suspected, most of the Yagas had entered the chambers, leaving only a few archers on the towers.

Now began the most bloody and desperate mêlée I have ever witnessed. Under the impact of the fresh forces, the weary Yagas gave way, and the battle streamed out through the halls and rooms. The chiefs tried in vain to keep the maddened Guras together. Struggling groups split off the main body, men ran singly down twisting corridors. Throughout all the citadel thundered the rush of trampling feet, shouts, and din of steel.

Few shots were fired, few arrows winged. It was hand to hand with a vengeance. In the roofed chambers and halls, the Yagas could not spread their wings and dart down on their foes from above. They were forced to stand on their feet, meeting their ancient enemies on even terms. It was out on the rooftops and the open courts that our losses were greatest, for in the open the winged men could resort to their accustomed tactics.

But we avoided such places as much as possible, and man to man, the Guras were invincible. Oh, they died by scores, but under their lashing swords the Yagas died by hundreds. A thousand ages of cruelty and oppression were being repaid, and red was the payment. The sword was blind; Yaga women as well as men fell beneath it. But knowing the fiendishness of those sleek black females, I could not pity them.

I was looking for Altha.

Slaves there were, thousands of them, dazed by the battle, cowering in terror, too bewildered to realize its portent, or to recognize their rescuers. Yet several times I saw a woman cry out in sudden joy and run forward to throw her arms about the bull-neck of some hairy, panting swordsman, as she recognized a brother, husband, or father. In the midst of agony and travail there was joy and reuniting, and it warmed my heart to see it. Only the little yellow slaves and the red women crouched in terror, as fearful of these roaring hairy giants as of their winged masters.

Hacking and slashing my way through the knots of struggling warriors, I sought for the chamber where were imprisoned the virgins of the Moon. At last I caught the shoulder of a Gura girl, cowering on the floor to avoid chance blows of the men battling above her, and shouted a question in her ear. She understood and pointed, unable to make herself heard above the din. Catching her up under one arm, I slashed a path for us, and in a chamber beyond I set her down, and she ran swiftly down a corridor, crying for me to follow. I raced after her, down that corridor, up a winding stair, across a roof-garden where Guras and Yagas fought, and finally she halted in an open court. It was the highest point of the city, besides the minarets. In the midst rose the dome of the Moon, and at the foot of the dome she showed me a chamber. The door was locked, but I shattered it with blows of my sword, and glared in. In the semi-darkness I saw the gleam of white limbs huddled close together against the opposite wall. As my eyes became accustomed to the dimness I saw that some hundred and fifty girls were cowering in terror against the wall. And as I called Altha's name, I heard a voice cry, "Esau! Oh, *Esau!*" and a slim white figure hurled itself across the chamber to throw white arms about my neck and rain passionate kisses on my bronzed features. For an instant I crushed her close, returning her kisses with hungry lips; then the roar of battle outside roused me. Turning I saw a swarm of Yagas, pressed close by five hundred swords, being forced out of a great doorway near by. Abandoning the fray suddenly they took to flight, their assailants flowing out into the court with yells of triumph.

And then before me I heard a light mocking laugh, and saw the lithe figure of Yasmeena, Queen of Yagg.

"So you have returned, Ironhand?" Her voice was like poisoned honey. "You have returned with your slayers to break the reign of the gods? Yet you have not conquered, oh fool."

Without a word I drove at her, silently and murderously, but she sprang lightly into the air, avoiding my thrust. Her laughter rose to an insane scream.

"Fool!" she shrieked. "You have not conquered! Did I not say I would perish in the ruins of my kingdom? Dogs, you are all dead men!"

Whirling in midair she rushed with appalling speed straight for the dome. The Yagas seemed to sense her intention, for they cried out in horror and protest, but she did not pause. Lighting on the smooth slope of the dome, keeping her perch by the use of her wings, she turned, shook a hand at us in mockery, and then, gripping some bolt or handle set in the dome, braced both her feet against the ivory slope and pulled with all her strength.

A section of the dome gave way, catapulting her into the air. The next instant a huge misshapen bulk came rushing from the opening. And as it rushed, the impact of its body against the edges of the door was like the crash of a thunderbolt. The dome split in a hundred places from base to pinnacle, and fell in with a thunderous roar. Through a cloud of dust and debris and falling stone the huge figure burst into the open. A yell went up from the watchers.

The thing that had emerged from the dome was bigger than an elephant, and in shape something like a gigantic slug, except that it had a fringe of tentacles all about its body. And from these writhing tentacles crackled sparks and flashes of blue flame. It spread its writhing arms, and at their touch stone walls crashed to ruin and masonry burst apart. It was brainless, sightless—elemental force incorporated in the lowest form of animation—power gone mad and run amuck in a senseless fury of destruction.

There was neither plan nor direction to its plunges. It rushed erratically, literally plowing through solid walls which buckled and gave way, falling on it in showers which did not seem to injure it. On all sides men fled aghast.

"Get back through the shaft, all who can!" I yelled. "Take the girls—get them out first!" I was dragging the dazed creatures from the prison chamber and thrusting them into the arms of the nearest warriors, who carried them away. On all sides of us the towers and minarets were crumbling and roaring down in ruin.

"Make ropes of the tapestries," I yelled. "Slide down the cliff! In God's name, hasten! This fiend will destroy the whole city before it is done!"

"I've found a bunch of rope ladders," shouted a warrior. "They'll reach to the water's edge, but—"

"Then fasten them and send the women down them," I shrieked. "Better take the chance of the river, then—here, Ghor, take Altha!"

I threw her into the arms of the bloodstained giant, and rushed toward the mountain of destruction which was crashing through the walls of Yugga.

Of that cataclysmic frenzy I have only a confused memory, an impression of crashing walls, howling humans, and that engine of doom roaring through all, with a ghastly aurora playing about it, as the electric power in its awful body blasted its way through solid stone.

How many Yagas, warriors and women slaves died in the falling castles is not to be known. Some hundreds had escaped down the shaft when falling roofs and walls blocked that way, crushing scores who were trying to reach it. Our warriors worked frenziedly, and the silken ladders were strung down the cliffs, some over the town of Akka, some, in haste, over the river, and down these the warriors carried the slave-girls—Guras, red and yellow girls alike.

After I had seen Ghor carry Altha away I wheeled and ran straight toward that electric horror. It was not intelligent, and what I expected to accomplish I do not know. But through the reeling walls and among the rocking towers that spilled down showers of stone blocks I raced, until I stood before the rearing horror. Blind and brainless though it was, yet it possessed some form of sensibility, because instantly, as I hurled a heavy stone at it, its movements ceased to be erratic. It charged straight for me, casting splintered masonry right and left, as foam is thrown by the rush of an ox through a stream.

I ran fleetly from it, leading it away from the screaming masses of humanity that struggled and fled along the rim of the cliff, and suddenly found myself on a battlement on the edge of the cliff, with a sheer drop of five hundred feet beneath me to the river Yogh. Behind me came the monster. As I turned desperately, it reared up and plunged at me. In the middle of its gigantic slug-like body I saw a dark spot as big as my hand pulsing. I knew that this must be the center of the being's life, and I sprang at it like a wounded tiger, plunging my sword into that dark spot.

Whether I reached it or not, I did not know. Even as I leaped, the whole universe exploded in one burst of blinding white flame and thunder, followed instantly by the blackness of oblivion.

They say that at the instant my sword sank into the body of the fire-monster, both it and I were enveloped in a blinding blue flame. There was a deafening report, like a thunder-clap, that tore the creature asunder, and hurled its mangled form, with my body, far out over the cliff, to fall five hundred feet into the deep blue waters of Yogh.

It was Thab who saved me from drowning, leaping into the river despite his crippled condition, to dive until he found and dragged my senseless body from the water.

You will say, perhaps, that it is impossible for a man to fall five hundred feet into water and live. My only reply is that I did it, and I live; though I doubt if there is any man on Earth who could do it.

For a long time I was senseless, and for longer I lay in delirium; for longer again, I lay completely paralyzed, my disrupted and numbed nerves slowly coming back into life again.

I came to myself on a couch in Koth. I knew nothing of the long trek back through the forests and across the plains from the doomed city of Yugga. Of the nine thousand men who marched to Yagg, only five thousand returned, wounded, weary, bloodstained, but triumphant. With them came fifty thousand women, the freed slaves of the vanquished Yagas. Those who were neither Kothan nor Khoran were escorted to their own cities—a thing unique in the history of Almuric. The little yellow and red women were given the freedom of either city, and allowed to dwell there in full freedom.

As for me, I have Altha—and she has me. The glamour of her, akin to glory, dazzled me with its brilliance, when first I saw her bending over my couch after my return from Yagg. Her features seemed to glimmer and float above me; then they coalesced into a vision of transcendent loveliness, yet strangely familiar to me. Our love will last forever, for it has been annealed in the white-hot fires of a mutual experience—of a savage ordeal and a great suffering.

Now, for the first time, there is peace between the cities of Khor and Koth, which have sworn eternal friendship to each other; and the only warfare is the unremitting struggle waged against the ferocious wild beasts and weird forms of animal life that abounds in much of the planet. And we two—I an Earthman born, and Altha, a daughter of Almuric who possesses the gentler instincts of an Earthwoman—we hope to instill some of the culture of my native planet into this erstwhile savage people before we die and become as the dust of my adopted planet, Almuric.

The Challenge from Beyond

by C. L. Moore, A. Merritt, H. P. Lovecraft, Robert E. Howard and Frank Belknap Long

Italicized phrases indicate the beginning of the next author's portion. Howard is also in bold print.

George Campbell opened sleep-fogged eyes upon darkness and lay gazing out of the tent flap upon the pale August night for some minutes before he roused enough even to wonder what had wakened him. There was in the keen, clear air of these Canadian woods a soporific as potent as any drug. Campbell lay quiet for a moment, sinking slowly back into the delicious borderlands of sleep, conscious of an exquisite weariness, an unaccustomed sense of muscles well used, and relaxed now into perfect ease. These were vacation's most delightful moments, after all—rest after toil, in the clear, sweet forest night.

Luxuriously, as his mind sank backward into oblivion, he assured himself once more that three long months of freedom lay before him—freedom from cities and monotony, freedom from pedagogy and the University and students with no rudiments of interest in the geology he earned his daily bread by dinning into their obdurate ears. Freedom from—

Abruptly the delightful somnolence crashed about him. Somewhere outside the sound of tin shrieking across tin slashed into his peace. George Campbell sat up jerkily and reached for his flashlight. Then he laughed and put it down again, straining his eyes through the midnight gloom outside where among the tumbling cans of his supplies a dark, anonymous little night beast was prowling. He stretched out a long arm and groped about among the rocks at the tent door for a missile. His fingers closed on a large stone, and he drew back his hand to throw.

But he never threw it. It was such a queer thing he had come upon in the dark. Square, crystal smooth, obviously artificial, with dull, rounded corners. The strangeness of its rock surfaces to his fingers was so remarkable that he reached again for the flashlight and turned its rays upon the thing he held.

All sleepiness left him as he saw what it was he had picked up in his idle groping. It was clear as rock crystal, this queer, smooth cube. Quartz unquestionably, but not in its usual hexagonal crystallized form. Somehow—he could not guess the method—it had been wrought into a perfect cube, about four inches in measurement over each worn face. For it was incredibly worn. The hard, hard crystal was rounded now until its corners were almost gone and the thing was beginning to assume the outlines of a sphere. Ages and ages of wearing, years almost beyond counting, must have passed over this strange clear thing.

But the most curious thing of all was that shape he could make out dimly in the heart of the crystal. For imbedded in its center lay a little disc of a pale and nameless substance with characters incised deep upon its quartz-enclosed surface. Wedge-shaped characters, faintly reminiscent of cuneiform writing.

George Campbell wrinkled his brows and bent closer above the little enigma in his hands, puzzling helplessly. How could such a thing as this have imbedded in pure rock crystal? Remotely a memory floated through his mind of ancient legends that called quartz crystals ice which had frozen too hard ever to melt again. Ice—and wedge-shaped cuneiforms—yes, didn't that sort of writing originate among the Sumerians who came down from the north in history's remotest beginnings to settle in the primitive Mesopotamian valley? Then hard sense regained control and he laughed. Quartz, of course, was formed in the earliest of Earth's geological periods, when there was nothing anywhere but heat and heaving rock. Ice had not come for tens of millions of years after this thing he held must have been formed.

And yet—that writing. Man-made, surely, although its characters were unfamiliar save in their faint hinting at cuneiform shapes. Or could there, in a Paleozoic world, have been things with a written language who might have graven these cryptic wedges upon the quartz-enveloped disc he held? Or—might a thing like this have fallen meteor-like out of space into the unformed rock of a still molten world? Could it—

Then he caught himself up sharply and felt his ears going hot at the luridness of his own imagination. The silence and the solitude and the queer thing in his hands were conspiring to play tricks with his common sense. He shrugged and laid the crystal down at the edge of his pallet, switching off the light. Perhaps morning and a clear head would bring him an answer to the questions that seemed so insoluble now.

But sleep did not come easily. For one thing, it seemed to him as he flashed off the light, that the little cube had shone for a moment as if with retained light before it faded into the surrounding dark. Or perhaps he was wrong. Perhaps it had been only his dazzled eyes that seemed to see the light forsake it reluctantly, glowing in the enigmatic deeps of the thing with queer persistence.

He lay there unquietly for a long while, turning the unanswered questions over and over in his mind. There was something about this crystal cube out of the unmeasured past, perhaps from the dawn of all history, that constituted a challenge that would not let him sleep.

He lay there, it seemed to him, for hours. It had been the lingering light, the luminescence that had seemed so reluctant to die, which held his mind. It was as though something in the heart of the cube had awakened, stirred drowsily, become suddenly alert . . . and intent upon him.

Sheer fantasy, this. He stirred impatiently and flashed his light upon his watch. Close to one o'clock; three hours more before the dawn. The beam fell and was focused upon the worn crystal cube. He held it there closely, for minutes. He snapped it out, then watched.

There was no doubt about it now. As his eyes accustomed themselves to the darkness, he saw that the strange crystal was glimmering with tiny fugitive lights deep within it like threads of sapphire lightnings. They were at its center, and they seemed to him to come from the pale disc with its disturbing markings. And the disc itself was becoming larger . . . the markings shifting shapes. . . the cube itself was growing . . . or was it illusion brought about by the tiny lightnings . . .

He heard a sound. It was the very ghost of a sound, like the ghosts of harp strings being plucked with ghostly fingers. He bent closer. It came from the cube . . .

There was squeaking in the underbrush, a flurry of bodies and an agonized wailing like a child in death throes and swiftly stifled. Some small tragedy of the wilderness, killer and prey. He stepped over to where it had been enacted, but could see nothing. He again snapped off the flash and looked toward his tent. Upon the ground was a pale blue glimmering. It was the cube. He stooped to pick it up; then obeying some obscure warning, drew back his hand.

And again, he saw, its glow was dying. The tiny sapphire lightnings flashing fitfully, withdrawing to the disc from which they had come. There was no sound from it.

He sat, watching the luminescence glow and fade, glow and fade, but steadily becoming dimmer. It came to him that two elements were necessary to produce the phenomenon. The electric ray itself, and his own fixed attention. His mind must travel along the ray, fix itself upon the cube's heart, if its beat were to wax, until . . . what?

He felt a chill of spirit, as though from contact with some alien thing. It was alien, he knew it; not of this earth. Not of Earth's life. He conquered his shrinking, picked up the cube and took it into the tent. It was neither warm nor cold; except for its weight he would not have known he held it. He put it upon the table, keeping the torch turned from it; then stepped to the flap of the tent and closed it.

He went back to the table, drew up the camp chair, and turned the flash directly upon the cube, focusing it so far as he could upon its heart. He sent all his will, all his concentration, along it; focusing will and sight upon the disc as he had the light.

As though at command, the sapphire lightnings burned forth. They burst from the disc into the body of the crystal cube, then beat back, bathing the disc and the markings. Again these began to change, shifting, moving, advancing, and retreating in the blue gleaming. They were no longer writings, no longer cuneiform- shaped. They were things . . . objects.

He heard the murmuring music, the plucked harp strings. Louder grew the sound and louder, and now all the body of the cube vibrated to their rhythm. The crystal walls were melting, growing misty as though formed of the mist of diamonds. And the disc itself was growing . . . the shapes shifting, dividing and multiplying as though some door had been opened and into it companies of phantasms were pouring. While brighter, more bright grew the pulsing light.

He felt swift panic, tried to withdraw sight and will, dropped the flash. The cube had no need now of the ray . . . and he could not withdraw . . . could not withdraw? Why, he himself was being sucked into that disc which was now a globe within which unnameable shapes danced to a music as alien. And the lightnings had stilled and had become sapphire suns that bathed the globe with steady radiance.

There was no tent. There was only a vast curtain of sparkling mist behind which shone the globe . . .

He felt himself drawn through that mist, sucked through it as if by a mighty wind, straight for the globe.

As the mist-blurred light of the sapphire suns grew more and more intense, the outlines of the globe ahead wavered and dissolved to a churning chaos. Its pallor and its motion and its music all blended themselves with the engulfing mist—bleaching it to a pale-steel colour and setting it undulantly in motion. And the sapphire suns, too, melted imperceptibly into the greying infinity of shapeless pulsation.

Meanwhile the sense of forward, outward motion grew intolerably, incredibly, cosmically swift. Every standard of speed known to Earth seemed dwarfed, and Campbell knew that any such flight in physical reality would mean instant death to a human being. Even as it was—in this strange, hellish hypnosis or nightmare—the quasi-visual impression of meteor-like hurtling almost paralyzed his mind. Though there were no real points of reference in the grey, pulsing, void, he felt that he was approaching and passing the speed of light itself. Finally his consciousness did go under—and merciful blackness swallowed everything.

It was very suddenly, and amidst the most impenetrable darkness, that thoughts and ideas again came to George Campbell. Of how many moments—or years—or eternities—had elapsed since his flight through the grey void, he could form no estimate. He knew only that he seemed to be at rest and without pain. Indeed, the absence of all physical sensation was the salient quality of his condition. It made even the blackness seem less solidly black—suggesting as it did that he was rather a disembodied intelligence in a state beyond physical senses, than a corporeal being with senses deprived of their accustomed objects of perception. He could think sharply and quickly—almost preternaturally so—yet could form no idea whatsoever of his situation.

Half by instinct, he realized that he was not in his own tent. True, he might have awaked there from a nightmare to a world equally black; yet he knew this was not so. There was no camp cot beneath him—he had no hands to feel the blankets and canvas surface and flashlight that ought to be around him—there was no sensation of cold in the air—no flap through which he could glimpse the pale night outside . . . something was wrong, dreadfully wrong . . .

He cast his mind backward and thought of the fluorescent cube which had hypnotized him—of that, and all which had followed. He had known that his mind was going, yet had been unable to draw back. At the last moment there had been a shocking, panic fear—a subconscious fear beyond even that caused by the sensation of daemonic flight. It had come from some vague flash of remote recollection—just what, he could not at once tell. Some cell group in the back of his head had seemed to find a cloudily familiar quality in the cube—and that familiarity was fraught with dim terror. Now he tried to remember what the familiarity and the terror were.

Little by little it came to him. Once—long ago, in connection with his geological life-work—he had read of something like that cube. It had to do with those debatable and disquieting clay fragments called the Eltdown Shards, dug up from pre-carboniferous strata in southern England thirty years before. Their shape and markings were so queer that a few scholars hinted at artificiality, and made wild conjectures about them and their origin. They came, clearly, from a time when no human beings could exist on the globe— but their contours and figurings were damnably puzzling. That was how they got their name.

It was not, however, in the writings of any sober scientist that Campbell had seen that reference to a crystal, disc-holding globe. The source was far less reputable, and infinitely more vivid. About 1912 a deeply learned Sussex clergyman of occultist leanings—the Reverend Arthur Brooke Winters-Hall—had professed to identify the markings on the Eltdown Shards with some of the so-called "pre-human hieroglyphs" persistently cherished and esoterically handed down in certain mystical circles, and had published at his own expense what purported to be a "translation" of the primal and baffling "inscriptions"—a "translation" still quoted frequently and seriously by occult writers. In this "translation"—a surprisingly long brochure in view of the limited number of "shards" existing— had occurred the narrative, supposedly of prehuman authorship, containing the now frightening reference.

As the story went, there dwelt on a world—and eventually on countless other worlds—of outer space a mighty order of wormlike beings whose attainments and whose control of nature surpassed anything within the range of terrestrial imagination. They had mastered the art of interstellar travel early in their career, and had peopled every habitable planet in their own galaxy—killing off the races they found.

Beyond the limits of their own galaxy—which was not ours—they could not navigate in person; but in their quest for knowledge of all space and time they discovered a means of spanning certain trans-galactic gulfs with their minds. They devised peculiar objects—strangely energized cubes of a curious crystal containing hypnotic talismans and enclosed in space-resisting spherical envelopes of an unknown substance—which could be forcibly expelled beyond the limits of their universe, and which would respond to the attraction of cool solid matter only.

These, of which a few would necessarily land on various inhabited worlds in outside universes, formed the ether bridges needed for mental communication. Atmospheric friction burned away the protecting envelope, leaving the cube exposed and subject to discovery by the intelligent minds of the world where it fell. By its very nature, the cube would attract and rivet attention. This, when coupled with the action of light, was sufficient to set its special properties working.

The mind that noticed the cube would be drawn into it by the power of the disc, and would be sent on a thread of obscure energy to the place whence the disc had come—the remote world of the wormlike space-explorers across stupendous galactic abysses. Received in one of the machines to which each cube was attuned, the captured mind would remain suspended without body or senses until examined by one of the dominant race. Then it would, by an obscure process of interchange, be pumped of all is contents. The investigator's mind would now occupy the strange machine while the captive mind occupied the interrogator's wormlike body. Then, in another interchange, the interrogator's mind would leap across boundless space to the captive's vacant and unconscious body on the trans-galactic world—animating the alien tenement as best it might, and exploring the alien world in the guise of one of its denizens.

When done with exploration, the adventurer would use the cube and its disc in accomplishing his return—and sometimes the captured mind would be restored safely to its own remote world. Not always, however, were the dominant race so kind. Sometimes, when a potentially important race capable of space travel was found, the wormlike folk would employ the cube to capture and annihilate minds by the thousand, and would extirpate the race for diplomatic reasons—using the exploring minds as agents of destruction.

In other cases sections of the worm folk would permanently occupy a trans-galactic planet—destroying the captured minds and wiping out the remaining inhabitants preparatory to settling down in unfamiliar bodies. Never, however, could the parent civilization be quite duplicated in such a case; since the new planet would not contain all the materials necessary for the worm-race's arts. The cubes, for example, could be made only on the home planet.

Only a few of the numberless cubes sent forth ever found a landing and response on an inhabited world—since there was no such thing as aiming them at goals beyond sight or knowledge. Only three, ran the story, had ever landed on peopled worlds in our own particular universe. Of these one had struck a planet near the galactic rim two thousand billion years ago, whilst another had lodged three billion years ago on a world near the centre of the galaxy. The third—and the only one ever known to have invaded the solar system—had reached our own earth 150,000,000 years ago.

It was with this latter that Dr. Winters-Hall's "translation" chiefly dealt. When the cube struck the earth, he wrote, the ruling terrestrial species was a huge, cone-shaped race surpassing all others before or since in mentality and achievements. This race was so advanced that it had actually sent minds abroad in both space and time to explore the cosmos, hence recognized something of what had happened when the cube fell from the sky and certain individuals had suffered mental change after gazing at it.

Realizing that the changed individuals represented invading minds, the race's leaders had them destroyed—even at the cost of leaving the displaced minds exiled in alien space. They had had experience with even stranger transitions. When, through a mental exploration of space and time, they formed a rough idea of what the cube was, they carefully hid the thing from light and sight, and guarded it as a menace. They did not wish to destroy a thing so rich in later experimental possibilities. Now and then some rash, unscrupulous adventurer would furtively gain access to it and sample its perilous powers despite the consequences—but all such cases were discovered, and safely and drastically dealt with.

Of this evil meddling the only bad result was that the worm-like outside race learned from the new exiles what had happened to their explorers on Earth, and conceived a violent hatred of the planet and all its life-forms. They would have depopulated it if they could, and indeed sent additional cubes into space in the wild hope of striking it by accident in unguarded places—but that accident never came to pass.

The cone-shaped terrestrial beings kept the one existing cube in a special shrine as a relique and basis for experiments, till after aeons it was lost amidst the chaos of war and the destruction of the great polar city where it was guarded. When, fifty million years ago, the beings sent their minds ahead into the infinite future to avoid a nameless peril of inner earth, the whereabouts of the sinister cube from space were unknown.

This much, according to the learned occultist, the Eltdown Shards had said. What now made the account so obscurely frightful to Campbell was the minute accuracy with which the alien cube had been described. Every detail tallied—dimensions, consistency, hieroglyphed central disc, hypnotic effects. As he thought the matter over and over amidst the darkness of his strange situation, he began to wonder whether his whole experience with the crystal cube— indeed, its very existence—were not a nightmare brought on by some freakish subconscious memory of this old bit of extravagant, charlatanic reading. If so, though, the nightmare must still be in force; since his present apparently bodiless state had nothing of normality in it.

Of the time consumed by this puzzled memory and reflection, Campbell could form no estimate. Everything about his state was so unreal that ordinary dimensions and measurements became meaningless. It seemed an eternity, but perhaps it was not really long before the sudden interruption came. What happened was as strange and inexplicable as the blackness it succeeded. There was a sensation—of the mind rather than of the body—and all at once Campbell felt his thoughts swept or sucked beyond his control in tumultuous and chaotic fashion.

Memories arose irresponsibly and irrelevantly. All that he knew—all his personal background, traditions, experiences, scholarship, dreams, ideas, and inspirations—welled up abruptly and simultaneously, with a dizzying speed and abundance which soon made him unable to keep track of any separate concept. The parade of all his mental contents became an avalanche, a cascade, a vortex. It was as horrible and vertiginous as his hypnotic flight through space when the crystal cube pulled him. Finally it sapped his consciousness and brought on a fresh oblivion.

Another measureless blank—and then a slow trickle of sensation. This time it was physical, not mental. Sapphire light, and a low rumble of distant sound. There were tactile impressions—he could realise that he was lying at full length on something, though there was a baffling strangeness about the feel of his posture. He could not reconcile the pressure of the supporting surface with his own outlines—or with the outlines of the human form at all. He tried to move his arms, but found no definite response to the attempt. Instead, there were little, ineffectual nervous twitches all over the area which seemed to mark his body.

He tried to open his eyes more widely, but found himself unable to control their mechanism. The sapphire light came in a diffused, nebulous manner, and could nowhere be voluntarily focused into definiteness. Gradually, though, visual images began to trickle in curiously and indecisively. The limits and qualities of vision were not those which he was used to, but he could roughly correlate the sensation with what he had known as sight. As this sensation gained some degree of stability, Campbell realized that he must still be in the throes of nightmare.

He seemed to be in a room of considerable extent—of medium height, but with a large proportionate area. On every side—and he could apparently see all four sides at once—were high, narrowish slits which seemed to serve as combined doors and windows. There were singular low tables or pedestals, but no furniture of normal nature and proportions. Through the slits streamed floods of sapphire light, and beyond them could be mistily seen the sides and roofs of fantastic buildings like clustered cubes. On the walls—in the vertical panels between the slits—were strange markings of an oddly disquieting character. It was some time before Campbell understood why they disturbed him so—then he saw that they were, in repeated instances, precisely like some of the hieroglyphs on the crystal cube's disc.

The actual nightmare element, though, was something more than this. It began with the living thing which presently entered through one of the slits, advancing deliberately toward him and bearing a metal box of bizarre proportions and glassy, mirrorlike surfaces. For this thing was nothing human—nothing of Earth—nothing even of man's myths and dreams. It was a gigantic, pale-grey worm or centipede, as large around as a man and twice as long, with a disclike, apparently eyeless, cilia-fringed head bearing a purple central orifice. It glided on its rear pairs of legs, with its fore part raised vertically—the legs, or at least two pairs of them, serving as arms. Along its spinal ridge was a curious purple comb, and a fan-shaped tail of some grey membrane ended its grotesque bulk. There was a ring of flexible red spikes around its neck, and from the twistings of these came clicking, twanging sounds in measured, deliberate rhythms.

Here, indeed, was outré nightmare at its height—capricious fantasy at its apex. But even this vision of delirium was not what caused George Campbell to lapse a third time into unconsciousness. It took one more thing—one final, unbearable touch—to do that. As the nameless worm advanced with its glistening box, the reclining man caught in the mirrorlike surface a glimpse of what should have been his own body. Yet—horribly verifying his disordered and unfamiliar sensations—it was not his own body at all that he saw reflected in the burnished metal. It was, instead, the loathsome, pale-grey bulk of one of the giant centipedes.

From that final lap of senselessness, he emerged with a full understanding of his situation. His mind was imprisoned in the body of a frightful native of an alien planet, while, somewhere on the other side of the universe, his own body was housing the monster's personality.

He fought down an unreasoning horror. Judged from a cosmic standpoint, why should his metamorphosis horrify him? Life and consciousness were the only realities in the universe. Form was unimportant. His present body was hideous only according to terrestrial standards. Fear and revulsion were drowned in the excitement of titanic adventure.

What was his former body but a cloak, eventually to be cast off at death anyway? He had no sentimental illusions about the life from which he had been exiled. What had it ever given him save toil, poverty, continual frustration and repression? If this life before him offered no more, at least it offered no less. Intuition told him it offered more—much more.

With the honesty possible only when life is stripped of its naked fundamentals, he realized that he remembered with pleasure only the physical delights of his former life. But he had long ago exhausted all the physical possibilities of pleasure contained in that earthly body. Earth held no new thrills. But in the possession of this new, alien body he felt promises of strange, exotic joys.

A lawless exultation rose in him. He was a man without a world, free of all conventions or inhibitions of either Earth, or of this strange planet, free of every artificial restraint in the universe. He was a god! With grim amusement he thought of his body moving in Earth's business and society, with all the while an alien monster staring out of the windows that were George Campbell's eyes on people who would flee if they knew.

Let him walk the earth slaying and destroying as he would. Earth and its races no longer had any meaning to George Campbell. There he had been one of a billion nonentities, fixed in place by a mountainous accumulation of conventions, laws and manners, doomed to live and die in his sordid niche. But in one blind bound he had soared above the commonplace. This was not death, but rebirth—the birth of a full-grown mentality, with a newfound freedom that made little of physical captivity on Yekub.

He started. Yekub! It was the name of this planet, but how had he known? Then he knew, as he knew the name of him whose body he occupied—Tothe. Memory, deep grooved in Tothe's brain, was stirring in him—shadows of the knowledge Tothe had. Carved deep in the physical tissues of the brain, they spoke dimly as implanted instincts to George Campbell; and his human consciousness seized them and translated them to show him the way not only to safety and freedom, but to the power his soul, stripped to its primitive impulses, craved. Not as a slave would he dwell on Yekub, but as a king! Just as of old barbarians had set on the thrones of lordly empires.

For the first time he turned his attention to his surroundings. He still lay on the couchlike thing in the midst of that fantastic room, and the centipede man stood before him, holding the polished metal object, and clashing its neck spikes. Thus it spoke to him, Campbell knew, and what it said he dimly understood, through the implanted thought processes of Tothe, just as he knew the creature was Yukth, supreme lord of science.

But Campbell gave no heed, for he had made his desperate plan, a plan so alien to the ways of Yekub that it was beyond Yukth's comprehension and caught him wholly unprepared. Yukth, like Campbell, saw the sharp-pointed metal shard on a nearby table, but to Yukth it was only a scientific implement. He did not even know it could be used as a weapon. Campbell's earthly mind supplied that knowledge and the action that followed, driving Tothe's body into movements no man of Yekub had ever made before.

Campbell snatched the pointed shard and struck, ripping savagely upward. Yukth reared and toppled, his entrails spilling on the floor. In an instant Campbell was streaking for a door. His speed was amazing, exhilarating, first fulfillment of the promise of novel physical sensations.

As he ran, guided wholly by the instinctive knowledge implanted in Tothe's physical reflexes, it was as if he were borne by a separate consciousness in his legs. Tothe's body was bearing him along a route it had traversed ten thousand times when animated by Tothe's mind.

Down a winding corridor he raced, up a twisted stair, through a carved door, and the same instincts that had brought him there told him he had found what he sought. He was in a circular room with a domed roof from which shone a livid blue light. A strange structure rose in the middle of the rainbow-hued floor, tier on tier, each of a separate, vivid color. The ultimate tier was a purple cone, from the apex of which a blue smoky mist drifted upward to a sphere that poised in midair—a sphere that shone like translucent ivory.

This, the deep-grooved memories of Tothe told Campbell, was the god of Yekub, though why the people of Yekub feared and worshipped it had been forgotten for a million years. A worm priest stood between him and the altar which no hand of flesh had ever touched. That it could be touched was a blasphemy that had never occurred to a man of Yekub. The worm priest stood in frozen horror until Campbell's shard ripped the life out of him.

On his centipede legs Campbell clambered the tiered altar, heedless of its sudden quiverings, heedless of the change that was taking place in the floating sphere, heedless of the smoke that now billowed out in blue clouds. He was drunk with the feel of power. He feared the superstitions of Yekub no more than he feared those of Earth. With that globe in his hands he would be king of Yekub. The worm men would dare deny him nothing, when he held their god as hostage. He reached a hand for the ball—no longer ivory hued, but red as blood . . .

Out of the tent into the pale August night walked the body of George Campbell. It moved with a slow, wavering gait between the bodies of enormous trees, over a forest path strewed with sweet-scented pine needles. The air was crisp and cold. The sky was an inverted bowl of frosted silver flecked with stardust, and far to the north the Aurora Borealis splashed streamers of fire.

The head of the walking man lolled hideously from side to side. From the corners of his lax mouth drooled thick threads of amber froth, which fluttered in the night breeze. He walked upright at first, as a man would walk, but gradually, as the tent receded, his posture altered. His torso began almost imperceptibly to slant, and his limbs to shorten.

In a far-off world of outer space the centipede creature that was George Campbell clasped to its bosom a god whose lineaments were as red as blood, and ran with insect-like quiverings across a rainbow-hued hall and out through massive portals into the bright glow of alien suns.

Weaving between the trees of Earth in an attitude that suggested the awkward lopings of a werebeast, the body of George Campbell was fulfilling a mindless destiny. Long, claw-tipped fingers dragged leaves from a carpet of odorous pine needles as it moved toward a wide expanse of gleaming water.

In the far-off, extra-galactic world of the worm people, George Campbell moved between cyclopean blocks of black masonry down long, fern-planted avenues holding aloft the round red god.

There was a harsh animal cry in the underbrush near the gleaming lake on Earth where the mind of a worm creature dwelt in a body swayed by instinct. Human teeth sank into soft animal fur, tore at black animal flesh. A little silver fox sank its fangs in frantic retaliation into a furry human wrist, and thrashed about in terror as its blood spurted. Slowly the body of George Campbell arose, its mouth splashed with fresh blood. With upper limbs swaying oddly it moved toward the waters of the lake.

As the veriform creature that was George Campbell crawled between the black blocks of stone, thousands of worm shapes prostrated themselves in the scintillating dust before it. A godlike power seemed to emanate from its weaving body as it moved with a slow, undulant motion toward a throne of spiritual empire transcending all the sovereignties of Earth.

A trapper stumbling wearily through the dense woods of Earth near the tent where the worm-creature dwelt in the body of George Campbell came to the gleaming waters of the lake and discerned something dark floating there. He had been lost in the woods all night, and weariness enveloped him like a leaden cloak in the pale morning light.

But the shape was a challenge that he could not ignore. Moving to the edge of the water he knelt in the soft mud and reached out toward the floating bulk. Slowly he pulled it to the shore.

Far off in outer space the worm creature holding the glowing red god ascended a throne that gleamed like the constellation Cassiopeia under an alien vault of hyper-suns. The great deity that he held aloft energized his worm tenement, burning away in the white fire of a supermundane spirituality all animal dross.

On Earth the trapper gazed with unutterable horror into the blackened and hairy face of the drowned man. It was a bestial face, repulsively anthropoid in contour, and from its twisted, distorted mouth black ichor poured.

George Campbell felt the round red god stir in his embrace. Vibrations flowed from it and as George Campbell sat enthroned, feeling the glow of empire in all his segments, Yekub's great deity spoke to him in accents that pulsed coolly through the corridors of his brain.

"He who sought your body in the abysses of Time will occupy an unresponsive tenement," said the red god. "No spawn of Yekub can control the body of a human.

"On all Earth, living creatures rend one another, and feast with unutterable cruelty on their kith and kin. No worm-mind can control a bestial man-body when it yearns to raven. Only man-minds instinctively conditioned through the course of ten thousand generations can keep the human instincts in thrall. Your body will destroy itself on Earth, seeking the blood of its animal kin, seeking the cool water where it can wallow at its ease. Seeking eventually destruction, for the death-instinct is more powerful in it than the instincts of life and it will destroy itself in seeking to return to the slime from which it sprang."

Thus spoke the round red god of Yekub in a far-off segment of the space-time continuum to George Campbell as the latter, with all human desire purged away, sat on a throne and ruled an empire of worms more wisely, kindly, and benevolently than any man of Earth had ever ruled an empire of men.

Miscellanea

A Twentieth Century Rip Van Winkle

(handwritten—dated October 13, 1920)

William McGarthy lived contentedly on his father's ranch in Western Texas until, at the age of twenty, he was suddenly smitten with wanderlust. He fought against the longing until it became unbearable and then he sold all the cattle and horses he had, drew all the money he had out of the bank and started on his tour of the world. His money, together with what his father had given, amounted to several thousand dollars. He saw the United States thoroughly, and then he took passage on a ship, a steamer, bound for Sydney in Australia. The ship stopped at Samoa to give the passengers a chance to go ashore and secure some of the fine fruit that was everywhere in abundance. There was no sign of natives but the captain warned the passengers and crew not to venture too far from the beach. "For," said he, "the Samoan of today is the same headhunter and cannibal that his ancestors were one hundred years ago."

Once ashore, however, amid the beauties of a tropical forest Bill soon forgot the captain's warning. He would have been more cautious if he had seen a pair of beady black eyes that peered from the shelter of the thick brush and that lighted with fierce triumph as the boat that brought the passengers ashore, pulled up at the beach. But McGarthy did not see and now as he heedlessly wandered further from the shore, a black, kinky-headed native was speeding silently inland.

For an hour the whites roamed the beach while inland McGarthy lay stretched at ease beneath a great mango tree. Came at dusk the shrill blast of the ship's whistle to recall the passengers to the ship. Instantaneously there came a wild chorus of yells and screams as a hundred ambushing bushmen broke cover and rushed down upon the terrified whites. A passenger and a sailor dropped, pierced by the arrows of headhunters, but the rest got on board the boat and by hard rowing got away to the ship. The Samoans cut off the heads of the dead whites and waved the ghastly trophies and yelled in triumph. But they were too wise to attack the ship so after dancing about on the beach awhile they silently departed. The captain knew better than to risk an expedition of revenge, so he weighed anchor and steamed away.

In the meantime McGarthy had been peacefully resting when the whistle and the yells brought him to his feet. At the same time something struck his head with a terrific "whack!" Several million stars flashed before his eyes; he wondered vaguely if a star had fallen on him or if it was merely an earthquake and then his consciousness soared off into space.

Slowly McGarthy drifted back to earth. When he opened his eyes and came to life with a jerk. He found himself lying on the earth floor of a rude native hut. He was not bound so he got on his feet but he was so weak and dizzy and his head ached so that he could hardly stand. Just then a native came in bearing a wooden tray on which was a bunch of bananas and other fruit and a portion of roasted pig. Being hungry McGarthy received the food with relief. The Samoan watched him with curiosity while the white ate. He was a hideous creature with long, krinkled hair, ear and nose rings, with a necklace made of dried human hands, and when he grinned he showed teeth filed to a sharp point. He spoke: "Good, you heap eat, when you get heap fat, fellow bushmen kai-pei you," and he smacked his thick lips in anticipation. McGarthy looked blankly at him. "You no savvy? Look, see!" and he opened the door. Bill looked out and felt his hair rise. There on two spears were impaled the heads of two whites whom he recognized, while in the center of the village the headhunters were preparing the bodies for their gruesome feast. Bill shuddered and turned sick then his strength returned with a rush. He struck down his guard and rushed out of the hut and down a side street of the village in a mad attempt to escape. The headhunters saw him instantly and gave chase with fierce yells. He had the start of them, however, and running like a frightened deer he distanced them and had nearly gained the jungle when a Samoan leaped from a hut full into his path. McGarthy stiff-armed him, receiving an ugly gash on his arm from a knife thrust, leaped over his prostrate body and hurdling the low boma he gained the jungle. For days he fled inland always eluding his pursuers but not daring to turn back toward the ocean for the bushmen were always between him and the beach.

Finally he crossed a small river in spite of the danger of crocodiles and the cannibals pursued him no further. And two miles beyond the river he came suddenly on a wide plain through which a river ran and on which lived a tribe of people neither bushmen nor saltwater people. They were not headhunters or cannibals. They were of Malay origin and were tall and brown skinned, not short and black like the Samoans. They were friendly to him and he stayed with them. They were ever at war with the blacks so none of them went to the sea. They could not get past the surrounding tribes of headhunters. However, in every battle almost they defeated the blacks and had held the plain between the main river and a tributary which had its source near the river and flowed toward the east and then back to join the main river ten miles further on. The Malays had held this plain for countless ages.

For years McGarthy lived among these people. He hunted with them, fought with them but he would not intermarry with them. The years sped by. Twenty of them. Three times Bill tried to reach the coast and each time he just managed to get back to the tribe with his head. The cannibals made it impossible. And then one day when he had given up all hope he heard a wild chorus of yells and rushing from his hut he saw a huge airship hovering over the village perhaps a hundred feet above ground. A wild surge of hope rushed over him. He clambered to the top of the hut and hailed the ship at the top of his lungs, "Come to earth! We won't hurt you!" and he shouted for the Malays to lay down their arms which they did. As the whites heard his cries they drifted slowly to earth and a man in khaki alighted. McGarthy rushed forward and seized his hand. "For God's sake take me home!"

As they sailed over forest and plain, over land and sea, McGarthy wondered at the great airship. Thirty men and three officers managed her. They had a cargo of wool exported from Australia and were sailing for England. "What date is this?" asked McGarthy to the captain.

"June the third, 1940," was the reply.

"Great Guns, and I left America in June 1920!"

They soon neared England for the ship was capable of making a speed of two hundred miles an hour and now the air was filled with airships and dirigibles. Tiny one-man fliers and monsters at ten thousand tons. At Bristol McGarthy parted from the captain who lent him sufficient money to get back to Texas on and then Bill took passage in a gigantic dirigible bound for Galveston. The ship was equipped with all the pleasures and comforts of the ships Bill had been used to and many more that he knew nothing of. They were two days crossing the Atlantic and then the big ship was held close over the docks and the passengers were lowered to the dock in elevators. McGarthy stepped into a drug store and asked for a cigar. The clerk looked over with a "fissy" eye and finally asked, "You been dead a few years? Don't you know that the twenty-first amendment forbids the use of tobacco in every form?"

Bill took a small flier for his home place and when he got there he was amazed. Instead of the rolling plains dotted with ranches and too numerous farms, he saw populous towns many only a few miles apart. He was bewildered. Finally he picked out a town which he thought was located close to the former site of his father's ranch and bade his chauffeur land him there. Once on the streets he knew not what to do. He walked the streets until he was in despair when he saw an old man he thought looked familiar. "Say, aren't you John Blake?"

"I am."

"You know Dave McGarthy who owned the Seven X Ranch?"

"I did know him. He has been dead six years."

"Dead!" repeated Bill dully. "He was my father."

The old man looked at him keenly. "Are you William McGarthy?" he asked.

"I am, for twenty years an exile in a cannibal isle."

"When your father died he was rich. He always hoped that you're not dead and that you would come back and he left half his fortune to you and half to your sister. She has married and lives here. I will go there with you."

As they went McGarthy asked him, "Where is Steve Burton?"

"Why, he was killed in the war of 1930."

"What war?"

"The war between England and America in which Ireland regained her freedom and Canada broke loose from England and established a separate republic."

"I'm rather behind the times," remarked Bill. "Tell me some more."

"Well besides the War of 1930 we had a war in 1925 with Japan. With the result that Japan was defeated and was forced to give up China and Manchuria."

"Who is the President?"

"A Texan by the name of Emerson Gans."

"Why, I knew him."

"Yes, he was only a few years older than you when you left and lived on the ranch adjoining yours."

"Have women ever gotten into politics?"

"Ah yes, Kansas has a woman governor and so has Ohio and West Virginia."

"Why is it I see so few automobiles?"

"No one uses them except people that are old-fashioned or live far out in the country and are too poor to buy a flier."

At last they came to his sister's house. They went up the steps and the door swung automatically open while an electric bell informed the occupants of the house of their visitors and a set of reflectoscopes in the sitting room showed the image of the visitors. They entered the room where they were greeted by Bill's sister and her husband.

"Alice, don't you know me?" asked McGarthy.

She stared at him for a moment then, "Will!" She cried and sprang forward with outstretched arms.

"I want to see a map of the world," announced McGarthy after he had related his experiences and heard an account of what had happened in his home place while he was gone. When it was brought he devoured it with eager eyes. "Where is Mexico?"

"Why, that was annexed to the United States in 1939."

"I see Australia is a separate republic."

"Yes, she broke from England in 1932."

After a dinner cooked electrically, McGarthy's sister and her husband took him on an "excursion of exploration." He saw the huge factories where airships were made at the rate of one in three minutes. They sailed to Galveston at the rate of one hundred miles an hour, as he had been in such a hurry when he passed through he had not noticed much of the town. Galveston was a great city of two hundred thousand people. They visited airplane factories much larger than those Bill had seen at Thuvia (his hometown). He saw the great guns guarding the harbor operated by radium and capable of a two-hundred-mile range. He saw things he had never dreamed could be invented. When he learned that in the thirtieth amendment the government had abolished the use of coffee he sank back exhausted. "Ye Gads," he murmured, "I'm a twentieth century Rip Van Winkle."

The Iron Terror

Outside the wind roared, snatching up the snow, whirling the flakes high in the air. The streets were deserted except for a few belated pedestrians hurrying home, heads bowed against the gale. Further up, in the business-proper part of town, even the crowds were scattered and few. Traffic had almost stopped. In a section where the streets were entirely bare, a house reared, bleak and dark among its lesser neighbors.

"At last!" A laboratory filled with weird contrivances. A withered old man seated at a table.

"At last!" What cared he for the wind and the cold outside? He scarcely knew of it, one of the worst blizzards that had ever swept New York.

"At last!" He rubbed his hands and chuckled.

A taxi drew up in front of the tall house that loomed so dark and forbidding.

A man alighted and made his way through the whirling snow to the door. The taxi whirled away.

The clang of an old-fashioned knocker rose above the shriek of the storm.

The man at the door shook the snow from his coat, stamped his feet and cursed beneath his breath. He raised his hand to knock again when the door swung open. An impassive Chinaman stood in the doorway.

The man handed him a card. The Oriental glanced at it and stepped aside, bowing.

"You are expected," he said, in almost perfect English.

The man stepped inside a dimly lighted hallway. The Oriental took his hat and coat. He carried no cane. The lights showed him to be a man of medium height and of a lithe, wiry build. His face was bronzed with the sun and his black eyes were clear, farseeing, with a certain compelling something about them. His whole form and features suggested an unusual mind and intellectual power combined with a tigerish physical power. His motions were quick but not hasty nor excited. Altogether, an unusual man.

The Chinaman led him up a flight of stairs, down a corridor and into a room.

"Wait here," he said and disappeared.

The stranger paced about the room restlessly. He seemed to be conscious of unseen eyes upon him and it gave him the feeling of a trapped wolf. His eyes took in the room rapidly but with every detail.

The room was not a large one. Several doors led from it. A few chairs, a costly Persian rug, a divan and a large mahogany table constituted the furniture. The walls were hung with weapons and the table was covered with them. Such a collection as is seldom seen outside a museum.

The stranger sat down at the table and began to examine the weapons upon it with an interest that was not feigned.

Then he looked up as a man came through one of the doors. An old, wrinkled man, small and withered, stooped with age, wearing a dressing gown, bedroom slippers and a red Turkish fez placed at a rakish angle on his nearly bald head.

The stranger rose.

"So you have come?" the old man said, a sneering note in his voice. "I have expected you."

He came forward to the table.

"You are interested in my collection?" he said. "What do you think of it, eh?"

"One of the most perfect I ever saw," the stranger replied, speaking for the first time.

"Ah, you think so? You are right." He waved his hands about the room, "This is but a part of my collection yet here you will find the weapons of all lands and all ages. Do you know them?"

"Yes."

"Aye, a good workman should know the tools of his trade. But," here the sneering note crept into his voice again, "do not flatter yourself."

He picked up a short dagger with a wide, wickedly curved blade. "What is this?"

"A cheray from Afghanistan, manufactured in Ghuzni," answered the stranger, scarcely glancing at the weapon.

"And this?"

"A Dyak parang-parang from Borneo."

"And this?"

"An Italian misericorde dagger."

"And this?"

"A bronze Kalmuck-Tartar peaked helmet of about the fifteenth century."

"And this?"

"A French anlace of the Middle Ages."

"And this?"

"A Zulu shield from Africa."

"And this?"

"A samurai sword of old Japan."

"And this?"

"A claymore from Scotland. But enough of this child's play!" he exclaimed impatiently. "There is no weapon here with which I am not acquainted. Few that I have not used. I know their use and their history as well as you.

"That tulwar was made by Yussef Abdullah of Kabul who prides himself on his work. That bowie knife was made in Missouri by James Black. That rapier is the work of Andrea di Ferrara. Antonio Picinino of Venice made that Italian schiavone. That Maharati gauntlet-sword was made in the workshops of Delhi.

"But I did not come here to speak of weapons."

"No." The old man seated himself across the table from the stranger, motioning him to sit down.

The old man cupped his chin in his hands, rested his elbows on the table and stared at his visitor.

"Aye," he said, scornfully, "you know the tools of your trade. The simple tools, steel and lead, edge, point and muzzle. But what does a soldier know of the higher arts of war? The triumphs of science?"

"I am no soldier," returned the stranger.

"No, you are a conqueror. An empire builder, is that not it, my friend?"

The stranger said nothing but his eyes flashed suddenly.

"Do you think I am a fool?" sneered the old man. "I know!

"War, conquest, power! Oh, it has been done before, I admit. Alexander, Caesar, Tamerlane! All those fools. Now you. Listen!" He leaned forward, "I know more than you think for, my friend. I know that you plan to unite the tribes of Arabia and make an empire!"

The stranger leaned forward, half-casually, but his hand played with the lapel of his coat.

"And how do you know all this?" he asked.

"I ask you again, am I a fool? Why have shiploads of rifles and ammunition continually landed at out-of-the-way ports of Arabia? Why do you come to me in the night in the midst of a storm? I have ways of knowing and learning things no other man may know. Oh, yes. Empire is your goal, Mr. Gordon. Sultan Gordon sahib! How does that sound to you?"

"If you know my plans, very well," Gordon answered coolly. "But," he leaned forward and his eyes glittered tigerishly, "it is not good for any man to know too much of my plans, my friend."

The old man laughed harshly. "I will not betray you. What care I for the country that disowned me? For the nations that laughed at me? And who am I to interfere with destiny? Aye, go your way. Be what you wish to be. Another Caesar, nay, rather another Genghis Khan! But trace the roads of the conquerors and try to be free from vanity."

"My road is my own," Gordon replied.

"Aye, and you will travel it. Like all conquerors. They came, they saw, they conquered! Where are they now?

"Here is a dagger that was carried by Genghis Khan. But where is Genghis Khan? So all conquerors go!"

"All men must go," Gordon replied. "It makes no difference whether he be slave or Emperor. But the Emperor is remembered."

"Yes, men go; but the works of man, stand. Genghis Khan has been dust for a thousand years, yet here I sit and hold his dagger! And a thousand years from now men will say, 'Here is the saber Gordon swung in the fore ranks of battle? Where is Gordon now?'" and the old man laughed, a cynical, mocking laugh. Gordon smiled.

"But science prevails!" the old man exclaimed. "Science, the work of man! What are soldiers, statesmen, workers of art? They pass. Science remains. Conquerors come and go like whirlwinds. The generations of man melt like snow on a mountainside. But the triumphs of science stand through the ages, outliving the pyramids!

"You, you conqueror, you empire builder, you man with great ambitions, you come to me for aid! Aye, well you may for I have perfected an invention that makes all others seem as grains of sand to a mountain! You are skilled in the use of all weapons, you say. But what do you know of the heights of attainment the mind of a scientist may reach? A man of war may wield implements of slaughter but first the man of science must make them!"

"Now we come to the real reason of my visit," said Gordon.

"You wish to buy my invention? One thing I tell you; that it will make you master of the world—if you gain control of it."

"What is it? I found out that you had perfected some machine of war. I must see it. If I do not buy it, be assured your secret will be safe."

"I should think so," sneered the old scientist. He leaned forward, his eyes blazing with scientific zeal.

"Man, I have worked out an engine of war that dwarfs all other such inventions. Come, you shall see it, at once, at once."

He sprang to his feet with a vitality amazing in one of his age. "Come."

Gordon followed him through a door and down a short, narrow corridor. Outside a heavy door, the scientist paused.

"You are now about to see what no man but myself has ever looked upon," he announced. "If you have treachery in mind, you had better not enter."

"Lead on," Gordon answered briefly.

The scientist turned the lock and swung the door wide. Gordon stepped into a large, brilliantly lighted room. The old man followed, pulling the door to. It locked with a click.

"Look well at the door, Mr. Gordon," the old man said.

Gordon did so. It was sheathed with heavy steel and was entirely bare of knob or lock of any kind.

"The walls are sheathed with steel," the scientist said. "This is the only door. The two windows are heavily barred. I, and only I, know the secret of the door. If I were murdered here my murderer could never escape."

Gordon's eyes wandered over the great room, taking in every detail. It was filled, but not crowded, with tables, cases and stands covered with scientific apparatus. Books of scientific subjects littered the room and here and there were more weapons. Some of them of weird type.

In one corner of the room, something, some object, bulked huge and forbidding. It was covered entirely by a heavy, dark, velvet cloth but even so there seemed to be something sinister about it. Gordon's eyes rested long upon it.

The scientist strode forward and stood before the veiled object.

"Beneath this cloth," he said, "stands an invention compared to which tanks, shrapnel, gas and submarines become the toys of infants!"

Gordon approached and leaned on a table. Mechanically he noticed that on the table were three or four broadswords of the Middle Ages. Long, massive, double-edged, two-handed swords.

"Show me," he answered.

The scientist gripped the cloth and dramatically snatched it away.

There stood revealed what appeared to be a metal statue, some eight feet high.

It was in the form of a man, and as a work of art alone it was a masterpiece. The face was terrifically powerful, there were no lines or curves of fineness or weakness. A face of crude, primeval, terrible power. A malignantly powerful face.

It appeared to be of steel and was jointed; shoulder, neck, elbow, hips, knee, ankle and fingers, protected by a steel mesh, somewhat like the joint-protections of Medieval armor.

"Well," the old scientist said impatiently, "what do you think of it?"

"Why, I hardly know," Gordon replied. "I see only a statue, a remarkable statue, I admit, but still a statue, such as I see everyday, barring the face."

The old man sneered. "A statue! You fool! Look here, this 'statue' is of metal. What kind?"

Gordon tapped it. His expression showed interest.

"I thought at first it was made of Harvard steel but I am not sure."

"Harvard steel! Bosh! Steel of my own invention. Twice as powerful as Harvard steel, twice as powerful as Krupp steel. No shell can shatter it. No bullet can pierce it. Listen while I tell you the secret of the Iron Terror."

Gordon drew nearer. The old man began, turning from the figure to his visitor as he talked.

"Inside this covering of iron, this manlike form, there is an incredibly powerful engine. No such engine as you have known. Not steam or gasoline or electric. What then? Can you guess?"

"Radium," Gordon suggested, his eyes aglitter.

"Yes, radium! But radium concentrated and strengthened a thousandfold. No man on earth but I know the secret of the concentrating of radium. The engine, which I shall not describe, has antennae similar to that of a wireless, but much smaller. Here," he turned to a machine which he had uncovered. It was a complicated affair of knobs and wheels and levers. "This controls my machine. But still you do not understand. But you shall. By manipulating this machine I can send my iron figure forward at any speed I wish!

I can regulate the speed, turn it any way or bring it back. No wires connect the machine. I guide the automaton by wireless!

"Ah, you see at last! This automaton, this Iron Terror, goes straight on in the direction that I guide it. Bombs, shells, shrapnel, cannot stop it. It may be knocked from its feet but it automatically rises. It tears down fortifications, climbs walls and mountains, wades rivers. Nothing can stop it, nothing but the pressure of a finger on a certain lever of the guiding-machine. Don't you see the terrible advantage of such a machine? A river can stop a tank but my machine strides straight through it. How many armies could stand before a thousand such monsters? See, I put a sword in its hand." He took up a great broadsword and placing the hilt in the palm of the metal hand, pushed down the metal fingers one at a time. Each finger clicked metallically as it closed around the hilt.

The old scientist stepped to the guiding-machine and worked a lever.

Gordon sprang back as the great arm rose and swept down, the long sword whistling with the force of the blow. The metal arm rose and fell, rose and fell, without stay or pause. Then the old man touched a lever and the arm stopped instantly, poising the sword in midair.

The scientist laughed eerily. "A swordsman, eh? You are a swordsman yourself; what could you do against such a swordsman as that?"

Gordon shook his head.

"Are you a strong man?" the scientist asked suddenly.

"Do I look like one?" Gordon asked, somewhat impatiently; he hated personal conversation.

"No, not especially. But your slim build is deceiving. You are built for speed, not strength. Oh, you are quick. I know what the tribes name you, 'El Borak, The Swift.' But you are strong. You have slain armed men with your bare hands. Your strength is a wonder. Yet, in the grip of my automaton, you would be as helpless as would be a young girl in your arms. Look."

He touched another lever and the other arm of the automaton went through the motions of throwing something. The fingers opened, reached to the figure's side, closed, and the arm swung back and forward.

"Bombs in a sack at the side," the old scientist said, bringing the figure to a stop. "Think of a thousand automatons charging into an army, hurling great bombs incessantly. Or sending forth clouds of gas. Or even hewing with great swords."

"A marvel," said Gordon. "Unless—"

"Unless what?" asked the old scientist sharply.

"Are you sure you can keep such a thing in absolute control? It would be a horror to have it free, charging at random, casting bombs or hewing right and left with such a sword as it now holds."

"Bosh!" cried the old scientist angrily. "Do you think I am a fool?"

Gordon shrugged his shoulders and did not reply.

"So you think I am a fool, eh?" the old man exclaimed in a fury.

"No, I know you are no fool," Gordon answered. "If I have offended you I sincerely apologize. But still I cannot believe that any invention can be perfected as you say this is. You say you have absolute control of the machine. Is it not possible for it to get from under your control?"

"It is not, sir," the old scientist retorted. "It is perfectly under my control, as much as any other inanimate object."

"A man might raise a storm," Gordon said, "but he could hardly control it after he had raised it. Understand me, sir; I realize that this is the greatest invention of the age. I consider you one of the greatest scientists that has ever lived. Still, there may be a flaw."

This but increased the old man's fury. "You fool!" he fairly shrieked. "You think there is a flaw in my machine? I'll show you!"

He whirled toward the controlling machine and jerked a lever. The great automaton moved out into the room with long, regular strides!

Only its metal legs worked, the arms were motionless, one hanging at its side, the other poised in the air, gripping the great sword.

It approached the scientist.

The old man turned to Gordon. "See?" he sneered, reaching for the control lever.

As he reached, his arm struck another lever. The great arm swung down! The old scientist was too near to the figure to receive the blade but the great arm itself struck him a glancing blow on the head and descending, crashed down upon the controlling machine.

Instantly, the thing charged out into the room, the great sword swishing the air as it rose and fell!

With incredible speed Gordon leaped back and jerked out a big automatic. The crashing reports filled the room with echoes, the bullets ringing on the metal figure as they glanced and smashed against the walls.

Gordon might have been throwing pieces of paper as far as the automaton was concerned. It strode straight on. One arm wielded the sword, the other by some freakish cause, swung out in a circular motion, swung back and clanged against the metal breast of the automaton. The smashing of the control machine had turned the metal horror loose and it was running amuck!

The old scientist lay where he had fallen, half across the battered controlling machine.

Gordon leaped across the room to the door. Then as he tried it the scientist's words flashed into his mind: "—only I know the secret of the door. If I were murdered here my murderer could never escape."

Gordon realized that he was trapped! Trapped in an inescapable room with an iron monster!

Then began one of the strangest battles that ever occurred on earth. Gordon had fought battles and fights by the hundreds. Again and again he had faced and overcome tremendous odds. But never in his life had he fought such a battle as when, in a room in New York, he fought for his life against a thing such as the world had never seen, a thing more terrible than a thousand armed men.

The thing came straight across the room and Gordon avoided it with ease. It struck a table and turned aside in its course. With no hands upon its control, its course was to an extent, dependent upon obstacles and other influences. It kept no straight course, but moved in an erratic manner. But nothing was irregular about the movements of its great arms. They kept up their motions with a terrible regularity.

Gordon avoided it and ran across the room to the old scientist. He raised him and found that he was alive. Gordon glanced around. He saw a large shelf high up upon the wall. With unbelievable strength and agility he managed to place the unconscious man upon it. There, at least he was out of the reach of the Iron Terror unless the thing developed a climbing ability.

As Gordon completed his task he saw the automaton had turned once more and was coming back.

He leaped to the guiding machine and sought to work the lever. They were bent and broken and the machine itself was nearly a wreck. Gordon was astonished. He would have thought that to smash the guiding machine would render the automaton useless.

The thing advanced across the room. Its sword clanged against the wall and Gordon hoped it would shatter. But the thing merely veered about and started on another course. Desperately Gordon jerked on a bent lever—the speed of the automaton increased! More than that it charged straight across the room towards him. He let go of the controlling machine and sprang across the room just in time to avoid the sweep of the automaton's sword. Then the Terror turned and came toward him again.

A rage came over Gordon. He was not used to running from his foes. He caught up one of the great swords that lay upon a table and charged in. He swung the great sword high into the air with both hands and struck a terrific blow. There was a clash and a clang like a mighty hammer-and-anvil and the great blade shattered from point to hilt. The automaton did not even rock and Gordon felt the wind of its sword as the thing swung about and struck.

He leaped back and hurled the useless hilt from him with a curse. The Terror was advancing toward him. He backed away and felt a heavy table at his back. Just in time he cleared it with a bound, as the Terror's sword came down and severed the table in half. The automaton strode over its ruins. A great metal cauldron stood in one corner of the room. It was for chemical experiments and must have weighed at least two hundred pounds. Gordon lifted it, swung it into the air and dashed it against the automaton! Even the Iron Terror could not stand before such a missile. It was knocked off its feet and crashed to the floor. But instantly it rose to its feet again, not once ceasing the motion of its arms!

Gordon watched, fascinated. It moved swiftly across the room and came into contact with a tall case. Instantly there was a rending and smashing of wood as the moving arm encircled the case and splintered it against the metal figure. Gordon shuddered in spite of himself. It was clear that if that arm ever closed on him, it would crush him.

"What a monster!" he said, aloud, wonderingly. "The old scientist was right. And I," he laughed sardonically, "I, who intended to hurl it against my foes, and he, who made it, are its first victims. The man who fought the cannon in the ship had an easy task, I think."

He looked about for a weapon. With one eye on the figure he opened several drawers. In one he found a bomb. He poised it in his hand, musing.

He remembered the scientist's words, "No shell can shatter it."

"A waste of time," he decided. "And dangerous."

He laid the bomb down and sidestepped as the automaton crashed into the opposite wall, swung around and charged in his direction. He watched and his eyes narrowed. At least he could break its sword. A great battle-axe of the Middle Ages lay near. He snatched it up and advanced.

He leaped in from the side, swinging the battle-axe as he sprang. It clashed against the sword and the sword-blade broke at the hilt and flew ringing across the room. Wolflike, Gordon recovered himself and leaped back almost simultaneously.

But though the sword was broken the great hand still rose and fell, gripping the heavy hilt. The other arm still swung out and back.

The room was a wreck. The automaton had knocked down, smashed, hewed or splintered nearly every piece of furniture.

As it lumbered across the room once more, Gordon did what he had tried to do before. He darted past the figure, raced across the room, and began to smash the controlling machine with the battle-axe. He believed that if that were destroyed the automaton would stop. As it had done before, the automaton charged back towards him. That showed that the controlling machine was still responsible for the thing's movements, thought Gordon, as he hacked desperately. Then the thing was upon him and he fled, dropping the battle-axe beside the machine.

And as if imbued with a mind the automaton followed him. Its speed was terrible. Its terrible face seemed the embodiment of the devil himself. Again and again Gordon dodged the thing, avoiding it by sheer speed and skill. He sprang to the machine again and swung the battle-axe. He thought of the scientist; his thoughts were short and disconnected: "A wonderful machine"—"if he built this he can build another—"

With a last swing he dropped the weapon and slipped under the arm of the Terror. But this time he was not quite quick enough. The hand holding the broken sword-hilt struck him a glancing blow and he staggered. In an instant the other arm was crushing him against the metal figure.

There was no sound; there had been no sound all along except the scuffing of feet, the crash of overturned furniture now and then and a slight sizzling sound from the controlling machine.

And silently, frenziedly, Gordon fought against the metal monster that gripped him. With all of his incredible strength he fought. And slowly he was being crushed.

And then suddenly the arm relaxed and Gordon slipped to the floor.

Wonderingly he rose and watched the Terror go blundering across the room, its arms now hanging at its sides. It went slowly. As he had known, the destruction of the controlling machine had stopped the automaton. Evidently he had done more with the battle-axe than he had thought. The Iron Terror stopped.

King of the Forgotten People

(synopsis)

Jim Brill came into the Gobi Desert, searching for the scientist Richard Barlow, who had disappeared into it four years before. Brill went at the plea of Gloria Barlow, the scientist's wife, whom Brill loved. She had not been happy with the brutal scientist, but she felt it her duty to try to effect his rescue. Brill's expedition had been attacked by Mongol bandits, and only he escaped. On a tired horse, during a sandstorm, he made his way across a trackless waste to a wild tangle of hills. The Mongols had followed him, but fled when they were attacked by a gigantic spider. He shot the spider and going on, nearly exhausted, topped a rocky crest and came upon a strange city in the hills. It was occupied by a degenerate race, descendants of the warriors of Genghis Khan, and Richard Barlow was their king; his consort was a yellow Chinese girl, captured from a caravan. Barlow told how he had made the monsters out of small spiders which frequented the caves of the hills, in order to protect the city. He showed Brill a chamber where he said the great Genghis Khan used to meditate for hours at a time, and he told a wild plan for invoking the ghost of that conqueror. Hie idea was that thought makes its imprint on material substances just as solid things do, and he was going to develop the walls just as a camera negative is developed. With the impression of the great conqueror to aid him Barlow expected to conquer the world. The man was already beginning to show Mongolian characteristics; and speak with a guttural accent. He sneered when Brill told him of his wife, then said that she should be brought to him. This Brill refused to do, and in a savage fight which followed, he knocked out the scientist, but was overpowered by his servants. The Chinese girl, who had overheard the conversation, stabbed Barlow, and just then the town was raided by a band of Mongols, led by a former friend of Brill's, who released him and escorted him back to civilization.

King of the Forgotten People

(earliest known draft)

Jim Brill licked his parched, cracked lips, staring about him with bloodshot eyes. He and his weary horse moved slowly onward, the only evidences of life amidst that grim desolation. Behind him lay the sand, curving in ridges blowing in long riffles; before him rose the stark outlines of the nameless mountains which were his goal. The sun hung above the western horizon, dull gold in the veil of dust which turned the sky to a sickly yellow. That dust pervaded the atmosphere, giving the taste to the very air he breathed.

Yet he was thankful for it. Without the storm that had masked the desert in a brown, driving cloud, he would not have been able to escape the doom which had overtaken his guides and servants.

The attack had come at dawn, sudden and unexpected as the stroke of a hidden cobra. From behind a bare ridge a swarm of squat riders on shaggy horses had rushed the camp, howling like devils, shooting and slashing. In the midst of the attack the storm had brought stinging clouds of dust rolling over the desert, and through it Jim Brill had ridden in a desperate dash for life, knowing that he alone remained alive of the expedition which had toiled so far on its strange quest.

Brill glanced behind him. The men who had pillaged his camp and slaughtered his followers were Mongol bandits. They would not let the one white man of the expedition escape if they could help it. It was almost certain that they would follow him, though the storm might be expected to confuse even their almost uncanny desert-bred instincts.

Brill's equipment consisted of the long-barreled .45 at his hip, a canteen with a few drops of water in it, and the weary horse which trembled at his weight after the long run.

Mindful of this, the man swung down from the saddle and plodded on, leading the animal. He scanned the rugged slopes ahead of him uncertainly. Sure death of starvation awaited him in the desert; what the mountains held, he could not know. No man knew what lay in this unexplored region. No white man had ever entered it, or if he had, he had never come out alive to tell what he had found.

A broad canyon mouth opened ahead of him. The floor was rocky and seemed to slope upward, narrowing as it climbed. As he entered the mouth, the weary horse snorted and threw up its head, reining back. Brill swore wearily and sought to quiet it. Its eyes rolled and its haunches quivered. Uneasily he scanned the slope for some sign of danger. He stiffened. Up on the steep pitch *something* moved, scuttled behind a boulder. What it was he could not say. He had a vague impression of something bulky and hairy, moving in a manner which suggested neither man nor beast. Then he forgot it.

Behind him sounded the clatter of hoofs, and whirling, he glared with a feeling of being trapped. The storm had not thrown off his pursuers, wolves of the desert that they were. They were riding into the canyon mouth—ten squat Mongols in wolfskins, flogging their horses and brandishing their sabers in exultation.

They did not pull their rifles from the boots beneath their knees. They knew their prey could not escape, and their lust for slaughter with cold steel was too much for their better judgment.

With a curse Brill dropped behind a rock, drawing and cocking his .45. His belt was empty; his only ammunition was the cartridges in the chambers of his pistol. Carefully he sighted across the crest of the boulder at the foremost horseman.

The man's course would carry him under the ledge on which he had seen the hairy thing move. As soon as he passed that point, Brill intended to pull the trigger, automatically judging the distance. But that shot was never fired.

As the leading Mongol neared the jutting ledge, some instinct caused him to look upward. And as he did so, a frightful change came over him. His yellow face went ashy; with a scream of mortal fear he threw up his arms, pitching far back in the saddle. And simultaneously something black and hairy shot from the ledge and struck full on his breast.

The rider was knocked out of the saddle at the impact, and the men behind yelled in dismay and jerked their horses back on their haunches to avoid trampling their companion. Above their clamor rose a scream of mortal agony. The horses wheeled and bolted, neighing in terror.

The fallen Mongol writhed on the canyon floor, pinned down by a great black shape that was like a creature from a nightmare. Brill swore in amazed credulity. It was a spider, but such a spider as Brill had never guessed existed, except in dreams.

In shape and general appearance it was like a tarantula, with a gross black body, bristling with stiff hair, and branching, crouching legs. But it was enormous, fully as big as a hog. It crouched on the writhing, shrieking Mongol, and suddenly his shrieks ceased in a bubbling gurgle. His twisting body stiffened out in an attitude that was unmistakable.

The other desert men had pulled up their frantic steeds some distance away, and sat shivering and chattering. One lifted a rifle and fired, but obviously what he had seen has shaken his nerves badly. The bullet ricocheted from a rock and screamed up the gorge. And as the monster turned in their direction, the Mongol yelled in terror and raced across the plain, crouching low like gnomes in their high-peaked saddles, and lashing their steeds ruthlessly.

Brill rose gingerly from behind his rock. His horse had bolted away up the canyon, twilight was approaching, and he was alone in the gorge with that hairy monstrosity crouched over the man it had killed like a black ogre.

He hoped to steal away up the canyon without molestation. The less shooting he had to do, the better. But the matter was taken out of his hands. The moment he rose into full view, the monster abandoned its stiffening prey and scuttled across the canyon floor at appalling speed.

Swearing with candid fright, Brill sighted at the hurtling black bulk and pulled the trigger. The impact of the big bullet knocked the thing sidewise, but it righted itself and came on. Again and again the gun cracked, waking the echoes in the narrow walled canyon, before the monster halted in its rush and lay writhing, working its hairy legs. Then from all sides sounded a sinister rustling, and cold sweat beaded Brill's skin as he saw other spiders appear. They seemed to dart from every cranny and boulder, all converging on the stricken bulk quivering on the gorge floor. None were so large as it, but all were big enough and poisonous looking enough to send chills up Brill's spine.

They ignored the man, and fell on their mangled king as wolves fall on the wounded leader of the pack. The giant was hidden in a writhing, working mass of black and grey-banded bodies. With a shudder of nausea Brill hurried up the canyon before they could finish their grisly repast and turn their attention to him.

He went up into the mountains because he did not wish to go down the gorge past that working hill of giant spiders; because only death by thirst lay in the direction of the desert; and because it was to find these hills that he had plunged into the Gobi in the first place.

Jim Brill was looking for a man, lost for four years; a man whom he hated more than anyone else on earth, yet for whom he was ready to risk his life.

It was certainly not love of Richard Barlow, eminent explorer and scientist, which had sent Brill on his quest; the latter had his own private reasons, and to him they were sufficient. Following dim clues and cryptic hints dropped by natives and caravan men, he had reached the conclusion that the man he sought, if he still lived, was to be found in the mysterious hills which stood in a portion of the Gobi, yet unmapped. He believed that he was within a day's ride from those hills when the bandits swooped down on him. And now he was striding through those very hills of mystery and horror.

He was without food, almost without water, without a horse, weaponless except for a pistol with three cartridges in it. He could not go back, he could not stay where he was, and probably death lurked for him further on. He went on because that course possessed the least certainty for death, and because he had a wild hope that he might find some trace of Richard Brent before he died.

He emerged from the canyon into a wild tangle of cliffs and ravines. There was no vegetation, no water. The turrets and ridges rose grim and stark and black in the dusk about him. He thought of the grim guardians of those hills and he shivered. A spider as big as those he had seen would carry enough poison to kill a whole squad of men. But the land lay desolate as the earth before man's creation, and the rising of the moon lighted the wild scene and carved out black shadows of ridges and cliffs.

At last he found himself climbing a long narrow path that wound up and up dizzily. He followed it for some time before he realized that it could not be a natural trail. It was manmade. It wound up between sheer cliffs to a notch that showed a square of star-flecked sky. When he came to the pass he halted. A heavy chain was stretched across the narrow notch. With his two hands resting on it, he gazed through the pass. It was narrow; beyond the path fell away into a valley where water gleamed in the moonlight, and he saw dense groves of trees. Among the trees rose gleaming walls and towers of a town, apparently of white marble. Even as he wondered, something moved in the shadow of the cliff in the pass. He caught a glimpse of a tall black figure with a curiously misshapen head from which glittered eyes like yellow balefire. A choking cry escaped his lips. No human ever had eyes like that.

Gripping the chain to steady himself, he snatched at his revolver. And in that instant the universe burst around him, showering the sky with red sparks which were instantly quenched in the blackness of utter oblivion.

.2.

When Jim Brill regained consciousness, his first impression was that he was lying on something soft and yielding, strange to his rugged frame after years of camp cots and pallets spread on the hard ground. Then he saw a soft oval of a face; a yellow face, with oblique eyes, yet a face undeniably beautiful. A voice spoke somewhere, a familiar voice, yet framed in an unfamiliar accent. The yellow girl answered and turned away with a lithe twist of her supple body. Then Jim Brill was fully conscious, and glaring about him in wonder.

He lay on a satin divan in a chamber whose ceiling was a fretted dome of gold and lapis lazuli. Satin hangings, worked with gilt dragons, adorned the walls. Thick carpets littered the floor.

All this he saw in a sweeping glance. Then his full attention was riveted on the figure which sat before him. This figure was a heavily built man, whose robe of watered silk sat strangely on him and did not conceal the knotted muscularity of his frame. A velvet cap was on his head, and from under this his cold grey eyes gleamed, matching the rugged hardness of his features. It was the aggressive jut of the jaw that woke recognition in Jim Brill's brain.

"Barlow!"

He sat up, gripping the edge of the divan, glaring at the other as at one risen from the dead.

"Yes, it's me." The man's voice was faintly sardonic. "Fancy *you* dropping in on me like this."

"I was hunting you, blast your lousy hide!" bristled Brill; yes, this was Barlow all right, with his gift of putting Brill's teeth on edge.

"Hunting me?" There was sincere surprize in Barlow's tone.

"Oh, it wasn't through any love of you," growled Brill. "I wasn't losing any sleep over you."

"Why, then?"

"Great Judas, man, can't you guess?" exclaimed Brill irritably. "Gloria—"

"Oh!" Barlow's expression was strange, as if he had just had something long forgotten recalled to his mind. "So my wife sent you?"

"Naturally. She waited four years. She never heard a word from you. Nobody knew whether you were alive or dead. You'd simply disappeared into inner Mongolia. Gloria came to me, because she knew no one else to come to. She financed the trip, and well, here I am."

"Sorry your welcome was so abrupt!" grinned Barlow.

"What happened to me?" asked Brill. "What was that devil-thing I glimpsed just before I went out?"

"Answering your last question," Barlow replied, the 'devil-thing' was merely one of my servants, garbed in a long dark robe and hood, with phosphorescent eyes painted on it. A little trick to discourage our superstitious neighbors, the Mongols. As for the other, well, you had your hand on the chain, and another faithful servant merely did as I've taught him to do. He pushed a little handle and sent a large number of electrical volts shooting along the chain. It's a little battery I brought into the Gobi with me; small, but powerful. If he hadn't seen you were a white man, you'd be dead right now."

Brill glanced at his hand. He knew little or nothing about electricity, but he had a vague idea that a shock hard enough to knock him senseless would be enough to burn his hand off. Barlow read his expression.

"No burns on you," he assured him. "You've seen men knocked cold by lightning without being burned, haven't you? Same principle. Elementary. I know more about it than any other man in the world. I've gone beyond that. I can control it as easily as I can write my name."

"Ever the modest one," grunted Brill. His dislike for the man had returned to more than its original vigor since finding him.

Barlow smiled with contemptuous tolerance. He had changed. There was more poise about him, a more certain air of superiority. And there was a vague difference in his face. Brill could not place it, but it was there, in his complexion, the shape of his eyes—somewhere. And his voice sounded strange at times. He slurred certain words in a manner strange to Brill.

"What is this dump, anyway?" Brill glanced about him. He afforded a strong contrast, in his dust-stained and tattered shirt, breeches and boots, to the figure in the embroidered silk. Brill was as tall as Barlow, and almost as heavy, a broad-shouldered, thick-chested man, with heavily muscled arms and a nervous energy that could fire him to the quickness of a big cat.

"This is the city of Khor," said Barlow, as if that explained everything.

"Khor's a myth," grunted Brill incredulously. "I've heard the Mongols spinning their lies about it—"

Barlow smiled coolly. "You are in the position of the man who looked at a camel and refused to admit its existence. Your denial is pointless. Khor exists, and you are at this instant lying in its royal palace."

"Then where's the king?" demanded Brill sarcastically.

Barlow bowed with mock modesty, then folded his hands in his lap and looked at Brill with eyes that glinted with some hidden meaning between slitted lids. Brill, looking at him, was aware of a vague uneasiness. There was something wrong about his appearance—

"You mean you're the boss of this city?" he demanded.

"And of this valley. Oh, it was not difficult. The people are slothful and unwarlike; grossly superstitious. My electrical battery and some other things I brought convinced them I was a magician to be obeyed. Their king, old Khitai Khan, was killed in a Mongol raid; he had no heirs, so I stepped into his shoes without any trouble. I'm not only the big sorcerer of Khor, I'm Ak Khan, the White Khan."

"Who are these people?"

"You'll have a chance to see them presently. They are a mixed race, Mongolian and Turkish with a strain of Chinese. Did you ever hear of Genghis Khan?"

"Who hasn't?" snapped Brill impatiently.

"Well, as you know, he conquered most of Asia in the early thirteenth century, and established a gigantic empire. He destroyed many cities, but he also built a few. Karakoram, for instance, and Khor. This was his pleasure city, and was erected by skilled Persian architects. Karakoram was built just like a big Mongol camp, without rhyme or reason. But Khor was a town of exquisite beauty—still is, for that matter. He filled it with his slaves, both men and women. When he died, people forgot about Khor, far up in these isolated mountains. The descendants of those slaves have lived on here ever since, under their own khans, raising their own food in the valley, getting other things they wanted from the few Mongol traders who dared approach the hills. They used to raid caravans until they became indolent and slothful."

He clapped his hands. "I was forgetting. You'll be hungry."

A hanging parted and a slender silk-clad figure swayed lithely in.

"Then she wasn't a dream," muttered Brill.

"Scarcely!" Barlow laughed. "The Mongols stole her from a Chinese caravan." He directed her to set down the vessels of food and drink she carried. Brill glanced curiously at her. Chinese women held no attraction for Brill, but this girl was undeniably beautiful. Her oblique eyes glowed with a soft fire, her features were delicately molded, and her slender body was supple as that of a young panther.

"Dancing girl," thought Brill, as he set to work ravenously on the food and wine she set before him. When he finished Barlow asked him if he felt like seeing the city. Brill rose with a snort of disgust that anyone should consider him so soft as to be knocked out long.

Barlow led him through a series of hallways, and out into a small court, surrounded on three sides by galleries letting into the palace, and on the fourth by a low wall. A fountain tinkled in this court. Over this wall Brill looked down into the city. It was much like other Oriental towns he had seen in the past, with market squares, narrow streets, open stalls where goods were displayed, and flat-topped houses. The main difference was in the unusual cleanliness, and the richness of the buildings. The houses were of marble instead of mud, and the streets were paved with the same substance.

"Quarries of marble in these hills," grunted Barlow, as if reading Brill's thoughts. "Made them clean things up after I got to be *khan*. Didn't want plagues breeding in filth."

The palace stood on a low hill in the center of the town. Brill could see up and down the valley, which was walled by sheer cliffs. Outside the pass through which he had been brought, and up to which a sort of natural ramp meandered, there was no break in the sheer ramparts. A stream flowed through the valley, and the vegetation which crowded its banks was relieving after the barren monotony of the outer desert. Small gardens checkered the valley floor, with tiny huts rising here and there. The city itself was furnished with a strong outer wall, and was of no great extent, though rather densely populated.

Close at hand, Brill saw the inhabitants. The were soft looking and moved indolently as they walked along the streets in their silk garments. Their skins were yellowish, their faces round and flat. Their slanted eyes were dreamy. They reminded Brill of the remnants of a race which had fulfilled their destiny and now waited drowsily for death, without hope and without interest.

Barlow's servants were of a different breed; they were Tonkinese, lean, wiry, dark-skinned men who seldom spoke but looked quick and dangerous as cats. Barlow said he had brought them with him to Khor.

"I'd show you my laboratory," said the scientist, "but I know your ignorance as to such matters. I'll content myself with telling you I've gone beyond the wildest dreams of western scientists. I was always cramped in America; fools with their laws were always interfering. Out here I have been able to do as I liked. Human life means nothing; the will of the ruler everything."

Brill scowled at the implication.

"You mean you've worked on human subjects?"

"Why not? These servants of mine do my bidding, and the Khoranese consider me the servant of Erlik, the god they have worshipped since before the time of Genghis Khan. The victims I demand of them are no more than offerings to the god, according to their way of looking. I only sacrifice them to the cause of science."

"To the cause of the devil!" snarled Brill, revolted. "Don't pull that stuff with me. You care nothing about the progress of humanity. All you've ever considered is your own ambitions."

Barlow laughed without resentment.

"At any rate, I've carried out my experiments unhindered. My will is law in this valley—a fact you will do well to remember. If I have occasionally used one of these fat fools in an experiment, I have also protected them. They used to suffer from the raids of the Mongols before I came. The only way into the valley of Khor is through that pass, but even so, the raiders would often cut their way through and devastate everything outside the walls of the city. Sooner or later they would have destroyed the city itself.

"I guarded the pass with that electrically charged chain, and have done other things that fill the Mongols with such fear that they seldom dare enter the hills."

"Those big spiders—" began Brill.

"Another of my experiments. They were originally small spiders which inhabited caves in the hills. By scientific means I enlarged their size. I could have made them as big as elephants fi it had been necessary. Elementary. I have gone far beyond all that. I am now exploring the greatest of all mysteries."

"What's that?"

"The human mind; the ego, spirit, soul. Call it what you will. In times past people have dabbled in what they called the occult in the manner of shamans and charlatans. It is time the mystery was approached in a deliberate and scientific manner. I have so approached it."

"Well, listen," said Brill abruptly. "I came a long way to find you, thinking you were a prisoner of a hill tribe. Now I find you master of the tribe. If you haven't been prisoner, why didn't you return to civilization?"

"I came here for a purpose," answered the other.

"Well," growled Brill, "you might at least have sent word to Gloria to let her know that you were still alive?"

"How?" demanded Barlow. "I have no one to send by. None of my Tonkinese could have gotten through the desert alive. I couldn't trust a Mongol trader to take the word. Anyway, when a man is absorbed in his life's work, he can't worry himself about a woman."

"Not even when that woman is his wife, eh?" sneered Brill, his resentment growing every minute. "Well, now I've found you, I want to know, are you coming back to America with me?"

"Certainly not. I have not yet completed my work."

"What shall I tell Gloria?"

"Tell her whatever you choose; you will anyway."

Brill's clenched his big fists. The man's attitude was intolerable. But before he could make the savage reply that framed itself on his lips, Barlow said: "Come, I'll show you what my work is. You won't understand it, and maybe you won't believe it. But I'll show you, anyway."

As Barlow led the way back through the corridors, Brill saw the Chinese girl watching them from an alcove and the look in her dark eyes as they rested on Barlow was unmistakable.

Barlow conducted him to an arched doorway of lacquered teak on which was worked a writhing dragon in gold. A great antique lock was manipulated by an equally antique key, and Barlow led Brill into the chamber.

Above it rose a dome inlaid with gold and ivory which was evidently the pinnacle of the palace. The walls were not hung with tapestries as in the other rooms, and were of some highly polished black stone that glistened. The floor was of the same material. There were no windows, the dome being craftily pierced to let in enough light dimly to illuminate the interior. On the wall was a great mirror, or what appeared to be a mirror, though when Brill glanced at it, he saw no reflection. Its hue was a frosty silver, and he could not determine whether it was metal or glass. For furnishings there was only a divan.

"This is the special room of the great khan, Genghis," said Barlow. "Only he entered it during his lifetime, and after his death the awe of him was so great that none crossed the threshold until I came. Here he sat and dreamed the dreams induced by wine, opium and *bhang*. And here I made the great discovery.

"Everything leaves its impression on its surroundings. Even thought, for thought is a tangible substance, invisible only because on a different plane than matter. I will admit that a chain of circumstances produced my success. When a man occupies a room a great deal, he leaves his impressions upon its walls. But other people come and go, likewise leaving their impression, which overlays his, and partly erases it. The stones that form these walls are of a peculiar quality I never met with before. I think they were part of a meteorite which once fell in this valley and which was sawed up and used for this purpose by the Mongols of Genghis Khan. They retain impressions a remarkable length of time and with remarkable clarity.

"No impressions overlie those of Genghis Khan. He left his impression indelibly imprinted on these walls, his dreams of battle, his memories of his power and the strategies with which he overcame his enemies. It is my purpose to 'develop' those impressions. Imagine these walls as negative of a camera film. That mirror is the focus point. On it I shall materialize the composite impressions of Genghis Khan."

Brill grunted scornfully.

"How? By waving a magic wand?"

"By processes I can no more explain to you than I could explain television to a Congo savage," answered Barlow imperturbably. "I could tell you, and when I was through, you'd know just as much as you know now. You'd have to have a special education of at least twenty years to get the slightest inkling of my explanation."

I'll tell you this much, that even you can understand: only a tyro is forced to make use of artificial and mechanical contrivances. An adept dispenses with such things. He no more needs them than an athlete needs crutches, to use an example concrete enough for your low-grade mind to grasp.

"I have developed my psychic powers—I use the term for lack of a more explicit one; I might better say my inner intelligence, or potential intellectual energy—to the extent that I do not need any mechanics of the profession."

"What about these walls and that mirror?" asked Brill skeptically.

"The walls are merely the vehicles laden with the potential power I intend to put into play," retorted Barlow. "The mirror is merely the focal point or, in another sense, the door I open upon the so-called unseen world. You forgot that I am not dealing with dreams or imaginative visions. I am dealing with substance as real on its plane of existence as that belt buckle of yours is on our plane. The universe is merely a giant chain, with each link inseparably bound up with every other link. The idealists are correct in reverse ration. Matter is *all*; all is matter, including thoughts. Dreams, visions, ideas, conjectures, all exist in material form and leave their imprint. Watch the mirror!"

Barlow seated himself on the divan and resting his elbows on his knees, sank his chin in his cupped hands, staring fixedly at the mirror. A peculiar change passed over the atmosphere of the room; the light faded to a twilight grey. Changing shades of darkness flowed over the gleaming walls. Brill glared about looking for some logical explanation. He saw none; nothing but the bare walls, the dim grey dome above them, and that cryptic figure sitting statue-like on the divan.

Brill looked again at the walls. The shadows still flowed across them in endless procession. The shadows were shapeless, nebulous, swiftly they passed, as swiftly succeeded by others. Sometimes a distortion of the dim light gave them fleetingly the appearance of misshapen human figures. Then he noticed something else. The shadows were not moving about the room in the same direction. Those on the left moved clockwise, those on the right counterclockwise. All converged upon the frosty mirror. It was like an opaque lake that swallowed the clouds.

And in its depths something began to grow. The frosty surface was strangely clouded; there was movement and unrest, a grotesque mingling and amalgamation of dim anthropomorphic shapes. As the shadows flowed into it, this amalgamation took more distinct outlines. Brill smothered a cry. In the mirror appeared a human figure, a squat giant in silk robes. The outlines of the garments and body were vague and unstable, but the face stood out more distinctly beneath the velvet skullcap. It was a broad, immobile face, with slanted grey eyes, and a wisp of a moustache drooping over wide thin lips. It was—

The cry burst Brill lips in spite of himself. He was on his feet, shaking like a leaf. Abruptly the image vanished. The shadows ceased to flow. Barlow was watching him cynically.

"Well?" demanded the scientist.

"It's a trick," snapped Brill. "You've got a picture projector hidden here somewhere. I've seen Genghis Khan's picture on old coins; it wouldn't be hard for you to fake up something—" But as he spoke he was uncomfortably aware of the cold sweat pouring off his skin, coupled with a tendency to nausea.

"I didn't expect you to admit you believed," answered Barlow, sitting like a silk-clad Buddha. In the dim light the unpleasant change in his countenance was more noticeable. It almost amounted to a deformity, and still Brill could not place it.

"What you believe matters very little," said Barlow placidly. "I *know* the figure in the mirror was Genghis Khan. No, not his ghost; not a phantom resurrected from the dead. But the combined image of his thoughts, dreams and memories, which together make up a sum as real and vital as the man himself. It *is* the man; for what is a man besides the total of his feelings, emotions, sensations and thoughts? When I materialize these things, the materialization is clothed in the flesh, as well as the silk and steel, that clothed the original materialization from which they in turn materialized. I told you the universe was a linked chain.

"I have sat here for hours and watched the great khan grow more and more distinct until he seems to step out from the mirror and stand before me. I can understand his thoughts, dreams, memories and ambitions, and more than all, the secret of his power.

"Genghis Khan was one of the freaks of nature—a natural conqueror. Born in a horsehide tent on the Gobi, son of a race of ignorant barbarians, nevertheless, he conquered all Asia and a great deal of Europe in his lifetime. He was, like all such geniuses, the result of a combination of circumstances not duplicated in a thousand years. And I am learning all he knew, the uncanny power by which he overthrew armies, kings, cities, empires!"

"And what of it?" demanded Brill.

"His power is to be mine. My ego absorbs all his power and knowledge. I shall be emperor of Asia!"

"Bunkum!" snorted Brill. "I'm sick of listening to your pipe dreams. What I want to know is, are you ever coming back to America, and Gloria?"

"No; you are going to bring Gloria to me!"

"What!" exclaimed Brill.

"Yes, I have decided. She will fit very nicely into my schemes. She will come, for she is a dutiful wife."

"Entirely too much so," snarled Brill. "Otherwise she'd have gotten a divorce from you long ago. Yes, she'd come, if I told her you wanted her to. Not because she loves you; her parents forced her into marrying you when she was only a child, and you've treated her like a dog; but she has an overdeveloped sense of duty. But I'm not going to take any such message—"

"Silence!" roared Barlow. "I say you shall—"

"Why, you dirty—!" Brill was on his feet, his big fists clenched. Then there came an interruption. The Chinese girl, entered. Her dark eyes were glowing with anger, and she spat something at Barlow in Cantonese which Brill understood only vaguely. But he realized she was objecting to Barlow bringing a white woman there. For answer the man struck her savagely in the face with an open hand, ripping out a volley of staccato gutturals that sounded Mongolian.

The girl crawled from the room, and Barlow turned back to Brill, who stood glaring at him, hair bristling with incredulous horror.

"I know now!" the explorer roared. "I've seen the change that's come over you! Your accent—it's Mongol. Your eyes have begun to slant; there's a copperish cast to your skin. You damned devil—*you're turning into a Mongol!* I realized it when you hit that girl!"

A wild flood of devilish exultation lit Barlow's countenance.

"And what of it?" bellowed the scientist. "I have absorbed the ego impressions of Genghis Khan, until I am becoming one with him. *I will be Genghis Khan!* His personality will replace mine, because his is the stronger. Like him I will conquer the world! You will return to America and bring me the little fool I married in a moment of weakness; she shall be my gift to Togrukh Khan, the Mongol chief who has promised me an alliance—"

With a maddened roar Brill drove at him, every nerve of his big muscular body straining with a primitive passion to smash and break and rip. With a guttural snarl the powerful scientist met the onslaught.

Brill scarcely felt the blows that rained on his face and body. In a red mist of berserk fury he drove Barlow backward with sledge-like smashes that ripped and cut skin and flesh and crumpled bone, until the scientist crashed over backwards among the ruins of a table, and Brill fell on him and sank his fingers into his bull throat. A worrying, wordless mouthing snarled from Brill's lips as he drove all the power of heavy shoulders and corded arms into his strangling hands, sinking his fingers deeper and deeper into his enemy's throat. All the enmity and resentment of years came roaring into life. Blood from Barlow's torn throat trickled over Brill's fingers; the scientist's tongue protruded between blue lips; his eyes were glazing.

All about there was a running and shrieking, but Brill, in the fog of his wrath, was not aware of the noise, or of the hands which tore at his corded forearms, striving in vain to drag him from his victim. Then a gun butt swung with desperate force, crashed on his head and the lights went out.

.3.

Brill was unconscious only for a few seconds. He came to himself with clear understanding of what had occurred and a fervent urge to renew the combat. But he was tied hand and foot, blood trickling from a wound in his scalp. The Tonkinese bound him to a chair, and Barlow sat facing him. Brill grinned wolfishly when he saw the damage he had done to the scientist's features. He knew Barlow's nose was broken, and that he had at least one cracked rib. One eye was closed and blue-black, and the other glared like balefire.

"Get out!" he croaked to his servants, choking with passion. They glided out and he glared at Brill. "You swine!" he panted. "When I get through with you—do you know what I am going to do to you? I'm going to turn you into a human ape! I've discovered how to disintegrate the human ego. A process of degeneration; I've tried it out on a Mongol and made an ape of him." He pointed at the stuffed horror. "Six months ago he was a man, as human as you. That's what you'll be in half an hour. Only I'll keep you alive and send you back to my darling wife with my complements—oh!"

Lala Tzu had glided through the hangings and driven a slim dagger to the hilt under his heart. The Tonkinese rushed in, knives glinting. The girl faced them, pale but fearless. Brill tore at his cords.

"Cut me loose, girl!" he roared. "I'll help you!"

She darted to his side, slashed the cords. With a bound he was on his feet, snatched from the wall the great Mongol scimitar. The Tonkinese rushed in, striving to reach him with their daggers. The great scimitar sung right and left and blood spurted. They gave back; three of their number lay crumbled on the red-stained floor. Brill seized the girl, ran through the corridors with the pack howling behind them. They ran up a winding stair, into a dome. They turned at bay. A howling Tonkinese charged up and around the stair, he came so quick he was thrusting a pistol into Brill's face before the explorer could strike. The scimitar hummed down as the gun cracked; the powder burnt Brill's face; the head of the Tonkinese flew from his shoulders. The rest fell back.

Outside, in the city, sounded a sudden din of shots and yells. A glance from the dome showed fur-clad riders racing through the streets, slashing and shooting. The Mongols had climbed the cliffs, scaled the walls and taken Khor. The chief of the desert men came into the palace, recognized Brill as a friend and gave him and the girl escort to civilization.

The Last Man

(originally untitled)

Chapter 1 – War

The flaming sun of the year 2000 looked down upon a war-swept world. In order that we may have a clear view, let us go back into the twentieth century.

The World War of 1918 was followed by an era of peace that lasted until 1960. Except for a brief war between Italy and Greece in which Greece was bested, almost universal peace reigned. Somewhat slowly and reluctantly the nations recognized the Soviet government of Russia and that country entered into an era of prosperity never equaled before.

One of England's conditions of recognition was the recalling of Russian agents who were teaching the principles of Sovietism among the Afghans and other Asiatics. This was done and the rising unrest in the Eastern world subsided.

Great Britain and the United States of America built great merchant marines and competed for the world trade. The winner was uncertain until commerce was revolutionized by the invention and perfection of the airliners. America was the first to see and seize the advantage of travel and commerce by air, with the result that she was soon supreme in trade.

Japan, with the persistence of the Orient, set to work to rebuild and set aside the damage and destruction caused by the great earthquake.

Italy slowly but surely progressed toward world power in trade and art, while Greece, having failed to thrust Turkey from the continent by war, began to wage a war of commerce with her. Turkey tenaciously keeping her hold on Constantinople.

France, a nation whose birthrate was at a standstill, made little or no effort to recruit her powers. The French people were themselves into a wild riot of pleasure—and vengeance. The vengeance was visited on Germany, the indirect cause of the French nation's downfall.

The nations of Europe looked with disfavor upon the crushing of Germany, but they did nothing more than protest. They were most of them too busy competing with America in trade and France was literally a nation whose back was up. She had the only large standing army in Europe, composed largely of black men and Arabs from her African possessions, and she was ready to use them if interfered with.

France did to Germany what Germany would have done to France if she had conquered in the war of 1918. Germany was so utterly smashed that the fear of an invasion from the north bank of the Rhine was forever removed from the minds of the French people. France seized the Ruhr, pushed the Germans back from the Rhine and from the sea and took possession of all advantageous seaports and the fertile Rhine Valley. Germany, as a nation, ceased to be. A vengeance well deserved.

And so peace was more or less universal until the year 1960.

In 1960 the United States gave the Philippine Islands their independence. Instantly Japan seized them. The United States cared little for the violation of treaties and the insults the Japanese government and people had offered the nation, but American capital and trade in the Islands was threatened, so war followed.

Japan recruited her powers from Korea and from China, whose rule she shared with Great Britain. Mexico formed an alliance with Japan and the war lasted until 1965. Japan's defeat was complete. America took possession of the Islands again and annexed Mexico, for her part in the war.

British corporations had interests in Mexico, and England presented an ultimatum to the United States. Instant war was the result.

War was declared in 1966. If England thought that America was weakened from her war with Japan too much to offer an effective resistance, she was surprized.

England gathered all her resources and, in 1968, launched a great drive against America. From the Isles, from Australia, from Canada, from all her colonies and possessions, England drew her power. Alaska fell into the hands of Canadian troops and British armies took Mexico. But try as they would, the British could not seize the Panama Canal, so England's strength was divided.

Warfare had changed greatly since 1918. Great planes, huge, armored tanks and gas and liquid firearms played a much greater part. Great air-navies shelled towns and fought titanic air-battles. America sprung a shred coup that nearly won the war. One of her greatest navies eluded the planes of the British, sailed to Australia and began to systematically overrun that country. Learning of that, armies of Australia, for years bound to England only by an alliance, sailed back to Australia to protect their country. Almost simultaneously, Ireland, given partial home-rule in 1940, broke into rebellion. Irishmen had steadfastly refused to enlist in British armies and, by the agreement of the home-rule act, could not be conscripted. In 1969 the Irish rose in a rebellion such as had never before been seen and England was forced to send back to the Isles troops enough to quell the rebellion. Thus deprived of the aid of Australia, who made a separate treaty with America, and with war at home, for British labor was hotly against war, England began peace negotiations. America was more than ready for peace.

Scarcely had the Anglo-American war come to a close, when war broke out between Russia and France. Germany started a war which was, in reality, little more than a rebellion against French rule. France quelled the Germans with the utmost barbarity. She turned her African troops loose and the last traces of Germany were stamped from the earth. Russia steadily pushed back the French armies and the war was about to result in France being conquered completely, when Greece, the Balkan States, and Poland, alarmed at Russia's close proximity and jealous of her rising power, allied themselves with France, the tribes of Russian Asia rose and made a furious effort to throw off Russian rule, and in 1980 the war was a bloody standstill.

Then the East, long quiet, began to rouse and shake her mane. All over the Orient war and rebellion spread like wildfire. China was invaded by wild hordes of Tatars and Mongols who, with the aid of the Chinese themselves, threw off both British and Japanese rule. Japan had long been seeking to rouse the East and lead her to conquest over the West. At last the East was roused and the Japanese saw that they themselves were apt to fall first.

The Franco-Russian war continued and other nations were drawn in. Nearly all the white nations were embroiled, England and America excepted. America put aside her armament and began to try to conquer the world by trade. England did the same, but was harassed by wars and rebellions in her Asiatic possessions.

In 1995 the war-weary nations of Europe met and decided on a peace. But that was all they could decide on. Peace they had, but nothing else. The jealousies and hatreds of nearly a hundred years of war are not easily forgotten. Unable to agree on any permanent peace plan, the nations drew apart and adopted a plan of isolation, more or less.

Then, from south of the Mediterranean, a people whose power was new and who were unwearied by war, came into prominence.

Such was the world in the year 2000.

Chapter 2.
"The circle goes 'round and the black man is on the upward turn."

I was walking down the streets of Richmond. That city had been almost destroyed by a British air-fleet in the war of 1966 and though nearly half a century had passed, the city still showed ancient signs of the bombardment.

Few people walked the streets. Few, that is, in comparison to the population, which was great as America had thrived in peace as the other nations had decreased in war. America at that time was the greatest power in the world.

The air car had supplanted the automobile of an earlier day almost entirely, except among the poorer people. All sorts of planes darted here and there, carrying passengers, joyriders, and cargoes. From tall, slim, steel towers, aerial trolley cars were passing every minute.

It was, I reflected, just such a scene as had been described by Edgar Rice Burroughs, a highly imaginative writer of fiction, who flourished in the early part of the twentieth century.

A citizen of Burroughs' time would have been astounded at the splendor and magnificence of the city, yet in proportion it was no more important than it had been a hundred years before, compared to the other cities such as New York, Washington, and that acme of luxury, Kamellia.

As I walked along I noticed a man ahead of me, swinging along with the long, easy stride of a man used to walking. He was tall, leanly but powerfully built, and dressed in plain garments that somehow seemed out of place in the city.

Three or four flashily dressed negroes rounded the corner. One of them bumped into the white man, intentionally, it seemed to me. I could not hear what they said, but the negro seemed to be threatening the white man, the other blacks backing him up, with the arrogance that the negroes had assumed of late years. And then the white man's lithe body lunged forward. The negro took his fist under the jaw, flew off his feet and rolled senseless into the gutter.

The other negroes started for the stranger. I reached the group about the same time. They stopped when they saw that they had two white men to face and just then a policeman hurried up.

"Here, here!" said he. "What's all this?"

"This white man attacked my friend," said one of the blacks, sullenly. "An' if yo' want to keep your job yo' better run him in."

The policeman flushed angrily. "Get up the street as fast as you can walk and take your friend with you," he ordered grimly. Sullenly the blacks obeyed, muttering to themselves. The policeman turned to us.

"The black devils," he said savagely. "When niggers are that impudent in the South, let alone in Richmond, what's the country coming to?"

As he walked back to his beat, disgruntledly, the stranger turned to me. His face was bronzed by the sun of deserts, his eyes were grey, narrow and rather sardonic. There seemed to be about his whole person something that spoke of far countries, of burning deserts and tropic jungles.

"I am obliged to you," he said. "Would it be too much to ask you to accompany me to my room?"

"I shall be glad to," I answered.

As we walked along, his cool, impersonal gaze scanned me from head to foot. "One does not often see such shoulders and hands as yours now-a-days," he said. "You are of an exceptional build."

"I was thinking the same of you," I answered. "The race has become physically degraded as well as morally, just as scientists and philosophers predicted nearly a hundred years ago."

"That's true," my new friend replied. "From a race of giants the Americans have become a race of weaklings. Years ago, six-feet men were the rule. Now they are the exception. Years of peace, prosperity and pandering to the senses have, as you say, degraded the nation physically and morally."

"Fat weaklings," I said, my disgust surging suddenly. "Only the working men approach the name of men, and they begin to yield to the lure of luxury and ease."

"What is your business?" he asked suddenly.

"Until 1990 I was a raiser of racehorses and a promoter of races," I answered. "Then I became so disgusted with the crookedness of the game that I quit. Since then I have been engaged in archeology work in Mexico."

"I may be wrong, but I should imagine that you took part in the Olympic Games."

"Yes," I replied, surprized. "I was winner in the two events in the last Olympics, fencing and wrestling. The only American to win first place in any event," I added morosely.

"The last Olympics was in 1990, was it not? Held in spite of the war."

"Yes, and in spite of the fact that most of the nations were at that time engaged in a titanic struggle, Englishmen, Canadians, Australians and Danes bore off most of the prizes. Some two score years ago, Americans regularly won nearly all the events."

"Have you ever thought," he said quietly, "that in the event of civil war or an uprising of the negroes, the citizens would find themselves practically helpless?"

"Thanks to the idiotic law which prohibits making, use or sale of firearms to citizens. The capitalist government, having pacified the laboring classes by higher wages and smooth promises, takes means to make helpless the middle classes. Why," I went on, my anger rising, "when I began to teach fencing I received a warning from the government to stop at once or go to prison. Having taken away all firearms, they do not wish the people to learn to fight with steel or even their bare hands. Witness the stopping of all kinds of wrestling and boxing. They are almost lost arts."

"The government fears a revolution," said my friend musingly. "But they need not. The people are so surrounded by luxury and idleness that they have become slothful and do not wish for a change. Morality, honest industry, art, science and philosophy have become almost submerged. No, the capitalists need not fear a civil war. But in putting down all things that might cause and make possible a civil war, they have disarmed and made helpless the people who fight any wars. And America must fall."

I was impressed with the stranger. "European nations—" I began.

"No," he answered. "Europe itself will fall."

"Then the invading people will come from Asia?" I asked.

"No, from Africa," he answered.

I was silent. I had never thought of Africa as a world power. By that time we had reached the hotel where he was staying. We stepped into a small plane, whose number corresponded to the number of the stranger's room, and rose swiftly up the wide central shaft of the hotel, to make a landing on the small platform before the door of the room, which was on the forty-first floor.

The hotels of that day furnished servants to their customers, but my friend had none in his suite. As we entered, a tall, bearded Oriental rose.

Leanly built, like the white man, and even taller, with a black beard, I supposed that he was a servant.

"My traveling companion, Chandra Singh of Delhi, Mr.—"

"Cameron. Stephen Cameron."

"And I believe I forgot to say what my name is," said he whimsically. "It is Frank Slade."

The name roused a train of half-forgotten recollections.

"Why," I exclaimed, "you are the man who tried to introduce the bill into Congress to forbid the sale of firearms to the natives of Asia and Africa, are you not?"

He nodded. "All I accomplished was to make enemies in Washington. But," changing the subject, "perhaps you wonder why I asked you to come here. I'll tell you. In the first place, your readiness to come to my aid showed you to possess courage, which is a rare virtue in these days. Then, your muscular ability is in your favor, with me at least. Please don't think I'm trying to flatter you. I am not given to flattery. But it is rare to see a man of the upper classes who possesses your build. And the nation, all the world, needs strong men, mentally and physically."

"If you're looking for a mental giant, I'm afraid you'll be disappointed with me," I told him.

He laughed. "Your conversation disproves that. You are one of the few men who see the evil of idleness and luxury. As to that, I suppose the government would consider our conversation approximating treason. I would not be surprized if it is not already jotted down at Washington."

"That's probable," said I. "And I suppose you are aware that most of these great hotels are full of government spies and that practically each room contains a concealed radio apparatus which transmits every word we say to the great receiving machines at Washington?"

"I am aware of that," he said dryly. "I think we can depend on Chandra Singh to attend to any spies, and as for the concealed radio, I found and disconnected that when I first occupied this suite."

"You have not told me yet what you wanted with me," I reminded him.

"First let me tell you something of myself," he said. "At the time I tried to introduce the bill into Congress, you possibly heard something of me, for press and public classified me as a fool and a fanatic. To begin, I went to Africa when a very young man, as a hunter of big game. Always, however, the study of men had appealed to me and in Africa I found many opportunities. Hunting became a minor part of my program. I studied the negro, the black man. I learned much of Africa.

"It is a known fact that the Negroid race doubles itself in a period of forty years. It requires just twice that long for the white race to double itself.

"The Africa of today is not the Africa of yesterday. White men came into Africa and, while exploiting the continent, stopped tribal wars, wholesale murder by black kings, and taught the negroes the principles of sanitation. With disease greatly reduced and no tribal wars to thin out the population, the black people have been growing steadily for nearly a hundred years. In 1910 the population of Africa was approximately 125,000,000, exactly the same as the population of all North America.

"Today, Africa numbers some 600,000,000 inhabitants, at least eighty-five percent of whom are pure negro and of whom ninety percent have negro blood in them.

"There are, in America, approximately 60,000 pure negroes and a third as many more people with negro blood in them. There are whole counties in America and whole cities that are wholly "negro." Race wars have kept them down to some extent or they would have pushed the white out entirely by sheer force of numbers.

"In 1941, South American plantation owners offered inducements for blacks to colonize in Brazil, Venezuela and other South American countries, and there are more than a million negroes in

South and Central America, besides thousands of mulattos. They came there from Madagascar, from the South Sea Islands, from Africa.

"In the South Sea Islands, black men outnumber the whites there, something like eighty negroes to one white man.

"Madagascar has a population of some 12,000,000.

"The negro is, comparatively, a new race. Each race must be supreme for a time. It is the law of evolution. While the white nations have been wasting their might in wars with each other, ignoring the black man, the black races have been growing, spreading out, advancing as much as the negro can ever advance. There has not been a tribal war of importance for nearly a century. First the white men put a stop to the wars and then the tribes saw the advantage of peace. They have been advancing physically, individually, as well as collectively. Always a race of giants, the black men have become even taller and larger during the last century. They are in truth, giants.

"The white races, on the other hand, have degraded. The men who sailed from America to conquer Germany in 1918 astonished the Europeans by their size and strength. Since then the Europeans have grown no larger and the Americans have decreased in size, especially during the long era of commercialism.

"In 1800, when white men went into Africa they found the natives, with the exception of the Kroomen, the Kaffirs and the Masai, as a rule not above average size. But as the white race rose mentally, they rose physically. Until 1850, when black men were excluded from all amateur and professional sports, negroes steadily won prizes from white men. For awhile athletics kept up the individual fighting trim of the nation and finally the reformers, with the aid of indolence, managed to abolish athletics of nearly all sorts. Now, fat men, small men, and small, slender or merely fat women are the rule in America as well as in Europe. The richer men and women hardly know what it is to use their feet. Horseback riding is almost unknown. But all this you know. You, yourself, though your build shows you to be extremely powerful and agile, are not over medium height, judged by the standards of fifty years ago.

"But it is of Africa that I was going to speak. A man, used to the effeminate form of manhood existing today in America and Europe, would be surprized and amazed at the magnificent physique of the black Africans. A man is hardly seen who is under six feet in height and large in proportion. Their strength and skill in any kind of combat is astounding. I myself have seen many warriors and chiefs who were over eight feet in height."

I exclaimed incredulously.

"But consider," said he, "for countless centuries the white race has trained the mind. And for nearly as many centuries, especially the last two, the black race has trained the body. They are all physical. Look at the progress we have made, mentally. Is it more astonishing that another race should advance as far on different lines?

"As I said, I was a young man indeed when I went to Africa for the first time. In the fifteen years that I spent on that continent I learned much. Most negroes are Mohammedans. The western missionaries have always failed to succeed among the blacks. The missionaries teach the negro to curb his natural instincts. The mullah tells him to give them full sway. The missionary would have him abolish war. The mullah would lean him to conquest. Aggressive Islam is dominant in Africa.

"The chiefs of Asia and Arabia have always sought to Islamize Africa. There was more than mere religious fervor in that desire. The Arab recognized the fighting quality of the black man long before the white man did. Moslems would be supreme over the world and they would win this supremacy by the means of black armies.

"France has aided them in their plan. She was the first and the only white nation to train and employ black men against white foes. England, the only other nation who might have done this, saw the folly of such a course.

"In Africa I found millions of warriors, splendid fighting material. I found hundreds, thousands, of chiefs as capable as any ever were, and as ambitious for conquest and military power as were ever Mosilizatze or Cetawayo. I found statesmen with the ability of Chaka and Unlimo. But there were no wars, no tribal raids. Why, I wondered? The white man's rule in Africa since 1860 has not been powerful enough to prevent war among the tribes. Then I found that all over the continent Arab mullahs were going. They taught peace and preparation for conquest. They made the black man see, after years of constant effort, that they but played into the hands of the white men by slaughtering each other. They taught black supremacy. They made no mention of their own plans.

"'Wait a while,' they would say to an ambitious chief who grew impatient and wished to lead his tribe to victory against other tribes. 'Wait a while. Do not fight among yourselves. Prepare for great conquest. Unite with the other tribes. Train your warriors in all the arts of war. Let your men enter white armies and learn their ways of fighting. Grow rich in peace and prosperity and with your money buy weapons. But do not let prosperity make you slothful. Some day the tribes shall unite and sweep the white races from the earth. When that day comes, you must be ready, lest some other chief seize the glory. Listen to me and you will become supreme on earth. The Arabs and all Mohammedans will aid you. The white races are on the wane. They have wasted their resources in war and have become effeminate with wealth.'

"Thus they speak craftily to the black tribes. And the black chiefs listened to them as they never listened to any white man. And in a long reign of prosperity and peace, the black grew and throve. But they did not grow idle and slothful. They paid little attention to their souls and their minds. They let their priests take care of their souls and their chiefs think for them. They developed the physical. And today the black man is the most perfect form of physical manhood that ever walked the earth. They even exceed the ancient Vikings of Scandinavia and the frontiersman of early America.

"American and European companies, first secretly and then openly, have sold weapons and ammunitions to Islanders, Asiatics and Africans. I returned to America and made all the efforts in my power to stop the sale of rifles and other weapons. I tried to make a law prohibiting it. And American capital defeated me. Why, give up a prosperous trade that was bringing in thousands of dollars? Hardly. So I went back to Africa.

"There I did my best. In America and Europe they called me a fool and a visionary fanatic and forthwith forgot about me. In Africa I did my best. I tried to stir up war between the tribes. And the British government put a price on my head. I met many Arabs teaching black supremacy—and the jackals picked their bones.

"The United Empire of Barbary sent great sums of money to be distributed among the tribes. One bulk sum fell into my hands and furnished me money to carry on my work with.

"Another vast amount I captured in the midst of the jungle. I had no way to carry it out of the jungle and the Zambezi flows above it, some two million dollars in gold and ivory.

"Gradually, working together perfectly, the Mohammedans formed the first part of a vast empire. The Kaffir tribes, always the most warlike and the highest type of negroes, were united first. The race of Dingan and Lobengula is far from extinct. Upon that solid foundation was built the empire. Little by little the surrounding tribes were drawn into alliance. And today, from the Straits of Gibraltar to Cape Agulhas, from Cape Verde to the Gulf of Aden, the black tribes form one mighty empire. Zulu, Matabele, Waganda, Masai, Sudanese, Senagalese, they all are wielded into one vast tribe, loosely bound, yet ready to be hurled against the white races.

"It is stupendous, it is incredible. A few men have foreseen and tried to stop the forming of such an empire. As well try to stop Victoria Falls with bare hands. The black man is ready for such an empire. Otherwise, not even the Moslems, with all the patience, all the craft of the East, could not have succeeded. The race is a new race and it must have its day. It is the law of evolution.

"And now the tribes are ready to throw off the last traces of white man rule and begin their conquest. In the Soudan a vast army is forming. From all Africa the tribes flock to it. They are armed as well as any European army. They have rifles, artillery, airships, all the implements of war except a navy, and the Barbary Empire will supply that. The Orient is ready to rise at a word, and the black islands and the blacks of America.

"When France turned loose the black hordes on conquered Germany, they got a taste, a mere tantalizing hint, of world power, black men over white. Germany was a flaming hell of looting, burning, slaying, ravishing. And the black men went back to their tribes, red handed and vainglorious, telling of the ease of conquering white men and the plunder, rich foods, fine wines, white girls. And their tales at once inflamed the black tribes and gave them power to curb their impatience until the time should come when the whole white race should go down beneath them. As Germany was, so shall the world be.

"The black man is all physical. His lusts, his primitive desires rule him. The red men could never be united in one vast empire because they were higher in the scale of evolution. They could think for themselves. The black man lets other men think for him and follows whoever can impose authority over him and gratify his desires. A black rule has always been, and always will be, a reign of beastliness, drunkenness and murder. The black rule will be brief, I think, yet it will rise supreme for a time.

"The prime factor, the emperor one might say of that empire, is one Ahmed el Bahran. He is an Arab with both Taureg and negro blood in him. He is a wonder of the age, of any age. He combines the ability of Genghis Khan with the generalship of Napoleon and the craft of Satan himself. He is a devil in human form. For years I tried to gain access to him, but failed. On the other hand, all the numerous attempts to have me assassinated failed also.

"Using Africa, the Orient and Europe as his pawns, he has laid the foundations of a worldwide empire, with himself as emperor. The new empire of united China and Mongolia with the wild Tatar tribesmen are ready to sweep over Japan, strike at Russian Asia and swarm into French Indochina. India, who has been refused home rule for nearly two centuries, is ready to strike for freedom. The wild tribes of Central Asia are clamoring to be led to battle.

"Asia will lead the black hordes to battle and when the whites are conquered, they will turn on Asia. Ahmed el Bahran foresees that. But it is part of his plan, I think.

"The black hordes will rule the world."

I sat silent. When I spoke, the question I asked was irrelevant.

"Why did you come back to America?"

"I was born in Virginia," Slade answered. "I wished to see the land where I was born before the black tribesmen sweep over it. Perhaps fifteen years of Africa have alienated me. Virginia, all America, has changed.

"Immigration should have been stopped eighty years ago. Americans are no longer Americans. Except in the South and West, nearly all trace of the American colonists have been submerged by foreigners. The labor unions are ruled by and composed principally of people of central and southern Europe. Czechs, Hungarians, Germans and Slavs work the farms and the great plantations. Jews control the capital of the nation. There are times when I feel that the real America has been submerged and that I owe no allegiance to the land and the government. But there are still thousands of real Americans in the South and in the West. It is to them that I hold allegiance. Not to a capitalist-owned, Jew-ruled government. Such is no more my land than Africa."

The Sikh entered the room. He seemed somewhat excited.

"The hotel radio is broadcasting, sahib," said he.

Slade stepped out upon the platform in front of his room, I following him. The voice of the radio filled the great building.

"Reports of native risings in South Africa. For the first time in almost a century, the tribes are in rebellion and are murdering white farmers and ranchmen in Natal and in the lake region of Uganda."

"The wheel goes round and the black man is on the upward turn," said Chandra Singh.

Chapter 3.

The details of the rising of the black empire would fill many books. Better men than I will record it, perhaps have already done so. I will give but the general outline of that great, worldwide conquest.

The black tribesmen, wielded into a great, compact fighting force, swept South Africa clean of all white people. Cape Town and New Gloucester were blotted out. All whites who could not escape by ships or airplanes were massacred.

Then the hordes moved north. The air-warships swept ahead of them, demolishing every white village and town. A combined fleet of British, French and Italian warships sailed to meet them and drove them back.

The blacks simply fell back within range of their artillery, where the European ships dared not follow. All over Africa the provinces rose and murdered white traders, settlers, and the few soldiers stationed there. Egypt rose in a red rebellion and the king of Abyssinia sent a great army to aid them.

Madagascar rose. In the islands of the South Seas, the natives rose. India rose. Rajput, Bengalese, Moslem, Buddhist, Hindu, all rose in united effort to expel the hated British. Only the Sikhs stood firm, and the Gurkhas of Nepal.

The Mongol hordes swept across Asia in a wild flood, bearing torch and sword.

The Turkomans rose against Russian rule. Arabia, Turkey and Persia hurled their united armies against England. The Afghans came down the Khyber Pass and plunged into the red chaos that was India.

Meanwhile, the mighty black army, having crossed the Sahara, swept into Egypt, whose people welcomed them with open arms. Khartoum fell and its entire white population was massacred. Above Khartoum a British army met the tribes.

And there I saw first how black men fought, for Slade, Chandra Singh and I sailed there from Richmond, in a powerful aircraft belonging to Slade, in which he had sailed from Africa.

The armies were well entrenched. There was no long drawn bombardment such as was usual in great battles. For a while great guns hurled their projectiles, for a while the air navies circled and maneuvered, then, from the black men's trenches, came lurching and lumbering huge tanks. They had more and greater tanks than the British, and they knew well their use. On came the tanks, impervious to rifle and artillery fire. When close to the British trenches, hatches were thrown back and from the great tanks swarms of black warriors leaped. Such men! Giants, as Slade had said, and armed and clothed not with rifle and bayonet and uniform, but with shield, spear, battle-axe, knob stick, and the full war regalia of the African brave, in loincloth, paint and feathers. Oh, he was crafty, Ahmed el Bahran. He did not intend to have his great army battered to pieces at long range. He counted most on their superiority in hand-to-hand fighting and he was shrewd enough to give his warriors their favorite weapons and opportunity to use them. And he was right. Hand-to-hand fighting of armies had almost become a thing of the past. And to see those huge, painted, black devils charging down upon the trenches, yelling and screaming like fiends of hell, swinging savage weapons, shook the nerves of the British more than days of artillery fire would have. Slade and I, with Chandra Singh, stood behind the last line of trenches. Our plane was nearly a mile behind, for Slade had foreseen defeat for the British and we had no desire to go down with them.

When the first charge of the black men broke on the trenches, Slade said, "We'd better get back to the plane. The British won't stand."

Nor did they. In an instant, it seemed, the charge had swept into and over the first trenches and the black warriors were leaping into the next line. The shrieks of slaughtered men mingled with the yells of the blacks and clashing of spear and bayonet. Much smaller physically than their foes, armed for close fighting with only the bayonet, a clumsy weapon at best, unused to such fighting, the British broke. Screeching with fear, they sprang from their trenches and fled in a wild riot, pushing, shoving, running, wild with fear, anywhere, anything, to get away from the flashing spears and whirling knob-sticks that rose and fell and whirled to fall again.

Such a rout had not been heard of for scores of years. Across the desert they streamed, a cursing, screeching mob, wild with fear. And among them raged the black warriors, drunk with slaying and with victory, smiting, stabbing, slaying.

Slade, Chandra Singh and I should have already been at our plane, yet we stood, fascinated at the scene. Then as the first of the fleeing horde reached us, we turned and ran for it, Slade turning from time to time to fire a long-range shot over the heads of the British. In some way I became separated from Slade and the Sikh and found myself surrounded by the soldiers, who had begun to scatter.

"'Ell!" gasped a little Cockney close to me. "This is h'awful." The next instant he threw up his hands and plunged forward, a throwing spear between his shoulders. The warriors were close behind. The white men did not fight back. They simply ran. And the sight of slaughter somehow drove me berserk. Recklessly I turned, drawing the revolver which was my only weapon. A great negro charged me, spear flashing, savage black face a study in cruel arrogance.

I shot him and he plunged headlong at my feet, his spear flying from his hand.

The flying British and their pursuers were scattering out over the desert. I retreated slowly, emptying my revolver. When it was empty I turned and ran, glancing over my shoulder presently to see a huge black close behind me, a Zulu, by his hair ring. I turned suddenly, by luck caught his thrusting assegai with both hands and held on. He was much taller than I, and a great deal heavier, and he jerked me this way and threw me that. I held on to the spear knowing that if I released it, he would run me through before I could move.

And he evidently did not care to let go with one hand and reach for the knife at his loincloth for fear I would wrench the assegai from his hand. So we struggled, until, in desperation, for I expected a spear between the shoulders any instant, I jerked the spear down, released it with my right hand and drove my fist crashing against his jaw. He pitched backward, unconscious, and I fled, not stopping to finish him with the spear which I took with me. During the fight many black men had streamed past us and were between me and the open desert.

I met a gigantic Masai, warded the yard-long blade of his spear and drove my assegai through him, pinning his shield to him. Then from all sides the blacks came leaping and I caught up the Masai spear to do my best before I should go down beneath their spears.

"Here goes Cameron," I thought as they closed in on me. Leaping, ducking and side-stepping to avoid the spears that flashed in from everywhere, I swung the six-foot Masai spear like a battle-axe, cleft a negro's skull, struck off an arm at the elbow and a hand at the wrist, and then a knob stick crashed against the back of my head, half stunning me. I went down and the black men swarmed on me, overcoming me by sheer weight of numbers. Why they did not riddle me with spears I did not know, but they bound me hand and foot and left me where I lay.

As I lay, I saw coming toward me a tall, splendidly garbed black, a chief I was sure. He came and stood, towering above me, a giant of a man, whose spear was red to the handgrip, who was clad in the barbaric splendor of a savage chief. No ancient barbarian king was ever more haughty, more arrogantly conscious of his power than that black chieftain.

His features would have been handsome had it not been for the cruelty and ruthlessness portrayed there.

"White man," said he, in my own language, "you fight like the white men of old. There are old men of the tribe who can remember when white men were men, not weaklings such as we slaughtered today. They screamed like women and ran like deer. Soon we will slay no more of them but make them slaves to do our bidding. But you, you have strength of a leopard and the courage. I commanded my warriors to capture any white man who fought well. That is why you were not speared."

I said nothing.

"Look at me, white man," he went on. "The rule of the white man is broken. Today the black man is the conqueror. Black men once were slaves. Now white men shall be slaves. Ha, ha! Slaves of black men! Look at me, white man! I am a man and a chieftain of men. Can the weaklings who fill the armies of Europe stand before such warriors as mine? No, we will smite them as a lion smites antelope."

I sneered. "You fool!" I taunted. "Perhaps the black race may rise for a time, but it will destroy itself. When did a black man ever rule but ruin? When the blacks have slaughtered each other the whites will rise once more."

He scowled. "White man, look well upon me. I am king of all Kafir-land. The blood of Dingan is in me, and the blood of Chaka and of Cetawayo. But two other chiefs rank me, and when the white men are all enslaved I will reign supreme. Brave men will do well to follow me. I could make you great, white man, great in Africa, in all the world."

"Turn renegade?" said I. "Fight with blacks against my own race? Follow a black despot? Are you a fool?"

"White man," he said fiercely, "who are you to insult a king? When my impis have swept over Europe I will be emperor."

"And dupe of Ahmed el Bahran," I laughed, "chief of Zululand."

"Ahmed el Bahran!" he hissed, starting. "What do you know of Ahmed el Bahran?"

I looked at him coolly and did not reply.

"Answer me!" he ordered savagely.

I shrugged my shoulders. In a transport of rage he lifted his assegai and drove it at my breast. I writhed aside and the spear drove deep into the ground. He wrenched it out and raised it again. Then over me leaped a great lean form, a saber whirled glittering in the air. The black chief went down as though struck by a piledriver and the next instant I was snatched up and whirled aloft. The earth seemed to spin away beneath me—then I saw that I was being carried up a rope ladder fastened to a swiftly moving plane, by a man I recognized as Chandra Singh.

Carrying me with apparent ease, he clambered into the plane, laid me down and cut my bonds. Slade was at the wheel and he greeted me with a smile. I saw that we were being pursued by a number of planes manned by black men, but we soon distanced them.

"That was a close call," quoth I, still somewhat shaken by my recent experience.

"We missed you," said Slade, "as soon as we had fought our way out of that mob of Britishers. Did you ever see a more complete rout? Then we circled about until we spotted you, and Chandra Singh went down the rope ladder and hauled you aloft."

"Slade," said I, "and Chandra Singh, all I can say is that you are men."

"It wasn't very risky," answered Slade. "The blacks were too occupied with looting the bodies of the soldiers to pay much attention to us. Oh, Chandra Singh, who was the chief you slew when you leaped down?"

"It was Amazaanda," said the Sikh slowly. "But I did not slay him."

"Not slay him!" I exclaimed. "Surely you clove him to the chin."

"No," answered Chandra Singh, "his spear turned the saber and it struck flat. There was not time for another blow."

Slade was silent. Then, "Oh, well, the chances are all that you'll get another chance at him."

"How will the nations receive the news of this battle?" I wondered.

"Most of them will say, 'What is that to us?'" Slade said cynically. "It is every nation for itself."

"But surely the men who viewed the battle personally and through the radio-cameras will be impressed?" I exclaimed. "Surely they will see that when the advance guard of the black army can smash a British army in a few minutes, that such an entire army might strike a blow at the dominance of the white race."

[. . .]

The Last White Man

The man shivered in the coolness of the early morning. He shifted his body to relieve the pressure on his elbows.

Cautiously he peered up over the great boulder in front of him, and down the mountain side. Fire twinkled there and the man cursed. An obscene song floated up to him and his curses deepened. The song was in a rich, guttural voice.

The man was a wonder, physically. Over six feet in height, his chest and shoulders were those of a giant. Weighing far over two hundred pounds, he yet gave the impression of sinuous speed. His face was sullen, savage, almost primitive; small black eyes glittering through tangled strands of sandy hair. In one great hand he clutched a rifle. A curved scimitar of surprizing proportions lay beside him.

He was a splendid example of a wonderful race. A race which reached physical perfection, sank to the depths of degeneracy, and then regained the heights just before their fall. He was the last.

He was thinking as he lay there, watching the camps of his enemies.

What heights his race had reached before luxuries, idleness and pleasures had sapped their might, had made of them a race of degenerate weaklings. He cursed beneath his breath.

There had been an age when his race had ruled the world. Their cities dotted the fertile plains. Their ships had furrowed the seas, bringing back the wealth of every land. Their armies had gone forth conquering and subjugating.

None could stand before them in the more peaceful sports. Their athletes defeated all others with ease. They were all giants, physically and mentally.

Then the decadence set in. It had been first noticeable in the sports and athletics. Fewer and fewer of the race had gained fame in the great games. More and more men of other races seized the prizes.

The ruling race forgot the art of war, forgot all except the search for newer pleasures, and in so doing, they descended to the depths of degeneracy.

Always some new strong race sprang up then, the man reflected, thinking of the hazy legends of the ancients, of great empires known as Greece, Rome, Nineveh, Sumeria.

And a new, strong race had risen. A race whose people had been enslaved for ages.

They were a mighty, a prolific race. First they overran their own continent. Rebellions swept Africa. The negroes pushed the Arab races to the north and the Arabs and Europeans slew each other, until from Cape Town to Tangiers, and from Kimberly to Suez, only black men ruled.

The whites should have seen that they could not stand before them. The black race doubles itself in forty years, the brown in sixty, the white in eighty. And the white race was exhausted by dissipation; birth rate almost ceased. Moreover, the race was decimated by fierce wars, wherein white man fought white man.

The whites had taught sanitation to the negroes, and had stopped massacres and tribal wars. The growth of the black race was uninterrupted.

In the almost incessant wars between the white nations, black men were pressed into service, taught the arts of war and then sent to their native lands—to teach others how the white man fought.

They were a strong, young race. Their day was yet to come. All they lacked was a leader.

And a leader had risen. A mixed-breed Arab, whose ambition was without measure, whose genius was Satanic.

He welded them into one great mass, gave them white man's weapons, furnished by Americans and Europeans, who would have as quickly and readily sold their own sisters' souls if the price were high enough.

He led them to the slaughter. At first the white race held its own.

But not for long. The blacks were physical giants, mighty fighting organisms, whose highest wish was slaughter and plunder.

That century-long warfare! The man thrilled with a savage pride as he reviewed the wonderful battle the whites gave, overwhelmed as they were with odds of a hundred to one.

If Asia had stood firm—but Asia did not stand. Whirlwinds of revolt swept from Kamchatca to Stamboul.

Japan called upon the East to strike for liberty and loot and put herself at their head. Like a pack of tigers the East rose and Japan herself, unable to stem the tide she had loosed, was the first to go down.

The Orientals allied themselves with the negroes to slaughter the hated whites. Only the Sikhs and Ghurkas in India and the Shans in Burma stood firm.

Spain, Portugal, Italy, the Balkans were overwhelmed with one rush. The black hordes spread out, until the tips of that vast army reached from Gibraltar to Siam.

They swept over Europe like a wave. In America a savage struggle was going on, for her black inhabitants, who numbered nearly half of her entire population, had risen.

Then over the ocean came the invaders from Africa. In less than ten years, the fight had changed from a war between two great nations, to a hunting down and slaughtering of scattered remnants of the great nation which once had ruled the world. Not with ease was this accomplished. The hunted life brought back the primitive might of the race and those who survived became giants, such as the man who crouched among the boulders and cursed.

Once the white race was scattered, the blacks turned upon their Oriental allies and slaughtered them. The Orientals always warred among themselves and had no unity, whereas the blacks were held together by the hand of their Arab ruler.

The Sikhs, the Ghurkas and the Shans had fallen with the whites. The Ghurkas withstood the negroes longest, for, with the fall of British rule, they had retreated to their Nepal hills and there they held the blacks at bay for a hundred years.

In the hills north of the Khyber, too, a long fierce battle was waged, and the Afghans, fierce and warlike as the blacks, held out longer than any other Asian race.

Followed years of slaughter and fleeing. All over the world, small bands of whites and Orientals fled, fought, stole into the camps of their conquerors to slay and burn, fled, fought, and were slaughtered, fighting and slaying to the last.

The last man reviewed the history and deep curses slipped from between his bearded lips.

Over a hundred years had passed since the first of the black horde swept up out of the Congo. A hundred years of battle, slaughter, pillage and rapine.

Now, over all the world, which the rising sun would soon light, to send the blacks bounding up the mountain, he was the only white man.

A world of black men. No white men, no brown or yellow men. No mulattoes. The women of the other races had slain themselves ere they could bear the children of the hated ravishers.

One white man in all the world.

And, he reflected, it would not be many years before the jackal and the wolf would wander unchecked. For sixty-five years the Satanic Arab emperor had held the blacks together, but when he was murdered, they fell into wars and even now a thousand small chiefs were fighting for ascendency. The last white man laughed with savage, unholy glee.

The black race was doomed. They were destroyers, not builders. When they slew the white men, progress ceased. The blacks reverted to savagery. They did not even know the art of making weapons. They had destroyed and could not rebuild. And they were going back to bestial savagery, and to a slaughtering of one another which even their animal-like rate of birth could not control.

It was dawning. The last white man looked about him, gathered his weapons. The rush would soon come.

And soon it came. A fierce shout, a chorus of yells, a glitter of spears, a firing of ancient rifles, and the black devils came leaping up the mountain slope.

Unable to make weapons themselves, the negroes had in truth gone back to the ways of their remote ancestors.

They were not the ebony giants who had smashed the armies of Europe, America and the Orient. Even as the whites had degenerated, so had the blacks.

The white man grinned savagely, shoved the muzzle of his rifle forward, and began firing. He had not many cartridges, but he wasted not one. Again and again his single rifle broke the rush and sent the remaining blacks scurrying for cover.

But the rush came when the white man stood up and hurled his empty weapon at the attackers. For a moment they halted, staring silently, fearfully, at the silent, savage white giant who faced them, great scimitar held aloft.

No five of them were a match for him, but there were thousands. They came with a rush, leaping over and across the boulders, spears flashing.

And the white man leaped to meet them, great blade swishing among the thrusting spears, hewing through limbs and bodies, smiting off heads.

They gave back before him, and for an instant he stood free. There, ringed about by his foes, he stood, the last white man, bleeding from a hundred spear-thrusts, his fallen enemies piled about him in a thigh-deep heap.

A moment he stood, drawn to his full great height, eyes fixed on the faraway skies, scimitar raised high above his head as if in salute to the spirits of the great ones he saw there—then a hundred spears whirled through the air.

The sun that rose above the mighty mountain shone upon a world of one race.

A Room in London

Report of Anthropological Bureau   2150 A.D.

A room in London

Antique furnishings

Professor Cameron

The University of Edinburgh

The giant

The mind of a scholar and the physique of a gladiator

Soul of a Celt in the body of a Viking

The rotations of Time

The cycles

The doorway to yesterday

Out of the past

The caveman

The races of man

Back through the centuries

Desert and canon

People of the cliffs

The trail of destiny

The red men

Catapults and bronze

Destiny

The Man Who Went Back

(incomplete and unfinished, originally untitled)

"The man at last—the right man—the only man!" Professor Jonas Worley rubbed his thin nervous hands together and his eyes glinted with an almost fanatic light. John Pendragon stood silent, immobile, his dark, strongly carved face inscrutable. They offered a strong contrast, those two—the professor, slight, white haired, a withered wisp of a man whose power lay altogether in his magnificent head. But the strength of iron was evident in John Pendragon, in his tall, squarely made form, in his low broad forehead, in the inflexible lines of the straight nose and square jutting jaw. And the cold flame of his iron will smoldered in his deep grey eyes.

"The man I need must have an adamantine will," exclaimed the old scientist. "I have tried scores—they failed. The weakness of the body overcomes the resolution of the mind—in the first whirling dizziness of the test many failed—in the titanic throes of the last moment, all have failed—but you will not fail."

"Let me get this straight in my mind once," said Pendragon in his deep harsh voice. "You claim to have invented some machine by which you can send men bodily into the future or the past—"

"Not the future," Worley made a swift gesture of denial. "I cannot hasten the sweep of change and interplay of forces men call Time; but I can turn it back in the individual. I can send you backward; not forward."

"And leave me marooned in some barbaric age for the rest of my days," said Pendragon. "Perhaps in a land and clime utterly foreign and beyond my ken."

"But it is for science," pleaded Worley. "Perhaps, as you argue, the race will not benefit one iota by the success of my experiment. But it will be another stepping-stone on the vast stair of progress. It will prove that greater things may follow. Discoveries lead to other discoveries. You owe it to your people."

John Pendragon sank his square jaw on his mighty clenched fist and into his eyes came a strange brooding gleam. "Aye," he muttered, "to—my people."

"You will do it?" the professor caught eagerly at his sleeve.

Pendragon shrugged his giant shoulders. "Show me this machine," he said.

Worley rose and limped around his desk, across the room, and opened a door. Pendragon followed unbidden. The strangely assorted pair crossed a broad laboratory and halted momentarily before a heavy steel-cased door. At the intricate mechanism of its lock Worley fumbled for a moment, then it swung back, more like the door to a bank vault than to a room in a dwelling. A light snapped on and Pendragon looked about him. Unversed in the more complex phases of advanced science, his gaze recoiled baffled from the intricate mass of wires, wheels, bulbs and machinery, which as far as his layman's mind could judge, clustered along the walls, ceiling and floor without rhyme or reason.

Stumbling about the room the professor began a highly technical description of the apparatus, but Pendragon stopped him.

"I cannot understand these terms. Tell me in the simple words of the basic, the fundamental elements of your invention."

"It is," said the professor, "in the last analysis, not an invention, but a discovery. Your eyes see but these mute and inscrutable wires and appliances. Forget them for the time being; they are but symbols of the power that lies behind—rather, the mechanisms by which we will release that power. Just as in coal, the power has always lain dormant, waiting but the proper combinations to release that power in heat and flame. The man who first burned coal was a discoverer, not an inventor. But behind him lay the discovery that fire could be induced from the elements. Mechanisms were necessary—the flint and steel—the twirling wood and bowl—just so I discovered the latent possibility lying dormant and built the mechanisms necessary to release that possibility—that power."

He pressed a switch. "Look!" A low whirl began to be noticeable; the whole room began to glow and pulse as if with life. Unexpected lights flashed on and vanished again.

"Do you not feel soothed, at ease? Can you not feel the sense of cosmic unity, the feeling of being attuned perfectly to all things animate or inanimate?"

John Pendragon nodded. "I feel as a babe rocked in its cradle; as a weary man, lulled to repose by the gentle sway of long waves flowing in eternal soft surges."

"Aye," the eyes of the old man lighted, "the slow rocking of the cradle—the motion of the waves flowing onward with the movement of the earth—attuned to the whole pulsing and deep throbbing of the universe, wherein all Life moves onward to some final, yet-unsighted goal. Your instinct has led you right. The secret of the universe is that same slow eternal flowing in long cycles onward—as the waves of the sea, untroubled by opposing winds, flow in accordance with the natural laws."

John Pendragon nodded. About the walls and the ceiling and the floor lights and globes of light and cycles of lights flowed on; great luminous globes revolved—all flowed and revolved in the same direction. There in that mysterious room, perfect rhythm had been captured. There was no flaw, no break, no discordant tone. All were bits of one great pattern, perfectly fitted, carrying out one common plan.

"They follow the trend of the earth, that follows the slow flow and revolution of all universes, the universes within, the universes without. They strike the tune of your own nature. They are in accord with the inner chords of your being. All is natural; all follows the set lines of universal change, which is called Time. Do not confuse the mechanisms with the Power. The Power is in you, as the power of fire and heat is in the coal. Mechanisms release the power in the coal. Mechanisms must release the Power in you. You are in tune with mechanisms here in action. I could confuse the workings and drive you insane by the discordant impact of jangling and howling chaos on your consciousness. I can reverse the entire system and send you back through Time and Space—a thousand years in an instant."

"Show me," said John Pendragon.

The scientist nodded. "Stand upon that pedestal. Good. Take hold of those handles—one in each hand. They are but means by which you signal me. From this soundproof, sight-proof cabinet I will direct the machinery. This of course is only a proof—not the real experiment. When you have reached the point past which you do not wish to go, press the handles."

Professor Worley vanished into the strange, polished cabinet and Pendragon stood erect upon the platform grasping the insulated handles, from which ran wires into the cabinet.

Again a low hum sounded that seemed, strangely, to recede further and further away, yet did not grow perceptibly fainter. The lights and globes were whirling again—this time counterclockwise. Pendragon had a queer sensation of unreality—unnaturalness. As if in a self-imposed hypnotism, he stared at the whirling globes—still they flowed on and on in perfect harmony, one with the other—but *backward.* This thought struck Pendragon—the trend was backward—in direct opposition with natural flowing lines of movement and change—the lights played and spun and wove about him. They wove a spell upon him—again he was one with his surroundings—in tune and in accord with them—and they were reversed—were flowing against the main tide of Life and Time and Space—were bearing him back with them, into the mists—

In whirling dizziness of his consciousness, he did not lose his iron grasp on reality. This was reality—not hallucination. He sensed that if he fainted or cried out, he would snap the chain that bound him to those spinning lights and luminous globes. He did not faint, but in full possession of his faculties, pressed the handles. The low hum died away, the lights ceased their play and interchange, and Pendragon came down from the platform with steady step, as the inventor rushed from his cabinet, trembling with ecstasy.

"I knew you were the man!" he cried in a voice that cracked with emotion. "You did not flinch—you did not allow the giddiness of change to overcome you. Only a man of iron will could have done that. I have seen powerful men fall senseless from that platform before much less than you endured. Are you convinced?"

"I am."

"And ready to go on with the experiment?"

"On my own conditions. Before I name them, tell me what you planned."

"I can control the distance I send you, as an engineer regulates the speed and power of his engines. It was my plan to send you back to, say the Golden Age of Greece, the Greece of Pericles; or the early days of the Roman republic. There you will hold converse with the great ones of the classic ages—with the great teachers and scholars who laid the basis of our civilization."

"I am neither teacher nor scholar," broke in Pendragon. "I am a wanderer and a fighter. You shall send me neither to Greece nor Rome; you shall send me to the wild western marches of Britain in the early days of the Saxon conquest."

The professor stared; "Man, are you mad! In those days Britain was a howling wilderness, beset by the yet heathen pirates beneath whose ruthless heels the last vestige of Roman civilization had vanished."

Pendragon nodded and his gloomy eyes lit with a curious gleam.

"To that land and to that age you will send me. Otherwise, you must get another."

Worley bowed his head. "I have no choice. I had hoped—"

"The choice is mine," said Pendragon. "Tomorrow night we will put the matter to the test."

"You can put your affairs in order? By that time?"

"I have no affairs; I am footloose and practically penniless; a broken soldier of fortune. One of the vast tribe of gentlemen adventurers, if you please. One moment—will I be hurtled into that other age naked and with bare hands to cope with its myriad perils?"

"All objects, inanimate as well as animate, are subject to natural laws," answered the scientist. "Your clothing and whatever you have on your person will accompany you on your journey."

"Good!" a fierce light flamed in Pendragon's eyes and he said something

[. . .]

At his humble quarters John Pendragon shook his clenched fist on high and swore in savage exultation. Floods of memory shook him—ancestral urgings that had haunted him since early childhood—a fierce love for a race long vanished into night.

Not alone in the ranks of religion and science are fanatics found. John Pendragon was as fanatic as Professor Worley—as Oliver Cromwell riding at the head of his Puritans.

His fanaticism dated far back and had its roots in a land across the sea. To America his Welch ancestors had fled from the oppressions of an English king. The legends and traditions of Wales—Old Wales and New—had formed the earliest remembrances of John Pendragon. He remembered sitting for hours at the knee of an old, old great-aunt, who told him stirring tales of old times—tales handed down by word of mouth, of Border wars and rebellions, and the older tales—legends of King Arthur and his knights who held the Saxons hard.

In his childhood dreams John Pendragon rode with Arthur—in the shimmer of naked swords and the shattering of lances he heard the war cry of the Christian knights and saw the long lines of mailed, horn-helmeted Vikings go down like windrows before a blast.

Raised in an Anglo-Saxon land, speaking an English tongue, he grew up an alien to the people about him; he was, in his own mind, a Briton—one with his ancestors. Aye, did not his very line claim direct descent from King Arthur Pendragon, and bore that ancient king's name? As the boy grew into youth, the dream, the desire, the strange loyalty to the long dead did not dim. Pendragon had told Worley he was not a scholar. In his own way he was. He studied the scanty chronicles of British days until he felt more a part of those long-gone days, than a part of his real work-a-day life.

From babyhood he had spoken Welsh, spoken in turn by the old, old aunt, though forgotten by most of his family. He delved deep into old books, musty manuscripts, half-forgotten folklore. The wars he had fought stirred him less than the narration of mighty battles in the lost ages when that horde, before they broke before the iron torrent and fled before it into the hills of Wales. Again and again John Pendragon had dreamed—picturing himself standing shoulder to shoulder with King Arthur—swinging a great sword that clove through iron mail and flesh and bone—and now—now the picture awoke in vivid reality. But it was with no paltry sword that John Pendragon saw himself now withstanding the iron warriors. He shouted aloud with wild joy and bending quickly, lifted a heavy case, a relic of wilder days in a wilder land.

The next night he faced Professor Worley in the scientist's study. Worley gaped in amazement. On Pendragon's back was strapped a bulky case and about his waist were belts with buttoned flaps.

"A machine gun," said John Pendragon grimly. "A little souvenir of a South American revolution I managed to salvage from the ruin when our little rebellion failed. It's a German gun—remarkably compact. And I know how to use it. I'm not going into a younger age unprepared."

"I had not foreseen this," faltered the scientist. "It seems almost sacrilegious, somehow—"

"No more so than sending a man born in one age, back into another," broke in Pendragon.

"But the power in your hands will then be unlimited," answered Worley. "A man with a modern weapon could well make himself king—change the whole course of history—"

Pendragon grinned mirthlessly. "How can I do that, when the history is already written and forgotten in the long past?"

"True," assented the scientist, "there are strange quirks to this business—you will use your power carefully, however, I trust?"

"Trust me," answered Pendragon grimly, and the scientist beckoned him.

Again he stood upon the platform, but this time he did not grasp the polished handles. Again he saw the flow and play of lights. The dizziness increased unbearably; he was racked and shaken by the throes as of some rebirth. About him reeled all planets and universes; the hum of the machinery blended with all universal and cosmic sounds; it was one with the whisper and rustling of the stars and the myriad suns—and on its wings he was borne back through time and eternity—through cold cosmic gulfs and vast rushing space winds all of which opposed him and beat against him in gigantic gusts. For a spinning blank instance, silence and unconsciousness enwrapped him, then John Pendragon stepped into the sunlight of a new land and a new age.

He knew it was Britain; not all the changing flow of the intervening century could alter the landscape beyond his recognition. Yonder were the western hills, brooding against the clear blue sky. To the east the down undulated to the horizon.

[. . .]

"Hunwulf, an American,..."

(untitled synopsis)

Hunwulf, an American, and John Brill, an Englishman, both sought the hand of Muriel Reynolds; knowing if either disposed of the other in a duel, he would appear abhorrent to her, they decided to settle it in a different manner. A certain scientist, known as von Scheck, desired two men for an experiment. This he explained as an attempt to send a human being forward several thousand years into the future. There were two parts to his experiment, only one of which was likely to be successful, but it required a sort of closed circuit. They volunteered for the feat, for the one sent into the future was scarcely likely ever to find his way back. The experiment was performed and Hunwulf found himself in a strange world of the incredible future. The scientist had projected his consciousness into that world and had told him what to expect. Long before, the white race had been overthrown and its remnants driven into the Arctic regions, whither their dark-skinned conquerors could not follow them. Now tribes of them, blue eyed and yellow haired, were drifting back into the world as restless barbarians. A strange race was dominant on earth, a people which had sprung from the mixed races of Mongolians, negroes, and white slaves; an exotic, perverse, dark-skinned race which lived in idleness and luxury in great cities, toiled for by darker-skinned slaves. But a monstrous thing had occurred; a race of cosmic monstrosities had flown to earth from the stars, and they were adored and worshipped as gods by the degenerate Tartarians.

ROBERT ERVIN HOWARD (1906-1936) grew up in the boomtowns of early twentieth-century Texas, eventually settling in Cross Plains where he lived for the remainder of his short life. Deciding early on a literary career, he spent the bulk of his time crafting stories and poems for the burgeoning pulp fiction markets: *Weird Tales*, *Action Stories*, *Fight Stories*, *Argosy*, etc. Howard's literary reputation was assured with the publication of "The Shadow Kingdom" in 1929, which featured a unique blend of Fantasy and Adventure which has since been termed Heroic Fantasy. The creation of Conan the Cimmerian in the pages of *Weird Tales* has earned him lasting recognition.

ROB ROEHM has edited more than a dozen Howard-related books for the REH Foundation Press as well as a couple with his own Roehm's Room Press. He has won multiple awards for his research and writings in a variety of Howard-themed publications. He has traveled to every location in the United States that Howard mentions visiting—from New Orleans to Santa Fe, and dozens of Texas towns in between—verifying and expanding our knowledge of Howard's biography. His research has also uncovered lost Howard stories, letters, and poems. He writes about these discoveries, infrequently, at howardhistory.com.

PAUL HERMAN, long-time engineer and intellectual property attorney, began publishing REH in 1999 via his own Hermanthis Press and later, Wildside Press; he has edited well over one million words. His etexts have been the starting material for a significant number of REH books published in the last 17 years. His REH bibliography, *The Neverending Hunt* became the new standard when it was first published in 2006, and is the basis for the HowardWorks website. His wife of 38 years, Denna, continues to tolerate his hobbies. Paul currently resides in Weatherford, Texas, a few miles from Robert E. Howard's birthplace.

MARK WHEATLEY holds the Eisner, Inkpot, Golden Lion, Mucker, Gem and Speakeasy Awards and nominations for the Harvey Award and the Ignatz Award. He is also an inductee to the Overstreet Hall of Fame. His work has often been included in the annual Spectrum selection of fantastic art and has appeared in private gallery shows, the Norman Rockwell Museum, Toledo Museum of Art, Huntington Art Museum, Fitchburg Art Museum, James A. Michener Art Museum and the Library of Congress, where several of his originals are in the LoC permanent collection.

MICHAEL A. STACKPOLE is an award-winning novelist, editor, game designer, computer game designer, graphic novelist, screeplay writer and podcaster. Back in the late '70s and early '80s he participated in REHupa and in he also wrote the novelization for the 2011 film, *Conan the Barbarian*. He has over 45 published novels to his name.

STÅLE GISMERVIK has been passionate about REH since discovering Conan in 1990. He established one of the earliest and largest Conan-focused websites, and currently manages the comprehensive REH resource at reh.world. Ståle also administers the Robert E. Howard Foundation website and its Press counterpart, and oversees the curation and editing of Foundation eBooks. Recently, he has taken on the role of preparing the new Ultimate Books for publication. His work contributes to the preservation and promotion of Howard's legacy.

www.ingramcontent.com/pod-product-compliance
Lightning Source LLC
Chambersburg PA
CBHW060700190726
48289CB00002B/487

* 9 7 8 1 9 5 5 4 4 6 1 5 0 *